Second Chances

A Buttermilk Falls Story

Deborah Flace-Chin

First Edition

PAGE PUBLISHING, INC.
New York, NY

First originally published by Page Publishing, Inc. 2015

ISBN 978-1-63417-582-1 (pbk)
ISBN 978-1-63417-583-8 (digital)

Printed in the United States of America

To my father, Danny, who always told the best stories; my mother, Joan, who has always been my own personal cheering section; and my husband, Mark, who, after all these years, is still the music of my heart.

Prologue

Eleven years ago

James looked out over the farm blanketed by fog and frowned. He and his wife, Rebecca, were supposed to fly to Martha's Vineyard that morning. He was an experienced pilot, but the fog was giving him reason to doubt their trip would happen. The dairy farm on which they lived had been in the Taylor family for generations. It was located outside Ithaca, in the town of Buttermilk Falls. It was a good size and did not rely heavily on equipment when it came to the milking of cows. Most were still done by hand. It was the way James's great grandfather, grandfather, and father before him had done it.

James and Rebecca had a ten-year-old daughter, Emily. Emily loved farm life. She was always eager to learn anything she could. She especially loved participating when the cows were being milked. Hanson Pierce (their foreman) and his son, Scott, lived in a small house on the property. He had a crew of about a hundred and fifty men. Some took care of the livestock, some handled the fields (they grew corn to feed the cows), while the rest handled milk production. Milkings were done several times a day in a center located on the south side of the property.

James's sister, Sabrina, was on her way from New York City. She would watch Emily while they were away. She had moved to New York to pursue a career in fashion design. She, James, and Rebecca all grew up together. As did the town sheriff, Ross Harris. He and James were best friends, brothers really. Ross had been in love with Sabrina since they were kids. Sabrina had no idea of his feelings for her.

Two hours later, the fog seemed to be lifting, and James's hopes for their trip were renewed. Rebecca had breakfast on the table. "James, come and eat. That fog isn't going to lift any quicker with you watching it." He smiled and opened the screen door. He kissed Rebecca, who was scooping eggs onto his plate. Emily ran into the kitchen and almost fell. He caught her before she went down. "Hey, slow down." "Sorry, Daddy." Hanson knocked and came in. "Mornin'. "Have you had breakfast, Hanson?" Rebecca asked. "I did, thanks." "Got a bit of a fog out there, James. Still think you'll be able to fly?" "Yeah. It'll be mostly gone by the time we take off." "I don't know, fogs tend to stick around especially where they aren't wanted." "You're wasting your time trying to tell him anything, Hanson, he won't listen." "By the time Sabrina shows up it will mostly have burned off. Trust me." The morning flew. Everyone was busy with their chores, and before any of them realized, it was nearly eleven by the time Sabrina arrived. James noticed Ross's squad car behind hers. He walked over. She parked and got out, looking very annoyed. "Anything you want to tell me, sis?" He smirked. "Don't start, James. You have no idea what I went through to get here." Ross got out of his car. "So, Ross, I'm curious. Does everyone get a police escort, or is my sister special? "Your sister was doing fifty in a thirty zone, and since she's in a different car, I didn't know it was her until I pulled her over." "My car is in the shop. James, he gave me a friggin' ticket!" She waved an orange piece of paper in his face. He let out a bellowing laugh. "It's not funny. I know I shouldn't have been speeding, but I knew I was running very late. I got called into work to handle an emergency." "What sort of emergency?" James asked. "One of our clients was having a fit because the dress she ordered for some big society party happening tonight had uneven seams. She insisted it be taken care of by me. So I lost 2 hours." "Uneven seams?" Ross couldn't help but laugh. She looked at him. "You're on thin ice as it is." He stopped laughing. "I'm sorry, James." He gave her a quick hug. "Forget it, there was a bad fog earlier, so we wouldn't have been able to take off anyway." She looked around. "Still seems kinda foggy to me." "It's a lot better than it was." She looked at Ross and frowned. "I still can't believe you gave me a ticket!" "Brina, I can't play favorites. You know that." "Fine. Whatever. Thanks for the escort, Sheeeriff!" She poked him in his chest and walked past him, annoyed. James watched Ross, watching her. "So I could be wrong, but I don't think giving her a ticket is the best way to win her affections." "Bite me, James." "Man, are you ever gonna tell her?" He shrugged. James shook his head. "Look, it's not that simple, James." "I think it is." "What if I tell her and she's uncomfortable with it. So much so that she says we can't be friends anymore. I couldn't take that. This way at least she's in my life." "Ross, life is all about taking chances. Tell her." "I'll think about it." He got into his squad car. "Be careful flying later, okay?" "Yeah, sure. No worries. See you when we get back. "Oh and Ross? "Try not to give my sister any more tickets while I'm gone." "Up yours." "Love you too, buddy."

That night Sabrina and Emily had just finished having dinner. Someone knocked, and when Sabrina went to the door, she saw Ross looking upset. She opened the screen door. "Are you okay?" He looked up and met her eyes. In that moment, deep down she knew something terrible had happened. "Brina." The way he said her name gave her chills. "It's James and Becca. They . . ." "They what, Ross?" "Their plane went down outside Canandaigua." "Oh my God. Are they okay? What hospital are they at? We need to go right away." He grabbed her arm. "They aren't at the hospital, Brina." She looked at him. "What do you mean they aren't at the hospital? Of course, they're at the hospital. That's where they take injured people." He took a deep breath. Brina . . . They didn't make it." He had tears forming in his eyes. She stood there, her eyes blinking. "There has to be some mistake. James could fly blindfolded." He took her hands in his, she tried pulling them away, but he only held on to them tighter. "Brina, please listen to me. The plane James's was flying crashed. They think it was because of the fog. They're gone, Brina. They're gone." She pulled away from him. "No! I don't believe it! I don't believe you! They aren't dead! They can't be dead!" She broke free from his hold and only managed a few steps before she stumbled to the ground. "Not James and Becca! Oh God, no!" Ross held her as she cried. Emily had been by the screen door listening and watching the whole time. Seeing her aunt curled up in a ball in Ross's arms was too much for her to bear. She ran up to her room and put a pillow over her head, trying to block out the sounds of her aunt's screams.

Chapter One

Emily heard a rooster crowing as she woke up. She went to her window to see the just-lightening sky overhead. Since today was her twenty-first birthday, she couldn't have asked for better weather. The weathermen had called for blue skies and sunshine today. As she looked out the window, she thought of her parents. After their deaths, her aunt had become her legal guardian and had given up a promising career. She had gotten an internship right out of college at a small design company in New York on famous Fashion Avenue as it was known in the industry. She dreamed of owning her own company one day. Sadly her dreams ended the day her brother and his wife were killed. Emily had decided long ago that she would take over running the farm, so her aunt could go back to New York. She attended SUNY in Syracuse. Her major was Agriculture, with a minor in Business Administration. She had a year left until she graduated.

Downstairs, Sabrina was preparing a birthday breakfast for her. "Emily, breakfast is ready!" "Be right down." She gave her hair a quick brush and went downstairs. When she saw the blueberry pancakes, she smiled. "Happy birthday!" Sabrina said as she hugged her. "Thanks." "So what's on the agenda for today? Hot date?" She laughed. "You know I'm not seeing anyone." "I know." "What about you? You haven't dated anyone since Johnny." "Robbie." "Robbie, right. It's time." "Don't worry about me. When the right guy comes along, I'll know it." "Sure, if you aren't too busy with book keeping to notice," she teased. While they ate, Hanson stopped by. "Happy birthday, Em." He hugged and kissed her. "Thanks, Hanson." Emily thought back to when he and his son, Scott, had first arrived. He had shown up looking for work, and her father had liked him so much, he hired him on the spot. Hanson had worked on ranches most of his life. He had been married, until the day his wife, Amanda, left him. After that, he decided that they needed a fresh start, so they moved near Seneca Falls. They probably would have still been there if the owner hadn't died and his family hadn't decided to sell the place. They ended up near Ithaca and the rest is history. Scott currently attended Morrisville State College. His major was Equine Science and Management. He would be graduating in June. "Pancakes, Hanson?" Emily's thoughts came back to the present. "Never could turn down your blueberry pancakes, Sabrina." He pulled up a chair and sat down. "So how does it feel to be twenty-one?" he asked as he dug into a stack of steaming blueberry hotcakes. "The same as it did to be twenty." He laughed. "Yeah, didn't think you'd feel much different. So what do you have planned for today?" He asked. "Oh I was thinking of doing a picnic by the lake." "Perfect day for it." "I know. How 'bout it, Aunt Sabrina?" Sabrina looked at him. "As much as I'd like to, Em, I can't. I've got to update the books." "Well, couldn't you do it later?" She paused, trying to come up with a believable excuse. "Hanson and I are having a meeting later tonight about some things, so I have to get it done earlier." Emily looked at him. "Yeah, we've kind of been putting it off." It was killing them to lie to her. "Em, I'll make it up to you. I promise." "Sure. I'm going to go take a shower." Sabrina and Hanson watched her go upstairs. "I feel like the proverbial stepmother." "Well, don't. She'll find out soon enough the real reason why." "Yes, I know but her face." "I saw. Look at it this way. She'll never expect the surprise party tonight." "You're right, she won't."

After having showered and dressed, Emily sat on the porch swing outside. Since her aunt wasn't able to make the picnic, she'd most likely go herself. Though the thought wasn't exactly appealing. She heard a car and looked up. Since she didn't recognize who it belonged to, she got up and started walking toward it. The car pulled over by the barn and a tall brown-haired guy got out. "Scott!" She leapt into his arms, taking him by surprise and nearly knocking him over in the process. "Whoa easy, Em." She smiled. "Sorry, I just didn't expect to see you." "Happy birthday!" "You came all this way for my birthday?" "Why do you sound so surprised. Turning twenty-one is a special birthday. No way was I going to let you celebrate it without me." He was tall, nearly six feet, had dark brown hair, hazel eyes, and great dimples. She then realized that his spring break hadn't started yet so how was it that he was here? "I thought your break started next week?" "It does. I cut out early. No big." "Scott, I didn't want you to cut classes for me." "I know you didn't. So I left a few days early. Really, Em, it's no big deal." "I bet your dad will think so." "I'll handle Dad. Don't worry. Anyway, come and meet my friend John." As her attention turned back toward the car, a blond-haired, blue-eyed guy emerged. "John, this is Emily. Emily, John." "Ah, so this is the famous Emily. Nice to meet you." "Nice to meet you." "Happy Birthday, by the way. Scott mentioned you were turning twenty-one. That's a big one." "Yeah, it is. Thanks for bringing Scott. It means a lot to have him here." "Glad to do it." He was looking at her and smiling. "So, Scott, you forgot to mention how pretty your friend is." She blushed. "Thank you." "You're welcome." Scott noticed the way he was looking at her, and a part of him didn't like it. "Em, where's Dad?" "In town ordering wood." "Good. I don't want to see him yet." "You're going to have to see him sooner or later." John said, "I know. I'd just rather it be later." Scott caught John's eyes go right back on Emily. "So I guess you should get going." "I guess. "Nice meeting you, Emily. Take care." "You too. Drive safe." "I will, thanks." He got into his car. Scott leaned over into the window. "Dude, how could you not mention how hot she is?" "Probably because I don't think of her that way." "What are you, blind?" "Come on, John, We've known each other since we were kids." "Yeah well, news flash, she's not a *kid* anymore." "Yeah, thanks for pointing that out." "Seriously, if you aren't interested, can I go for her?" "*No.*" "Why not?" "Because I know you, that's why." "Ouch! Come on, I'm not that bad." "Ah, yes you are." He laughed. "Maybe I am." "Drive safe and thanks again for the ride." "You wanna really thank me, give me her number." "Dream on." "Some friend you are." He said grinning as he drove away.

Emily was still waving when Scott came back over to her. "Your friend seems very nice. "Yeah, he's a good guy." "And very good looking. I've never seen eyes that color blue ever." He wasn't sure why her comment about John bothered him, but it did. "Yeah, well, he couldn't take his eyes off you." She giggled. "I noticed." He decided to change the subject. "So what's on the birthday agenda?" "Well, I'm not sure. I wanted to do a picnic, but Aunt Sabrina can't go." He scratched his chin. "How come?" "She's got to update the books." "Well, if you wouldn't be too disappointed, I could go. That is if you want me to?" He was teasing her and she knew it. "Of course I do. I'll go pack us a basket. Be back in a flash." "Okay." He watched her walk back up toward the house, and for the first time appreciated the view in a very different way. When he caught himself he shook his head. "What the hell am I doing? It's Em for God's sake." He shook his head again and put it out of his mind.

Emily rushed into the kitchen and began taking things out of the fridge. "Hey, where's the fire?" "You'll never guess who's here?" "Hugh Jackman?" She laughed. "No, Scott. We're going to the lake for a picnic." "Whoa, slow down a minute. Back up to the part about Scott?" "Oh well, it's only a few days before his break starts. Not a big deal according to him. "Well, I bet his father will think it's a *very* big deal." "Aunt Sabrina, could you not mention Scott's being here to him when he gets back?" "I won't lie, Em." "I'm not asking you to. Just if he doesn't ask where I am, you could just not say anything." She laughed. "Have you ever considered a career in politics?" "Okay, seeing how Scott did it for you, I'll cut him some slack. I won't mention anything unless he asks. But if he does ask, I won't lie. Understand?" "Yes, you're the best." She hugged her, grabbed the basket, and raced out the door.

They were walking up toward the lake when they saw Ross's squad car coming up the road. He stopped and got out. "Hey, Emily! Happy birthday!" He gave her a big hug then looked at Scott. "What are you doing here?" "Walking to the lake. You?" "You know what I mean. Aren't you supposed to be in school?" "So I keep hearing. Look, I left a few days early, that's not a crime. Is it?" "No, it's irresponsible. You know your dad is going to blow a gasket when he finds out." "Wouldn't be the first time. Don't worry, I'll handle it." "Sure you will." Emily explained that they were heading to the lake. "Real nice day for a picnic. Well, you two have fun. Scott, enjoy your last meal." "You're a riot." Ross grinned, got back in his car, and left. He was on his way to Sabrina's to deliver party supplies.

He drove up to the house and she opened the door. "Hi, Ross. Did you get everything?" "Yep. On my way here, I bumped into Emily and a truant Scott. Hanson around?" "No, he's in town." "Man, I'd love to be a fly on the wall when he finds out." She laughed. He got all the bags out of the car and brought them inside. She gave them a quick once-over. "This looks great." She smiled and she was beautiful. Long light brown hair (usually worn back), dark green eyes, (almost the color of emeralds), and creamy white skin. "Always happy to lend a hand." "Don't forget, be here by five. "No problem. See you then."

Emily and Scott found the perfect spot for their picnic. In a grove of trees that gave shade but still allowed sun too. They set the blanket down and continued talking. "So you really think you can run things?" "Well, I've taken every agricultural and business course there is." "Yeah, well not to rain on your parade, but courses aren't real life." "You sound like you don't think I can do it?" "No, that's not what I'm saying. While the courses definitely help, you'll need more than that. It might be better to train alongside your aunt and my dad first. Get to know the ins and outs of how everything works." "Scott, I've been here all my life. I know how things work." "Well, so have I, but that doesn't make me an expert. Believe me, they make it look easy. There's more to running the place than pulling on cow udders all day." "I know that," she said, sounding slightly annoyed. "Look, I'm just saying there's a lot that goes on behind the scenes. Just think about it." "Okay, I will."

The afternoon had been perfect, but it was time to head back. "So how are you going to handle your dad?" "I'll just tell him I did it for you. He'll understand." "You think so?" "Sure." She looked at him. She had many words to describe Hanson's reaction, and understanding was not one of them.

They arrived back to find Hanson sitting on the porch looking pissed as hell. He stood up and started walking toward them. "Scott, get your ass inside!" "Dad, if you would just let me—" "Let you? Let you? I don't have to let you do a damn thing." "Inside . . . *now!*" He walked inside, head down, looking ten years old again. "Hanson, please don't be angry. He did it for me." "I know that, Emily, but that doesn't make it less wrong." He followed Scott inside. Emily decided to wait outside for now.

"I don't care why you left, all I know is you are going back!" "But, Dad, you aren't being fair. I did this for Em." "Emily did not ask you to skip school for her." He took a deep breath to try and calm down. "Look, you can do something with her next week. She'll understand." "But I won't. Dad, please just let me stay today. I promise I'll leave first thing in the morning." Emily overheard some of their conversation as she walked back inside. She felt she needed to speak up for Scott. "Hanson?" He turned around. "I know what Scott did was wrong. But he did it for me." He shook his head. "I can't condone his actions." "I'm not asking you to. What I am asking is that you let him stay for my birthday." He looked at his dad and could have sworn he heard a crack forming in that icy exterior. "Please, it would mean so much to have him here." He looked at her and shrugged in defeat. "They sure could use you at the UN." "Does that mean he can stay?" "Yes, but first thing in the morning you go back. Got it?" "Got it. Thanks, Dad." He huffed and left the room. "I can't believe you got him to change his mind. You're amazing!" "I know." He laughed as he hugged her.

Sabrina had been over at Hanson's, baking a cake for the party that night. He came in scratching his head. "Trouble, Hanson?" "That niece of yours sure knows how to chip away at a man's resolve." "I know. James was like putty in her hands, used to drive Rebecca crazy." Hanson told her what happened. "I just don't know what I'm going to do with that boy." "First of all, he's not a boy, he's a man. You need to start treating him like one. He'll be a college graduate come June." "You're right. Anyway, if this surprise party of ours is going to have any real chance of being a surprise, then we better get Emily out of the house." "Ross is coming at five to . . ." She paused. "Wait a minute, Scott's here. He can take her out. He'd have a much easier time keeping her out than Ross would." "Makes sense." "Okay, I'll call Ross and tell him about the change in plans. You handle Scott." "Okay."

He found Scott brushing Sugar. Max and Pete were with him. They had worked on the farm for five years. They worked at the same ranch as Hanson, along with Steve, Riley, and Dave. Over the years they had kept in touch. Then one day Hanson received a telegram from them informing him that the ranch where they had been working had gone belly-up. They wondered if he knew of any places looking for help. Their timing could not have been better since they needed help on the farm. He vouched for them, and Sabrina hired them. It was a decision neither one of them ever regretted. They not only were solid workers, but they were also fun to work with. Scott was busy feeding Sugar carrots. Sugar had been James's horse. When they had first come there, Scott would visit her daily. James noticed how happy Sugar made Scott. So he gave her to him. "Earth to Dad. Earth to Dad." Scott was snapping his fingers in his face. "Oh sorry, just remembering something. Listen, I have something I need you to do." "Dad, can't you cut me a break. I'm only here—" "Hold on, I'm not giving you a chore, all right? We're throwing Emily a surprise party tonight. We need her out of the house so we can set up for it." "So there is a party?" "Of course there's a party. Did you really think there wouldn't be?" "I didn't but Em does." "Good, we need her to go on thinking that." "Hey, if you guys need help decorating, count us in," Max said. "We'd definitely appreciate the help." "Come by around five." "Right." Pete and Max left. Scott was putting Sugar back into her stall. "So, Dad, how long do I need to keep her out?" "Well, Sabrina has everyone coming here around eight thirty. So I'd say nine to play it safe." Scott looked at his watch. "Dad it's four o'clock. What are we going to do for five hours?" "Son, you're the college man, figure it out." He said grinning as he walked away.

Scott told Emily that he was taking her out for a birthday dinner at the new Italian place in town. To kill even more time, he came up with the idea of birthday shopping. He just hoped it didn't kill him first. After debating what to wear, Emily decided on the red dress her aunt had made for her. It was perfect. When she was finished getting ready, she took one last look at herself in the mirror. Her chestnut hair flowed in loose waves, her green eyes popped against the crimson of her dress, and her porcelain complexion glowed. Though she didn't usually wear makeup she had put some on. Brown eyeliner, mascara, and red lipstick. Her curves were brought to attention by the sweetheart neckline and darted waist of her dress. The crimson ended about two inches above her knee. On her feet, she wore black kitten heels, which she had borrowed from her aunt. As she came downstairs, everyone stopped talking and stared. The one who stared the most was Scott. The dress-hugged curves he didn't know she had. Her skin seemed to glow from within. Her eyes seemed greener then he remembered. And her legs. When had they gotten so shapely? She was simply breathtaking. "Emily, you look amazing," Sabrina said. "Honey, you look beautiful." "Thanks, Hanson." Scott wanted to say something but he couldn't. He just kept staring. Finally, his father gave him a nudge. "Say something, idiot." He cleared his throat before speaking. "Sorry, it's just . . . You look . . . I . . . You look *amazing*." "Thank you, Scott." They smiled at one another, and Sabrina recognized the looks between them. Her brother and his future wife had looked at each other the same way. "Well, you two get going and have fun." Hanson said practically pushing them out. "Have a lovely time. See you later," Sabrina said as they left.

Since it was an unusually warm spring night, Emily only needed a shawl. While walking to the car, Riley, Pete, and Max were walking toward the house. "I think I have died and gone to heaven 'cause there's an angel standing in front of me." "Why thank you, Riley. Aren't you sweet?" "Isn't he, though?" Scott said sarcastically. "You sure look pretty, Miss Emily." "Thanks, Max." Pete didn't say anything. He was too busy catching flies with his mouth. Scott noticed Riley closing it for him. "Well, we'd better get going if you want to shop before dinner." The guys stopped dead in their tracks. "Shop?" Max asked. "You're joking, right?" Riley said. "Nope." "Guys, I'm the one who'll be doing the shopping, not Scott." "Doesn't matter, guilty by association." Riley joked making her laugh. "All right, enough. See you clowns later." Scott said sounding slightly annoyed. "Hey, make sure you bring me back something' pretty." Riley joked as they walked away.

On the drive into town, Scott decided that thinking was getting him into the kind of trouble he couldn't hide. So he decided talking was safer. "So where did you get that dress?" "Aunt Sabrina made it for me. I don't usually wear red because it's so bold but—" "You look great in it." She looked at him, and he was finding it increasingly difficult to drive. *When she did get this hot?* His eyes looked down at her chest. *And when the hell did she get those?* "Are you all right, Scott?" His attention came back to her face. "What? Oh yeah, sorry." "Were you just looking at my chest?" "Er, well . . . I . . ." "Scott . . ." "I was. Sorry. It's just I never noticed them before." She laughed. "Well, they've always been there." He laughed. "Yeah, I'm sure they were but they never . . . well . . . you never . . . shit I sound like an idiot." She laughed. "No, you sound like a typical guy." He laughed. "That's me, Mr. Idiot Guy. In my defense, the dress doesn't make it easy on a guy. I mean Christ, it shows off every curve." "I think that's the idea, Scott." "Yeah, I guess it is." They both laughed.

Ross pulled up behind the farmhouse. He couldn't park in front because then Emily would see his car. He rang the bell and heard several voices yelling to come in. When he walked into the living room, he saw Riley and Pete hanging up streamers. Max, Dave, and Hanson blowing up balloons. And Steve and Sabrina were hanging up the birthday sign. "'Bout time you got here. We must have blown up about a hundred of these." "Don't worry Dave, I'm sure you've still got plenty of hot air left." Hanson joked. "Ha-ha. Why don't you use some hot air of your own." He tossed a handful of balloons at him. After they were done decorating, they got to work setting up the folding tables and food.

Scott and Emily had shopped till he dropped. Shopping wasn't one of his favorite pastimes. It ranked right up there with having a prostate exam. They arrived at Portofino's where the Maître d' seated them at a cozy corner table. "Man, am I pooped. Why can't girls shop more like guys? We need a pair of pants, we just buy 'em." She laughed. "Shopping wears you out?" "Shopping wears *every* guy out." She smiled, and their waiter came over to tell them the specials. They ordered wine and appetizers first. After the waiter brought their wine, Scott raised his glass. "To being legal. Happy Birthday, Em." "Thanks, Scott." Their glasses clinked and they drank their wine. They talked about how he couldn't wait to graduate. That the only courses he enjoyed were the ones have to do with horses. "I'm just itching to move on already. After all, there's more to life than school and books." "You really are serious about opening that center, huh?" "Why shouldn't I be?" She paused. "No reason, just that it won't be easy. It will take time and money.

The time you have, the money not soo much." "I have some money saved." "Yes, but I'm sure whatever you have saved isn't enough." "It's a start." "Do you have any idea how much you'll need to start up?" "No, I was hoping you'd help me figure that out." "Me?" "Well, sure you are Miss Business Administration after all." "Scott, even with loans from the bank, which in all likelihood your dad will have to co-sign, it's going to be costly. "Yeah, I know, but dreams are worth the price. Aren't they?" "Of course they are. You know I'll do anything I can to help." "Thanks." He found himself looking at her red lips, wondering if they'd taste as good as they looked. "Is there something on my mouth? "No, it's just you don't normally wear lipstick." "Oh does it look bad?" "No, just different. As a matter of fact everything about you tonight is different." "Well, it is a special birthday. I wanted to look different." "You look beautiful." She smiled, and he leaned across the table and took hold of her hand.

Chapter Two

Back at the house everything was ready for the party. The tables were arranged, food trays placed, and decorations up. Thanks to the guys and their help, they were slightly ahead of schedule. Sabrina thanked them as they left to get ready for the party. Ross and Hanson remained while she put the finishing touches on the cake. It was a ten-layer chocolate cake with raspberry filling and chocolate icing. As she finished, Ross came from behind and tried to get a taste. "Don't!" "Oh come on, you can fix it." "No! Get away!" She gave him a shove. It does look mighty tempting." Hanson said. "Either of you touches this, you'll be singing soprano permanently." "Message received," Ross said. "Loud and clear," Hanson said. "Good. Now go get ready. I've got to shower and get ready myself."

Scott and Emily finished their expensive but completely-worth-it dinner. Scott had the veal saltimbocca, which he said melted in his mouth. While Emily opted for the seafood Fra Diavolo. Scott had been enjoying dinner so much he hadn't given any thought to time. When he finally looked at his watch it was near nine. *Crap! We're late!* "Gosh, I didn't realize it was that late already." "Late?" She looked at her watch. "It's only nine, Scott." "Yeah, I know it's just . . ." He almost slipped about the party "Just what?" "I need to get back because Dad will have me up at the crack of dawn tomorrow." She felt a little disappointed that the evening would be ending soon. Scott got the check and they left.

When they arrived back at the house, it was completely dark except for the porch lights. "That's strange. Why's it so dark? Aunt Sabrina was supposed to have a meeting with your dad." "Maybe they decided to have it at our house instead." "Maybe." As she opened the door, she was greeted by shouts of surprise. "Surprise!" She took in the large group of friends and neighbors who were there. Her aunt came up to her. "This is why I couldn't go on that picnic." "I should have known." "Yes, you should have." "Aunt Sabrina, thank you so much. I love you." "I love you too, honey." Emily looked over at Scott. "You knew didn't you?" "Guilty. It was your Aunt's idea." *They made him take me out.* Scott saw her face change. "Something wrong, Em? "Just a little overwhelmed. That's all." She walked away leaving him feeling a distinct chill that wasn't from the cooling night air.

The whole evening, whenever Scott got close to Emily, she would find some way to avoid him. He was slowly getting annoyed. She was chatting with a few of the guys when he came up behind her. "I had no idea about any of this." "That's the way it should be," Max said. "So are you enjoying the party?" Pete asked. "It's great." "You deserve it," Dave said. "Thanks, Dave. "You still look like an angel," Riley said with an exaggerated smile. Scott wanted to smack him. "Em, I need to talk to you." "Not right now, Scott." "Yes, now. Excuse us." Before she could say anything else he pulled her away and outside. "That was incredibly rude." "So is avoiding someone half the night." "I don't know what you're talking about." "Oh, I think you do." "Well, there are a lot of people here." "That's bull and you know it." "Scott, you're being ridiculous. I'm going back inside." He blocked her way. "Not until you tell me what's eating you." "I was just giving you space." He looked at her. "Space? What are you talking about?" "I thought taking me out was your idea." "Your Aunt came up with it, but she didn't have to twist my arm. I mean, I probably would have taken you out anyway. Em, everything that happened tonight was all us. Hell, I was having such a good time that I forgot to check the time. I was supposed to have you back here by nine. You were late for your own surprise party." "I'm sorry, Scott." "It's okay. I'm glad we got it straightened out. Now let's get back to your party."

Everyone was having a good time, including Em's friend, Samantha. They had met during freshman day and had been friends ever since. She noticed the looks passing between her and Scott and wanted to know the deal. Emily was chatting with Mr. Smith, the town pharmacist. Sam walked over and tapped her shoulder. "Can I talk to you?" "Yeah, sure. Excuse me, Mr. Smith." They went into the kitchen. "So you wanna tell me what's up with you and Dimples. "To be honest, I'm not entirely sure." "Just that something is happening between us." "Well, that much is obvious to anyone with eyes." She laughed. "He even took me birthday shopping." She put her hand up. "Hold up. He took you shopping?" "Yes, can you believe it?" "Em, no guy in their right mind would ever volunteer to go shopping. Give any guy a choice between shopping and being tortured by terrorists, and they'd pick torture." She laughed. "I'm dead serious and very jealous right now. I have yet to find a guy who'd take me shopping for gum, let alone clothes." "Then you'll be really jealous when I tell you he picked out an outfit, too." "You're right, I'm pea green with envy." Then we went to Portofino's and had a great dinner." "So he took you shopping, picked out clothes, and spent money on you. It's a date." "It was not a date, Sam." "Fine, whatever, but it was definitely a date." Just then Scott walked in. "Hello, ladies." Sam looked at him. "Hey, Dimples." "Sam, you are the only person in the world who gets away with calling me that." "I know. So what's new?" "Not a whole lot." You?" "Oh you know me." He laughed. "Yeah, I do. So who's the latest sucker?" She laughed. "Excuse me, I don't date suckers. Just guys who like to have fun. He laughed. "Face it, Sam, you're a man-eater." "Why? Because I like variety?" "No, because you devour 'em." She knew he was teasing her, so she laughed. "So Em tells me you took her shopping?" "Yeah, what about it?" "Well, guys hate shopping. One guy told me he breaks out in hives if it's even mentioned." He laughed. "Well, no hives, so I guess I'm safe. Though it's not my favorite pastime." "You and every other guy in America. Still you took her and picked out clothes that she could actually wear, in public." "As opposed to clothes she couldn't wear in public?" "Exactly." He shook his head. "Sam, that makes no sense." "It does to me." She patted his cheek affectionately. "So, Em, I want to dance with you." "But there's no music, Scott." "So we'll improvise." "Go on, dance. I'm going to see if I can't round myself up another *sucker*." They all laughed.

After Emily and Scott left to most likely find a place to make out, Sam decided to scope out the male prospects. Which were pretty slim since most were either taken, married, over fifty, or wore dentures. While scanning the living room, she took notice of one particular guy. He wasn't real tall, probably around five eight, just three inches taller than her, but what he lacked in height he made up for in looks. He had dirty blond hair, sky blue eyes, and a tight little rear that she could not stop admiring. She decided to walk over and strike up a conversation. "Hi, we've never met. I'm Em's friend, Sam." She was slim, had light mocha skin, and golden brown eyes. She was downright gorgeous. "Emily's mentioned you." "Only good things, I hope." "Well, mostly." She laughed. "I'm Riley." "Nice to meet you, Riley." "Likewise. So you enjoying the party?" "Definitely How 'bout you?" "I'm enjoying it a whole lot more now." He gave her an appreciative glance. She recognized a player when she met one. Maybe she'd finally met her match.

Emily and Scott walked out to the barn. "So you enjoying the party?" "Yes. It's even better because you're here. I'm glad your dad let you stay." "Thanks to you. He was this close to kicking me all the way back to Morrisville." "I know. I heard him yelling from outside. He was loud." "Yeah, I've always told him if farming hadn't worked out, he could have had a career in replacing bullhorns." She laughed. They stood inside the barn now. "Scott, I still don't get how we're going to dance without music?" "You have no imagination." He put his arms around her waist and began humming. After a few minutes, she asked, "What is that you're humming?" "Rhapsody on a Theme of Paganini." "Classical? Since when do you like classical music?" "I don't really. It's just I had a new roommate this semester, Brian, and he was big into classical music. Boch, Chopin, Beethoven. Out of everything he played I liked this best." "It is very nice." They were surrounded by livestock and hay bales, yet it was the most romantic place on earth. He brushed her cheek with his finger and. "Em, I'm sorry." "For what? You haven't done anything." "Exactly. All these years, I never noticed *you*." My friend John thought you were hot. And you know what. He's right." "Scott, to be fair we never noticed each other." He cupped her face in his hands. "Well, I'm noticing now. You're beautiful, and I'm going to do something I've been dying to do all night." She didn't have to ask because she knew it was the same thing she'd wanted him to do all night. "So sweet. I knew they'd be sweet." Sabrina walked in and caught the tail end of what had just happened. She cleared her throat loudly to get their attention. "Sorry to interrupt but it's time for cake." "We'll be right there." "Okay." "Well, birthday girl, time for you to go blow out your candles. So what will you wish for?" "I already got it without even wishing." He smiled at her took her hand, and they went back toward the house.

It was near two by the time the last of the guests had left. Only Scott, Hanson, and Ross remained. Sabrina was thrilled that the party had gone so well. Her cake had been a big hit. Everyone's adrenaline rush was wearing off, and they started yawning one by one. Sabrina looked over at Ross. "You're tired. Stay in the guest room." "Not like I live far." "I know, but I'd feel better if you stayed." "All right." Hanson got up to leave and reminded Scott that they would be leaving bright and early. Sabrina yawned. "My turn to hit the sack." She got up and went over to kiss Emily. "Night, honey." "Night. Thanks for a great party." She looked at Ross. "Ready for bed?" *You bet I am*. "Ross. Did you hear me?" "Yeah, sorry. Lead the way." "Night, Em. Night, Scott." "Night, Ross."

At the top of the landing, Sabrina paused. "There are fresh sheets on the bed and an extra quilt in the closet in case you get cold. "Thanks. It was a great party. You outdid yourself with that cake. Which I would have known a lot sooner if you'd let me sample it." She smiled. "I'm glad you enjoyed it. I want to thank you for all you did today. You're just the sweetest man." She kissed him and started walking toward her room. Suddenly, he reached out for her hand. This took her by surprise. She turned around and her eyes locked on his. "Did you want something?" *You.* "Ross?" "Brina, I . . ." "Yes?" "Nothing." "Night, Brina." "Night, Ross." He waited until her bedroom door was closed before he smacked himself in the head.

Scott and Emily sat on the sofa holding hands. "So not too shabby as far as birthdays go, eh?" She looked over at him. "No, not at all. The best actually. Thank you for everything. Shopping, dinner, the dance. And most of all thank you for this." She leaned over and softly brushed his lips with hers. He really wanted to stay, but he knew if he did things would get out of hand fast. Instead he pulled away. "Em, I can't believe I'm saying this, but I think it's a good idea if I go. I need to get up really early. And to be perfectly honest, I don't trust myself right now. Before I go, I want to give you something, though." "Oh, Scott, you've already given me so much." He reached into his pocket and pulled out a tiny tissue-wrapped package. "What is it?" "Open it." Inside were two green dangling crystal earrings. "They reminded me of your eyes." "They're beautiful." "You like them? If not I can exchange them. The girl in the shop said so." "They're perfect." They looked at one another and moved in for one last kiss. He pulled away grinning, showing off those devastating dimples. "Try not to miss me."

"Rise and shine, Sleepin' Beauty," Hanson said as he flipped on the light. Scott covered his face with his pillow. "What friggin' time is it? "Six." He rolled onto his stomach, putting the pillow over his head and growled. "Told you I'd be getting you up early. You're lucky I didn't wake you up at five like I originally planned." "Ugh." "Don't mention it." He rolled onto his back and was now staring up at the light that seemed brighter than the sun. "Can you shut off that damn light? It's giving me a headache." He flipped the switch. "Dad, why go back for three days?" I mean exams are over. There's nothing for me to do. It's stupid." "No what was stupid was your doing it in the first place." "Yeah, I know." "Scott I told you—" "That I would go back today. I know but things are different now. A lot has changed." "What the heck are you talking about? "Em and me we ah, well . . ." "For Pete's sake, spit it out." "We kissed last night." "What? Get up." "You're still making me go back?" "No, I'm making you get up, so we can have coffee." "Oh."

They sat in the kitchen with their piping-hot coffee. "You kissed her?" He took another sip of his coffee. "You kissed Emily?" He looked at him, annoyed. "I think we've established that already." "Sorry, it's just taking some getting used to." "Yeah, I know. It just kinda happened."

"It just happened? Do you hear yourself? You sound like when you were thirteen and I caught you with Susie what's her face?" "Jenkins. And no it's not the same. I didn't grow up with Susie. I've known Em half my life. It's weird but in a good way. Know what I mean?" "No, and I don't think you know what you mean either." "Oh man, give me a break. I'm trying here." Hanson sipped his coffee and smirked. "Try harder." Scott rolled his eyes. He didn't see his son get this worked up very often. It was kind of fun. "So how was it?" "Dad!" "What? Can't I ask?" "Different." "Different?" He asked. "What I mean is kissing Em was different from other girls." "Good different or bad?" "Good, definitely good. Amazing actually." Hanson's lips curled up. "So what's the problem?" Scott paused. "Well, I don't know if I'd say there is one. It's just what if today she regrets it?" Hanson picked up his mug and got up. "There's only one way to find out and that's to ask her." He paused in the doorway. "Listen, about school, I'll make a deal with you. You can stay as long as you promise to help out with the chores around here." "Thanks, Dad."

Emily opened her eyes and looked at the clock and jumped up. She had overslept, and Scott was now on his way back to school. This meant she'd have to wait to talk to him. She put on her robe and went downstairs. The living room was a mess. Since there wasn't any coffee brewing, that meant her aunt was still sleeping. She decided she would make breakfast for them. A short time later, she heard footsteps, and her aunt came around the corner. "Morning. I haven't slept this late since I lived in New York." "I know. I only woke up at ten myself." "I guess Ross isn't up yet?" "No, I don't think so. By the way, I'm making breakfast." "That sounds great." "Good. I'll get things started while you wake Uncle Ross."

Ross was already awake. He had been thinking about how he had the perfect opportunity last night and blew it. But what else was new? While he was busy beating himself up, Sabrina knocked at the door. Since he only slept in boxers, he covered himself with the sheet. "Come in." She opened the door and was treated to his well-defined chest. *Hello, abs.* "Morning Ross. Emily's starting breakfast, so you should come down." "Sounds good." "Sleep well?" "Not really." "Oh why?" *Because I couldn't stop thinking about you.* "I guess I was wound up.

Took me a while to unwind." *Yeah, like half the night.* She couldn't help looking at his chest, but this time he caught her. "Were you just checking me out? "No!" "Yes, you were. I saw you." "I was not." "Deny it all you want, but I saw you checking me out. Not that I blame you." He was grinning. She let out a frustrated sigh. "Fine, I looked. Happy?" "Yeah. Except now you've got me wondering." "About?" "Why were you looking in the first place?" "Oh for Pete's sake." "You are making much more out of this than you have to. You are in good shape. *Great* shape. Much better than in high school." He laughed. "Well, I would hope so. Back then I was just tall and awkward. Whereas now, I'm tall and studly." He winked and she rolled her eyes. "You left out modest." "That too." "You know you are quite the catch. You'll make some girl very happy." Her last remark struck a nerve. He sprang out of the bed and took her by the shoulders. Surprised by his reaction, she gasped. "God . . . You just don't get it do you?" "I don't want some girl. *I. Want. You!*" He moved quickly, ravaging her mouth with kisses. They ignited a fire in her which she hadn't known existed. As they lowered themselves onto the bed, he got on top of her. His hands traveled to her breasts, and he opened the buttons on her pajama top. He tossed it on the floor and stared. He had imagined seeing her this way for so long. "God you're beautiful." He kissed each nipple. It felt good and she moaned. *Wait, what am I doing?* "Wait . . . I need to think." "No. You don't. What you need is to relax and let me pleasure you." He flicked her nipples and she ached for more. Then he teased them with his tongue. When he had finished with them, he moved back up to her lips, and their tongues mated. The moment was brought to an abrupt end when they heard Emily shout that breakfast was ready. Ross ran his fingers through his hair. "Talk about bad timing." Sabrina picked her top up off the floor. "I'd say it was perfect timing. Another minute or two and God knows what would have happened." He looked at her. "And that would have been a bad thing?" "Oh I don't know. I'm so confused right now." Ross came up behind her and wrapped his arms around her. "That was—" "Wildly erotic?" He said, hugging her from behind. She laughed. "What was that?" "Well, see it's like this. When a man and a woman are attracted to each other—" "Be serious, will you!" "You want serious fine, but it's a conversation we'll need more than five minutes for." "Okay, well, Emily is waiting." "Fine, we'll do it later. But we will do it, Brina," he said, sounding very determined. "I promise you we will.

Chapter Three

Emily looked at the breakfast she prepared. "Looks good if I do say so myself." Her Aunt and Ross walked in. "Wow, this looks great. Thanks for making it." "Sure, Uncle Ross, it's the least I could do after everything you guys did for me." They sat and began eating. A while later Hanson and Scott came in. When Emily saw him, she couldn't contain her enthusiasm. "Scott!" she said in a voice that was a whole octave higher than normal. She cleared her throat and tried speaking again. "I thought you left?" "Scott talked me into letting him stay. It seems that lately I've turned into a softie." Scott chuckled. "Oh yeah, you're a regular soft-serve at Dairy Queen. Besides, I don't call adding extra chores going easy on me." "Oh well, perhaps you think you've been treated unfairly?" "No." He smiled. "That's what I thought." "So I guess you can start after breakfast by helping clean up." "I was already planning on doing that anyway." "Good."

After breakfast, while Sabrina was clearing the dishes, Ross picked up his plate and brought it to the sink. As he handed it to her, he brushed her hand with his fingers. His touch gave her goose bumps. "I'm heading to my place to shower, then I'll head to the station. I'll come back later for our talk." She nodded. "See you later."

A few hours passed, and operation clean sweep was well under way. Ross had come back and was helping too. Scott was putting empty cups into a bag. "Parties are fun but party cleanup sucks." "Well, I don't mind especially since it was my party." "Yeah, well I have more work after this. Dad is really piling it on." "Would you like some crackers and cheese to go with that wine, Scott?" "Not right now, maybe later." Ross looked over at Sabrina who was once again struggling with her vacuum. "Brina, when are you going to get a new one? That one is practically an antique." "There's nothing wrong with it." "Except for the fact that it weighs more than you." "It does not." "Aunt Sabrina, it is pretty old. Maybe getting a new one isn't such a bad idea." "See, she agrees with me." "Well, I don't. It's a vacuum not an heirloom. It stays and that's final." She looked upset like she was on the verge of crying. "Brina, what's—" Before he could finish, she excused herself and went upstairs. "What was that all about?" Scott asked. "Uncle Ross?" "I'm not sure, but I'm going to find out."

He knocked and when he heard nothing went in. She was sitting on her bed, wiping her eyes with a tissue. He never could stand to see her cry. He sat next to her. "Why are you crying? Please don't tell me it's because you've developed some strange attachment to the vacuum." She sniffed into a tissue and laughed. "You must think I'm crazy." "No, at least not yet. I'm just wondering what the big deal is about an old vacuum." "It was James's." He looked at her. "I didn't know. If I did I wouldn't have pushed you." "No, you're right. It' old, and it's an absolute horror to use. Still every time I think about getting rid of it, I just can't." "So buy a new one and put that one in the attic." He took a tissue and wiped the rest of her tears away. "Besides, you aren't the only one who keeps things past their expiration." "What are you talking about?" "Remember that set of tools James had?" "The ones that had belonged to our grandfather?" "Yeah. They were pretty old when he got them, but he still used them. Anyway, I have them." "You do?" "After he died, Hanson and I were going through some of his things in the barn, and we found them. They were pretty worn done, some not even usable anymore, but I still couldn't bring myself to throw them out. They're in my garage." She smiled. "You're such a sweet man." She kissed him on the cheek. "Thanks, but I'd rather be sexy." "Well, you were definitely sexy this morning." "And you, Ms. Taylor, were incredibly hot. Still are." "Thanks." She felt herself flush from the heat he was sending at her. "Ross—" "Don't say another word. I'm going to kiss you again because I have to." His kisses felt like flames that made her burn hotter with every caress. She moaned softly into his mouth, and it drove him wild. "Do you have any idea how much I want you right now? So bad I can taste it." "This can't keep happening." "I'm definitely not complaining." "Ross, be serious for a minute." "Joy kill." She couldn't help but laugh. "Ross, please." "Oh all right. What do you want me to say, Brina?" "Well, for starters. Why do you suddenly want me?" "You silly woman. I don't just *suddenly* want you. I've always wanted you." "Ross . . . I—" "Hear me out, Brina." "All right." "All these years, I kept hoping you'd realize how I felt. When that didn't happen, I had to make a decision. Did I tell you or keep my feelings to myself? If I told you, you might decide to end the friendship. I couldn't risk that. For me the price was too high. So I kept it a secret. But now I'm tired of hiding it. I love you, Brina. I can't remember a time when I haven't loved you." "Oh, Ross, I don't know what to say." "You don't have to say anything. What I'm hoping is that you'll give me a chance. Maybe in time you'll come to love me." "I do love you." "I know but not the way I love you. I'm hoping that will change." She looked at him. "I'm not telling you this to pressure you." She walked to her window. "I'm so sorry. It couldn't have been easy all these years. Keeping those feelings a secret." He laughed. "They were only a secret to you. Everyone else knew." "Actually, to be perfectly honest it was hell." "How could I have been so blind? How could I have not known?" He decided to lighten the mood. "My Oscar-worthy performance?" "Please don't make jokes, now. Not about something as important as this. I care for you, Ross." "I know you do. I also know that I can make you happy. Just give me a chance." Maybe dating was the next logical step. They were after all extremely close had been since they were kids. She already knew the kind of man he was, trusted him completely. "All right I'll give us a chance." He was so happy. "You will? Great! I thought I'd have to do a lot more convincing. Throw in more kissing to wear you down." "Am I that bad?" "Sometimes you think too much." "You're right, I do. Well, not this time. I'm going to throw caution to the wind." "I'm glad, Brina."

Scott and Emily were halfway through with the cleanup when he decided it was time to take a break and talk. "Em, let's take a break." "Okay." They walked out onto the porch. "Listen, about last night." She braced herself. "I didn't get much sleep. I kept thinking about it. I want you to know that I don't regret it, and I hope you don't either." She breathed a sigh of relief. "I don't. I was afraid you would." He smiled. "I'm glad. Listen, I'm not entirely sure where it will all go, but I think we owe it to ourselves to find out." "What if things don't work out? I wouldn't want to lose you as a friend." "You won't. Trust me." He moved closer and his body brushed hers. "I've been thinking about kissing you again ever since last night." "Why don't you stop thinking and start doing?" She said making him smile. "Yeah, why don't I." He pulled her in for a steamy kiss and when they pulled apart Scott was trying to catch his breath. "Em, you've got me so turned on right now. "Would a cold drink help?" He looked down at himself and smiled. "Not unless I poured it down my pants." She laughed.

As they headed inside for something to drink, they bumped into Sabrina and Ross who were on their way out. Ross wore a huge grin on his face. Emily took out a pitcher of tea and poured some. "Uncle Ross looked really happy." "Yeah, he did. There's only one thing that puts a grin like that on a guy's face. He's either gotten lucky or about to." She handed him his tea. "You can't be serious?" "Why not? They're both single, right? Plus I've always thought he had a thing for her." "They've been friends since they were kids." He looked at her. "So were we." She looked at him. "That's different." "How?" "It just is." He laughed.

Ross and Sabrina stood by his car. "So when do you want to go out?" "Boy, you don't let the grass grow under your feet." "Why should I?" "How about Saturday?" "Saturday sounds good. Pick you up at seven?" "Sure. Looking forward to it. I haven't been out on a date since . . ." "Robbie." He cringed. "That guy was a jerk. I never understood what you saw in him." She couldn't resist teasing him. "He had a great butt." He gave her a dirty look, and she burst out laughing. "Very funny." "Sorry, I couldn't resist." She started to walk away when he took hold of her arm. "I know what you mean, I can't resist either." He took her mouth and when he was done, she couldn't feel her legs.

"Betcha Robbie never kissed you like that." He said with a smug smile. "Ah . . . no." "I thought so. That'll give you something to think about 'til Saturday." He got in his car and drove away, leaving her leaning against a barrel for support. *Think? Who could think after being kissed like that?*

When her legs felt strong enough to walk again, she headed back into the house. She found Scott and Emily kissing in the kitchen. When they realized she was there, they pulled apart. "Relax, you two. I had a feeling something was going on." "That obvious eh?" Scott said, grinning. "If the looks during the party weren't enough, finding you in the barn was." "You're okay with it right, Aunt Sabrina?" "Oh course, honey. Why wouldn't I be? I love Scott." "Thanks," he said, blushing. "No thanks necessary. You were a good boy, and you've become a wonderful man. I'm happy you two are together. Now while we are on the subject of sharing, I want you both to know that Ross and I have started dating." Emily looked at her with surprise in her eyes. "Wait, you and Uncle Ross?" "I knew it! What did I tell you." She rolled her eyes. "Great, they'll be no living with him now." "How did you know, Scott?" "When you were going out to his car, the look on his face. Guys only look that happy when they've either gotten lucky or are about to." She burst out laughing. "Sorry for being so blunt." "That's all right. We're all adults." "So you and Uncle Ross? I can't believe it. I mean, I'm happy for you. It's just going to take a while to get used to." She nodded. "For me too. Believe me." "So when are you guys getting together? "Saturday. He's picking me up at seven for dinner and a movie." Scott looked at her. "Why don't we do the same, Em?" "Sure, why not." "Well, I have invoices to catch up on, so have fun."

Later that evening, Sabrina was having a hard time focusing on her work. Ever since Ross had planted that searing kiss on her, she had been good for nothing. *God can that man kiss.* Her thoughts were interrupted by her phone. "Sabrina Taylor." "Sabrina, Michael Harding." "Oh, Mr. Harding, I was just putting your invoice together." "Was wondering if maybe mine got lost in the mail since I usually get it sooner." "I apologize. It was Emily's twenty-first birthday and we had a party." "Gracious is that child twenty-one already?" "Yes, I can't believe it myself. I'll get your bill out first thing tomorrow. You know you are the only customer who calls to find out where their bill is. No one else wants theirs." He laughed. "I'm anal that way." "Well, thanks for understanding about the delay." "Sure. Good-bye, Sabrina." "Take care, Mr. Harding."

Emily and Scott sat in a booth at their favorite diner, Danny's. It was one of those retro diners with big red leather booths and black-and-white checkered floors. It even had a jukebox. They had finished their burgers and were just sitting and talking. "Hey you two. Been a while. So how are things?" Danny asked. They looked at each other. "They're good. Really good." Danny noticed Scott looking and winking at Emily. "What's with the looks?" They laughed. "Let me show you, Danny." He leaned across the table and kissed her. Danny's eyes opened wide with shock. Danny's hand slapped Scott's back. "Well, it's about friggin' time." "I mean, if I was thirty years younger I would have gone for her myself." "Well, then I guess I'm lucky and you're not. Otherwise, I'd have some serious competition." "Damn right you would. This calls for a celebratory sundae. I'll have Flo bring one over." "Thanks, Danny." The movie Emily wanted to see didn't start for another hour, so they had time. "Em, do we have to see *Big Miracle*?" She laughed. "Didn't you say I could pick the movie?" "Yeah, but I didn't think we'd be seeing a movie about whales." "It's based on a true story. It got good reviews. Give it a chance. You might like it." Flo came to their table holding what was probably the biggest, most delicious-looking sundae either of them had ever seen. "Compliments of Danny." "Thanks, Flo."

By the time the movie ended, Scott was eating his words. "I told you that you'd like it." "Yeah, I still can't believe how good it was." She smiled at him. He opened the car door for her, and she got in. "You know you're lucky to have a guy like me. Most guys, like my friend John, would only see a movie like that if you tied him up and made him watch it." She giggled. "So how about rewarding me?" "What did you have in mind?" "How about I take us someplace more private. Then I can show *exactly* what I have in mind." "Okay."

Ross was trying to catch up on paperwork, but he wasn't having much luck. All he could think about was Sabrina. The way she looked half-naked under him. The way she moaned when he kissed her. It was nearing ten o'clock when he decided to call her. "Sabrina Taylor." "Brina, it's me." "Oh, hi. Why are you calling on the business number?" "I figured you'd be working." "You figured right. I had to get out some invoices. I thought you had paperwork." "I did, I do. I am having the hardest time concentrating." *When did he start sounding so sexy?* "That's funny because I've been having the same problem." "Have you? Wonder why that is?" "I haven't a clue." "Brina, I don't think I'm going to make it to Saturday." "It's two days Ross. You'll be fine." "It may be kind of early for me to be saying this, but I miss you." "Actually, I have been sitting here missing you." He was so quiet, she thought they lost connection. "Ross, are you there?" "You miss me?" "Yes, and I'm looking forward to Saturday, but don't let that go to your head." He leaned back in his chair and grinned. "I'll try not to." "Oh and by the way, Scott and Emily are dating." "He dropped the phone. "Sorry. Did you say dating?" "I did." "When did that happen?" "The night of the party. Evidently, that red dress made him wake up and smell the hottie." He sat back in his chair. "'Bout time. Not sure why it took so long for him to notice." "Not everyone is as observant as you." "Tell me about it. Well, as much as I hate getting off the phone with you, I should get back to work." "I need to finish up myself." "Good night, Ross." "Night, Brina."

Sabrina decided to call it a night. She was about to shut off the lamp when she noticed an old picture of her, Ross, and James as teenagers. It was taken during one of the school picnics. She looked at the photo carefully. James was on her right, Ross on her left. Both looking at her while she made funny faces at the camera. She remembered Rebecca had taken the photo. For the first time she noticed the way Ross was looking at her. *He loved me even then didn't he?* She looked at it for a few more minutes and then turned the light out and went upstairs to read.

Scott drove to Hunt's Point or Make-Out Point as it was better known. Both the high school and college crowd brought their dates here, hoping to get lucky. He parked the car and turned off the engine. "So I see that Make-Out Point is just as popular." "Yeah." "I'm sure your dad and Ross brought their dates here." "Probably."

He unfastened both their seatbelts. "What are you doing?" she asked. "I think you know what I'm doing." She smiled and they started kissing. Things quickly escalated. "Let's move to the back, Em." He sat her on his lap and began undoing the buttons of her top. He pulled it over her head and went for the zipper on her jeans. She placed her hand on top of his and helped him pull it down, which drove him crazy. In his haste he yanked the jeans down, and one of the seams ripped. Neither of them paid any attention. She was wearing only her bra and panties now. Which he slowly began to take off. This was one time she wished she wore sexier lingerie. "So why do guys get girls naked while they're still fully clothed?" "Don't know. Guess we just like staring." "Well, you've stared long enough. It's my turn now." "I like the way you think." She unbuttoned his Henley and pulled it over his head. His jeans were button fly and one by one the buttons opened. Pop, pop, pop. No sound was ever more erotic. He wore only boxer briefs now. "I like these. They're sexy." "Thanks. I try." He teased. She pulled them down and took in every inch of him. His body was tight and lean. "I want you, Scott. Every inch you inside me." That nearly made him come right there. "Em, I do want you. Badly, but if you aren't ready, we can wait." She took his hand and placed it on the delta between her thighs. "This is how ready I am." Feeling how wet she was, he lost all control. He pulled out a condom and guided himself into her. It felt so damn good, so right. They were both nearing that edge, but she was first to go over it. He followed, and afterward they lay holding each other in post-coital bliss. "So that was new for us." She laughed. "Man if I had known it would be like that between us I would have made a move on you years ago." She laughed. "I think it happened right when it was supposed to." "Yeah, I guess it did. They stood that way for a while, holding each other. "Um Em, I hate to cut this short, but I have to get up in a couple of hours. I have a lot to do tomorrow. Dad gave me a long list of supplies and then there's the barn repairs, too. If you want we can hang out after I'm done though." "That sounds good." He kissed her, and they started getting dressed. He picked up her jeans and handed them to her. "I'm afraid they've seen better days." "Ya think?" She was laughing. "I'm not as talented with a needle and thread as my

Aunt is, but I can fix them." "I'm glad she's okay with . . . us." "Me too." "Em that was . . . I mean . . . I've been with other girls—" "And I've been with other guys." "I know, but that was pretty amazing?" "It was."

A short time later they were nearly back home. "Scott, there's something we didn't think about." "Oh, what's that?" "Well, I won't be home the full two weeks. I go back sooner, remember?" "Oh crap, your right. Well, I'll just drive out to see you." "Scott, it's like two and a half hours." "Not the way I drive." He joked. "Besides, you're worth it."

Chapter Four

While Scott was in town getting supplies, the guys got started on the barn repairs. The list Hanson had given Scott was pretty long. Not only had they needed their regular supplies but also the wooden planks, which Hanson had ordered previously. Which meant Scott would also be making a trip to the lumberyard. He grinned. When he had first woken him up, he rolled over and put his pillow over his head. Hanson knew it was because he'd been out late with Emily. When he got back, Hanson walked over to him. "What took you so long?" "I would have been back sooner, but someone gave me a list almost as long as *War and Peace*." He raised his brow, Scott looked at him, and they laughed. "So did you get everything?" "Yep, everything but the kitchen sink." "Smart-ass." Hanson eyed the wooden planks loaded on his truck. "Those don't look like the oak I ordered." "That's because they're not. Johnson said the shipment he was expecting got delayed. Won't be in till next week. The oak he had left wasn't enough, so he suggested we use maple instead. Since we already stripped those rotted sections, we don't really have a choice." "Okay let's get this done."

Later that morning, Emily came out wearing fitted jeans, a white T-shirt, and denim jacket. Scott was already hot from working on the barn, but once he saw her, he grew even hotter. The guys began whistling. Emily knew they were teasing her, so she laughed. "Were you guys raised in a barn?" Scott joked. "Actually, I think Pete was. Right, Pete?" Max said. "Yep, spent years next to the cows. Then one day, someone tried to milk me. Damn near killed me." They all roared with laughter. "So where you off to, Miss Emily?" Max asked. "Oh, I thought I'd take Katie up to Miller's Pass." "Nice day for a ride," Hanson said. "That's what I figured." "Hey, maybe you can join me later?" "Sure, as long as Dad doesn't plan on adding a new wing next." "No, I figured we'd save that for after graduation." "Great. I can hardly wait." "We should be finished in a few hours," Max said. "Okay, I'll be in my usual spot." Riley and Dave came out with Katie, already saddled. "Aren't you sweet. Saddling her for me." "Always a pleasure doing anything for you, Em." Riley flirted. "You wanna tone it down, the lady's spoken for." Riley looked at him. "It was the red dress. Wasn't it?" The corners of Scott's mouth curled up. "Something like that." Scott placed a soft kiss on her lips. "Be back in a minute, guys." When they were far enough away from them Scott grabbed hold of her. "Did I tell you how hot you look in those jeans?" "No." His roaming hands found her butt and squeezed it. "Well, you do. I mean you fill them out real nice." "If Dad and the guys hadn't been here I think I would have taken you in one of the stalls." "Control yourself, Mr. Pierce." "I'm a guy, I don't have control." She laughed as she got on Katie. "See you later." The guys came out of the barn in time to see her leave. "Now it's not real often that a woman looks just as good leaving as she does coming, but she sure does make one pretty exit." Riley said. "She sure does." Scott said, smiling.

Three hours later, the barn was good as new. "Looks good if I do say so myself," Scott said. "It sure does." Hanson said. "Good job, fellas." Sabrina came out with a tray of lemonade and sandwiches. "Hi. Figured you could use this right about now." "Bless you," Pete said. The guys scooped up the sandwiches and drank the lemonade to quench their thirst. "The barn looks great." "Yeah, we were just saying that," Max said. "So, Scott, I hear you're joining Emily at Miller's Pass." He looked at his father. "Boy, news travels fast around here." "Well, I made some scones. Take some with you." "Okay, thanks." "Dad, we're good here, right? "Yeah. Go on." "Ah, you might want to do one thing first," Max said. "What?" "Take a shower." "So sorry if my manly scent offends you, Max." "No, not me, but that's cause I smell the same way. But our Miss Emily, on the other hand, smells like a tulip in springtime." "She sure does," Riley said. Scott gave him a look. "Lighten up Pierce. I'm just busting your balls." "Yeah, well you busted them enough this week." "That's your opinion." Riley said grinning. "Whatever. Anyway, you can all relax since I'm going to go shower." "Believe me, you'll thank us later." Riley said trying not to laugh as Scott walked away.

An eager and freshly showered Scott rode Sugar to meet Emily. When he finally came across her, she was asleep in the grass, a book resting on her chest. He got off Sugar and lay down next to her. As he watched her, thoughts of last night aroused him. He kissed her until she woke up. "Hi." "Hi." "Barn done?" "Yeah, it took longer than we thought." "Another Nora Roberts?" "She's the best. You must be tired. You didn't have to come." He raised his hand to her cheek. "I had to. I had to be with you, Em. He kissed her, and before either of them knew what was happening, he was carrying her to an area hidden by trees. "Last night's darkness robbed me from really seeing you. But now I'm going to see every inch of that gorgeous body of yours." He pulled off her shirt, unhooked her bra, and marveled at her perfectly shaped breasts. "You're perfect." He teased each nipple with his tongue, and they peaked in response. She took off his shirt and ran her hands down his back, feeling every muscled inch of him. She flipped him on his back, and she was on top now. She was wet and ready when she guided him inside her. "Em, that feels . . . that is just . . . sooo good." As the excitement continued to build, so did the intensity and pace. Their lovemaking was even better now that they weren't hindered by the backseat of a car. He flipped her on her back, and they moaned in ecstasy as they both came together.

Afterward, they lay in the grass covered by a blanket. They were snacking on the scones Sabrina had given them. "God, I can't believe we did this." "This area is pretty well covered by trees. We would have seen them before they saw us. Besides, it added to the excitement." "Tell, that to Uncle Ross when he arrests us for sex in a public place." He grinned. "He'll probably be doing the same thing with your aunt."

"Please, that's one picture I don't need floating around in my head." He laughed "Just saying. When a man waits that long, self-control is in real short supply." "Well, it's been a long time for her too." "Right. She hasn't seen anyone since that guy, Ron was it?" "Robbie." "Oh right, Robbie. Guy was a jerk. Never liked him. Ross hated him." "How do you know that?" "Believe me, he'd hate any guy she was dating just on principle." "Can we talk about something else besides my aunt and Uncle Ross's sex life?" He laughed. "Sure, how about our sex life?" "Is that all you think about? "No, not all. Besides you know what they say?" "No, what?" "Practice makes perfect." She laughed.

The rest of the week went by, and it was Saturday night. Sabrina was nervous. *I can't believe I'm nervous. It's Ross for heaven's sake. I've known him most of my life.* Emily knocked. "Come in." "Hey, just wanted to see if you needed help getting ready." "Normally, I'd say no but it seems I have a case of first-date jitters. Which I can't believe 'cause it's Ross." "Okay, why don't you show me what you're wearing." "Well, that's the thing. Since he's known me forever he's seen everything." "Well, what about those dresses you made last year?" "I forgot about those." "I'm sure one of them will be perfect."

Ross had gotten held up at the station because two guys got into a fight at the Feed N Seed. Apparently, one of them was flirting with the other's girlfriend. Idiots. Who tries to pick up a woman over chicken feed? He needed to grab a shower and change his clothes before heading to Sabrina's. He called and Emily picked up. "Em, its Ross." "Hi, Uncle Ross. Shouldn't you be on your way?" "Yeah, I should. But I'm not because of two idiots. I'm leaving work now. Could you please tell Brina that I'll be there by seven-thirty?" "Sure and don't worry she's running late too." He grabbed his keys and left.

It was near seven thirty by the time Sabrina was ready. They had decided that she should wear her green dress. It was cotton jersey, so it would be comfortable throughout the night. The dress had a boat neck and three-quarter sleeves. It was A-line and came a few inches above her knee. She wore tan flats and gold hoops. She wore her hair down and loose for a change. "You look great." "Thanks to you. I would have still been scratching my head." "Uncle Ross is not gonna know what hit him." "Yeah, I just hope we aren't going for pizza, otherwise I'm definitely overdressed." "I doubt after waiting all these years, he'd take you for pizza." The doorbell rang. "He's here! Course, he's here. It's seven-thirty and Ross is always on time. He's never late. Oh God, I'm babbling aren't I?" Emily walked out, shaking her head and laughing. When Emily opened the door, Ross had a bouquet of tulips in his hand. "What beautiful tulips." "Well, they're her favorite. I got ready in a bit of a hurry. Do I look okay?" "Better than okay. I'd say very handsome." "Thanks." He was wearing taupe-colored khakis and a sapphire blue shirt. She could tell he was nervous. "Would you like anything to drink? Water? Scotch?" "Very funny. Do I look that nervous?" "Yeah, but if it's any consolation so does she." "Really?" "She took almost an hour trying to figure out what to wear. But you didn't hear that from me." He smiled. "My lips are sealed." Sabrina took one last look in the mirror and went downstairs. Ross and Emily were busy chatting, but the minute Ross caught sight of her he stopped talking. *God, she's beautiful.* "These are for you." He gave her the flowers. "They're lovely." "Not as lovely as you." "Em, could you put these in water?" "Sure." Ross was looking at her. "Is that a new dress? I don't remember seeing it." Sabrina and Emily winked at each other. "Actually I made it." "Oh. Well, wow is all I can say." She laughed. "Wow, works just fine. By the way you look pretty *wow* yourself." She kissed him on the cheek. Emily was watching them and smiling. "Okay, you do know that in order for the date to start you have to leave the house?" "You know I think Scott's sarcasm is rubbing off on you." She laughed. "Have fun." As soon as the door closed behind them, he pulled Sabrina in for a passionate kiss. "What was that for?" "For looking that way for me." He then pulled her in for a second kiss. "And that?" "Just because I wanted to." "So where are we going?" "Rose Hill. There's this French bistro that's supposed to be really good." "Sounds lovely."

Citron Bistro was everything Ross hoped it would be. It was lit by candlelight, and their table was near a fireplace. Ross noticed every man's eyes on Sabrina as they were shown to their table. He couldn't blame them. *Eat your hearts out boys. She's with me. Finally, she's with me.* Once they had gotten their wine and appetizers, Sabrina asked about the restaurant. "So how did you find out about this place?" "Well, Mrs. Haugtry stopped by the station earlier this week." "Was this before or after you found Sammy?" He laughed. "After, but that's another story. "So we got to talking, and I mentioned that you and I were having dinner. That's when she suggested this place." "Great suggestion. It's lovely." "No, you're lovely. I swear when you came down those stairs, my heart stopped." "Oh, Ross. You always know just what to say." "I should. I've been rehearsing for years." She laughed. "Thank you, Ross." She reached for his hand. "You're welcome." After dinner, they discussed the movie they'd be seeing. "So am I going to hate it?" "No, it's based on a book called *The Help*. It's about segregation and the lives of African American housemaids back in the sixties." "Okay. What time does it start?" "Eleven." He looked at his watch. It was almost nine thirty. They could have dessert and make the movie if they ordered within the next few minutes. After perusing the dessert menu, they decided to share the chocolate lava cake. Several minutes later, their dessert arrived and looked positively decadent. Ross asked the waiter to bring the check. "This looks sinful," she said. "It does." He broke off a piece with his fork, dipped it in whipped cream, and fed it to her. Her eyes rolled back she let out a low moan. Which had him thinking of other things. "Better than sex." "That good?" "Taste it and you'll see." She fed it to him. He let the dessert swirl around inside his mouth. His tongue was singing. "Well, since by agreeing I'd be putting my own skills down I'm going to say comes pretty darn close to sex." They laughed.

A few hours later, the movie was over and they were walking back to the car. "So can I pick a movie?" "You can." "I still can't believe stuff like that happened. I mean making people use different toilets, it's crazy." She nodded. "Glad none of that goes on here. I'd have to personally kick anyone's ass if they even tried it." Sabrina looked at him. "I know you would." He looked at her. "So now what?" she asked. He thought for a second and grinned. "Ross, I know that grin. What are you up to?" "You'll see. Come on."

By the time Ross parked the car, Sabrina was laughing so hard she had tears in her eyes. "Hunt's Point!" I can't believe you brought us to Make-Out Point!" He was laughing too. "Well, we are on a date. "Yes, but we aren't pubescent teenagers." "So?" Still laughing, she looked around. "I didn't even think this place still existed. I see it's still just as popular, though." "Yeah, everyone comes here." "I'm surprised you haven't cracked down on it more." "They aren't doing any harm. Just working off some hormones. Besides, if I did that then I wouldn't have any place to bring lovely ladies such as yourself to." "Oh, so who else have you brought here?" He realized he put his foot in his mouth." "No one lately." Her eyebrow went up. "I think the last person I came here with was Susan." She remembered Susan. They went to school together. She was nice, very pretty. Sabrina thought they made a nice couple. Susan ended things and she always wondered why. She had asked him, but he never told her the reason." "You never told me what happened between you." He looked at her. "Well, she was nice and we had fun together but . . ." "But?" "She just wasn't you." She looked at him. "I tried moving on. Told myself it was the smart thing to do. So I'd date. The problem was, I ended up comparing them to you." She cleared her throat. "I don't know what to say." "You don't have to say anything." "Ross, I'm sorry." He gently took her face in his hands. "Listen to me, no more apologizing. What's important, what matters is now and *this*." His kisses stirred her. They kissed again and again, hoping it would fan their flames down to more controllable embers. "So I guess Make-Out Point still has its magic." She was trying to catch her breath but still managed to laugh. "Apparently." He looked at her. "Brina, I know we said we'd go slowly, but I just can't. I have been dreaming about making love to you since I was fifteen. I don't want to dream about it anymore. I want to do it. I want you over me, under me, wrapped around me." She had never felt so wanted in her entire life. "I want you, too. It's just . . ." "Just?" "Sex can complicate things. I'm not sure I'm ready." "You're ready." "Ross, it's been a long time." "It's been a long time for me too." She paused to think. No this time she would just *feel*. "I think I'm ready for complicated." His first impulse was to take her right there, but he pulled back. He fastened her seatbelt, then his and started the car. "What are you doing?" "I'm not some horny teenager who'd be happy doing it in the backseat. When I make love to you it's going to be in my bed." "Ross?" "Yeah?" "Drive fast." He laughed. "Happy to."

As sheriff, Ross always set an example. He never abused his position or the power that came with it. Never broke any traffic laws until tonight. "I know I said to drive fast, but I didn't mean this fast." She teased. "Sorry, I'll slow down. It's just I can't wait another damn minute to get you into my bed." "Remember, patience is a virtue." "Not now it isn't." She laughed. They arrived at his house, and the minute he turned off the engine he reached across the seat and kissed her. He stopped suddenly, and then he was at her door, pulling her out and against him. He couldn't get enough of her. His hands were everywhere. She grabbed at his shirt and pulled him closer. "Ross, I want you, *now*." He picked her up and got to his front door. He put her down to get his keys out of his pants pocket. She fondled him from behind. "Brina . . . oh God . . . just let me get the damn door open." He opened it, scooped her up, and kicked the door shut behind him. She was biting his earlobe and he felt his eyes roll. Somehow they managed to stumble to the sofa while tearing at each other's clothes. She was having trouble with the buttons on his shirt, so he ripped it open. He unzipped her dress and exposed her breasts, which were showcased in black lace. "Thank you." "For what?" "For wearing *that*. You look so god damn sexy it should be illegal." "Maybe you should arrest me?" "I am going to do more than that." He made her stand up, and her dress dropped to the floor. Not only had she been wearing one hell of a sexy bra but a matching thong too. "I want you to know that if I die tonight, I die happy." She laughed. "Guess I should take my pants off." "Yeah, they might get in the way." He took both his pants and boxers off at the same time. Then he wrapped his arms around her, and with a flick of his wrist, her bra came undone. He knelt down in front of her and pulled her thong down using his teeth. He lifted her, and she wrapped her legs around him. Their movements were slow at first, but soon their pace quickened. "Brina . . . so good . . . I can't . . ." She felt herself peak. They let go and came together in a swirl of ecstasy.

Afterward, they lay on the floor in each other's arms. "We'll make it to the bed next time," he teased. "That was . . . you're incredible." He kissed her. She propped herself up on one arm. "You weren't so bad yourself. By the way, how did you do that thing with my bra?" "Just another skill." "Fine, don't tell me." "How 'bout we move this to my nice, soft bed?" She cuddled closer, practically purring. "Sounds heavenly." He swept her up into his arms and carried her into his bedroom.

"You know I've dreamed of this." "You have?" "Yeah, but the real thing is so much better."

Emily woke to find her Aunt's bed hadn't been slept in. She went downstairs and saw Scott walking toward the house. She opened the door. Scott noticed she was wearing a very short nightshirt. "Do you always sleep in that?" "No, but after yesterday I didn't feel like wearing much to bed." He was trying to get his mind off her poor excuse for a nightshirt. "So where's your Aunt?" "With Ross." "What doing errands?" "No, she never came home last night." "Really? Go, Ross!" She watched him and laughed. "What's so funny?" "You are. You should see how you look." "Well, I'm happy for the guy. He's been waiting a long time." "He has, and I'm happy for them both." The phone rang and she picked it up. "Oh hi, Uncle Ross. Yes, I figured she was with you. Not a problem. Tell her not to hurry home on my account. Right. Bye." "Ross?" "Yeah. He just wanted me to know that she's with him." "Like we didn't already figure that out." He grinned.

Sabrina put on one of Ross's old jerseys and went out to the kitchen. "I'm making us breakfast." "Oh that's nice of you." "Nice has nothing to do with it. I'm friggin' starving after last night." "I'm pretty hungry myself." "Okay, so pancakes or French toast?" "Pancakes." "Coming right up." He gathered the ingredients and began making the batter. "I should call Emily. I don't want her to worry." "I already called her." "Oh. What about the station?" "I called them too. Andy is taking care of things." "Well, you seem to have thought of everything." "Yeah, I have." "At least let me make the coffee and set the table." "If you insist." She put on a pot of coffee and set two places at the table while he heated up the griddle. "So what do you want to do today?" She drank some water. "Do?" "Yeah I thought we'd spend the day together." "Oh, Ross, I can't. I have so much work waiting for me." "Like?" "Well, I have to put together a ton more invoices that need to be sent out. Some are already late." He poured the batter into the pan and it sizzled. "When was the last time you played hooky?" She looked at him and laughed. "High school." "Hmmm. Well, if anyone deserves a day off it's you." "What you're suggesting can't be done. There's too much to do." "There's always stuff that needs to be done. Sometimes you just have to take a break. Everyone needs an MH day." "MH?" "Mental Health Day." She laughed. "So what would you have me do on this MH day?" "I've got a few ideas." "I'll bet you do." She smiled back. "I'll make a deal with you." "I'm not going to like this, am I?" "Oh stop. I'll spend half the day with you. Then I have to get back and do some work." He was pouring and flipping pancakes. "So till like five? "That's too late. I was thinking more like two." He continued to stack the cooked pancakes on the plate. "Not long enough. Four." "I have a ton of work. Three. Take it or leave it." "Woman, you drive a hard bargain." He turned off the griddle and brought the pancakes over. She looked at them. "Chocolate chip?" "They're your favorite." "They look delicious." They sat down and both couldn't want to dig in. She took a bite and her taste buds thanked her. "These are delish! I may make the best blueberry pancakes, but your chocolate chip ones kick ass." He couldn't help but laugh.

Chapter Five

Hanson and crew were busy putting fresh water and feed in the stalls when Scott came in. "So, Scott, how did things go the other night?" Riley asked. "That would be none of your business." "Struck out huh?" "You ever think there's more to women than just sex?" "No." "I'm not surprised." "Anyway, I need to talk to my dad. So if you could give us a few." "Yeah, sure. We'll take our union ten. Come on guys." "So I'm sure you are wondering what this is all about." 'Must admit that my curiosity is piqued. He walked over and sat down on a hay bale. "I want to talk about Mom." Hanson was surprised since he never wanted to talk about his mother. He sat on the hay bale next to him. "Okay, what do you want to know?" "Well, how old were you?" "Well, I was twenty-two, and she was turning twenty-one, I think." "What was it like, being with her?" "What's with all the questions about your mother? You were never interested before." "I guess maybe I'm finally ready to try and understand. You loved her, right?" "Son, I was a goner the first moment I laid eyes on her. She was singing, our eyes met, and that was all she wrote. "She sang?" "Yeah, sexy as hell too." "So what went wrong? I mean you still loved each other right?" "Son, you're young and, well, you'll learn that sometimes love isn't always enough." "I don't get it. How could she just leave us like that?" "I've often asked myself that same question. The only one that could really answer it would be her. She'd always thought if she could get somewhere, a big city, she'd get discovered. I guess after we had been married a while she realized that wasn't going to happen." "Do you ever think about her? "I loved her and she gave me you. Of course I think about her." "What about you, Scott? How do you feel about her?" He shrugged. "I always thought I hated her, but I don't. Dad, do you ever regret the choices you made? I mean if you moved somewhere else, Mom might have stayed." "True, but then we'd have both been miserable. She and I had several good years together, and wherever she is, I hope she's happy."

After they finished breakfast, Sabrina cleared the dishes and started washing them. "Brina, I said you didn't have to do that." "I know I don't. But I want to." "How about a compromise? You wash and I dry?" "Fine." She handed him the dish towel. "So I've been thinking, you up for a picnic?" "A picnic sounds perfect actually. Wait." "What?" "I can't wear the dress from last night." "You can borrow one of my old T's and a pair of shorts. They'll be big on you, but a belt should hold them up." "I'll probably look ridiculous but okay." "You look good in anything. I've got the rest of this. Go pick something out and get ready." "Okay."

An hour later, they were at the lake, picnic basket in tow. They walked around the lake, hand in hand. Stopping to steal kisses from one another. "You were right, Ross. This is just what the doctor ordered." "I'm you're your enjoying it." "You getting hungry?" "A little." "Okay, let's find a nice spot and eat."

Ross had packed a really nice lunch, which included grilled chicken, pita bread, goat cheese, and fresh figs. He even brought a bottle of chilled wine. "Ross, I still can't believe that you packed all this while I got dressed." "Just another skill." "Well, it's great." "Hold on. We aren't done yet. He pulled out a container of the ripest-looking strawberries. He opened the container and held one up to her mouth. "Try this." She leaned in and took a bite. The ripe berry juices dripped down her chip. He learned in and kissed it. "Hmm, very juicy." She picked a berry and offered it to him. He gladly took a bite. Licking the juices off his lips with his tongue, he went in for another bite, taking what was left of the berry and her fingers into his mouth. She felt her breath catch. "Hmm, so sweet. Though I can think of something else that would taste even sweeter." He pulled the T-shirt up over her head, revealing her lacy bra. "God, I love this bra." He moved his arm around her back, and with a flick of his wrist it came undone. She felt herself shudder as the air hit her nipples. He planted a single kiss on each of them. "For what I have in mind, I think we need more privacy." He carried her to a secluded area surrounded by trees. As he laid her down, her hair fanned out in the grass. He undid the belt and then slowly pulled the shorts off. She was licking her lips in anticipation. He kissed her moving downward though he took his time, not wanting to miss a single inch of her. When he arrived at the place he sought, he paused. "Now, we'll see what's sweeter you or the berries." She felt his tongue brush her lightly, and she moaned. He used his tongue over and over to whip her into an erotic frenzy. She was practically breathless. "Ross . . . please." He stopped and looked up at her. "Please what?" "I . . . I . . . can't take anymore." He smiled and licked her as if she were an ice-cream cone melting in the summer heat. She moaned in pleasurable torture. "Ross . . . I . . ." He stopped momentarily to look up and meet her eyes. "You what? I wanna hear you say it." He moved his tongue in continuous circles. Driving her closer to the edge but not allowing her to fully go over it. She reached out and grabbed at the grass. She was panting. "Ross . . . please." He smiled, and with one swift motion, sent her over the edge.

Emily was working on her economics project due upon her return. "God, could this be any more boring?" Someone knocked. "Come in." Scott walked in, hands behind his back. "What are you doing? You know I have to work on this." "Yeah, I know. I just thought you might need a break." "Boy, do I ever." "Supply and demand. Inflation, deflation. Always put me right to sleep." "So what's behind your back?" "Nothing." "Oh really? Then show me your hands." "Can't right now." She got off her bed and walked over to him. "Come on, let me see." "What are you, five?" He pulled out bouquet of wildflowers that had obviously been picked. "Oh they're beautiful." Yeah, I figured after dreary economics you'd need a lift." "Definitely. Thank you." "You're welcome. Anyway, I have to go help Riley fix the chicken coup. Why don't you stop by when you're done?" "Sure see you in bit."

Ross and Sabrina were dressed and putting the remnants of their picnic away. “You outdid yourself, Ross, really.” “Thanks I aim to please, in *every* way I can.” She shook her head. “You are shameless.” “And proud of it.” She looked down at her watch. “We should start heading back.” “Yeah, okay.”

When Emily felt as if her eyes were about to bleed, she closed her book and went to find Scott. He and Riley were still working on the chicken coup. “Hey there, lady in red.” “Don’t you ever stop?” Scott asked. “If I do its cause I’m dead.” Scott laughed. “So how’s it going?” She asked. “We’re just about done. How about we go into town and grab some dinner at Jake’s?” “I can’t, I still have more work to do.” “Oh,” he said, sounding disappointed. “We could go for a quick walk?” Scott looked at Riley. “You got this?” “Yeah.” “Thanks. Later.”

Hanson, Pete, and Dave were outside the barn when Ross and Sabrina got back. “Well, it’s about time you showed up. We were about to send out the search parties.” Hanson teased. “Glad you didn’t because I would have been too busy to answer.” He grinned. “So is it safe to assume that the big-assed grin you’re wearing is because you two are finally together?” Dave asked. She answered by planting a long steamy kiss on Ross. “That sound you’re hearing is my ego deflating since no one has ever kissed me like that.” Pete said. “Eat your hearts out, boys,” Ross said, grinning from ear to ear. “We should go to Jake’s and celebrate.” “You down, Ross?” Steve asked. He looked at Sabrina. “Go, have fun.” “Count me in.” “Great,” Pete said. “Well, I’d better get inside. I have lots of work waiting for me,” she said. “Yeah I’ve got stuff to do back at the station.” She kissed him good bye, and he watched her walk back to the house. “We’re real happy for you, Ross,” Pete said. “Yeah, we know you’ve always been crazy about her,” Dave said. “Thanks, boys. Call me later and let me know when you’re heading to Jake’s. I’ll probably meet you there.” “Will do.” Pete said.

A while later, Emily and Scott arrived at the milking parlor, which was on the south side of the farm. It wasn’t as large as some of the surrounding farms, but it held its own. Max was there. “Hey, you two.” “Hi, Max, would it be okay if I—” “Sure, go ahead. Why don’t you go over there and milk that group?” “Okay.” She went over and got work. “How ’bout you Scott?” “No thanks, Max. Horses are my thing, not cows." He laughed. "Oh before I forget, a bunch of us are going to Jake's tonight to celebrate Ross's finally getting with Sabrina. You interested?" Scott looked at Emily. "You should go. I have work to do anyway." "Count me in, Max." "Good."

Chapter Six

Emily knocked on Sabrina's office door. "Come in. Hey, Em." "Hi, I came to get all the deets of your date with Uncle Ross." "Deets?" "Details, Aunt Sabrina." "Oh right. What is it you want to know?" "Everything." She laughed. "Okay then we're gonna need some ice cream." "Before dinner?" "Screw dinner." She laughed. "Whatever you say, Aunt Sabrina." She followed her into the kitchen. "So rocky road or cookie dough?" "Gotta be cookie dough." "Exactly what I was thinking." She took out the container and placed it in front of them. She got them both water and handed Emily hers. She was just taking a sip when she asked her, "So how was the sex?"

She nearly spit out her water. "What? I mean I know you guys did it. You weren't spending all those hours playing board games." "No, we sure weren't. Okay, first I need ice cream." She gave them each two scoops. After putting the container away, she sat down at the counter with her. "Okay, now fortified with cookie dough, I am ready to answer your questions." "Again I ask, how was the sex?" She laughed. "So I guess we won't move on until I answer right?" "Right." "It was good. *Really* good." "You're glowing." "Am I? I feel great. I haven't felt this good in a long time." "I'm happy for you." "Thanks. I'm happy for me too." She took another spoon of ice cream. She thought about saying something else, but then she didn't. Emily noticed. "Something else on your mind?" "Oh you know me. I think too much." "Yes, you do. What are you afraid of?" "Just that he's wanted me for so long, and now that we're together—" "You're afraid he'll get tired of you?" "Yes." "That will never happen. He's head over heels for you." "You think so?" "I *know* so." "What about Scott?" "The truth? I think I'm falling for him." "I know." "That obvious huh?" She laughed. "Oh yeah on both ends." "What?" "Oh come on, Em, he's crazy about you." "I know he likes me." "Likes? Honey, he's falling for you like a ton of bricks." "Then I guess the feelings mutual." She said it sounding a little down. "What's wrong, Em? You say that as if it's a bad thing." "It just makes me a little afraid, that's all." "Why?" "Well, being in love is great but sometimes things don't stay that way. Like with Sam and Jason." "Jason cheated on Sam, Em." "I know. Which is why she's the way she is with guys." "She's afraid of them doing to her what Jason did. So she dumps them before they can hurt her." "Em, Scott would never ever do that to you." "I know." "There's something else going around in that pretty head of yours. What is it?" "It's just couples break up, and well—" "You're afraid if you did, you won't be friends anymore?" "Yeah, I mean we've been friends since we were kids. I'd hate to lose that friendship." "I understand your concern, but don't let fear stop you from taking a chance." "You're right. So getting back to Uncle Ross. You know the guys are all heading to Jake's tonight right?" "Yes." "Well, then you know they're going to want to know about you two." "You think so?" "Are you kidding? Those guys are worse than the old ladies down at the book club." She laughed. "Well, Ross isn't the kind to kiss and tell, so they won't get much." "Boy, I'd love to be a fly on the wall when Jake finds out." "He'll definitely be surprised." "Surprised? He's going to be shocked as shit." She laughed. "You're probably right." "You know I had a crush on him when I was a teen." "Really, Em? You never told me." "Well, I never told anyone. It was just one summer. I was sixteen, and Jake was the classic bad boy. He had a bar, rode a bike, and wore a leather jacket. Plus all that dark wavy hair and pale green eyes." "Did he ever figure out you had a crush on him?" "He must have. I mean I was at the bar almost every day." "Yeah, that should be a dead giveaway." "Anyway, it was only one summer, and then I was over the whole bad boy thing. That's when I started dating Mike who was the epitome of holy." "Mike Miller? Wasn't he the one who wanted to be a minister?" "Yep, like I said, holy." She laughed. "Well, as much as I hate to break up girl time, I have to get back to work." "As much as I hate to admit it, I have to get back to boring economics myself. See you when my eyes start bleeding again." They both laughed.

A while later, the phone rang. "Sabrina Taylor." "So formal. I almost believe you're civilized on that farm of yours?" She smiled. "Nico, so nice to hear from you." "Isn't it though?" "Still modest I see." "Always." She had interned at his design company back in New York. "So what's new in Mayberry?" "Nico, Buttermilk Falls is a lot bigger than Mayberry." "It may be bigger, but it's about as exciting as Mayberry. Anyway, talk to me. Tell me you've met some gorgeous man who will steal you away from life on the prairie?" "Well, as a matter of fact there is someone." "Really? Do tell and don't leave anything out. Is he Rock Hudson or Cary Grant handsome? How did you meet him? Have you had sex? If so is he good in bed?" "Whoa, slow down," she said, laughing. "You've already met him." He paused. "I have? When?" "At my brother and sister-in-law's funeral." He thought back. "Refresh my memory. What does he look like." About six feet tall, light brown hair, and chocolate brown eyes." "Wait, the sheriff?" "Yes." "I remember him now. He's not really Hudson or Grant, more like Cusack, but after *Say Anything*, though." "I never thought about it but you're right." "You know he's had me ever since he showed up outside Ione Skye's bedroom window playing 'In Your Eyes.'" "Me too." "So longtime friend turned lover. How delicious." "Well, if you like that, wait till you hear the rest." "Oh do tell. I'm all ears." "Well, it seems that I was dumber than wood because I never knew he'd always felt that way." He paused. "Wait, so he was into you, and you never knew?" "That's exactly what I'm saying." "I always knew you were slow but—" "I know, I know." "An unrequited love. Oh this is almost tragic. I think I'm going to cry." She heard sniffling. "Nico, I don't have time for this. I have work to do." "Fine. Scoff at my pain. Go feed a chicken, cow, or whatever it is you do there. Lord knows it's not designing." She grew annoyed. "Nico, we've been over this like a hundred times." "So I mean I don't get it. Why can't you design for me again? I mean, I'm willing to let you do it from that farm you call home. You could overnight them to me." "Nico, I'm flattered but—" "Honey, be anything you want, but just do it. It's a crying' shame to waste talent like yours. Believe me, I've seen a lot of flash-in-the pan talent over the years, and that isn't you. You've got a real creative flare and you love doing it." "I do." "You must miss designing the over-the-top stuff? Things that can only come from working in a big city like New York? I mean just last week Ivanka Trump came in wanting me to design something outrageously bold for the Met Costume Gala." "Ivanka Trump? Really? Nico, that's wonderful." "It is, isn't? I almost fainted. Anyway, think about it. I miss you. I miss your work." "I miss you too. It's just I have so much to do. It just doesn't fit in." "Well, maybe you just haven't tried hard enough." "You're being pushy again." "Honey, I'm a New Yorker, we invented pushy." She laughed. "Just promise me you'll think about it." "Nico." "Promise me." "Fine, I promise." "Anyway, back to your man. "He's a sheriff, so he comes complete with handcuffs. I love men in uniform. Don't you?" "Yes, who could forget Richard Gere in *An Officer and a Gentleman*?" "Oh please, don't get me started, honey." She laughed and glanced at her clock. "I have to run." "Wait, let me guess. Timmy's stuck in the well again." "You're terrible." "I know, but you love me anyway." "Yes, I do." "So I'm thinking of visiting you and that hunky lawman of yours." "Really? I'd love for you to visit. It's been ages. Last time you only stayed overnight. This time you should stay for a few days." "Oh I don't know. I mean moí on a farm for that long. It just seems wrong somehow. Doesn't it?" She couldn't help shaking her head. "You'll be fine. I'll be with you the whole time." "Well, why the heck now! How's June for you?" "Well, Scott will be graduating then." "Scott? Foreman's son, right?" "Yes, actually he and my niece just started dating." "Really? What's their story?" "Nico, I have to go. I have work to do." "Oh please Timmy can stay in the well a few more minutes." "Fine. Quick version. Friends since childhood. Red dress, which I made and *bam*." He sighed. "Ah, nothing like a red dress to stir up the passions of the young. I remember those days. Francois was his name. I met him in Paris during Fashion Week. He was the one that got away." "You don't talk about him much." "I don't like talking about it. It was difficult to get over him." He grew quiet. "I'm sorry, Nico." "Why are you sorry? It's water under the bridge at this point. Anyway,

I'll give you a call to discuss dates." "Sounds good. Can't wait to see you." "And I can't wait to see your local lawman, again. Yum." She smiled. "Be in touch. Ta-ta." "Ta-ta, Nico." She hung up and thought back to when she first started working for him. *"Remember the number one rule in fashion, honey, and you'll never go wrong." "What is that?" "Never design what you yourself wouldn't wear." She looked at him with a conflicted expression. "You disagree?" "Well, I—" she hesitated. "It's okay to have your own opinion. In fact, I encourage it." "All right. In that case, I disagree because I've designed things that I wouldn't wear but could see someone else wearing. I thought that was part of being a designer?" He looked at her for what felt like an eternity. "Oh, darling, we are going to get along famously." "I'm sorry but I don't understand. You said the main rule was to never design what you wouldn't wear." "I did. However, it's not true." "It isn't? So why say it?" "Because I wanted to see what kind of person you are. A yes gal who will never disagree with the boss, which, to be honest, I have no use for or someone who will not only disagree but vocalize it too." She looked at him. "So it was test?" He nodded. "Bingo. Which you passed with flying colors." She smiled. "So now that we've established that you have a mind of your own, let's get to work."* Sabrina smiled at the memory. Nico had tested her a few more times during her tenure there. Feeling tired, she shut her office lamp and headed upstairs to read.

The guys walked inside Jake's, and when Jake saw them, he came out from behind the bar to greet them. "Where's Harris?" "He's finishing up at the station. He'll be here soon." "So what'll it be, boys?" "Whatever you got on draft." "Comin' right up." "So, Scott, what's new?" "Em and I are dating." He looked at him with surprise in his eyes. "When did that happen?" "The other night at the party." "Yeah, I was sorry I missed it. I heard it was good." "It was." Ross walked in. "Well, look who the cat dragged in. 'Bout time you got here, Harris," Jake said. "Oh were you missing me, Jake?" He flipped him off and Ross smiled. "Sorry, Scott, back to you and Emily." "One minute we were friends, and the next we were making out." Jake laughed. "I've had that happen myself, but usually there was alcohol involved." He laughed. "Yeah, well, no alcohol here." "You know, it was that red dress." Ross teased. "Can't blame the man. She was hot," Riley said. Scott gave him a look. "What? I'm just sayin'." "Yeah, well don't." "Jeez, so touchy."

"Anyway, enough about me and Em. Ross is the one with the *really* big news." Jake looked at him. "Oh?" He sipped his beer. "You gonna tell me, or do I have to shine a bright light in your eye?" "No bright light required. Sabrina and I are together." Jake almost dropped the glass he was holding. "Are you shitting me? Son of a bitch!" He came out from behind the bar and gave him a hard slap across his back. "So you finally grew a pair, eh?" "Yeah, I finally did." "About fuckin' time. This calls for a celebration! Drinks are on the house!" He lined up eight shot glasses and began pouring tequila into each one. Hanson put his hand over the top of his glass. "None for me, Jake, I'm driving." "Okay." The rest knocked back their shots. Jake wanted details. "So how did it happen? When did it happen?" He looked at him. "Since when did you become so interested in my love life?" "Since I've been single for way too long." "Sorry, but I don't feel like sharing right now," he said, trying not to grin. "Stop being an ass." "Yeah, come on." Dave said. Ross took another sip of his beer and grinned. "Maybe later."

A few hours and several shots later, the boys had talked about everything from farming to school to sports but nothing about Sabrina. Jake was really pushing now. "Come on, Harris, I thought we were friends. I thought we shared stuff?" "We are and we will at our next mani/pedi appointment." "Come on, at least tell us how you made your move. You owe me that much." Ross looked over his glass. "How you figure that?" "Well, all I heard about for years was Sabrina this, Sabrina that. Sabrina's my sun, my moon, my starlit sky." They all looked at him. "Hey, I never said that." "True but you probably thought it." He laughed. "Yeah, I probably did." "You owe me, Ross." "Jeez, all right already." "Sabrina had come upstairs to get me for breakfast. When she came in, I was in my boxers." Jake interrupted. "Which ones?" "What does it matter?" "Humor me." He rolled his eyes. "The ones with envelopes on them." Jake shook his head and started laughing. Scott interrupted. "What's so funny?" "The boxers he had on were a gift from Susan, his ex." "So you were wearing the boxers your ex-girlfriend gave you when you made your move on your current girlfriend? Nice." Riley said. Ross made a frustrated face. "You guys want to hear this or talk about my boxers some more?" "Sorry buddy, go on." "I caught her looking at my chest." "Makes me hot." Jake teased.

"Fuck you, Jake." "Sorry, you're not my type." He smirked and took a sip of his beer. "Then what happened?" Steve asked. "Well, I called her on it. She denied it at first but then she admitted it." Hanson ate some peanuts. "Then?" "Well, after I bragged about my studly status, she told me I would make some girl very happy. That's when I got upset. I grabbed her and told her that I didn't want any girl. I wanted her. Then I kissed her." "Then what?" Dave asked. "Then Em called us down for breakfast." The guys all made sounds of disappointment. Jake poured him another beer. "Well, that timing sucked." "Yeah, but it all worked out, so I'm fine with it." "Ross, I'm glad things worked out," Hanson said. "Thanks." "And on that note, I think we should get going. Morning comes real early." Hanson said. "I'll walk you out. Hey, Nick, cover me." "Sure thing, Jake." Jake walked them to Hanson's truck. As everyone loaded into Hanson's truck, Jake took Ross aside. "Hey, you know I'm real happy for you about Sabrina, right?" "Yeah I know, and thanks." "For what?" "For all those years." "That's what friends do. Besides, you did the same for me after Angela and I broke up." Scott poked his head out of Hanson's truck. "Hey, if you two are done with your bromance moment we'd like to get home." They flipped him off, and he went back inside the truck, smiling. Jake waved as they drove away, and he went back into the bar.

Chapter Seven

The next morning, Ross sat at his desk, holding his head. "You want me to give you some aspirin?" He looked up at Linda, the station's receptionist. He shook his head gingerly. "That's the last time I let Jake talk me into doing tequila shots." Andy came in. He was the deputy. "What's the matter with him?" "Oh, one too many tequila shots at Jake's." "Been there, done that. Which is why I'm reformed. I never get near anything named Jose." She laughed. "Would you two mind keeping it down?" "Not our faults you had too much to drink." "We were celebrating." "Celebrating what?" Andy asked. "Him and Sabrina finally getting together." "No shit! Really? That's great." Andy forgot about Ross's hangover and slapped him on the back. Which made Ross turn slightly green. "Oops, sorry, boss. How come I didn't know about this?" "You left early the night they went out. So you missed all the hoopla." Ross looked up at her. "Hoopla?" "Well, you know. You coming in from that fight at the Feed N Seed, all upset 'cause it made you late for your date. You just went on and on about it." "Well, any man dumb enough to attempt picking up a woman in a place that sells fertilizer deserves to have his butt kicked. Am I right, Andy?" "Absolutely, I mean there are other places far better." "Like?" Linda asked. "Like the supermarket." She looked at him. "You can't be serious?" "I am. In case you haven't heard, supermarkets are the new pickup spots." "That's ridiculous," she snapped. He shrugged. "You asked." "So how does that work?" Ross asked. "Pretty well, actually. I've gotten a few dates while scoping out produce. "So tell me, what lines did you use in these situations?" she asked. "Well, if I saw a cute girl husking corn, I'd walk up to her and say, 'I like the way you husk your corn.'" Ross laughed and Linda rolled her eyes. "You're joking, right?" "Nope. Another good one, melons. They open up all kinds of possibilities." Ross looked at Andy and laughed. "Jeez, who knew I could have been in the produce aisle racking up dates?" "For heaven's sake, who are you kidding? There's only one girl for you. Always has been always will be." "You know me, Linda." "'Course I do." "Anyway, Sheriff, the reason why I came in was because Mrs. Haugtry has managed to lose Sammy again." Linda threw her arms into the air. "When is that woman going to learn? She keeps using the same puny leash, and he just keeps getting away from her. Why a petite woman like that would want a huge dog like Sammy is beyond me." "For protection most likely," Andy said. "Protection from what? Squirrels?" she countered. "Well, like it or not he's on the loose. So someone needs to track him down." Andy looked at Ross. "Sheriff, don't take this the wrong way, but you look like crap." "None taken. 'Cause I feel like crap." "I'll take this one. It's been a while since I had to find Sammy. It'll be fun." Linda looked at him. "Fun?" "Sure, I figure I can ride him back." They laughed and Ross held his head. "That's it. You are going to do two things. The first is to put some carbs in that there stomach of yours." "And the second?" "Take two aspirin and call me in the morning." "Cute, Linda real cute." "I'll radio when I find Sammy, Sheriff." "Okay and please tell Mrs. Haugtry for the thousandth time that we have better things to do than locate Sammy." "Will do." He left. "Now you go on down to Danny's and get some pancakes. They'll soak up all that excess acid wreaking havoc in your stomach." "Yes, ma'am."

By the time Ross got to Danny's, his head was slightly better. Danny saw Ross come in and he walked over to his table. "Mornin' Sheriff." Ross winced. "Looks like someone is hungover." "Yeah, and if you don't mind, could you keep it down? My head hurts." "Keep it down!" Ross put his head on the table. "I run a business. You want quiet go to the friggin' library." "Fine." He said meekly. "So what'll it be?" "I'll take an order of pancakes." "Short or long?" "Long." "Any toppings?" Ross looked up at him. "Do I look like I'm up for toppings?" Ross knew his balls were being busted. "No toppings." "You sure you don't want some strawberry or blueberry compote?" Ross was growing greener by the minute. "Just the pancakes." "What about whipped cream?" That was the last straw. Ross felt his stomach lurch, and he ran to the bathroom. Danny chuckled all the way back to the counter. "What's wrong with the sheriff, Danny?" One of the customers asked. "Oh, he just doesn't like whipped cream on his pancakes."

Meanwhile, Scott was feeling a bit hungover himself. His father was eating a breakfast of scrambled eggs, bacon, and toast. "Mornin', Sleepin' Beauty." "Thanks for not waking me." "Well, I took pity on you. Tequila tends to do a number on you the next day." "Tell me about it. Oh let's do shots to celebrate. Should have stopped after the second one." How many did you have?" "Six." "Well, you'll be good for nothing today." Scott looked at him. "Is that all you care about? Chores? A little sympathy for the man with the migraine." "You want sympathy, you'll find it in the dictionary between shit and syphilis." He sat down and attempted to drink his coffee. The smell from his dad's breakfast was making him sick. "God, that smell." "Go sit over there then." He moved but he was still able to smell it. "I can still smell it." "So don't breathe." He looked at him, annoyed. "What do you want me to say? All I've been hearing lately is how I don't treat you like a man. Well, I am now. You're hungover. Deal with it." "Great, now you decide to listen to me." Hanson grinned. He decided to have a little more fun at his son's expense. "Why don't you come back over here and have some of this greasy bacon?" Scott felt his stomach turn. "Thanks, but I think my liver needs to recover first before I start working on clogging my arteries. Hanson looked at him and laughed. "If you want I can make you pancakes. They'll help." "You think so?" "That's what I usually eat when I was hungover." "All right." He made the batter and heated the griddle. Someone knocked. "Come in." Hanson yelled and Scott winced. "Mind keeping it down?" "Wear earplugs." Emily walked in. "Morning." "Morning, Emily. I'm fixing pancakes for a hungover Scott. Would you like some?" "No, thanks. I already ate." She looked at Scott. "Hungover." She walked over to him. "Poor baby. Are you feeling really bad?" "Nah." "That's not what you were saying just a few minutes ago. You should have heard him. I'm hungover. Poor me. Blah-blah." She laughed. "Here, eat your pancakes." Scott looked at the plate set before him. He didn't feel as nauseous as he thought he would. He took a small bite and waited to see how it would react. When the first bite went down okay, he took a second, and then a third. A short time later, he had finished the whole stack and was feeling better. "You were right. My stomach does feel better." Hanson walked over to Scott and put his hand to his ear. "What? I'm sorry could you repeat that?" Scott rolled his eyes. "You were right." "Well, will wonders never cease." "So, Em, did you finish that project?" "Just about." "What's the subject?" Hanson asked. "Economics." Hanson shook his head. "That stuff is Greek to me." Emily laughed. "To me too." "So are you up for a walk?" "You want to milk the cows again, don't you?" She smiled. "What is it with you and cows?" "Probably the same thing with you and horses." "Got me there. I just need to shower. Give me an hour, and I'll meet you by the barn." "Okay."

Sabrina sat at her desk trying to print out the invoices she had finished doing. So far she wasn't having much luck, thanks to the printer. Every time she tried printing, it jammed. She'd remove the jam, but it would just happen again. "Piece of crap." She picked up the phone and dialed. After several rings, it was finally answered. "Mellow." The voice sounded groggy. "Jake? He took a minute to process the voice. "Sabrina?" "You were expecting the girl from last night?" "There is no girl from last night." "What kind of bartender are you?" "Evidently not a very good one." She laughed. "Did I wake you?" "Yeah, but I had to get up anyway." "I'm sorry. I figured you'd be up by now. It's after twelve." "Yeah, usually I am, but it was a bit of a rough night." "What did you guys end up doing last night?" "Before or after the tequila?" "You have my sympathies." He laughed. "Thanks." "So what's up?" "Well my stupid printer is acting up again." "So you want me to have a look-see?" "If you don't mind. I'm sorry to bother you, but you're the only one who's ever able to fix it. I'm sorry, you're probably hungover." He laughed. "Just a bit of a headache and one heck of a cotton mouth. Harris called earlier to curse me out for giving him that much Cuervo. Anyway, I need to shower and eat something first. How's one thirty sound?" "That's fine, but don't eat, I'll fix you lunch." "That's not necessary." "Nonsense, it's the least I can do since you are going to fix this piece of crap for me." Jake heard her bang it. "Easy, we need it in one piece if I'm going to fix it." She laughed. "Good point. See you soon."

Since she couldn't do anything without a printer, she sketched while she waited. She had lost track of time because it wasn't until the doorbell rang that she realized what time it actually was. She put the pad down and went to let him in. "Hey Jake." She kissed him. "Hey. Sorry I'm late. Slow going." "You have José to thank for that." "Well, you're half right. José and *you*." "Me?" "Sure, if you hadn't finally given Ross a tumble, we wouldn't have been celebrating." "Oh no, you can't pin this one on me. The blame lies squarely on your broad shoulders. You're the one who gave out the shots." He laughed. "Got me there." He stepped in. "I appreciate you coming. I mean I know you have better things to do than fix my printer." "Nah, not really." She smiled. He walked into the living room and noticed the sketch pad on the table. "Doodling again?" "Yeah, I decided to sketch while I was waiting." He flipped through them and whistled. "These are good. I mean, I've seen your work before, but these are different. More ah . . ." "Over the top?" She finished. "Yeah. I mean no one around here would wear these." She nodded. "Right you are, Jake. That's cause I sketched them with NYC in mind." "Oh?" "My old boss has been after me to come back and work for him. It's something I'm actually starting to consider now that Emily is older." "How would it work?" "Well, he said I could sketch and overnight them to him." "That sounds easy enough." "It does but finding the time to sketch is the tricky part." "I hear that. When you own and run your own business, there's always shit that needs to be done." "Exactly." She led him to her office and showed him where it was jamming. "See, it's right in there." He looked. "You got that tiny screwdriver, the one I used last time? "Yes, I kept it." "Good, I think I'm going to need it again." "Okay, I'll get it." Sabrina went and got the toolbox out. She handed it to him. "Thanks." "So have you spoken to Harris?" "Not yet." He was tinkering with some screws. "So how surprised were you when you found out about us?" "I don't think surprised really covers it. Shocked as shit was more like it." She laughed. "Emily said that would be your reaction." "She was right. The guy has had it bad for you for years. I used to tell him to come clean, but he was always afraid to. At times it was downright pathetic." He looked at her. "I didn't mean it the way it sounded." "I know." "I wanted Ross to tell you because I thought you'd be good together." "Apparently, you knew that before I did." "And he's over-the-moon happy. I've never seen him this *up* before." "That's sweet of you to say, Jake." "Hey, it's the truth. He loves you a lot." "I know he does. I just wish . . ." "That you loved him back?" "Well, I do but . . ." "Not the way he does, I know." I feel bad." "Well, don't. Believe me he's happy just knowing you care about him and enjoy being with him. The rest will come in time." "You sound just like him." "Good, 'cause that means he's using his brain finally." When did you get to be so smart about relationships?" "Oh right after Angela and I split. It's amazing the clarity that comes with a breakup." She grew quiet. "Jake, I'm sorry." "Hey, don't be. Things didn't work out." He had the entire back panel off the printer. She decided to change the subject. "So . . . any ideas?" "I think so. I noticed one of the rollers was bent, so every time it takes in the paper it pulls it through on slant, which—" "Makes it jam." "Exactly. So if I can just fix it your problem should be solved." "Great. I've got lots of work waiting for me." "I know you do. I know what it's like running your own business." "How's the bar doing?" "Good. I mean when we opened five years ago I was scared shit, but it's been doing really well. I can't complain." "Good, I'm glad." Jake put the cover back on the printer and turned it back on. "Now for a test. Send something to print." "Here goes nothing." The printer made a slight creaking noise but then it took the paper and printed. "You did it! You're wonderful!" She grabbed and hugged him. "Well, if I had known I'd get this kind of reward I'd have bent that roller myself." She laughed. "Well, looks like I got here just in time." She turned around and saw Ross standing in the doorway. "Moving in on my girl, Jake?" She was just thanking me for fixing her printer." "Not the old let me come over and fix something for you?" "You would know since you've used it, too." Ross frowned and Sabrina laughed. "All right you two, I feel like we're back in high school." "Jake never left." "Two words, F and U." "Those are letters, not words." "Yeah so. You know what they spell." "That I do." Ross grinned. "Enough. Let me say hello to my girl." Come here." She went to him and they kissed. They were still kissing when Jake looked at his watch and said, "What is this, a Big Red commercial?" "Don't you have a bar to run?" Ross asked, feigning annoyance. "Yeah, but annoying you is so much more fun. Sabrina could not stop laughing. "Come on, you two, time to eat."

"So it seems you recovered nicely from your hangover?" Jake said. "Yeah, well, in a strange way I have Danny to thank for that." "How so?" He kept asking what toppings I wanted on my pancakes, and next thing I knew I was praying to the porcelain god. After that I felt a whole lot better." Jake laughed. "Bet you did." Sabrina placed the chicken she grilled on their salads. "You didn't have to go to all this trouble, Brina." "Yeah, I feel bad. I mean I had food back at the bar." "Please I just grilled some chicken. It's no trouble at all. Besides you always eat bar food. That's got to get played out." "It does but I'm lazy." "I think the last time I had someone other than my mother cook for me was . . ." He dropped off when he realized. "Angela?" Ross finished. "Yeah." Sabrina saw his face. "If you don't want to talk about it." "No, it's fine." He chewed a piece of chicken and swallowed. "Funny but sometimes it seems like just yesterday." "Hey, look it's her loss. If she couldn't appreciate you, then she didn't deserve you. Believe me, the right girl is out there. You just have to find her." "Yeah, does she answer the want ads?" He laughed. Sabrina wiped her mouth. "Jake, you're a great guy, and if Angela was dumb enough to let you go well then screw her." Ross looked at her. "That's my girl." "Thanks for the support, guys." "Anyway, Brina this might be the best damn grilled chicken I've eaten." "Sure beats what I would be eating down at the bar." "Well, I'm glad you guys enjoyed it. "Are you kidding? I'm ready to move in." Ross joked. "Who are you kidding? You were ready to do that ten years ago." Ross shoved him and he almost fell off the chair. "Touchy aren't we?" Jake joked. She was laughing and holding her stomach. "Boys, play nice, otherwise I'll have to call a time-out," Sabrina joked. "Well, I guess I better get back," Jake said, bringing his plate to the sink. "Jake, thanks again. I really appreciate it." "Anytime." "I'll walk you out," Ross said. "Bye, Sabrina." She kissed him. "Bye, Jake." When they got to the door, they stopped. "I assume you're staying?" "Not for long, I have to get back to the station. Andy is out looking for Sammy." "Again? What the fuck is wrong with that woman?" He shrugged. "I've tried talking to her. We all have. She just doesn't get it." "No, she doesn't want to get it. Next time, play hardball. Tell her all your people are tied up. Let her sweat. Then she'll think twice about it." "She's an old woman who lost her husband. I feel bad." "I know, but it's not your job to look for her dog every friggin' week." "You're right. I'll get tough next time." "Sure you will."

Ross walked back inside and saw the sketch pad. He flipped through it and brought it into the kitchen. Sabrina was busy washing the dishes. "I would have done that." "I don't mind." "So I just looked at your sketches. They're amazing." "You think so?" "Sure. I mean you have designed some nice things in the past, but these are just, wow." "Thanks. I did them while I was waiting for Jake. Nico's on me to design for him again." "That's nothing new." "True but for the first time I'm actually considering it. Emily will be graduating next year, the farm is solid." "So you'd move back to NYC?" he asked, trying not to let the fear he felt show in his voice. "Wouldn't have to. I would sketch here and overnight them to him." He breathed a sigh of relief. "That doesn't sound so bad." "It's not. It's just there's always something to do, and I don't have much free time." "Brina, you've spent the past eleven years doing for everyone else. Don't you think it's time to start doing for yourself?" "I guess so. It's just hard to switch gears. For so long it's been only Emily and the farm." "I know." "Speaking of switching gears." He pressed against her and she felt his desire growing." "Hmm, you smell good." She laughed. "I smell like chicken." "Good enough to eat." "You're terrible." "That's not what you said the other day." She turned around. "What did I say?" "That no one ever made you feel so good. That you love it when I do that thing with my tongue on your—" "Ross!" He smiled. "You asked." "That'll teach me." "Speaking of teaching, I could show you a few things." "Is that all you ever think about?" "No, but it's a close second." They laughed. The phone rang, and she dried her hands to get it. "Hello. Oh hi, Nico. I wasn't expecting to hear back from you so soon. Yes, I understand. Four hundred thread count. No, I won't use flannel. Yes, I know anything under three hundred gives you hives. Uh-huh. Right. Got it." Ross couldn't help chuckling. "Don't worry, Nico, everything will be fine. You'll get to see Ross again, sure. Yes, I'm sure he remembers you. How do I know? Because who could forget you. Uh-huh. Okay, see you then. Ta-ta." She hung up and started to laugh. Ross laughed too. "Is that guy for real? Talk about affected." "Oh I know, but he's such a great person. "So you remember him?" "Remember him? How could I forget? He showed up wearing a veil." They both laughed. "Anyway, he's coming for a visit." "When?" "Right after Scott's graduation." "He's staying here?" "Yes. I need to get four hundred thread-count sheets before then." "Yeah, I heard about how he breaks out in hives from anything under three." She laughed. "I'm looking forward to seeing him. He's a lot of fun." "Hmm, if I didn't know he was playing for the other team, I might be jealous." She kissed him. "No reason to be. I only have eyes for you." His face lit up like a kid at Christmas. "Hearing you say that just made my year." They stood motionless, looking into each other's eyes. Then he kissed her. She laid her hand on his fly and felt how hard he was. "Looks like someone is in need of some attention. Why don't you step into my office?" she teased. "Lead the way." She led him to the sofa and stroked him. Her hands moved up and down his shaft. The buildup was both unbearable and incredible at the same time. He'd die if he didn't find sweet release soon. "Brina, I—" "You what? Want me to stop?" She took her hand away. "No! Don't stop." She continued to tease and taunt him. He was brought to the brink again and again, only to be pulled back each time. "You're killing me." She took him in her mouth, and it felt like pure magic. She sucked, licked, and swiped every inch of him until he was panting like a wild animal. "Do you want more, Ross? Tell me what you want." He could stand it no longer. He flipped her onto her back and took her mouth. "It's your turn to be tortured." Within minutes, she was naked and panting until finally he entered her, and they came together in a vortex of heat.

Afterward, they lay on the sofa together. "We'll make it to a damn bed yet," he said, trying not to laugh. "You are one wicked woman." She laughed. "And you are just as wicked." "I can't feel my legs." "What legs?" he asked, grinning. Once the feeling in their legs came back, they got dressed. "All this great sex has made me hungry. How 'bout you, Brina?" "I could go for a snack." "We could head over to Danny's get something sweet. Though I doubt they'd have anything that tasted better than you." "Ross!" She smacked his arm. "What? It's true." "As tempting as it sounds, I can't. I have work." "Joy kill." She laughed. "All right, I guess I'll go back to my lonely post at the station. But before I leave, I want one more taste." He pulled her into him for a kiss. "Try not to miss me too much." "I'll try but I'm not making any promises." He left smiling.

Chapter Eight

Emily was waiting by the barn for Scott when Riley came by. "Hey, Em, Pierce stand you up?" "No, he's just hungover." He laughed. "Tequila will do that to you." "How come you aren't hungover?" "I only had two shots, since I know José and I don't get along." "Got ya." "So some party, right?" "It was great. I still can't believe I didn't know." "Well, that means we did a good job of keeping our mouths shut." "I never had the chance to thank you and the guys for all your help with the party." "Happy to help. By the way, I met Sam." "Oh yeah?" "Yeah, she's crazy cool." She laughed. "Crazy sums her up well." "So have you spoken to her?" "No. Why?" Just wondering." She looked at him. Something was different about him. He hadn't flirted once. Also, he usually made stupid comments about the women he met, but he hadn't done that with Sam. *He likes her.* "Okay, spill." "What?" "You heard me." "We talked a while and then we went for a walk, and then we . . . kissed." "No way!" "Way, and I haven't been able to stop thinking about her since." "Why don't you call her?" "I don't have her number." "Why didn't you get it?" "I didn't want to look desperate." "Hello, you could have asked me." He stood there, looking awkwardly uncomfortable. "*Men*." He laughed. She jotted it down and handed it to him." "When are you going to call her?" "Now." He smiled and walked away. He passed Scott who noticed his grin. "What's he so happy about?" "A girl." He looked at her. "He met her at the party. Says he can't stop thinking about her." He whistled. "For him, that's huge. Who is she?" "*She* is Samantha." "You're shitting me?" "Nope." "I don't believe it. Mr. I Don't Remember Her Name, hooked by man-eating Sam. That's rich." "They could be good for each other." "I don't know. If the guy didn't spend all his spare time busting my balls, I'd almost feel sorry for him." "Don't. I think they've both met their match." "Maybe they have."

Ross arrived back at the station, sandwich in hand. "Andy back yet?" "Not yet. When last he checked in, he was making his way toward Hunt's Point." "Was he bringing a date?" She chuckled. "Let me know when he radios." "Sure." He went into his office to eat his sandwich. A short time later, she knocked. "Andy has Sammy. He's bringing him back to Mrs. Haugtry now." "Great. Thanks, Linda."

Emily and Scott sat on a tree limb, talking. Their walk had taken them to a lilac-filled meadow. It was beautiful and smelled amazing. "The view from here is so pretty." "Not as pretty as you." She blushed. "Thanks, I can't believe it's almost time for me to go back." "Don't remind me." "You still planning on visiting?" "Better. Not only will I be visiting, but I will also be driving you back." "That's so nice of you." She kissed him. He looked at her. "Em, there's something I want to talk to talk to you about." "Sure, what?" "My mom." "What about her?" "I've been thinking about her a lot lately." "Why?" "I don't know. Dad said one look was all it took for him to fall for her." "Were they happy?" "At first, but part of the problem was that she had big dreams, dreams of becoming a singer. I asked Dad if he regretted any of it." "What did he say?" "That he loved her, and they had a lot of good times together. He also said that she gave him me so how could he regret it." "You're dad's an amazing man. You're lucky to have him." "Yeah, I know. Even though he drives me nuts sometimes." "Ever think about trying to find her?" "I could but why? She left. Never bothered to see if we were dead or alive. How could anyone do that, Em?" "I can't answer that. Only she can." "Well, enough about MIA parents. Let's talk about something else." "Like?" "Like, when are you going to talk to your aunt about running the diary?" "Oh that." "Yeah, that. You can't start until you actually talk to her." "I know. I just." "You just what?" "I'm scared."

"Of your aunt? She's a cream puff." She laughed. "Don't let her hear you say that?" "Don't worry, I won't." "I'm just afraid she's going to say no." "So if she does, you convince her to stay yes." "You're right. I'll talk to her before I head back to school." "Good."

Andy arrived back at the station looking a little worse for wear. "What the heck happened to you?" Ross asked, trying to hide his smile. "Sammy. That's what." "Did he sit on you again?" Andy frowned. "No, I had to chase him, and I fell trying to grab on to him." "So did you talk to her? "Well, I had every intention of doing it, but then she brought out freshly baked pie and started talking about how lonely she is." "Folded like a cheap suit, didn't you?" Linda asked. "I did." "Nice work, Deputy Chicken." Andy looked at her, annoyed. "I'll have to talk to her again," Ross said. Linda and Andy walked out. "You think he'll be able to stand firm with her?" "Honey, a snowball has a better chance in hell." He laughed.

Sabrina finished putting the last invoice in its envelope. Now she just had to run them to the post office. She grabbed her keys and walked outside. She saw Hanson near the barn tinkering with something. "Hey, Sabrina. Going somewhere?" "The post office. Need to get these bills out. Some are already late, like Mr. Harding's." "Oh he's a pussycat." "I know he was very understanding. Unlike Mr. Peters." Hanson cringed. "Peters is an asshole." She laughed. "No arguments there. He smirked. "Anyway, do you need anything while I'm in town?" "Actually, more chicken feed." "Oh, but didn't Scott just get some?" "He did but not enough. They were running low, and Ryland asked him not to take all their supply." "Okay." "Want me to come with you?" "No, it's fine. Mr. Ryland can have Charlie load it for me." Hanson took out his keys. "Here, take my truck. It'll make things easier." "Okay, thanks."

Jake was busy stocking the bar with freshly cleaned glasses when the phone rang. "Jake's." "Hey, man." "Harris. Miss me already?" "Yeah, I'm counting the moments till we're together again." "Wiseass." "What's up?" "I thought you'd like to know that Andy found Sammy." "Good. Where was the dumb mutt this time?" "Up near Hunt's Point." "He got that far?" "Yeah. Should have seen poor Andy. He was covered in dirt." Jake laughed. "Like riding a bull at a rodeo." Ross laughed. "Yeah. So after you left, Sabrina got a call from her old boss, Nico."

Jake smiled. "Nico? What is he Greek?" "No, gay." He laughed. "Okay that would have been my second guess." "Sure it would have. Anyway, he's coming in June and staying for a few days. The guy is a real trip. He wants four hundred thread-count sheets. Says he breaks out in hives if anything less is used." "Sounds high maintenance." "Tell me about it. He showed up at James and Rebecca's funeral wearing a veil." "Get the fuck out of here?" "It's true. It was like Sunset Boulevard." "I have no idea what you are talking about when you talk Broadway." He laughed. "You just don't appreciate the finer things in life." "Do too. Remember that hot redhead that was in here a few weeks ago?" "Yeah." "She was fine, and I appreciated her plenty." He laughed. "I stand corrected. Anyway, he's been after Brina to work for him again." "I know." "You do?" "I saw the sketches. So what are you worried about? She said she'd work from home." "Sure, that's what he says now. Then after a while it will be you really need to come here." "Think so?" "I *know* so." "Okay so let's say she does have to go to NYC. What's the big deal? It's like three hours from here." "Yeah, but I can't compete with that world." "No one says you have to. Besides, you are getting way ahead of yourself. She hasn't accepted yet." "No, but she's considering it." "Don't you want her to be happy?" "Of course I want her to be happy. I love her, damn it." "I know you do. Believe me, no one knows that better than me. But she's got a gift that's being wasted. You know that, right?" "'Course I do." "Anyway, the guy isn't coming till June. If she decides to do this thing, you'll need to support her." "Jake, I don't know if I . . ." "If you what? If you can? That's a cop out." "It is not a cop out. I'm not cut out for city life, you know that." "Yeah, I do, but you won't have to move there. You'll just have to visit. Do you think Sabrina wants to live in New York? Raise a family there?" "No." "Don't make the same mistake I made with Angela." Ross sat up in his chair. "What are you talking about?" "Angela left because I didn't give her a choice." "You never told me that." "I didn't want to admit that I was the one who fucked things up. I loved her, but I was afraid." "Of what?" "You know I don't even know anymore. All kinds of crazy things were running through my head back then." "I always thought she just left without even a second thought about you. Damn, Jake." "Yeah, it's something I'll regret for the rest of my life. That's why I'm telling you. I don't want you to make the same mistakes I did. You have loved that woman most of your life. Whether she stays or goes, you'd be a complete fucking idiot not to make it work." "You're right." "You bet your ass I'm right." "Jake, thanks for telling me." "Sure." "Well, I'd better run." "Okay, later."

Emily and Scott found the guys putting down fresh straw in the barn. "Hey, nice to see you finally showed up to meet your lady, Pierce," Riley said. "She said you were hungover." "What about it?" "Wouldn't have happened if you laid off the Cuervo." "Yeah, well some of us like to do more than one shot." "I did two." "Whoa, two whole shots. And maybe someday you'll be a real drinker." "Up yours." "You started it." "And I'm finishing it," Max said. Emily figured this was a good time to pull Riley aside. "Riley, got a minute?" "For you, I've got two." Scott rolled his eyes. She brought him outside, Scott followed since he knew it was about Sam. "So did you call her?" "Yeah." "So how did it go?" "Okay." "Riley, you're killing me." He laughed. "Sorry." "Was she happy you called?" "I think so." She shook her head. "Okay, why don't you tell me the whole conversation." "I don't want the guys to hear." She gave a look saw Scott hiding behind the hay bales and rolled her eyes. "They're all inside, except for Scott." Riley looked over and saw him. "Eavesdropping?" "Come on, cut me a break here. I am dying to know what happened." "Why?" "'Cause Sam has been a man-eater for years, and it's high time she got taught a lesson by a player such as yourself." Emily looked at him, eyebrow raised. "A gentle lesson of course." "I thought you wanted Sam to teach him a lesson?" Riley looked at him, eyebrow raised. "Okay, could you stop doing that? It's freaking me out." "Look, I think it's time they both got taught a lesson. Okay? You know I'm not wrong, Em." Riley looked at her. "Well, your attitude toward women has been sorely lacking." "I know." They looked at him. "It's not like I went out of my way to be a dick. I'm just not the flowers and candy kind of guy. At least I never thought about it till Sam. Crazy huh?" "I'll say. You picked the wrong chick to start thinking about flowers, man." "I know." "She said she's dated and things never really work out. I'd like to think I'm up for the challenge." "She told you all that?" Emily asked. "Yeah, we talked for like two hours." "Two hours? He's gone." "Look who's talking, Mr. I'm Going for a Walk in the Meadow so I Can Skip." "Hey, I haven't skipped since I was eight." "You know what I mean." "Yeah, I guess I do," he said, looking at Emily. "Anyway, she wants me to come up and see her. She figures I can hitch a ride with you." "Um, yeah, that's not going to happen." "Why not?" "Because." "Because why?" "How about because you're always a dick to me?" "Come on, do a guy a solid." Scott blew out an exaggerated breath. "Fine." "But you start with me, and you'll be thumbing your way there. You got me?" "Yeah." "Good."

After Sabrina finished up at the post office, she drove over to the Feed N Seed. She went in and found Mr. Ryland. "Evenin', Sabrina." "Hi, Tom." "What brings you here so late in the day?" "I was at the post office, so I figured I'd stop by and get the chicken feed we needed." "Oh right. I told Scott to come back, but he never did." "He's a bit preoccupied these days." "Oh?" "He and my niece are dating, and well, you know how young love makes you forget everything." He chuckled. "I remember those days. Seems like an eternity ago. So how many bags do you want?" "How many did Scott get?" "Twenty." "Let's say ten to be safe." "You got it. I'll get Charlie to load it up for you." "Great thanks. I have Hanson's truck, so it should make things easier." A few minutes later Charlie Ross came charging down the aisle, flatbed in tow, loaded up with chicken feed. "How ya doing, Ms. Taylor?" "I'm good, Charlie. You?" "Five by five." She had no idea what that meant. "Glad to hear it." "Would you please speak English to the customers. No one understands your babble." "It's not babble, Mr. Ryland. Five by five means I'm doing good. It's an expression." "Yeah well, express yourself in English." Charlie shrugged his shoulders. She could not help but laugh. "Charlie, bring that out to Ms. Taylor's car, ah correction, she has Hanson's truck today." "'Kay." She walked out behind him. They got to the truck, and he began loading the feed. "Hey, did you hear about the fight?" "I think Ross mentioned something about it." "It was so damn funny. These two guys got into it over hitting on the other's girlfriend. I mean how stupid is that? Hitting on a girl in this place? Lame-o, man." She chuckled. "Anyway, Sheriff Harris showed up and tried to get them to break it up, but they wouldn't stop. One of them almost punched him. "He did?" she asked, surprised. "Yep. After that he tossed the guy into that barrel of water." "He didn't?" "He sure did.

It was the coolest thing I've ever seen." His face looked a bit starstruck. "Who were they?" "I'm not sure. I still don't have everyone's names and faces down yet." Charlie was new. He'd only been working at the Feed N Seed for a few weeks. "That's okay. As long as Ross took care of it." The truck was loaded and ready to go. "Thanks, Charlie," she said, handing him a tip. "Thanks, Ms. Taylor. See you next time." He ran back inside. *Looks like Ross has a fan*, she said to herself, smiling.

Linda was walking out as Sabrina was coming in. "Hey, Sabrina. How's it going? "Oh it's going." Linda laughed. "So you here to see our favorite boy in blue? Well, technically he's in light khaki, but you know what I mean." She laughed. "I do." "Listen, I just wanted to say that I'm thrilled for you both. I mean it's about time." "Thank you. It wasn't all his fault." "Nonsense. He's the man. He should have manned up and told you years ago. Serves his ass right having to wait." "Oh, Linda, I love your sense of humor." "Thanks, I'll be here all week." "Hey, what's all the ruckus?" They both turned to see Ross, arms crossed, standing against a doorjamb. "I was just saying how it's about damn time you manned up and told her how you felt." "You been talking to Jake?" "No but sounds like great minds think alike." "Well, since we are together now—" "Finally." He rolled his eyes in annoyance. "Moot point, Linda, since we are now together." "Oh all right. I'll grant you that." He walked over to Sabrina and gave her a soft, yearning kiss. "Why can't I find anyone to kiss me like that?" "Because you're already married. To Ed." "Oh right. No wonder." They laughed. "What are you doing here, Brina? Not that I'm not happy to see you." "I was at the Feed N Seed and thought I'd stop by. Charlie Ross sends his regards." "Nice kid, but I can't understand half of what comes out of his mouth." She laughed. "I know. I asked him how he was, and he said five by five." "What the heck does that mean?" Linda asked. "Apparently, it's Charlie's way of saying he's okay." Linda laughed. "Okay? That doesn't make any sense to me. The future of America. A little scary if you ask me." "Anyway, he seems to think Ross is the coolest." "Oh?" "Yeah, he told me about how you broke up that fight and tossed one of the guys into a barrel full of water." "The jerk took a swing at me." Linda looked at him. "You didn't tell me that." "I was in a bit of hurry that night to get to a certain someone." He smiled at Sabrina. "So now

Charlie thinks you are the greatest thing next to sliced bread." "Smart boy, that Charlie." "Oh spare me," Linda said. "Hey, I did what I had to do." "Yeah, you're a regular Clint Eastwood." "Don't you have to get home? To your husband?" "Oh I could tease you all night, but yeah I should get going. Ed is helpless without me. Nice seeing you, Sabrina. Don't take any crap from this one." Ross frowned. "So to what do I owe this unexpected pleasure?" He wrapped his arms around her. "I got a kick out of Charlie and wanted to tell you. He really looks up to you." "Great, now I have to top myself." "What are you talking about?" "Well, he's like what twenty? He probably thinks every day is that exciting. He'll expect me to do something like that again. He should know that most days are spent chasing Sammy." She couldn't help but laugh. "But enough about that. How about we go into my office, lock the door, and I frisk you?" "Oooh, I like the way you think." "So do I. Let's go." He pulled her down the hall, and they bumped right into Andy. "Hey Sheriff, Sabrina." He looked at both of them and knew something was up. "I'm gonna go work on some more of those files." "Good." "See you, Andy." She could barely get his name out before she was yanked into his office. Before she knew what was happening, she had been backed up against the door and stripped down to her bra and panties. "Stand against the wall, legs apart." "Yes, sir." She was playing along and he liked it. He slowly moved his hand up her leg and stopped at her essence. "Someone's ready for me." He continued to run his hands up along her torso stopping at her breasts. He cupped them and gently squeezed her nipples. She moaned. "I think you may be hiding a concealed weapon, I'm going to have to go in deeper. She licked her lips in anticipation, and he grew harder. He moved her panties aside and worked his fingers inside. First one, then two, and finally three. "*Ross . . .*" she said, sounding breathless. "I'm not done yet." He pulled down his pants and wrapped her leg around his thigh and plunged into her. Back and forth he rocked as the tension built. "How's that feel, baby?" "Good. Please don't stop." "I don't intend to." He moved faster and went deeper. She felt her legs buckle, and he grabbed her legs and wrapped her around him. "Hold on." They rode each other to that glorious edge and peaked together. They fell to the floor, spent, and unable to move. "Next time a bed or bust." She laughed. "I think we both 'busted.'" It was his turn to laugh. "Yeah, I guess we did." "Ross?" "Yeah?" "Do you think Andy heard us?" "So what if he did? He's had sex before. I think." She looked at him. "Relax, Brina. He's a big boy. Besides, he probably didn't hear anything, since he is constantly listening to Lady Gaga."

Ross was right. Andy had heard the start of what he deemed to be a private moment and turned up Lady Gaga. They found Andy dancing and singing along. "Can't read my, can't read my, no you can't read my poker face." They stood, trying not to laugh. Ross looked at her. "Told you." He walked up behind him and tapped his shoulder. He jumped. "You scared the shit out of me!" "Sorry." "How long were you two standing there?" "Long enough." He grinned. "Stop teasing him. I think you've got some nice moves, Andy." "Thanks. I try." "Try harder." "Pay no attention to him. He's just jealous." Ross looked at her. "She's right. I wanna dance just like you." He rolled his eyes. "I'd tell you to go do something but there's a lady present. Instead, I'll use hand gestures." He flipped both middle fingers up and Sabrina laughed. "I definitely have to come here more often. Anyway, I should really go. Hanson's probably wondering what happened to me." "I'll walk you out." They stood by Hanson's truck holding hands. "You sure you don't want to come back in. We could go for round two?" "Hmmm, tempting but I can't." She got in and started it up. "By the way I like the way you frisk a girl, Sheriff." She gave him a sexy smile and drove away. "I am so gonna marry that woman."

When she got back, Hanson had the guys unload everything. "Thanks, guys." "No problem." She turned to Hanson. "So there's this new guy at the Feed N Seed." "Yeah, I met him. Charlie. Nice kid. Doesn't speak English though." "Five by Five." They said at the same time and laughed. "Last week, Ross broke up a fight between two guys." "He told us all about it at Jake's. Trying to hit on someone else's girl is stupid enough, but doing it surrounded by chicken feed and fertilizer is downright pathetic." "Agreed. Anyway, Charlie's starstruck over it." "Sounds like Ross has a fan." "He definitely does. Oh, I almost forgot. I have a letter for you." "A letter? I'm not expecting anything. Who's it from?" She looked at it. "I don't know there's no return address." He opened it and began reading. After just a few lines, she saw his face change. "What's wrong?" He handed her the letter. "Amanda? Your ex-wife? What does this mean?" "It means she wants back into our lives." "Hell, I need a drink." "Come inside." "Has she ever tried contacting you before?" "No. Never." "Sabrina, beer's not gonna cut it." "Okay. She opened a cabinet and took out a bottle of scotch. He poured what looked like three fingers' worth. "I just can't believe it. Twelve years." He knocked back the scotch. "How did she even find you?" "Probably through one of the guys I used to work with. I keep in touch with most of them." "Do you think she's sincere?" "How the hell should I know?" He snapped. "I'm sorry." "No need to apologize. I know this comes as quite a shock." "Pardon the language, but it's a fucking huge one." "What are you going to do?" "I don't know." "What about Scott?" He poured himself more scotch. "I don't know that either." "Why don't you take some time with this?" "Yeah, that's a good idea."

Chapter Nine

The day of Emily's return to school came, and she wasn't looking forward to it as much as usual. Mostly because it meant being apart from Scott. "Do you have your economics project?" Sabrina asked. "Yes." "Okay good. That was a fast two weeks." "Tell me about it." "It's nice of Scott to take you back." "Yeah, it is though he's not too thrilled about Riley tagging along." "I know. I still can't believe it about him and Sam." "You're not alone." "Um, Aunt Sabrina, before I leave, I wanted to talk to you about something." "Sure, honey, what is it?" *It's now or never.* "I want to run the farm." She looked at her. "Since when?" "Since always. Don't sound so freaked out about it." "I'm not." She looked at her. "Okay, I'm a little freaked just because it's a huge undertaking." "I know, but I still want to do it. You gave up everything to come back here. So now that I'm old enough, I'd like to give you the chance to make your dream come true." "Em, I appreciate it more than you know, but I just don't know if it will work." "Why, because you don't think I can do it?" "No, you can do anything you set your mind to, it's just it takes time. I worked with Hanson for a long time before I felt comfortable to handle it all on my own." "So I'll spend the summer working alongside both of you." "Honey, one summer is not going to be enough. Believe me." "But it's a start. Right?" "Right. You are stubborn, aren't you?" "I take after my father. I just want a chance to make it up to you." "You don't have to make up anything to me. I did what I did because I love you. And I'd do it all again if I had to. I love this farm, it's a part of me." "I know." "It may not be that simple to get back into it. Even if I wanted to." "Now why do you say that? When your old boss is practically begging you?" "You were eavesdropping?" "I prefer to call it being in the right place at the right time." "You sure you don't want a career in politics?" She laughed. "I'm sure. Anyway, he wants you back. So just do it." "It's not that simple." "Sure it is. You are just making it way harder than it has to be. You sketch and overnight them to him and train me. Once you feel I've got enough experience, then I'll take over. Leaving you to design something gorgeous for the next Heidi Klum." "You have this all figured out, don't you?" "Yep. Believe me I've been thinking about it for a long time. I even changed my major to agriculture." "Well, sounds like your mind is made up." "It is. So . . . will you hire me as your intern this summer?" Sabrina looked at her and smiled. "As if I had a choice." They both laughed.

With her bag in tow, they walked out to where Scott and Hanson were waiting by Sabrina's car. "Where's Riley?" "Right here." He came up alongside them, holding flowers. Scott looked at him. "Did you just pick those?" "Yeah so?" "How the mighty have fallen." "Bite me." "Touchy aren't we?" "I think it's sweet," Emily said. "So do I." "Thanks, ladies." "Can we go? Or do you want to go pick some more daisies?" "Just for that, you drive." "Oh no, you're driving. I want to sit in the back with Em." "No, you want to sit in the back and *make out* with Em. I'm not being subjected to that for three hours." "Relax, don't get your panties twisted. We'll share the driving." "Damn right we will." Emily shook her head. "This is going to be one loooong trip."

Sometime later, they were on the road, and Scott was driving. He and Riley had been arguing over who'd drive first, and to shut them up, Hanson had flipped a coin. Scott called heads and lost. "So what do you plan on saying to her?" "I'm not sure." Scott looked at him in the rearview mirror. "You're joking, right?" "What?" "You have lines, use them." "Lines?" Riley asked, trying not to smile. "Sure, every player has lines." "Good to know," he said, grinning. "What if I don't want to use them on her?" He looked at him. "Oh jeez, this is worse than I thought." Emily giggled. "Look that's the way it's been with every girl. Meet them, talk them up, then . . ." He stopped talking and looked at Emily. "Damn, I've been a real asshole. Haven't I?" "Yes, but I think that's all about to change." She said to him. "Look, I love Sam. She's great, but she's a little messed up when it comes to guys." "Scott, you know why Sam's the way she is." Riley looked at her then Scott. "Something you're not telling me?" "Sam will tell you when and if she's ready to," Emily said. "Em, he should know." She paused. "Fine. Sam was in a serious relationship with this guy named, Jason." "Go on." "She was head over heels for him." "Let me guess what comes next. He dumped her." "Worse," Scott chimed in. "He cheated on her." "Was he blind or just plain stupid?" "I know, right? I mean Sam is a hottie." Em looked at him. "The point is she opened up her heart and—" "Got it handed back to her in pieces," Riley said. "Yes, I'm afraid so." "And every guy after that—" "Pays the price," Scott finished. Riley let out a steady breath. "So she gets rid of them before things get serious, before she can be hurt again." "Yes," Emily said. "You sure you still want in, buddy?" Scott asked. "Yeah, I do. More than before."

Sabrina was in the kitchen cleaning when the phone rang. "Hello." "Hey, gorgeous. Miss me?" "Sorry, I'm too busy to miss anyone." "Ouch. You really know how to hurt a guy." "Would it help if I promised to kiss it and make it better?" "It might." "So what's up?" "I was just sitting here trying to do my job, and a certain someone kept popping into my head." "Anyone I know?" "She's about your height, emerald eyes, great curves, sexy as hell." "Oh, she sounds mighty hot." He laughed. "So what are you up to?" "I was just cleaning the kitchen. It's funny since I was thinking of calling you just now too. I wanted to talk to you about Emily." "Everything okay?" "Yes, it's just well we had a talk before she left." "What about?" "It seems she wants to take over running this place." He sat up in his chair. "Really?" "You sound like me." "Well, it's just that's a huge undertaking for someone with no experience." "Well, when I said that, she got upset." "What did she say?" "She said she'd be willing to train for as long as I felt necessary." "Did you say yes?" "Of course. Her mind was completely made up. Should have heard her. She sounded so much like James. She said 'I'm doing this one way or the other.'" "That does sound like James, but it also sounds a lot like someone else I know." She knew he meant her, but she kept on talking. "She wants to do this, so I can go back to working for Nico." He felt his insides shake. "Nico, right. Well, Hanson will help her." "I know, but he's got his own stuff to deal with right now." "Why? What's going on?" "I guess you haven't talked to him?" "No." "He got a letter from Amanda." "His ex? Are you serious?" "Yeah, he's pretty upset." "I'll bet. The woman left them without so much as a backward glance." "I know, but she says she wants to make amends." "What's he going to do?" "He hasn't decided yet. I told him to give himself some time." "Does Scott know?" "No." "That's probably best for now." "I agree. Anyway, they should be back at SUNY by now. You should have been here, Ross. Riley and Scott were going at it like an old married couple." He laughed. "What is it with those two?" "They were arguing over who'd drive, who wouldn't drive. Hanson couldn't take it anymore. He made them flip for it. Scott lost." He laughed. "I feel bad for Em trapped in a car for three hours with those two." "What was Riley going up to Em's school for anyway?" "To visit Sam." "Wait, what?" "They met at the party and apparently they hit it off. Riley's smitten." He laughed. "A ladies' man like him, smitten? Will wonders never cease?" "Well, I think he'll find he's met his match in Sam. She's got a trail of broken hearts in her wake too." "So Love 'Em & Leave 'Em meets Man-Eater, sounds like a bad sci-fi movie." She laughed. "It does. Though Riley seems to think he's up for the challenge." "Well, I wish him luck." Linda knocked. "Hold on, Brina. Yeah, Linda?" "Andy caught Tommy Johnson tagging up by the old Cutter place again. Andy thought you'd want to talk to him. He's outside." "Give me a minute." She went back out. "I guess you heard?" "A little. Something about Tommy getting caught tagging up." "Yeah and it's not the first time either. Andy's talked to him before, but it didn't seem to stick, so now it's my turn." "What are you going to do?" "Scare the crap out of him, of course." She smiled and shook her head. "Maybe you should call Charlie Ross. Have him come down, so he can see you in action again." "Very funny." "Well, I'd better go. Let's get together tomorrow for lunch." "You know I do have a farm to run." "I know but you gotta eat right." She smiled. "I sure do. Come around noon." "See you then."

Ross saw Tommy sitting on a bench, scowl on his face. "What the hell did you think you were doing?" He shrugged. "Don't give me that.

You were caught tagging up at the old Cutter place. It's not the first time either." "So what were you writing, huh?" "My name." "Oh your name. Why, were you afraid you were gonna forget it?" "No." "You know that's a crime, right? If you were eighteen, we'd be having a very different conversation." Tommy looked at him. "You're real lucky you aren't. Means there's still time to get your act together. A few more of these, and you'll end up in juvey." He was starting to look scared. "You wouldn't want to go there believe me. Tough place, full of mean, nasty kids." "I, I won't do it again, Sheriff. I, I promise." "Good. I don't want to see you here again. Now get out of here." "Don't worry, you won't." Ross smiled as he ran out. Linda walked over to him. "Scared the crap out of him, huh?" "Yep." "Nice job." "Thanks."

Hanson sat on the porch reading, the letter over and over again.

Dear Hanson,

I am sure this letter comes as quite a shock, since I am probably the last person you ever expected to hear from again. It's taken years for me to get up enough courage to write to you. I have so many things that I want to say to you, and to Scott. I took the coward's way out when I left, because I knew I'd never be able to leave if I looked either of you in the eye. I wish I had done things differently. That I'd never left, because it cost me everything. I know I have no right to ask but I'd like to see you. Here's my phone number. (212) 754-3377. If our time together meant anything, please call me.

Fondly,
Amanda

"If our time together meant anything? She's the one who left." Max came walking up. "Talking to yourself again?" "Yeah." "You okay?" he asked. "I've been dealing with some stuff." "Anything I can help with?" "It's complicated." "I got time." "All right, why don't you start by reading this." He handed him the letter. A minute or two later, he folded it and handed it back to him. "Well, ain't that just a kick in the ass. Amanda? I just can't believe it." "You and me both, Max." "What are you gonna do?" "I don't have a fucking clue." "She sounds sincere." "So does a con artist." "Does Scott know?" "No, I don't even know if *I* want to see her. She broke my heart, Max." "I know. Do you still have feelings for her?" He looked at him. "Are you crazy? After what she did? I should hate her." Max shrugged. "But you don't." "No, I don't. Though Lord knows I've tried." "You two have history together." "Ancient history." "You were crazy about her." "I'm over her. I've been over her." "Who are you trying to convince? Me? Or you?" He walked away, leaving him more confused than before.

Riley pulled into the SUNY parking lot. "We made good time." "Yeah, and we would have made even better time if someone hadn't stopped to pick daisies." He ignored him and Emily was glad. After being in the car with them for nearly three hours, she had had enough of them. They walked inside and ran into one of Emily's classmates. She hugged him and Scott sized him up. Tall, good looking. Scott didn't like him one bit. "Oh where are my manners. Brad, this is my boyfriend, Scott. And Riley." "Nice to meet you." He shook their hands and couldn't help noticing the looks Scott was giving him. "So you work on the farm?" "I do. He just takes up space." Scott gave him a shove. "My dad is the foreman. I go to school at Morrisville." "The Equine School, right?" "You know it?" "Sure do. My sister went there. She actually has her own ranch in Kentucky. It's small but she hopes that will change some day." Scott's enthusiasm could not be contained. "Really? Wow that sounds great. I have plans for something like that myself. A place where horses can be raised, trained, lessons given, the whole shebang." "Brad, maybe you could put him in contact with your sister." "Sure, she'd be more than happy to help out a fellow horse lover." "Excuse me. This is all very interesting, but I need to go see a girl," Riley said, walking away rather quickly. "Must be some girl to have him moving like that." "You don't know the half of it," Scott said, laughing. "What's so funny?" "The girl he can't wait to see is Samantha," Emily said. Brad took a minute. "Our Sam?" "Yes." "Isn't she? Well, I mean I've heard she's a—" "Man-eater. You can say it. Everyone does," Scott finished. Brad laughed. "Does your friend know?" "He does." "And he's going for it anyway? He's either incredibly brave or incredibly stupid." It was Scott's turn to laugh. "He's a player. Former player." "So what cupid's arrow straight to the heart?" "Somethin' like that." "They met at my birthday party. According to Riley he hasn't been able to think of anything else since." Brad whistled. "Sounds serious." "It's been very entertaining so far," Scott joked and Brad laughed. "I'm sure it has. Well, I should get going. I'm meeting some people. You guys are welcome to come," he said, looking more at Emily than Scott. "Thanks for the invite, but we want some to spend some time together before Scott has to go back." "Well, if you change your mind, we'll be at O'Casey's." "Thanks. See you around." "Gee, I almost feel sorry for the guy." "Why?" "Because he's into you." "What? Don't be silly. We're friends." "So were we." She looked at him. "Believe me he's into you." "Well, since I'm with you, it doesn't matter." He smiled. "Good point. I do like the fact that his sis went to my school and has her own ranch. Contacts like that make a huge difference." "I agree. I'll make sure he gives you her number." "You're the best girlfriend ever." "I know." He laughed.

Hanson sat by the phone wondering if what he was about to do was right. "To hell with it." He picked up the receiver and dialed. It rang several times before she finally picked up. "Hello." Hearing her voice even after all these years still got to him. "Amanda, it's Hanson." She stood silent. "Are you there?" "Yes, sorry I just . . . I wasn't expecting to hear from you this soon." "You mean at all, don't you?" "Yes." "Listen. About your letter. Give me one good reason why I should let you do anything." "Because I need to make up for all the hurt I've caused." "Make it up with what? Flowers?" "You're angry, you have every right to be." "Damn right I'm angry. You can't imagine the shit sandwich you left me with." "I can only imagine how bad things were." "No, you can't. If you want to come, come." "Thanks. I know this is more than I deserve." "You're right, it is." "What about Scott?" "Like you care." "Okay, I deserve that." "Scott's back at school. You'd better hang up before I change my mind." "I can be there tomorrow, if that works?" "That's fine. Come around two." Before she could say anything else, he hung up.

Riley stood at Sam's door, and for the first time ever, felt nervous. He knocked and felt his pulse speed up. "Hey." "Hey." "What's that you're holding?" "Oh right. These are for you." "Pretty. They look like they were just picked." "That's 'cause they were." "Well, thanks. Come on in." "Thanks." He stepped inside and looked around. It was simply furnished with a desk, sofa, TV, and microwave, what every student needed. "Nice place." "Thanks. It's not bad for a dorm room." She was putting his flowers in water. "So where are Dimples and Em?" "Dimples?" "It's my nickname for Scott." "Is it?" "Don't go getting any ideas. I'm the only one who gets to call him that. Got it?" "Yeah, sure. They were talking to some guy, Bob?" "Brad?" "Brad, that's it. Anyway, I think Scott picked up on the fact that Brad's into Emily. Should have seen the poor guy's face when she introduced us." "Yeah, he's been crushing on her for a while now. Em, of course, is clueless." "Of course." "How about something to drink?" "Sure what do you have?" "Ginger ale, ice tea, beer." "Ice tea sounds good." She got out two glasses and poured tea in them. "So did you have a nice break?" "I had some work to do, but it was good just the same." She handed him his glass. "Thanks. You know ever since the party I just haven't been able to stop thinking about this one girl." She sat down next to him. "Really? That's funny 'cause I've had the same problem. There's this guy I can't get off my mind." He smiled. Anyone I know?" "Good looking, bit of a player." "Sounds promising. I like him already." They laughed. Someone knocked and Sam opened the door. "Girl, I missed you." "Me too." They hugged. "Hey, Dimples, want some iced tea?" "Yeah, thanks." He walked over to the couch and sat near Riley. "Hey, Dimples." "Shut up." "Now, Riley, I told you only I get to call him that." "Sorry I just couldn't resist." "So I heard you bumped into Brad." "Yeah, he was on his way to O'Casey's. He invited us, but I told him Scott and I wanted time alone." "Did he cry?" Riley asked. Scott smirked. "Almost." They both grinned. "Stop being so mean. He's a nice guy," Emily said. "Who just happens to be interested in you. I mean it's written all over his face." "Riley, tell him he's overreacting." "Sorry, no can do. He's definitely into you." "Sorry, Em, but you're outnumbered, darlin'." "You too, Sam?" "Yeah. Sorry. The guys got a classic case of the hots for you." "Why didn't you ever tell me?" "Because you wouldn't have listened anyway." "I can't believe this. Brad?" She stood there in disbelief. "It's okay, he hides it well. Only trained pros like Sam and me could see it." "Really, Riley?" "No, just trying to make you feel better about it." She laughed. "Thanks, that helps." "Anytime."

Hanson pulled into the lot at Jake's. He walked inside and sat at the end of the bar. Jake saw him and came over. "Hey, Hanson. The guys coming?" "Not tonight, Jake." "Want a drink?" "I wouldn't say no to a beer." "You got it." He poured him his favorite pale ale. "So you wanna tell me what's bothering you?" "How do you know something is bothering me?" "I'm a bartender, we always know." "Well, you know the story about my ex-wife, right?" "She left when Scott was a kid, right?" "Yeah. She left twelve years ago, didn't even have the decency to say good-bye. Just left a note." "That's pretty shitty." "It was and Scott was fucked up afterwards." "I'll bet. Must have been a real tough time for you both?" "It was. Anyway, fast forward twelve years and I get a letter from her." "Are you fucking kidding me?" "I wish I were. She's sorry, and wants to make it up to us. I was tempted to tear up the letter." "Why didn't you?" "Not sure. I called her." "Really? How did that go?" "About as you'd expect." "I expect angry and awkward." "You'd be right. She's coming tomorrow." "But Scott's here?" "Right now he's up at SUNY with Emily, Sam, and Riley. They drove her back this afternoon. He'll probably stay overnight and come back tomorrow." "Does he know about any of this?" "Hell, no." "Do you think he'd want to see her? "A year ago I'd have said no, but now I'm not so sure." "Why?" "Well, he asked about her. Said he's been thinking about her lately. That he's trying to understand why she did what she did." "That's rough. I mean it's still gotta hurt." "I'm sure it does. I mean, I'm twisted up about it myself." He looked at him. "You still got feelings for her?" "Why the hell does every one keep asking me that?" He shrugged. "Maybe 'cause you do." "When I heard her voice it felt like I'd been punched in the gut. Know what I mean?" "Yeah. If Angela contacted me, I'd feel the same way." "Jake, I'm sorry. Here I am going on and on never even thinking about you and Angie." "Look, no worries. I've moved on." "Famous last words, my friend. I told myself for years that I was over Amanda, but you know what I'm starting to think?" "What?" "That I'm full of shit." He finished his beer and got up. "Well, I'd better get back. Thanks for the beer and the listening ear." "Anytime. Hanson?" "Yeah?" "Good luck." "Thanks, I'm gonna need it."

Riley and Sam decided to head to O'Casey's, giving Scott and Emily the alone time they wanted. "Could this have worked out any better?" They were sitting on the sofa cuddling. "So I was thinking of spending the night and heading back tomorrow." "What about Riley?" "What about him?" "Scott." "Fine. He can sleep in the trunk." "You are so bad." "Don't worry, the way he and Sam were looking at one another, I have a feeling he'll be staying with her." "Are you going to call your dad?" "Yeah, give me five minutes and then I'm all yours." "I can hardly wait," she said, smiling.

O'Casey's was a small pub where the college kids hung out. Riley and Sam walked in and sat at the bar. Riley noticed the bartender noticing him. "You want anything?" "Rum and coke, please." He moved down toward the other end of the bar and got a closer look at the bartender. She was a very attractive redhead. She turned to him and smiled. "What can I get you?" "Rum and coke and what beer you got on tap?" "We have Harpoon, Pete's, Sam Adams." "I'll have a Sam." "You got it." She walked away and quickly returned with their drinks." "Thanks." "Anytime, handsome." Normally he'd sit down, strike up a conversation, and flirt like mad until closing. Then more than likely they'd seal the deal. Not tonight, though, because he found himself in very unfamiliar territory. He could care less. He came back with their drinks. "Looks like you've got an admirer." He tried to brush it off. "She's just trying to get a bigger tip." "I don't think so. She was looking at you like you were a snow cone in the desert." He let out a big laugh. "So what do you think the two love birds are doing?" "Oh I think we know exactly what they're doing." She laughed. "I guess we do." "You know what else?" "What?" "I can't believe how badly I want to kiss you right now." "So what's stopping you?" "Nothing." He leaned into her and brushed his lips against hers. After that she noticed the disappointed look on the bartender's face. "Looks like your admirer is disappointed." "She'll get over it." He went right back to kissing her.

Brad had been eyeing them since they came in. "Hey, you two." "Hey, Brad." "Brad." "Riley, right?" "That's right." "So where are Em and Scott?" "Oh they're getting busy." Riley chuckled. "You do have a way with words, Sam." "So I've been told." "How long have they been seeing each other?" "Why do you want to know?" "Just curious." Riley gave him a look. "Is there something you wanted to say?" Brad asked. "It's none of my biz." "True but I'm still asking." "It's just you shouldn't be asking about another guy's girl." "What are you, best friends or something?" Sam laughed. "Hardly. I'm just looking out for them. I like Em, she's good people." "I know she is." "Good, then you'll agree with me when I say she doesn't need anyone messing with her life, right?" He got the message. "Look, I don't know what you think about me but—" "What I think is not your concern. But what I know is. And I know that you have a case for her." "Riley?" Sam said. "No, it's fine, Sam. Let him have his say. You know for someone who you're not really friends with, you seem to be doing a pretty good job." "It's all about the bro code. You should read up on it." "I would never try to steal her from him. I'm not that kind of guy." "That's good, 'cause if you did, he'd kick your ass and then I'd have my turn. Understand?" "Yeah, I do." "Good." "Okay, you two, there's enough testosterone flying around to make me grow facial hair." They looked at her and laughed. "You'd look awful in a beard," Riley said, looking at her, smiling. "Everyone's a wiseass. I'm going to the bathroom. Either you two change the subject, or one of you change seats." She walked away, strutting her hips, and Riley loved every minute. "She told us," Brad said. "You bet your ass she did. What a woman." Brad looked at him. "What?" "Nothing. Just seems that the player is about to get played." He grinned. "Don't I know it."

Chapter Ten

Hanson picked up the ringing phone. "Hello?" "Hey, Dad." "Scott, what's up?" "I'm staying overnight. Em doesn't have class till noon so I'll leave then." "Figured that. Listen, don't rush home on my account. We got things covered." "Really? You mean you aren't plotting the next project I can do?" "No, but I will now." "Great, nothing does it for me like manual labor." Hanson chuckled. "How are things going with Riley and Sam?" "Oh they're out at a pub right now. Should have seen him, Dad. He was practically making a fool of himself over Sam." He laughed. "I'd have loved to see that one." "Anyway, see you tomorrow." He hung up and immediately dialed Amanda. Her machine picked up. "Amanda, it's Hanson. Look I've got some things to do in the afternoon, so if you could come in the morning, say, eleven instead of two. Call me if that's a problem." Riley and Sam came back to find Scott and Emily in make-out session on the couch. "Oh man, this is hurting my eyes." "Then don't look," Scott said. "Did you have to pick the couch?" "You'd prefer we used the bed?" "Good point. Sofa was a good choice." "So how was O'Casey's?" Emily asked. "It's cool. Mostly a lot of collegiates trying to tie on one." "Collegiates?" Scott teased. "What, you don't know what that is?" "I do. I just didn't think *you* did." "There was this bartender who had a yen for Riley." "Really? She hot?" "Red hair, hazel eyes and—" "I thought you weren't interested?" "I wasn't, but as long as I have a pulse, I will always notice attractive gals such as yourself." "Nice save." "Thanks." "So listen, we'll head back tomorrow. If that's okay." "Like I have a choice." "You could always hitch a ride." "No thanks. Sam, is it okay if I sleep on your sofa?" "That's fine. I appreciate you're not assuming you'd be allowed in my bed. Besides, my bed is a twin, so you sleeping in it with me wouldn't work so well." "Really?" "Yeah. Em has the same bed. All the rooms do. Limited space. "Oh, man. I wanted to fall asleep holding you, Em." Riley made gagging noises. "Stow it, Finn." "Em could I talk to you a minute? Alone?" "Sure." "What's that all about?" Scott asked. "No idea." "You think it's about us?" "Probably." "What's up?" "Riley kissed me at the bar." "So on a scale of one to ten how would this time rate?" "About a hundred." "And let me guess, you'd like some alone time. Right?" "See, this is why you're my best friend. You totally get me and know what I'm going to say before I ever say it." "Of course, what kind of best friend would I be if I didn't?" "A bad one." They walked back out. "Everything okay?" Riley asked. "Fine." "Come on, Scott. Time to go." "Yeah, okay. So tomorrow Em doesn't have class till noon. How 'bout you, Sam?" My first class is at eight, it ends around ten. Then I'm free till noon." "Okay, so why don't we meet at ten." "We could meet in the cafeteria, they have pretty good food," Emily said. Sam and Riley looked at one another. "Sounds like a plan." Scott and Emily left. "Whew. Alone at last. I thought they'd never leave." "Hey, that's my best friend you're talking about." He grabbed her by her waist and pulled her down onto his lap. "Em's cool but *he's* a pain in the ass." Sam shook her head. "What?" "You guys should just get married." "Bite your tongue." "Bite it for me?" He drew her in for a steamy kiss, playing with her tongue until she moaned. "You're getting me all worked up." "That a bad thing?" "No, but the bed isn't big enough." "We don't need a bed." He picked her up and carried her to the kitchen and sat her on the counter. He unbuttoned her shirt, slowly. "Are you trying to seduce me?" "Is it working?" "*Oh yeah.*" "You know, you are wearing way too much." "Am I?" "Why don't you help me lighten the load?" he said. "My pleasure." She began unbuttoning his shirt. He had taken hers off already, leaving a metallic gold push-up bra. Her breasts looked amazing in it. They stood, staring at each other. "Damn, had I known you had those abs, I would have taken your shirt off the night of the party." "Thanks and just so you know, if I had I known your breasts looked this gorgeous, I'd have helped you out of yours too." "So now that we've got our tops off, what's next?" She asked. "I was kind of hoping we'd lose our bottoms." She laughed. "Sounds like a plan." He grinned and went on to the zipper of her jeans. She decided to unzip his at the same time. The sound they made together was incredibly erotic. "Matching panties?" "Always. You like?" "Oh I like. I like a whole lot." "Boxer man? I figured you for briefs." "I'm just full of surprises." "Yeah, you are." Their lips met again, but this time it was no holds barred. All the passion that had been brewing threatened to boil over. "God, Sam, you taste." "I know. You too." "So will you promise to respect me in the morning?" She gave off a throaty laugh that made him grow even harder. "Isn't that my line?" "Nah, you're the man-eater. I'm at your mercy." "I'm not that bad. Casualties have been greatly exaggerated." "Good to know." "Besides, you're the player." "I'm turning over a new leaf." "Since when?" "Since you." She looked at him. "Really?" "Yeah, really. Enough talking." He swept her off the counter and lowered her to the floor. "I'm going to pleasure you now. And when I'm done, you won't remember any of those putzes who couldn't keep you interested." "Is that a fact?" "Yeah, it is." He kissed every part of her, starting at her lips and working his way down. With every kiss she felt herself moving closer to the edge. He played with her breasts in ways she'd never dreamed of. He went lower and moved her panties aside with his teeth. He put his tongue on her sensual spot, and she writhed in ecstasy. "You like that?" "Hmmm." "More to come. No pun intended." He swirled, licked, and sucked. It was more than she could stand. He used his fingers to work magic inside too. He fingered and teased her with his tongue and felt her body quiver. "Oh my God," she whispered. "God's not doing this." She let out a sexy laugh. "I know." "Say my name. I want you to say my name when you come." She felt the floodgates opening, and she let go. "*Riley*." After that they lay holding each other on the floor. "Whew, that damn near killed me." He laughed. "I take it you enjoyed it?" "That's putting it mildly. There are no words for what that was." He smiled. "Glad I could be of service." "Why don't you let me return the favor?" "No." She propped herself up with one arm on his chest. "No?" "No. I want tonight to be about you. Which you can't believe how huge that is for me. Since I'm ashamed to admit it I've never been concerned with that much before." "I thought when you put me on that counter you were going to—" "Do you?" "Yeah." "I know, but I want to do things differently with you. I don't want to have sex with you the first time I see you. I want things to go slower than what's usual for me. I hope that's okay?" "Are you kidding? I'm used to most guys wanting to get lucky after a cup of coffee." "Yeah, well, been there done that. I'm trying to change all that. I hope this is a good start." She kissed him. "It is."

The morning came and Scott woke up first. He looked over at Emily who looked so beautiful that it took his breath away. She stirred, and her eyes fluttered as she awakened. "Morning." "Morning, beautiful." He kissed her gently. "How long have you been watching me?" "Long enough." "I must look terrible." "Are you kidding? You look amazing." "I doubt that very much, but thanks for saying it." "You look amazing all the time. Awake, asleep, when we're making love." They kissed. "We should shower. We have to meet them in an hour." "Five more minutes." "'Kay." A few minutes later, she sat up. "Time's up." "Joy kill." She laughed. "You want to shower first or should I?" "I was just thinking I have a hard time reaching my back." "Do you?" "Yeah, I can never really get it that good. But if you were there with me, you could—" "Get it for you?" "Exactly." "You are so transparent." "I know, but just thinking about you in the shower, all slippery and wet . . ." He came up behind her and caressed her breasts. "Scott, you're not playing fair." "I know." He moved his hands down to her warm and already-moist center. "You could always get even." She moaned. "I could." She turned around started stroking him and pulled away. She stood in the bathroom doorway. "You coming?" "Not yet, but soon." She laughed.

Riley and Sam had been waiting in the cafeteria. "They're late." "And you're surprised by this?" She laughed. "No, I guess not." Then they spotted them and waved them over. "Sorry we're late," Em said. "Yeah, we got hung up in the shower." She slapped his arm. "What? Like they don't know *why* we're late. Riley?" "Sex in the shower." "See." "How do you know that?" Emily asked, blushing. "Your hair is still wet." "Nice bit of detective work, Finn," Scott said. "Thanks, I try."

After they had eaten, they went for a quick walk on campus. "This really is nice," Riley said. "We like it," Sam said. Emily looked at her watch. "I've got to get going soon. I don't want to be late, since I need to turn in my project." "Economics?" Scott asked. She nodded. "Shoot me now." "I should get going too. I've got calculus with Mr. Excitement." "Mr. Excitement?" Riley asked. "Yeah, he's about as exciting as a wet mop." "Calculus isn't exactly a riveting subject, Sam," Scott said. "I know, but he doesn't even try and make it more interesting. He just reads from the book. It's soo boring." "So what would you like him to do? Juggle?" "Smart-ass." "Til the day I die. Anyway, why don't we walk you two lovely ladies to your class?" "Sure."

They stood outside Emily's economics class. "Why don't Sam and I give you two a little privacy. Scott, we'll meet you near Sam's calculus class." "It's room sixteen ten, Dimples." "Okay." "So this is it," she said, sounding sad. "I'll be back real soon." "Scott, if you can't make it—" "I will *definitely* be making it. God I'm going to miss you." "Me too." She felt herself tearing up. Brad walked by on his way into class. "Everything okay?" "Yes, just saying bye." "*For now*," Scott stressed. "Right. See you inside." "He's in your class?" "He's in a few of my classes." "Well, I'll sleep a whole lot better knowing that." "You're jealous." "Am not." She looked at him. "Okay, maybe a little. Come on, the guy could be a model for Christ's sake." She smiled. "Maybe but you're the one I want." "Come here." He drew her in for one last kiss. "I'll see you soon." He watched her walk in and sit right next to Brad. He frowned. *Friend my ass.*

Scott walked down the hall and saw Sam and Riley in a major lip lock. He was tempted to bust Riley's balls but instead he gave them their moment. After all, they had done the same for them. When they pulled apart, Riley put his hand on her cheek. "You know I have never said this to another woman, but I'm going to miss the hell out of you." "That so? Well, I *might* just end up missing you too." He laughed. "Scott's right. You are a man-eater." She laughed. "I'm just teasing. I'm going to miss you too. A lot. Maybe we could work out another visit. Scott's coming back, you could come with him?" "I could, and that might work if we don't end up killing each other on the drive here." "I'd better go inside. Class is about to start." "Okay. If you want to call me later, feel free." "I just might just do that." She winked at him and went inside. He stood there, staring. That's when Scott came up behind him. "I know the feeling. Been there, just did that." "It's amazing 'cause if you had told me a month ago that I would be like this over a woman, I would have said you were crazy." "Buddy, I would have thought so too." "This is all new to me. I'm used to—" "Wham, bam, thank you, ma'am?" "Was I really that bad?" "Yeah. You were." He shook his head. "Don't worry, I can give you some pointers." He rolled his eyes. "Great, I can hardly wait."

Hanson got his morning chores done early, so he could be free when Amanda arrived. As he walked toward the main house, he saw Sabrina on the porch. "How are you holding up?" "Not that great." "I know it's rough, but you'll get through it." "Hope so. What are you doing?" "Waiting for Ross. We're having lunch." A few minutes later, he pulled up in his squad car. "Ross, I thought we said noon." "We did, but I couldn't wait to see you." He kissed her. "Well, that's my cue to leave." "No, don't go. We'll wait with you until Amanda comes." Ross looked at him. "She's coming? Here? Now?" "Yep." "Holy crap. What time is she due?" "Eleven but originally it was two. I left her a message asking her to come earlier. She's already thirty minutes late. Maybe I should call her." "She probably got a little lost. It's a bit tricky finding this place if you've never been here before," Sabrina said. "Yeah, you're probably right. Just then they spotted an SUV coming up the stretch of road. "That must be her." Sabrina grabbed hold of his hand and gave it a gentle squeeze. "You can do this." "I don't think I have much of a choice. Unless, I sic Ross on her." He looked at him. "Sorry, I don't do long-lost ex-wives." "Chicken." He laughed. The SUV stopped, and they all seemed to be holding their breath as the door opened and a petite brunette got out. Ross whispered to him. "You never said she was hot." He gave him an annoyed look. "Are you fuckin' kidding me?" "I'm just saying." "Well, don't." As she walked toward them, her eyes met Hanson's and both felt an old familiar jolt. *Crap.* "Hello, Hanson." "Amanda. This is Sabrina, she's the owner, and Ross, he's the sheriff. She shook both their hands. "Nice to meet you." "Likewise." "Amanda, can I get you something to drink?" "Actually, I would love a glass of water." "Sure. Ross would you help me, please." "Sure." They stood together in awkward silence. "You look good, Amanda." "Thanks. You look pretty good yourself." Sabrina came out, holding a glass of ice water. "Here you go." "Thanks. The road was pretty dusty." "We haven't had much rain lately, which makes the roads a lot more dusty." "Nice place you have here." "Thank you, but I don't do it alone. I have lots of help." "So, Amanda, where did you drive from?" Ross asked. "New York." Sabrina grew interested. "Really? I worked there briefly." "You did? Where?" "Seventh Avenue, for a small design company." "How did you end up here?" "My brother and his wife were killed in plane crash." "Oh I'm so sorry." "Thank you. It was an extremely difficult time, but we managed. Mostly because I had these two amazing men supporting me." "In times like that, having support makes all the difference." "Like you would know anything about that," he quipped. Sabrina and Ross looked at each other. "Well, if you'll excuse us. We have lunch plans. Nice meeting you, Amanda." "Nice meeting you." She waited until they were inside before speaking. "Feel better after belittling me in front of your friends?" "A little." "I'm prepared for angry." "Well, that's good since you are going to get that and a whole lot more." "I'm ready. Let it fly." After waiting twelve years, the only thing he could be was blunt. "What the fuck were you thinking leaving like that? Didn't you care about Scott? Do you have any idea what it did to him?" "Please lower your voice. To answer your questions, I wasn't thinking, of course I cared about Scott, and I know my leaving screwed him up." "No, you're leaving *fucked* him up." "Fine it fucked him up. That's why I'm here." "You left without a second thought to either of us. I just don't understand how you could have done something like that. It shouldn't have taken twelve years to develop a conscience." "It didn't. I just didn't know how to come back after." "That's horseshit, Amanda." "Fine. I didn't come back because I couldn't." "Couldn't? What do you mean you couldn't?" She paused, debating whether she should tell him the truth. "You mean you didn't want to." "That's not true. When I left I was confused." "Please, you are going to have to do a whole lot better than that." "I'm trying." "Yeah, well, so far you're doing a shitty job." She looked at him with frustration in her eyes. "I'm not the same person anymore. I've changed." "Well, *whoop-d-fucking-do*!" "Can you please stop being angry for five minutes and actually *hear* what I'm saying!" "Oh I *hear* you just fine. I'm just not buying any of it." She let out an exasperated sound. "God, I'd forgotten how stubborn you are! You never listened!" "So you're blaming me?" "No! Please for once in your life listen!" "Why should I?" "Because Scott's happiness depends on it." "Oh right, like you *care* about that." "I know you find this hard to believe but I do. Not a day has gone by that I haven't thought of him, haven't missed him." "Well, allow me to nominate you for the Mother of the Year Award!" She felt herself losing control. "You know what, I thought I could come here and you'd at least hear me out. But I was wrong, I'm leaving!" He stopped yelling and spoke calmly. "Go ahead. It's what you do best anyway." She turned around, walked back over to him, and slapped him. "You bastard!" He held his jaw. "Try that again, and I just might forget you're a woman." "Is that supposed to scare me? Because it doesn't. Ever think that you're not the only one I screwed by leaving? I lost the only man I've ever loved and my child." "Whose fault was that?" "Mine! But I was hoping we could put aside the anger and hate long enough to have a civil conversation. Two people who want what's best for their son." "What's best for Scott doesn't concern you. It hasn't for a very long time. I've been doing just fine without you." "She took a calming breath. "This was clearly a mistake." She started walking toward her car. He stood there, remembering another time when she had walked away. *"Manda, I'm home." He had gotten off work a little early and picked up flowers. She had been down and he hoped the flowers would cheer her up. He laid them on the table and noticed a folded-over piece of paper, his name written on it. He opened it and began reading,*

Dearest Hanson,

I hope one day you will be able to forgive me for what I'm about to do. Please know that my coming to this decision was difficult but it's the right thing to do for all of us. Hopefully, one day you'll understand. I love you.

Always Yours,
Amanda

Her walking away from him again made something inside him snap. He came up behind her and turned her around to face him. "What are you doing?" "Something I've been wanting to do for the past twelve years." "Oh and what's that?" "This." He crushed his mouth against hers. It had been twelve years since his lips touched hers. Since his arms held her. It still did something to her. She pulled away breathless. "What are you doing?" "Kissing you, damn it." He took her mouth again, realizing that he'd never completely gotten over her. "We need to stop this." "I know." "You're still a good kisser," she told him. He grinned. "Thanks and your still one hot little number." "Is that a compliment?" "Yeah, but don't let it go to your head. In no time at all you'll be back to slapping me." She laughed. "Why don't we go to my place and try to have that civilized conversation?" "Sure. I think we're both safe for now."

Ross and Sabrina finished eating. "So how do you think it's going?" "Well, if the shouting's any indication I'd say not good." "They were pretty loud. I feel bad. I just wish there was something I could do." "Look, he's a big boy, he'll handle it." "I saw the way he looked at her, I think he still has feelings for her." "Probably. I mean they were married and have Scott together. Plus, she's hot." She gave him a look. "Hey, I'm not dead." She laughed.

Hanson and Amanda sat at his table. "I need a drink. How 'bout you?" "Definitely." He got out scotch and poured a healthy dose for each of them. She took a swallow and coughed. "God, how do you drink this?" "There's a time and place for everything. Right now we both need something strong." "True. So I'll be the one to go after the elephant in the room." "Which one?" He asked jokingly. "Well, how about what just happened." He took another sip. "Which part? The slap, you're calling me a bastard, or the kiss?" She laughed. "I see your point. Maybe I shouldn't go after any elephants." He laughed. "Honey, to handle all those pachyderms we'll need something a whole lot stronger than scotch." She smiled. "I've missed this." "What?" "You. Me. Talking. Laughing." He paused before drinking again. "To be honest, I haven't let myself miss anything it was too damn painful." "I'm sorry. You didn't deserve any of it. You were a good man, husband, and father. The fact that you even let me come here today speaks volumes about the kind of man you are." "Yeah, I gotta be honest though. I almost tore up your letter." "I wouldn't have blamed you if you did. I hurt you and Scott deeply. I know it's too late for us, but I'm hoping it's not for Scott." "What do you want, Amanda?" "I want to make amends somehow." "He's asked about you, you know." "He has?" "Yeah. He also wanted to know about us. It kind of surprised me because for years I couldn't even mention you." He looked up at her. She was tearing up. "I'm sorry." "No, he has every right to feel that way. I abandoned him. He probably hates me." "He doesn't hate you." "How do you know?" "Because he told me." "So what did you tell him?" "I said that I fell for you the first moment I laid eyes on you. That we were happy for a time, and I never regretted any of it because it gave me him." She got up and walked over to the window. He heard muffled sobs. "Ah, geez, 'Manda, don't cry. You know I always hated to see you cry." She sniffled. "You haven't called me that in twelve years. Feels good to hear you say it again." He looked at her. "It's just I never expected you to be so nice about things." She sobbed. "See, all these years I thought you hated me." "I don't hate you, 'Manda. I've been pissed off as all hell at you, but I've never hated you. Though I did try." She looked at him. Her eyes were puffy red, and her face wet with tears. "Here, let me get you something." He came back with a box of tissues. "Thanks." She blew her nose and dried her eyes. "I'm sorry, there's so much pain because of me. I hate myself for what I did to Scott, to you, to us. If I could go back in time, I would." "I believe you. The thing is you can't." So what are we going to do?" "Why don't you let me talk to him first. I can feel him out. If he's interested in talking to you, then I'll have him contact you." "All right. So do you want to tackle the last elephant?" He looked at her. "The kiss." "Oh that." "Yes, that." "What do you want me to say?" "How about why you did it?" "I honestly don't know. When I saw you walking away something snapped. You still haven't told me anything about you." "Let's save that for another time. If there is one," she said, sounding sad. "You think there won't be?" "I honestly don't know." "I'll walk you to your car."

Chapter Eleven

Scott and Riley were halfway home, and Riley was being given a crash course on relationships. "Look, I appreciate what you are trying to do, but I *knoooooow* women." "No, you think you do. Just because you sleep with them doesn't make you an expert." Riley looked at him with a raised brow. "Okay fine, so you're an expert in *that* area." "Damn straight. I know what turns them on, off, and revs 'em up." "You think you're the only guy who knows all that? 'Cause you're not. Besides, what about the other stuff?" "What other stuff?" Scott looked at him. "I rest my case." Riley looked at him, annoyed. "I'm just trying to help." "I get that but I got this." "No, you only think you do. Women need to feel special." "Sam is an almost-female version of me. She doesn't need all that other stuff." "Okay, have it your way. Just remember I tried to tell you." "You told me. So leave it alone." "Fine."

Sabrina was walking Ross to his car when they saw Hanson and Amanda heading to her car. "So you're leaving?" Sabrina asked. "Yes, I think we've done enough talking for one day." Ross noticed a car approaching. Sabrina was trying to see who it was. "Ross, is that?" He squinted. "It's your car, Brina." "Damn." Hanson said, looking upset. "What is it?" He looked at her. "It's Scott." She looked at him, confusion and panic in her eyes. "You told me he was back at school." "I lied." "What?" "I didn't want him here. I wasn't sure how it would turn out." "But my letter?" She looked at him. "You did tell him? Didn't you?" He let out a breath. "No, I didn't." "I see." The car was getting closer. "Are you all right, Amanda?" Sabrina asked. "Not really." "Amanda, when I got your letter, I was a mess. All that pain came flooding back." "You don't have to explain, Hanson. I probably would have done the same thing. But he's here now, so what are we going to do?" "We could say you were lost and stopped to ask for directions?" Ross said. They all looked at him. "Or not." "Ross and I will leave. You don't need an audience." "I should get back to the station, anyway." "Amanda, if you need to talk, my door is always open." "Thanks." The car pulled over and stopped. Riley and Scott came out, arguing as usual. Amanda felt her heartbeat quicken. The moment she had dreamed about for twelve long years was finally here. Her boy was standing in front of her. Though he was no longer a boy. He was a man. Hanson shook his head. "You two at it again?" "Yeah, but you'll be happy to know we bonded." Hanson felt the corners of his mouth curl up. "That's great boys." "Yeah, he's my new BFF," Scott teased. "BFF?" Hanson asked. "Best friend forever," she said, smiling. Scott and Riley looked at her. She was petite but definitely a looker. For some reason, she looked familiar to Scott. "And *who* is this?" Riley asked flirtatiously. Hanson rolled his eyes. "Aren't you with Sam?" "Yeah, but that doesn't make me blind." Amanda couldn't help laughing. Scott gave Riley a shove. "You'll have to excuse my friend, having a girl for longer than one night is a new concept for him." He smiled, showing his dimples and her heart melted. "It's fine and I'm flattered." "I'm Scott and this idiot is Riley." "Pleasure to meet you both." *She looks so familiar.* "Scott, this is Amanda." "Nice to . . ." *My mother's name was Amanda.* He took another look at her and saw himself staring back at him. "Wait, my mother's name was Amanda?" She looked to Hanson for approval, and when he nodded, she spoke. "Hello, Scott. I'm Amanda, your mother." He stood there stunned. He had been having thoughts of coming face to face with her after all these years. And now it all seemed too much. "Scott, I know this is a shock," Hanson started to say. "Shock? You gotta be kidding me." "I know my being here is hard, and that I'm the last person you expected to see but—" "You're right, you are." "But I'd like to try and make it up to you if I can. Make things right again." "Right? You can never make things right." "Scott." "Dad, don't, all right?" He walked away, and they all knew better than to follow. All except Riley. "I'll stick with him. Make sure he doesn't do anything stupid. "Thanks, Riley," Amanda said. "By the way, you are way too hot to be *his* mom." He winked at her and walked away. Despite the situation, both she and Hanson laughed.

Scott sat in the same tree that he and Emily had. "I wish you were here, Em." "Will I do?" He looked down and saw Riley. "Not even close." "Well, tough 'cause I'm all you've got." "Lucky me." "You gonna come down, or should I come up?" He didn't answer him. "Fine. Move over, I'm coming up." He climbed skillfully and sat on the branch next to him. "So that's your mom?" "Evidently." "She's too hot to be a mom, let alone *your* mom." "You're an idiot." "I'm just saying. She's a nice little package." "Okay, we are not having this conversation." "So let's have another one." He looked at him. "Look, I appreciate what you are trying to do, but I came here to be alone." "I know. If it's any consolation, she seemed genuinely worried." "Yeah, well, it's about twelve years too late." "Is it?" "What's that supposed to mean?" "Look, I never really knew my mom. She died when I was very young." "I'm sorry." "Thanks. I gotta say that not a day goes by that I don't wish she was still alive." "And your point?" "My point is my mom is gone. She can't come back, but yours can." "She left us." "She made a mistake, which I'm sure she's been paying for ever since." Scott climbed down and he followed. "Riley?" "Yeah?" "Do you still miss your mom?" "Every damn day."

Hanson and Amanda sat on the porch. "This is all my fault." "No, it's mine. I should have told him." "At least Riley's with him," she said and he laughed. "If you knew those two the way I do, you wouldn't find that comforting."

Scott and Riley were walking back. "Hey, thanks for telling me about your mom." "Sure." "Do you remember anything about her?" "Only that she was pretty and had a great smile. The kind that always made things better." "Guess that's what being a mom is all about." Scott said nothing. "So are you going to talk to her?" "Probably. It's funny but I just asked Dad about her." "Really?" "I wanted to know why she left." "Well, it looks like you'll have your chance to ask." "Yeah, looks like I will.

Sabrina sat on the porch with Hanson and Amanda. "That must have been awful for him." "It was. The look on his face damn near broke my heart," she said. "Mine too," he said. "Do you think he'll come around?" "I hope so," she said nervously. "They're back," he said. "Oh God. I'm soo not ready for this." "Just take it one step at a time." "Right. "Looks like they're waiting for you, Scott." "Yeah." "You want me to stick around?" "No, I'm good." "Riley?" "Yeah?" "Thanks." "Good luck."

"I'm glad you came back, son. We were worried." "Yes, we were." There was a long and awkward pause. "Scott, do you feel up to talking?" He seemed hesitant. "If not, I can come back another time." "No! I mean I'm not sure I want you to come back." "Well, I can't say I blame you." "Look, I'm sorry, I didn't mean—" "No, please, don't apologize. You have absolutely nothing to be sorry for." "Why don't we go into the barn, talk there?" "Whatever you want." They walked inside and Pete, Dave, Steve, and Riley were there. "Hey, Scott." "Hey." They were all looking at Amanda, and Scott got annoyed. Riley must have told them who she was because they made their excuses and left. As they were walking out they overhead them talking. "Man, Riley, you were right. She is hot." Scott shook his head. "Why don't you sit down?" He pointed to a hay bale. "Okay, sure." "So," he said. "So." "Well, this is going well." "Why don't I start?" "All right." "First, let me apologize for the way this went down. I had sent your father a letter, and when we talked about meeting, I assumed he'd tell you." "Dad didn't tell me anything." "Please don't be mad at him. He was only trying to protect you." "I'm a big boy, I can take care of myself." "I'm sure you can, but when you're a parent, you never stop trying to protect your child." "You did." His sharp words cut through her like a knife. "Oh, Scott, no. I know this is going to be hard to believe, but I never stopped thinking about you." "Right." "When I left I wasn't myself. After you were born, I became moody, easily irritated. I thought it was because of the life I was living." "You mean because of Dad and me?" "Yes. I loved you and your father, but I felt trapped. I had delusions about the life I should be living. "So how'd that work out for you? Get everything you wanted?" "No." "That's a damn shame." He got up and turned his back to her. "No, what was the real shame was my giving up our life together." "Our life together? Do you even remember any of it?" She stood up. "I remember. And I've thought of nothing else for years." "Well, that makes me feel a whole lot better." "There are no words to excuse what I did." "You're right. There aren't." "I know you're angry." He laughed. "Angry? That doesn't even begin to cut it. I hated you for years. Dad couldn't even say your name around me." "I understand," she said with sadness in her voice. "No, I don't think you do." "When you left, Dad was ripped apart, we both were. He tried to hide just how fucked up he was from me, but I knew. He would cry at night when he thought I was sleeping. Imagine a grown man reduced to tears night after night." He felt his anger growing. "I loved your father." "Yeah, you loved him so much you left." She felt tears welling up in her eyes. "I never meant to hurt either of you." "Yeah, well, newsflash. You did. And those scars run pretty damn deep." "I know they do." "You don't know anything." "So tell me?" "What for? A tear dropped down, and she wiped it away. "I know I hurt you, but I promise things will different. I'm different. I screwed up, but I'm going to make things right." "And just how do you plan on doing that? Because aside from building a DeLorean and traveling back in time, I don't see how you can." "Believe me, if that was possible, I would do it in a heartbeat." "Why should I believe anything you say?" "Because even though I left, I'm still your mother, and you're still my son." "That's just biology." His words stung. "I love you, Scott. And I'd like a chance to prove that to you." "A chance? You don't deserve anything, least of all a chance. "You're right. I don't but I'm still asking for one. No, I'm begging for one." "I find begging very unattractive in a woman." She laughed. "God, you remind me so much of your father. You have his wit and good looks. You must have a ton of girls after you." "I have a girlfriend." "Oh. Is she pretty?" "She's . . . everything." She looked at him. "You're in love with her?" "That's none of *your* business." "I guess I haven't earned that right yet." "That's right, you haven't." "I'm just happy that you found someone. I mean your face, it—" "What?" "Nothing." "You wanted to talk and now you clam up?" "It's just it reminded me of the way your father used to look at me." "He loved you." "I know." "And you broke his heart." "I know that too." He stood with his hands on his hips. "So how would this work?" "We can take it as slow as you want. If you just want to talk on the phone, we can do that. Or if you want me to visit you or you could visit me. It's up to you." He looked at her. "I loved you, you know." She sighed, more tears falling now. She caressed his cheek with her hand. "I know you don't believe this, but I never stopped loving you." She kissed him and started walking out. "You're leaving?" "Yes, I think we've talked enough. Your father has my number. If you contact me, great. If not, I'll respect that too. Take care of yourself, Scott." Just like that she was gone again. The only difference was this time it wouldn't be for good if that is what he wanted. Trouble was he didn't know what the hell he wanted.

Amanda was inside her car when she shut down the engine and got back out. She walked up toward the house and knocked on the door. "Come in." When she went inside, she saw Sabrina at the dining table surrounded by drawings. "Sabrina?" She looked up. "Oh, Amanda. I'm sorry I thought you were Hanson or one of the guys." "It's okay. I can see you're busy so I'll just—" "No, it's fine. I need a break anyway. I'm getting ruffle vision." "Ruffle vision?" "It's what my old boss used to say when everything he drew had the same feature in it, like a bow or a—" "Ruffle?" "Exactly." "So what's your ruffle?" Amanda came closer and started looking at the sketches. "These all have sashes." "Yes, they do." "You drew these?" "I did." "These are amazing." "Thank you." "You're very welcome. I'd wear these in a second." "Good to know. So you need to talk?" "I'm sorry, I feel bad just dropping in like this." "Nonsense. How about a snack?" "Oh I don't want you to go to any trouble." "It's no trouble at all. I made fresh apple pie earlier." "That sounds great." "Let's go into the kitchen and talk."

Scott wasn't sure what he was going to do, but he was tired of thinking. His head hurt. As he walked inside, his father was coming out. "Hey." "Hey." "Did your Mom leave?" "Don't call her that." "All right. Did Amanda leave?" "Yeah, she did. And if you want a play by play, you're out of luck. I've got a headache and not in the mood to talk right now." "Okay." He looked at him. "When you're ready, I'm here." "Thanks, Dad."

Ross was driving around town when he saw Mrs. Haugtry walking Sammy. Or rather, it looked more like Sammy was walking her. *Oh for the love of Pete.* He pulled over. "Hey, Mrs. Haugtry, you okay?" "Fiiiine." "You don't look fine." "He's just a little high strung today." *He's high strung every day.* "Well, just be careful." "Not to worry, Sheriff, I've got him." And with that, she was jerked down the block. *Got him my ass.*

Sabrina and Amanda sat eating pie and drinking tea. "So am I to assume that things didn't go well?" "That would be a safe assumption." "I'm sorry." "Me too, but I didn't expect him to welcome me with open arms." "At least you're realistic about it." "I have to be." "So how did you two leave things?" She sipped her tea. "If he wants to get in touch he will. If not . . ." "And you're okay with that?" "No. To be honest, knowing I might never hear from him again scares the crap out of me, but there's nothing I can do. If he decides to shut me out, I won't ever get over it. But deep down, I know that's what I deserve." "You know, Hanson never really told me what happened between you." "I'm not surprised." "How did you two meet?" She smiled. "I sang for my supper. Literally. I got jobs singing in clubs and bars. One night, while singing, I felt this pull from across the room. I followed it to the most intense pair of brown eyes I'd ever seen. I sang the rest of the song looking into those eyes. They were Hanson's." "Wow that sounds intense." "Oh it was. I swear I heard the air crackle when our hands brushed as he handed me a drink that night. Before either of us knew what hit us, we fell madly in love and got married. He continued working on the ranch, and I continued singing. We were so hot for one another. That's how I ended up pregnant soon after we were married. We couldn't keep our hands off each other. After Scott was born, things went downhill. I started feeling sad a lot of the time. In my mind, I could attain these dreams if I wasn't married and didn't have a child. *They* were making me feel the way I did. *They* were holding me back. After I left, those feelings didn't change. Eventually, I was diagnosed with postpartum depression." "Does Hanson know?" "No." "When we talked earlier, I merely hinted at it. I don't want a second chance to come from pity." "I understand, but don't you think they have the right to know? I mean, postpartum isn't a joke." "It's a lot more complicated. Believe me. Anyway, I should get going. I've taken up enough of your time." "Nonsense, I needed a break from all those sashes." They laughed. "I'll walk you out." "Sabrina, thank you for everything." "Anytime. I hope to see you back here soon." "So do I."

The next day, Scott was up early brushing Sugar when Riley walked in. "You're up early?" "Yeah, I didn't get much sleep." "I imagine you wouldn't. Thinking about your mom?" "Don't call her that!" he snapped. "You wanna take it down a notch?" He let out a frustrated breath. "Sorry." "I get it, sore subject." "It's just a person needs to earn the right to be called mom." "Okay, how about Hot mama?" "You're an idiot." "I'll take that as a no." They looked at each other and laughed. "Thanks. I needed that." "Anytime. Look, I know this is rough, but you'll get through it." "I'm not so sure." "You will." "I hope so, 'cause this sucks. A part of me wants to hate her, so I just won't give a damn." "And the other part?" "The other part wants to maybe give her a chance." "I'd listen to *that* part." Scott looked at him. "When did you get so smart?" He laughed. "I've always been *this* smart, you just never noticed." "Why aren't you being your usual dick self?" He smiled. "I figured you deserved a break." "I'm touched." "You should be. So what's on the agenda for today?" "I'm going to see Em." "That's not a good idea." "Why not?" "Well, don't take this the wrong way, but you're a fucking mess right now. You aren't thinking straight. Hell, I wouldn't trust you with my cat right now." "You don't have a cat." "You're missing the point." "You might do something even more stupid than usual." "Like?" "I don't know I'm just saying whenever I feel the way you are, I avoid people. It's safer." "I need her, Riley." "I'm sure you do, but just hold off till you're in a better place." "I'll think about it." He finished brushing Sugar and walked out. Riley shook his head. *He's going. Idiot.*

Emily slept and dreamed of making love with Scott. Just when it was getting really good, she heard banging in her dream, which woke her up. Someone was at her door. She sleepily looked at her clock and noted that it wasn't even eight. *Who could that be?* She looked through the peephole and grew excited when she saw Scott. She had just been dreaming of him, and now he was here. She opened the door and smiled. "Hey, handsome, I was just dreaming about you." She noticed that he looked upset. "What's wrong." He took in her flushed appearance, grabbed her by the hair, and started kissing her. He moved them inside and pushed her up against the door. He was pawing at her clothes like an animal. Suddenly, she was naked and he was inside her. He wasn't even looking at her. Just thrusting, and then it was over. He withdrew and zipped up his jeans. She reached for her clothes. "You wanna tell me what that was." "What? I wanted you. We made love." "There wasn't an ounce of love in that." He looked at her. "I hadn't realized you switched your major to psychology, Em." "Yeah, well, I hadn't realized you switched yours to wham, bam, thank you, ma'am." "What the hell is that supposed to mean?" "You know exactly what it means." "Hey, I drove a long way to see you." "No! You drove a long way for a fuck. Which is all that was. I don't know what's gotten into you, but you'd better start talking and it had better be good." "I wanted you." "You've wanted me before, and it's never been like that." "Like what?" "Like I was just some no name girl you picked up." "Em, I—" "Do you even realize that you didn't use a condom?" He put his head down and felt like a total asshole. "Is it . . . are we?" "A little late to be concerned about that now." He looked at her. "But lucky for us I'm due any day for my period." "Thank God." "Scott, something is wrong. You're hurting. Let me help you." The way she looked at him, pleading in her eyes, was more than he could take. "I can't. I'm sorry." Just like that he was gone. She dropped to the floor and cried. He stood there listening. And hated himself. He almost went back in. But almost doesn't count.

A few hours later, Scott was back home. He was lucky to have made it there in one piece, since he was speeding most of the way. Riley was out by the barn. He could see from his face that something had gone down. "You look miserable." "I don't want to talk about it." He went into the barn and Riley followed. "What happened?" "What are you deaf? I said I don't want to talk about it?" "I heard you but I don't give a shit." "I'm fine." "Bullshit!" "Fuck you!" "No, *fuck you*. I'm trying to help, but if you don't want my help, then that's fine too." He started walking out, when he heard what sounded like muffled sobs. He turned around and saw Scott on his knees. "Oh Christ." Pete and Dave came in and saw Scott on the ground. "Riley?" "He's fine. I got this. Just go." They looked at one another and left. "Great, now they'll think I'm a pussy." "Nah, a sissy maybe but not a pussy." Scott looked at him and laughed a little. "You done falling apart? Or should I go get some Kleenex?" "You're an ass." "Yes, I am and proud of it." He helped him up. "So you wanna tell me what happened?" "I hurt her." He let out a long breath. "I don't like saying this because I hate it when people say it to me, but I told you so." "You did, but I was too stupid to listen. Why didn't I listen?" "'Cause you're a guy. It's in our genetics not to." "It was awful." "I'm sure it was. Tell me." He started telling him. "I mean it was just going through the motions. Like sex with a . . . with a . . ." "Stranger?" "Yeah." "How did you leave things?" "I freaked out and left." "Smooth. I'm sure when you left she bawled her eyes out." "She did." "How do you know?" ""Cause I was standing on the other side of the door, listening." "Nice." "I almost went back in." "Almost doesn't count." "I know. I should go back, apologize and—" "Whoa, no friggin' way am I letting you go back now." "You don't understand, I'm in love with her." "Took you long enough to figure it out." "You knew?" "You're kidding, right? Everyone knows. The way you look at her. The way she looks at you." "Not after what I did." "Give her some time." "Right. I think I need a drink. You mind dropping me off a Jake's?" "Sure, what the hell. I got nothing better to do."

Chapter Twelve

Riley drove up to Jake's and Scott got out. "You sure about this? Remember the tequila incident?" "Yeah, well, since I plan on drinking whiskey this time, it shouldn't be a problem." "Oh that makes me feel *much* better." "Relax. I'll be fine." "Well, if you want me to come pick your drunk ass up, just call." "Okay, thanks." He went up to the door and knocked. The bar wasn't open yet, but he knew Jake would be there. Jake came to the door and was surprised to see him. "What are you doing here?" "I've had a rough couple of days, and I need a drink." "Something wrong with your dad's scotch?" "No." Jake looked at him. "Come on in." "So what'll it be?" "Whiskey." "You sure about that?" "Positive." He grabbed the bottle of Jameson and poured. Scott knocked it back in one gulp. "Whoa, easy! That's not your grandma's lemonade you're drinking." "Believe me, I need it. Pour me another." "What's going on, Scott?" "Pour me another and I'll tell you." "Start telling me and I'll pour." His mouth corners turned up slightly. "Fine. I came face to face with my mother yesterday." Jake looked at him. "The same mother that left when you were eleven?" "The one and only." Jake took out another glass and poured. "What are you doing?" "Now *I* need a drink."

When Emily missed both economics and agricultural studies, Brad became worried. So he tried calling, with no luck. He decided to go there. He knocked. "Em, are you there? Say something please." He listened and heard muffled sounds. "Honey, please let me in." Nothing. "Okay, if you don't let me in, I'll get Sam." He heard what sounded like a clicking sound. The door opened, and he went in. "Are you sick?" "No, sorry I scared you." She wasn't looking at him. He moved around her and saw her. Her eyes puffy and red, cheeks wet with tears. "You've been crying." "Go away, Brad." "I'll leave when you tell me what's got you so upset." She sat on the sofa and started crying. He sat down next to her and held her as she wept.

Scott filled Jake in on Amanda's surprise appearance. "I don't know what to say." "That's okay, neither do I." "So what are you going to do?" "That's the million-dollar question. Plus, it gets worse." "How the hell could this get worse?" "I did something." "To?" "Em." "What did you do?" "For that, I'll need another shot." "You aren't driving are you?" "No, Riley dropped me off." "This is the last one. Deal?" Scott blew out an annoyed breath. "Deal." Jake poured. "So what did you do?" "Well, after all this with my . . . with Amanda, I really needed Em. So this morning I got up extra early and left to go see her. Of course, before I left Riley tried to warn me about it not being the best time for a visit." "I take it that you didn't listen?" "Nope." "What could you have possibly done that was so bad? I mean, from what Ross tells me, you're crazy about her." "I'm in love with her." "Okay, I hadn't realized you were *that* crazy about her." "I am." "So you still haven't told me what you did." "I screwed her. No hellos, nothing. I didn't even look at her. Just grabbed her, pushed her against the door, and got my rocks off. And you know, even after that, even after I treated her no better than a one-night stand, she still wanted to help me. That got me. So I left." "Smooth." "Tell me about it. Then I stood there listening to her cry. I almost went back in." "Why didn't you?" "Because I figured I'd done enough." "Man, you weren't kidding. You screwed up." "I know." "Em is one sweet gal who deserves to be treated with respect. You showed her none. And right now she's hurting because of it." "So what do I do?" "First, you are going to get this shit with your mother straight. And yeah, I called her your mother 'cause that's who she is, like it or not. The sooner you deal with and accept that, the better off you'll be. If you want to give her a whirl, fine. If not, tell her adios and move on. Second, tell Em everything. And I mean *everything,* and pray she's willing to give you a second chance." "Okay, thanks, Jake." "Don't thank me, just do it."

Brad convinced Emily to shower while he fixed her something to eat. "Sorry, it's not a better meal." "It's fine. I appreciate it." "Growing up, my sister was always the one to cook. I should have paid more attention." "Scrambled eggs are fine." "So are you ready to tell me what happened?" "Not really." "At least let me call Sam. It's obvious you need to talk to someone." "All right." He dialed Sam and told her the situation. "She's on her way." "Thanks. You're sweet to take care of me this way." *That's because I'm crazy about you.* "Well, Mama always said a gentleman never leaves a distraught lady alone." "Is your mother from the South?" "No, she just watched *Gone with the Wind* a lot." That got her laughing a little. "Now that's more like it." "You made that up?" "Guilty as charged. You're much prettier when you smile." He paused, looking at her, taking in every inch of her face. "You're being upset. It has to do with Scott, doesn't it?" "Yes." "What did he do? I'm sorry I don't mean to push, it's just finding you upset like this pisses me off." "I'm fine." "You are not fine." "I'm sorry, you missed class because of me." "I don't care about that. I care about you." Sam came in. "Hey, I used my spare key." He went over to her. "What happened?" "That's what I've been asking, but she won't tell me. I figured she'd be more inclined to talk to you." "I appreciate that, Brad." "Right. Em, if you need anything call." "I will. Thanks." "You don't have to thank me, honey. I'm here if you need me. Feel better." He kissed her head and left. Sam closed and locked the door behind him. "Boy, the guys were right, he's got it bad. Too bad your hooked up with Dimples." She started crying. "Hey, what's with the tears?" "Scott was here." "Really? He didn't say anything about coming. I would have asked him to bring Riley." "He didn't stay long." "Then why did he come?" "It seems he came to *come.*" It took Sam a minute to understand what she meant. "Are you saying what I think you're saying? That he came for a booty call?" "That's exactly what I'm saying." "I don't believe it. He's one of the good guys." "Not today he wasn't."

Jake pulled up near Hanson's and Scott got out. "Thanks for the lift, Jake. I could have walked." "Not after all those Jamesons." Scott smiled. “Thanks for the listening ear and the advice.” “You’re welcome. Remember what I told you. I will.” “Take it easy, Jake.” “Yeah, I’d say the same to you, but I know nothing will be easy right now.” “Don’t I know it.”

Hanson saw Scott get out of Jake’s truck. “Hey, saw Jake drop you off. You have a few?” “Quite a few actually, and I would have had more if he’d let me.” “Look I know you’re upset, but alcohol isn’t the answer. It won’t make you feel better.” “Funny ’cause I feel *much* better.” “That’s only temporary. After you’re sober, all the problems that made you drink in the first place will still be there.” “I really don’t care.” “What’s going on, Scott? This isn’t just about your mother, is it?” “Don’t fucking call her that! She is *not* my mother!” He took a deep breath. Hanson looked at him with surprise in his eyes. “I know you’re trying to help, but you can’t. At least not now.” “Fine. Enjoy the alcohol haze while it lasts. When you’re ready to deal, you know where I am.”

Sam sat next to Emily. “I just can’t believe he treated you that way. I mean, he’s not a ‘wham, bam, thank you, ma’am’ kind of guy. Trust me, I know.” “I know he’s not. Yet, that’s just how it was. I mean he didn’t even look at me. I could have been anyone up against that door.” “I don’t think that’s true.” “You’re defending him?” “No, I think he’s a total asshole right now, but I don’t think he’d do anyone. He’s too head over heels in love with you.” “I thought so.” “Look, guys are idiots. Dimples is no exception. He screwed up, but I’m sure there was a really good reason for him to act that way.” “That’s what I keep telling myself. But what?” “I don’t know, honey. You’ll have to wait for him to tell you.”

The next day Emily felt better and went to class. Brad was there. “Hey, you look better.” “I am. Thanks to you and Sam.” “Glad I could help. By the way I copied my notes from yesterday’s class for you.” He handed them to her. “Thanks. That was nice of you.” “No problem. I was thinking if you’re up for it, we could have lunch.” “I might not be the best company.” “You’ll be fine.” She thought about it a minute. “Okay.” “Great, I’ll even spring for ice cream.” “Big spender,” she teased, making him laugh. “Well, I’ve always felt ice cream makes everything better.” “I won’t disagree with you on that. Besides, better sounds good." "Great, I'll pick up everything and meet you on the Great Lawn." "Kay."

After class, Emily had seen Brad make a beeline for the door. She took her time walking to the area where they were to meet. She sat down in the grass and just soaked up some sunshine. A short time later, Brad showed up carrying a canvas bag. "I got here as fast as I could. There was a line in the cafeteria." "It's okay, I've been enjoying the sunshine." He pulled out a blanket, and Emily helped him lay it on the grass. They both sat down and began eating. "Now isn't this better than eating in the cafeteria?" "Definitely. Thanks again for lunch, Brad." "My pleasure." "Actually, I should be buying *you* lunch. After what you did for me." "Don't mention it." "No, I will mention it because it wasn't something just anyone would do." "I'm just glad you're feeling better." Sam spotted them and came over; she had just gotten out of class. "Hey, you two. Picnic?" "I talked her into it." "I'm heading back to my room. Forgot my calculus book. You okay?" "Better than I was." "Good. I'll catch you later." "Later." "Brad, this was so nice of you. Really." "My pleasure. I've enjoyed spending time with you outside the classroom." "Me too." She looked down at her watch. "Wow, is that the time?" He looked at his watch. "Yeah, I guess so. Time flies when you're having fun." "I'll say we didn't even get to the ice cream." "Chute, your right." "How about this. Whenever you want, I'll bring over a pint." "You don't have to do that, Brad." "You're right. I don't have to do it. I *want* to do it. Just let me know when." "How about tonight?" "Tonight, sure. What flavor should I bring?" "Cherry Garcia." "Oh so you're a Ben & Jerry's girl eh?" "Since birth." He laughed. "Well, I should get to class." "All right, see you tonight."

Scott sat by the phone debating who he'd call first. Either way he really wasn't looking forward to it. He decided to call his mother first. He dialed, and a few rings later, she picked up. "It's Scott. I want to talk some more." She let out a breath she hadn't realized she was holding out. "I'm not making any promises, though." "That's fine, I don't expect any. When did you want to get together?" "Well, I head back to school Monday, so before then?" "I'm free tomorrow afternoon?" "That works." "How about we go for a ride?" "We could do that." "I should be there around three. Scott?" "Yeah?" "Thank you." "Don't thank me yet, since this thing might be over before it even gets started." "I understand. See you tomorrow."

Evening came, and Emily was setting up the ice cream bar. She loved ice cream, so she always kept lots of toppings on hand. The phone rang. It was Sam. "Hey, just checking on you." "I'm fine." "Has he called?" "No." "He will. What are you going to say?" "That all depends on what he says." "What are you doing now?" "Brad's coming over with ice cream." "Hmmm." "What?" "Oh nothing. It's just yesterday he practically broke down your door, today a picnic, and now ice cream." "Okay, first he didn't break down my door, I opened it. Second, it was just lunch, and third it's just ice cream." "It's never *just* ice cream." "Your being silly, Sam." "Really? What flavor is he bringing?" "Cherry Garcia." "I rest my case." "You're being ridiculous." "He's making a play." "He is not. He's just being a good friend." "Guys don't go out of their way like that if they aren't interested. Knowing you and Scott had a falling out, he figures he has a shot." "Well, he's going to be very disappointed if he does think that." "Call me after you've crushed his hopes." "Good-bye, Sam."

After she hung up, the phone rang again. She thought it was Sam calling back. "Sam, I said I'd talk to Brad." "It's not Sam." "Scott?" "Yeah." She grew quiet. "Em, are you okay?" "Not really." "I'm sorry. More than you could ever know. There's no excuse for what I did, but I'd like to explain why I was so messed up." "I'm listening." "I met my mom." "What? How?" "Apparently, she sent Dad a letter, and he arranged a meeting while I was at SUNY with you. He figured by the time I got back, she'd be long gone. Unfortunately for us, Riley broke the sound barrier, and she was leaving when we got there." "What's she like?" "Light reddish brown hair, brown eyes. Very pretty and petite. I can see why Dad fell for her." "What did she say?" "Look, I'd rather not go into that now." She grew annoyed. "Fine." "What's wrong?" "Nothing, it's just you're shutting me out." "I'm not shutting you out. I just don't want to talk about *her* right now." "Well, you brought it up." "I know. It's just she's not what's important, you are." "Sure didn't feel that way yesterday." "I know. I said I was sorry." "Yeah, well sorry isn't going to cut it. I missed classes, and Brad practically broke down the door to make sure I was okay." "What a guy." "He took care of me."

"Of course he took care of you, Em. He wants you." "He's been a very supportive friend." *I'll bet.* He's even bringing ice cream." "Well isn't that sweet of him." "Stop it's completely innocent." "On your part but not his." "Now you sound like Sam." "Well, I'm glad someone else sees through him." "Pleeze, he wished us both well. Remember?" "That was an act put on for your benefit." "You don't really believe that, do you? You're starting to sound paranoid. Besides, he doesn't have to work all that hard to get me away from you, since you're doing a bang-up job all by yourself." "What's that supposed to mean?" "I think you know what it means." "This is about Amanda. Isn't it?" "Partly. Look, Brad will be here soon. So I'd better get going." "Yeah, wouldn't want to keep him waiting." "Good-bye, Scott." "Em, wait. Please." "What?" "I know you want me to tell you everything, but right now it's too raw." "Well, don't wait too long. Otherwise, I might not be here waiting to listen."

Brad was on his way to Emily's when he bumped into Sam. "Hey, Sam." "Brad. What's in the bag?" "Ice cream. I'm on my way to Em's. Figured I'd cheer her up." "Aren't you sweet?" she said sarcastically. "What gives, Sam?" "Why don't you tell me?" "I'm not sure I know what you're talking about?" "I'm willing to bet you do." "Since I don't, why don't you save us both time and spit it out?" "Fine. You're into Em." "You're right. I am." She looked at him. "You aren't even going to try and deny it?" "Why should I? It's true." "I knew it." "Kudos to you. Now if you'll excuse me, the ice cream is melting." She blocked his path. "What?" he asked, annoyed. "What's your game?" "To make sundaes." "Wiseass." He grinned. "Look, I just want to cheer her up. If you had seen her the way I did, crying like that, it was heartbreaking." She looked at him. "You're in love with her?" "Maybe I am." "What are you going to do about it?" "Nothing. She's too vulnerable, and I don't work that way. I care about her." "Look, I know you're a good guy. But so is Scott." "Could've fooled me. He did something to upset her like that." "He did, and I could kick his ass right now, myself but it's between the two of them. You got me?" "Remind me to never piss you off." She laughed. "My money's on you, Sam." She laughed again. "Flattery will get you *nowhere.*" "I'll remember that. Now can I please deliver the ice cream before it's soup?" "Sure, just remember what I said." "I will."

Emily answered the door and took the bag from Brad. "That's gonna have to go in the freezer for a bit. I was delayed." "Okay. I got us all set up." He looked at the counter. There was an array of toppings. Reddi-wip, sprinkles, nuts, chocolate syrup, cherries, caramel sauce. "Wow, you don't mess around." "As my mother used to say, anything worth doing is worth doing right." He laughed. "Your mother sounds like a smart lady." "She was. Have a seat. Can I get you something to drink?" "Water would be great." "Sure." She poured water and handed it to him. "Thanks." "So why was the ice cream so melted?" "Well, a certain friend of yours stopped me and did everything but shine a bright light in my eyes." "I'm sorry, Brad. She and I were on the phone earlier, and I told her you were coming over. She said after seeing us together earlier, she wondered about us." "What did you tell her?" "I said you were being a good friend." "Right. So the ice cream should be good by now." "Okay." She took it out, and he did the scooping. They each made their own sundae and sat down to feast. She was making various noises. Noises that sometimes sounded sexual. He tried not to focus on it. "It's been a while since I've had ice cream." He told her. "Why?" "Mostly because I could eat a few of those pints myself." "I don't blame you. I'm pretty addicted myself. Cherry Garcia is my absolute favorite. Hard to stop sometimes." "A moment on the lips, a lifetime on the hips," he joked. She laughed. He was looking at her. She was beautiful when she laughed. "Do you know how beautiful you are?" She blushed. He got up, walked over to where she was, and knelt down beside her. "What are you doing?" "Getting a closer look." He looked at her lips and contemplated something he knew he shouldn't. "Brad . . ." He decided to throw caution to the wind and moved in gently, brushing her lips with his. She pulled away and got up. "I'm sorry. I shouldn't have done that." "It's my fault too. I didn't stop you. I'm sorry." "What are you sorry for?" "Because I'm about to hurt you." After that, he knew. "You're a wonderful guy but—" "If this is the part where you tell me you only like me as a friend, or worse, a brother, let's not and say we did." She looked at him sympathy in her eyes. "Will you be all right?" "I'll be fine." "At least we can still be friends," he said, sounding hopeful. "No, we can't. Friends don't kiss each other,

Brad." "It won't happen again." "You're right it won't." He looked at her. "So that's it?" "I can't hang out with you knowing you feel this way. I just wouldn't feel right." "I understand." He pulled her to him. "Brad? What are you doing?" He brushed her lips with his fingers. "Saying good-bye." He pulled her in for one last kiss. When their lips uncoupled, he held her. "You're an amazing woman, Emily Taylor." "And you're a great guy, Brad." "If you ever change your mind, I'll be here." And on that note, he left.

Sam was reading the latest from her favorite author, Nora Roberts, when someone knocked. "Who's there?" "It's Brad." She opened the door. "You're supposed to be stuffing yourself with Cherry Garcia and making a pass at Em." "Been there. Done that." "What happened?" "Oh exactly what you said would happen." "You didn't?" "I did. And I feel like an idiot." "Well, at least you're not alone. You've got Scott for company." "Yeah, somehow I don't find that comforting." She laughed. "Okay, so tell me what went down." "Can I get a beer?" "After ice cream?" "I'd ask for root beer but I need something stronger." She opened the fridge. "You're in luck. I have one left." "Thank God." She handed him the beer and he chugged it. "Hey, slow down. Make it last." "Doesn't matter. After this, I'm heading to O'Casey's." "To get drunk?" "No, to get *very drunk*." "What happened?" "I'll tell you only if you promise not to say 'I told you so.'" "Fine, I promise. Now spill."

Emily finished washing the bowls when her phone rang. She wasn't in the mood to talk, so she let the machine pick up. "Em, it's me, Scott." She turned off the water. "Listen, I know I was a total ass. I just . . . knowing how much I hurt you, it's killing me. I know you want me to tell you about my mom, and I want to. It's just not easy to open up about something that I've kept locked up inside all these years. I don't know where to start. Damn it, if you're done eating ice cream with *him*, could you please pick up. I'm afraid I—" She picked up. "Hi, Scott." "Did you hear what I said?" "About Brad?" "No, not about him. The other stuff?" "Yes." "What do you think?" "Come tomorrow, I don't have class until noon. We can talk then. I'll meet you in the cafeteria." "I'll see you around eight." "That's fine." "Em?" "Yeah?" "Is *he* still there?" "No, he left." "So soon?" he said sarcastically. "How come?"

"Let's just say he wanted more than ice cream for dessert." "Told you." "Yeah, you did. See you tomorrow."

Brad told Sam everything. "Why don't men listen?" "I don't know, faulty wiring or something." "You'd think you'd learn after a millennia of making the same dumb-ass mistakes. History is full of idiot men whose lives would have turned out a lot better if they had just listened to their women." He was looking at her and smiling. "What are you grinning at?" "You. Any minute, you'll start listing those men." "That would take *waaay* too long." They laughed. "So any words of wisdom for *this* idiot?" "Yes, don't do it again." "Right." He finished his beer and got up. "Well, it's time to move on to O'Casey's." "Thanks for listening, Sam." "Sure. See you in class tomorrow."

Chapter Thirteen

The next day, Scott was once again up bright and early to drive to SUNY. He walked into the kitchen, and his father was eating breakfast. "You're up?" "Yeah, busy day ahead. I'm driving up to SUNY. Then Amanda's coming at three." "You sure you want to do this?" "No, I'm not sure of anything right now." "Scott, this isn't something that can be put right in a day." "I know. I just need to get things to a better place because it's affecting my relationship with Em." "How so?" "I don't want to get into it." "You two have a fight?" "You could say that." "What did you do?" "I hurt her." Hanson stood up and brought his plate to the sink. "You love her, don't you?" "Yeah, I do. I've never felt this way about anyone." "That was the way I felt about your mother back in the day." "What was it like, seeing her again?" "Like hell and coming home all at the same time. If that makes any sense?" "It does, which is probably because I'm so screwed up right now." That made him laugh. "It's funny because I was kind of hoping she'd let herself go. But she's still just as beautiful." Scott looked at him. "What went down that day she came?" "*A lot.*" Scott recognized when someone didn't want to go into something. Mostly because he had been the king of it lately. "Do you think she's sincere?" "Seems to be." "I wanna hate her, Dad, but I can't." "That's okay. I can't hate her either. Though Lord knows I've tried." He looked at him. "You still have feelings for her. Don't you?" "Hard not to. Considering all that's happened. Anyway, forget about that right now. Go make up with your girl." "That's the plan."

Emily sat in the cafeteria, eating her yogurt. She hadn't gotten much sleep thinking about Scott and what had happened with Brad. She knew she'd hurt him. Her eyes were on the entrance to the cafeteria when Brad walked in. Looking very hungover. She wondered if he would come over or pretend like he hadn't seen her. He started walking toward her. "Hi." "Don't take this the wrong way, but you look terrible." He laughed. "Believe me, I feel worse." "Rough night?" "You could say that. I went to O'Casey's and had one too many." "Because of me? I'm sorry." "Stop apologizing. What are you doing here so early? Economics isn't till noon?" "I'm meeting Scott." "To talk things through?" "Hopefully." "Well, I'd better get some carbs in my stomach, otherwise I might toss my cookies in Mr. Carter's class." She laughed. "Oh he'd love that." "I know. I'm almost tempted *not* to eat." They laughed. That's the way Scott saw them together when he walked in. He decided that he'd had enough of Brad. "Brad, you look like shit." "Thanks I feel like it too." "What's the matter? Too much Cherry Garcia?" "Scott, don't." "Stay out of this, Em." "You got something to say, Scott. Spit it out." "Gladly. You got nerve hitting on Em." "That wasn't my intention." "The hell it wasn't." "Scott." "Em—" "I was trying to clean up *your* mess." "Thanks, but I can clean up my own messes." "Didn't seem that way to me." "Guys, people are starting to stare." "What the hell does that mean?" Brad was in his face now. "Just that where were you when I found her crying? Oh that's right *you're* the reason she was crying." He poked Scott in his chest. "You're going to want to take a step back, *friend*." "I don't think so. She was hurting, because of *you*. You *don't* deserve her." "Oh and I suppose you think you do?" "I'm a hell of a lot better for her than you. At least I didn't make her cry." Before Scott knew what was happening, he threw a punch that sent Brad flying back, landing with a thud on the floor. Emily stood staring. Scott stood over him. "That's right I did make her cry, and I have felt like shit ever since. I came here to make things right. *I love her, damn it*. Not that it's any of *your* business." Brad looked stunned. As did Emily. "You love me?" "A little." The corners of her mouth curled up. "You *love* me?" "I'm fucking crazy about you." "Then why don't you kiss me?" "I was getting to it." She smiled and he pulled her in for a kiss. Brad collected what was left of his dignity and left.

Brad sat in class, holding his jaw. Sam came in and sat down next to him. "Morning." "Morning." She looked at him. "What the hell happened to you?" "Scott happened." "What?" "Em and I were talking, he saw us, we exchanged words, and he decked me." "He decked you?" "Yeah." "How's it feel now?" "It's throbbing like a mother." She turned his face toward her and looked at it. "He got you good." "Tell me about it." "What did Em do?" "She tried to stop us, but neither of us would listen." She looked at him. "I know, I know. More dumb men to add to the list." She laughed. "You didn't try hitting back?" "I didn't have a chance. I was knocked on my ass, and then he went off on me. The grand finale was him saying he loved her." "What?" "You heard me." That's great!" He looked at her. "Though not from where you're standing, I suppose. Cheer up, things can only get better from here." He laughed. "I certainly hope so."

Emily and Scott went back to her room. "I can't believe you punched Brad." "He deserved it. Jackass." She was smiling at him. "What?" "Nothing, you're just really cute when you're jealous." "Damn right I'm jealous. Em, look, what Brad said was true. I don't deserve you, but no one will ever love you as much as I do. Say you'll give me another chance. Say you love me, too." She paused. "I will and I love you." "Oh, Thank God. Come here." She went to him and felt her body melt into his. "You are just so beautiful." They made love for hours, their bodies becoming one. Afterward, they lay in bed cuddling. "So are you ready to talk about your mom?" "Yeah. She's coming by at three." "I hadn't realized you'd want to see her again so soon." "I don't but I think I have to. There's a lot of crap I need to sift through." "Does your dad know?" "Yeah." "How's he doing with all this?" "He's holding his own. I think he still has feelings for her." "He probably does. After all, they had you together. That bonds people for life." "Yeah, I guess." "Did she tell you why she left?" "She said she was different after I was born. Irritable, lots of mood swings." "Hmmmm." "What?" "Just it sounds like postpartum depression to me." "I hadn't thought about that. Why wouldn't she tell us, though?" "Probably because at the time she didn't realize what was going on." "So why not tell us now?" "Maybe because she doesn't want her second chance to come from a place of pity. She wants to know she got a second chance because you wanted to give her one. What else did she say?" "That she always loved me. Always thought of me." "Did your dad mention their conversation?" "No, he just said a lot went down." "I'll bet." "I didn't push him since he didn't push me about Mom and you." "So what are you going to do with her?" "She suggested going for a ride." "Sounds like a good idea. I can't imagine how it must have felt coming face to face with her." He laughed. "What's so funny?" "Riley." "What about Riley?" "He was being all flirty with her." He laughed again. "He told me that she was too hot to be my mom." They were both laughing now. "Pain in the ass, but he was the one who got me through it." "Really?" "Yeah, he told me some really personal stuff. His mother died when he was young, and so he doesn't remember much. He made me realize that I was being given something most people don't ever get." "A second chance." "Exactly." She kissed him. "I hope it works out for you." "Me too." She looked at the clock. "We should shower. I have class in an hour." "You go first." "You don't want to join me?" "I do, but if I do, you'll never make it to class." She laughed.

Emily was late to class anyway because halfway through her shower a very turned-on Scott decided to join her. "Call me and tell me how things go with your mom." "I will. I love you." "I love you too." They kissed and she went inside. This time she did *not* sit next to Brad. And he couldn't help smiling. As Scott walked down the hall, he heard his name being called. He turned to see Brad walking toward him. "Here." "What's this?" "My sister's number." "You're giving this to me after I hit you?" Brad shrugged. "I figured I owed you. I was out of line with Em." "Yeah, you were." He looked down at the folded piece of paper. "Thanks." "Well, I'd better get back to class." "I'll call my sister and let her know you'll be calling her." "What's her name?" "Vanessa." "Got it, thanks. Hey maybe you aren't as big an asshole as I thought." He laughed.

Sometime later, Scott was back, and he was wearing the biggest grin. He wanted to tell Riley all about it. He went in the barn and saw Max. "Hey, Max." "Scott." "You see Riley?" "He's up at the milking parlor. They needed extra help today." "Where you coming from?" "Seeing Em." "Must have left real early." "I did." You two have a falling out?" "Something like that." "Did you make up?" "Yeah," he said, grinning. "You look like the cat that swallowed the canary. Glad to hear it. You look good together." "Thanks, Max. Catch you later."

When Scott got there, Riley was busy milking a line of cows. "Hey." "Hey, yourself. Back already?" "Yeah." "Well, I can see by the stupid grin you're wearing that things went well." "They went great after I decked Brad." He stopped. "You did what?" "I decked him." "You're shitting me?" "Nope. He hit on her last night." "What about the bro code?" Riley said. "I know, right? Sneaky bastard. Anyway, we had words, and my fist ended up connecting with his chin." "You know, it's called throwing a punch." He laughed. "Yeah, I know. Laid him out flat." "Nice." "The best part wasn't punching him though." "No? What was?" "When I told Em that I loved her." He stood up. "Right there? In the cafeteria?" "It just came out. I was on a roll." "Apparently." "So I assume by the grin that she said she loves you, too?" "Yep." He grinned wider. "Look at you. Pathetic." "So what's next?" "Well, I've got Amanda coming a little later. We're taking the horses out for a ride." "Sounds like a plan." "Well, I'll let you get back to milking heifers." "Very funny. Hey, maybe I'll happen to be around when she shows up later." "Why, so you can hit on her again?" "I wasn't *hitting* on her. I was *admiring* her. There's a subtle difference." "Sure there is. Maybe I should give Sam a call. See if she thinks there's a *subtle* difference." "Some friend you are." "You know, I'm growing on you." "Yeah, like fungus grows on trees."

Sabrina sat looking over her sketches. They were quite good, if she did say so herself. Good enough that she was seriously considering sending them to Nico. She decided to call him. The phone rang, and he picked up on the first ring. "Nico, it's Sabrina." "Is Timmy out of the well?" "Very funny. Listen, I've been doing some sketching, and I think you might like to see them." "Well, it appears hell has finally froze over." "If you aren't interested—" "Now, don't go getting your bikini brief twisted. Of course, I'm interested. So what brought about this renaissance?" "Well, Emily told me she wants to run this place so I can get back to doing what I love." "How entrepreneurial of her."

"I have to admit that I'm worried. I mean this place is a lot of work. She has no idea what she's asking." "Nonsense, she comes from tough stock. It will take time, but there's no doubt in my military mind she can do it." "You were never in the military, Nico." "True but fashion is very similar. People telling you what to do, what to wear, and when to do it." "I see your point. Anyway, I'm sure she can do it too. But my impression is she wants to run things like yesterday." "Ah, the impetuosity of youth. I can relate. After all, when I first started, I had people telling me I didn't know shit from Shinola. And look where I am today." "Tooting your own horn?" "Sarcasm doesn't become you, dear. At my own successful design company, that's where." "You've done very well." "Yes, I have. Anyway, the point is, sometimes you just have to go with your gut. I commend your niece. Someone her age wanting to take on something so you can come back to the civilized world shows a great deal of guts. She reminds me of a certain someone who interned for me. Oh, you have no idea how happy this makes me. I can finally die happy." "Don't go dying on me just yet." "No worries, I'm as fit as a fiddle. Just had my annual physical." "Glad to hear it. So I'll overnight the sketches to you." "Please do. I can't wait to see them. I'm practically drooling, and I'm wearing silk. So not good." She laughed. "It will be good to have you back." "Nico, I won't be *back*." "Yes, yes. By the way, how are things going with that delicious man of yours?" "Good." "So you never told me how he is in the sack." "Nico!" "Is he naughty or nice? Or is he a combination? Which has always been my personal favorite." "Nico!" "What? I'm suffering a dreadful dry spell. Don't deny me." She shook her head and laughed. "Well, I'm sorry, but you're going to continue to suffer because the only thing I'm going to say is that he's very skilled." "Oh please. That could mean anything." "I did tell him you would be visiting." "Does he remember me?" "Of course he remembers you. Who could forget a man who wore a veil to a funeral?" "I was channeling Dorothy Dandridge." "Well, you nailed it." "I did, didn't I? Hard to top that one, but I'll do something equally memorable when I see him again." "Just make sure you don't scare him." "I'm going to pretend I didn't hear it. Sketches. Send." "I'll get them out today." "So will they be delivered via Pony Express?" "No, carrier pigeon." He laughed. "I do love you." "I'm hanging up." "I'll call you when I get them. Ta-ta." "Ta-ta, Nico."

Sabrina waited on line at the post office. When it was her turn and she was called, she could not believe her eyes. "Susan? What are you doing here?" "I work here." "You're back?" "Yes, I've really missed everyone." She hoped that everyone still didn't include Ross. Susan had left right after their breakup. "So what have you been up to?" *Dating your ex.* "Oh the usual." "Nothing new?" "Well, actually, the reason I'm here is to overnight sketches to my old boss in New York." "Sketches?" She took them out and showed her. "These are great. Do you want to send them priority overnight?" "Yes." "Okay, give me a minute." She walked away and came back holding a small tube. "This is used mostly for blueprints and posters, but your sketches will fit nicely and be protected." "That's great. Thanks, Susan." "Don't mention it. No sense you drawing stuff that looks like this only to have them look like crap when they arrive. So how's Ross?" *Crap.* "He's good. Same old Ross. You know how he is." "I do. So what about you? Seeing anyone?" *Double crap.* "As a matter of fact, I am." "Who?" "Ross." She looked at her. "Susan, I—" "Sabrina, please. Ross and I dated, but the key word in that sentence is *dated*." Besides, I've moved on. I've been seeing this really great guy. Things are pretty serious." "That's great. I'm happy for you." "Thanks. So you and Ross. All I can say is it's about friggin' time." She looked at her. "You knew?" "Honey, everybody knew." "Except me. How ironic." Susan laughed. "The truth is that I loved him. After we had been seeing each other a while, I realized that he was in love with someone else. Eventually, I figured out that the someone else was you." "Is that why you broke up with him?" She nodded. "Susan, I don't know what to say." "Sabrina, you don't have to say anything. It was a long time ago. Really, I'm over it and I'm happy for you both." "Thanks, Susan."

Scott sat on a fence post, waiting for Amanda. Hanson came up to him. "You know that saying about a watched pot never boiling?" "I know. I just wanna get this over with." "Don't sound so excited." "Come on, Dad. What do you expect?" "I expect my son to make an effort." "Yeah, well you're expecting too much." They spotted Amanda's SUV. "She's here so could you wrap up the lecture." "Just remember, we all make mistakes, Scott. Even you." He walked away. Amanda got out and walked over to him. "Hi." "Hi." "So you still up for a ride?" "I'm not really sure." "Then why am I here?" "I don't know." "Well, you're just full of answers, aren't you?" "Look, I'm trying, all right?" "If you aren't up it, it's fine." "I thought you'd be pissed." "Oh I'm the last person who has any right to get pissed. Especially since this is all courtesy of moí." I'll come back another day." As she started walking back toward her car, he felt a sudden twinge of guilt, which annoyed him. He got down from the fence. "Amanda?" "Yes?" "You coming?" "But I thought?" "Changed my mind." "Okay, sure." "I'll take Sugar, you can ride Lavender." She's older. Won't give you any trouble." "I've ridden before." "When?" She paused. "Okay, so it's been a while, but it'll come back." "Sure," he said in a tone that irked her.

Chapter Fourteen

Sabrina sat at the counter at Danny's. She was treating herself to a piece of chocolate cream pie. A specialty of Danny's. She was celebrating finally sending her sketches to Nico. "Hey, Sabrina. How's it going?" "Okay, Flo. How 'bout you?" "My feet hurt, my back hurts. The usual." Sabrina laughed. "I swear I want to trade myself in for a younger model." "I know the feeling. My energy level isn't half of what it used to be. Thank God for caffeine." "Amen to that." Danny came over. "What are you griping about now, Flo?" "You." "Figures." "How's things, Sabrina?" "Oh they're good, Danny." "How's Harris treating you?" She looked up. "How do you?" "I know everything." Flo snorted. "Sure you do." "Flo, there's a table needs waiting." "I'll get to them in a minute." "Get to them now." "Yes, sir!" She saluted him and walked away. "See what I put up with?" "Oh stop. You'd be lost without her." "Lost? I'd be in heaven. So how are things with our local lawman?" "Great." "'Bout time he got his head out of his ass and asked you out. In my day, when you liked a girl, you didn't wait years to tell her." "I'm sure the guys today could learn a thing or two from you, Danny." "Damn right, they could." Flo came back with an order. "Go, cook." He looked at her, huffed, and went back into the kitchen. "So where were you before this?" "At the post office. I sent some sketches to my former boss." "That's great." "Yeah, I'm pretty excited about it. Feels good to get back into it." "How's Ross feel about it?" "He's happy for me. Why?" "Oh I just thought he might be upset." "Why?" "He might be worrying what it would mean down the road." Before she could answer, Danny rang the bell. "Order up!" "I'd better get that before he starts bitchin'." "I said *order up!*" "*I heard you!* Jeez. Well, enjoy the pie." "Thanks, Flo. I hope your aches improve." "The only way that will happen is if I kill Danny." She laughed as she savored her pie.

Amanda finally made it to Miller's Pass. She had tried to keep up with Scott, but it simply wasn't possible. Scott had given her the slow horse on purpose. "Does this horse even know how to gallop?" He almost forgot himself and laughed. "Sure, as long as her rider does." *Smart-ass.* She got off Lavender and wrapped her reins around a branch. She sat in the grass, and he sat about a foot away from her on the opposite side. "Why don't you sit on the other side of the pass?" "Don't tempt me," he mumbled under his breath. "So is this how it's gonna be?" "Seems that way." She got up and wiped the seat of her jeans. "Leaving?" "As a matter of fact, yes. It's obvious you aren't interested in making a go of this." "And this surprises you?" "No, not really. I expected it to be difficult, but I never expected you to be this big an ass about specially since you were the one who asked me to come." His face got beet red. He was on his feet, closing that once large gap to just a few inches. "I'm an ass?" "That's right. You are. And I'm leaving." "Go ahead, that's what you do best, anyway." She turned back around. She was tired of the Pierce men throwing that in her face. "That's right, I left then and I'm leaving now, unless you really want to *try* at building a relationship." "No thanks, I think I'll pass, *Mom*," he said sarcastically. She looked him dead in his eyes. "Look, I get you're pissed at me. And you have every right to be. I was blessed to have you and your father, and I threw it all away. I can't take any of the mistakes I made back. And believe me not a day goes by that I don't wish I could. The only thing I can say is that sometimes in life not everything is black and white." "What's that supposed to mean?" She paused, debating disclosing the truth to him. She decided to wait. He looked at her, waiting for answer. "Just that sometimes things aren't always as they seem, sometimes there's more." "Great, more riddles," he said, annoyed. "I know you don't believe this, Scott, but I never stopped loving you, and I never will. Now if you'll excuse me, I'll do what everyone seems to think I excel at, leaving." She walked over to Lavender, and then decided she needed to gallop like she had never galloped before. She knew Lavender wouldn't be able to give that to her. She went over to Sugar. "Sugar, it's been years since I rode, but I really need to without making an ass of myself. I'm putting my trust in you, girl." Scott turned around in time to see her mounting Sugar. He rushed over. "What the hell do you think you're doing?" "I need to actually move ahead instead of backwards." "No, what you need is to get off Sugar and take Lavender. Sugar is too much horse for you. Now come down." She grew angrier by the second. *I'll show you.* "I can manage." "No, you can't. I might be pissed, but that doesn't mean I want to see you get hurt." "I'm touched." "Get down, Amanda." He tried to yank the reins from her hands. "No! I *know* how to ride a damn horse." She jerked away and rode off in an uneasy gallop. "Great." He got on Lavender and went after her. Or at least he tried to.

Sabrina arrived at the station, and since Linda was on the phone, she sat down on one of the benches. Linda mouthed to her that she'd be off in a minute. Andy came by. "Hey, Sabrina. How are you?" "Good, Andy. How about you?" "Well, the sheriff's been riding me lately." "Why?" "Oh he says I need to load other songs to sing to besides Lady Gaga." She tried to hold in her giggle. Linda got off the phone. "Sorry, it was my daughter calling with another crisis." "Is everything okay?" "Yes, I should have explained that her idea of a crisis is running out of Crisco before she's supposed to bake six dozen cookies for the school bake sale." "How are you?" "Fine." "Here to see the sheriff?" "You know I am." "Ah, does my heart good seeing you two finally together." "Thanks, Linda." "Yeah, you two are just like Ross and Rachel on Friends." Linda looked at him. "Why don't you go play some more Gaga." "You mean Lady Gaga." "*Whatever.*" "Fine, see you, Sabrina." "Bye, Andy." He walked away, and Linda shook her head. "He's a good guy, but sometimes I just want to smack him." "That's funny, Linda, I thought I was the only one you wanted to smack." They turned around, and Ross was standing behind them. "It varies." "What about Ed?" "I've been slapping him around for years. It's no fun anymore." "I feel bad for Ed." "You know, I don't think I like you anymore." "No, well then, I guess that means you aren't interested in a Mocha Sensation from Perk?" "Mocha Sensation?" She cozied up to him and smiled. "You've always been my favorite person." Sabrina could not stop laughing. "Just a minute ago, you wanted to slap me." "I've seen the light." "Hmm, more like the caffeine fix." They laughed. "Brina, wanna come?" "Sure." He grabbed her hand, and they walked out together. He stopped on the stairs. "What?" "I just like looking at you," he said as he moved in to kiss her. "God, I could kiss you all day." "Don't stop on my account," she said. "I wasn't planning on it." He kissed her again. "Ross, at this rate, we'll never get to Perk." "True. We can make out some more in Perk." She laughed.

Amanda had a little trouble at first but eventually got the hang of it, and was running against the wind. She knew Scott had come after her, but Lavender was no match for Sugar. "Who's riding Miss Daisy now?" She smiled. Sugar needed a break, so they stopped at the lake. She sat near the lake. Scott finally caught up, and she couldn't help grinning. He tethered Lavender to a nearby tree and came over to her. "Nice to see you're still in one piece." She said nothing. "Are you proud of yourself?" "Actually, I am. I showed you." "You sure did." He sat down on the rock next to her. "Where'd you learn to ride like that?" "I dated a former polo player for a time." "He must have been some teacher. The way you were weaving in and out of those trees scared the crap out of me." "He was a great rider. If you're interested, I could show you some moves." His face shot up. "Really?" *Ah there it is, the way in.* "Then again, you said you weren't interested." He looked down and kicked some dirt. "Oh right. I did say that. Didn't I?" "That's why I left." "Yeah, and then I had to chase you." She was laughing now, picturing him trying to get Lavender above a trot. "Hey, it's not funny, all right? You could have been hurt. I was worried." She stopped laughing. "You were?" He quickly covered it up. "Yeah, well, Dad would have kicked my ass." "Oh so you weren't worried about me, just what your dad would do?" "Yes. No. I don't know. Jeez, do you always twist people's words around?" "Not always, just after they've put me on the slowest horse in the barn." He looked at her and laughed. "Okay, I deserved that." "Yes, you did." They smiled at each other, and for the first time in a long time, she felt something—hope.

Sabrina sat on a sofa at Perk, waiting for Ross to come back with their drinks. She sat there, thinking how life was about to change again, but this time the focus would be on her. Ross came over with their drinks. "One vanilla kiss for my lovely lady." "Thanks." "Wait, I'm not done yet. And one sheriff's kiss." She smiled as he leaned over and kissed her. "Hmmm, better than anything they have here." "What did you get?" "Café latte. Boring but it's what I like." "Where's Linda's?" "I didn't get it yet. Figured I'd get it on the way out, so it would be nice and hot." "That's thoughtful." "Thoughtful has nothing to do with it. I want her to burn her mouth." "Ross!" "What? I'm kidding. Though the idea does have merit." "You're terrible." "That's not what you said the other night." They laughed. "So what brought you to town?" "Oh, I overnighted some sketches to Nico." He grew quiet. "You did, huh?" "What, you don't sound happy about it." "Well, it's just what if you get to be this big designer and end up back in New York." "Don't you think you're putting the cart ahead of the horse here?" "Maybe, it's just that now that I have you, I don't want to lose you." "First of all, the kind of success you're talking about takes years to achieve if it happens at all. And even if it did, I wouldn't want to live there. I'd miss it here. Most of all, I'd miss you." She kissed him. "I want you to succeed, Brina. I do." "I know you do." "I want you to know that no matter what does or doesn't happen, I'm already proud of you." She looked at him and could feel herself falling deeper. She kissed him, and this time, he was the one who felt his toes curl. "What was that for?" "For being you."

Amanda and Scott were riding back to the farm. The difference this time was that they were riding at the same pace. "So how did you get interested in horses?" "Well, after Dad became foreman, James and Dad became good friends. Dad told him what happened, how I put up a lot of walls after you left that." "You were afraid someone else would leave." "Yeah. Being with Sugar helped. I visited her every day and got to taking care of her. Anyway, James noticed how different I was with her, so he gave her to me." "That was quite a gift." "James was a great guy. I still miss him." "I assume James was the brother Sabrina spoke of who died in the crash?" "They hit a patch of fog, and as good a pilot as he was, even he couldn't fly in it." "That must have been so horrible." "Em was only ten at the time." "She's the girl you spoke of, right? The one you're seeing?" "Yeah." Again she noted his face when he spoke of her. "I can't imagine how hard that must have been for her losing both parents. I mean, how do you get through something so tragic?" "The same way I got through what you did." She looked at him. "You just go on." "Some people would just give up." "Not Em, she's no quitter. Sabrina's strong that way too." "After your father and I went a few rounds, I talked to her." "You did?" "Yes, normally I wouldn't open up to a stranger, but I felt comfortable with her." "Sabrina's great. She gave up her life's dream to come here." "Yes, I saw some of her sketches. They were impressive." "Yeah, I've seen her stuff too. She can design her ass off." She smiled. "Well, we're almost there." She was sorry the ride would be ending, especially since this was the first time they had actually talked and not argued. "I have to ask you something." "Okay." "What happened between you and Dad that day?" "What do you mean exactly?" "I think you know what I mean." "He was yelling, and I was yelling. Then I ended up slapping him." His eyes grew wide. "You slapped Dad?" She nodded. "Not one of my finer moments." "What did he say to make you do that?" "The truth, which always hurts." "How did you leave things?" She hesitated, thinking back to their kiss. "To be honest, I'm not really sure." "Hmmm." She looked at him. "What?" "Nothing." "Don't give me that. You're thinking something." "Just that Dad seemed to be holding something back too. So now you've both got me wondering what it is you don't want me to know." "So tell me about Emily. What's she like?" "You're trying to change the subject." "Correction, I *am* changing the subject." "Fine, have it your way for now."

Ross and Sabrina finished their drinks. "Well, I guess coffee break's over," he said. "I have to go to Landy's, myself." "Well, I guess I'll get Linda her Mocha Sensation." She watched him swagger up to the counter. He looked very sexy. A short time later, they were walking back to the station. "So you'll never guess who I saw in the post office." "Who?" "Susan." "Susan? What was she doing there?" "Apparently, she works there." "Really?" "Yeah, she said she's moved back for good. She asked about you." "That must have been awkward." She chuckled. "Slightly. She asked if I was seeing anyone." "Shit." "I had a similar reaction." "What did you tell her?" "The truth." "And?" "She was perfectly fine with it. Happy for us even. She said she's seeing someone and it's serious." "I'm glad, she's good with people." "She also mentioned that she knew how you felt about me." He knew what was coming next. "That it was the reason you two broke up." "I told you that." "Yes, but I didn't know that she knew. That must have hurt. She liked you a lot." "I liked her too, but it was never going to be more than that for me. I guess I'll have to make a trip to the post office." "I think you should." He stopped walking and looked at her. "I'm sorry I wasted *so* much time. I should have told you how I felt years ago. James warned me." "James? Ross, what are you talking about?" "The day of the crash. I was watching you, and he asked me if I ever planned on telling you." "James wanted you to tell me?" "Yeah, he pushed me for years. I should have listened." "I had no idea." "I know."

Chapter Fifteen

Hanson was by the barn, thinking things over. He hadn't been happy with Scott's attitude about Amanda. Not that he blamed him for being angry; it was just he felt that if Scott wasn't interested, then he shouldn't bother. Why get her hopes up? Then again, why did he care about her feelings? She'd never given his consideration. If she had, she would have at least talked to him before leaving. He looked up toward the road and saw them riding side by side, and was that an almost smile on Scott's face? He went inside, got two glasses of water, and came back out. "I figured you could use this after a dusty ride." "Thanks, Dad." "Thank you." When she took the glass from him, their hands touched, and there was a quick spark. "So how was the ride?" They looked at each other and started laughing. "What's so funny?" "Do you want to tell him or should I?" Scott asked. "Oh, I think I'd like to hear your version." Hanson looked at the horses. "Wait, you took Lavender?" Riley was walking by. "Looks like someone came off a hard ride." "Yes, we just got back." He looked from her to Scott and back to her again. "Well, can I say that trail dust looks good on you." She smiled. "Could you stop flirting with my mother?" She looked over at him. He hadn't ever referred to her that way. Ever. "Sorry, no can do. That would be like asking me to stop breathing." "Whatever." Riley looked at the horses. "Who took old Seabiscuit out?" Amanda burst out laughing. "Here's the story. She hadn't ridden in a few years, so I thought better to be safe than sorry." "So you put her on her?" he teased. "I gave her Lavender because she's gentle, and—" "Slooooow," Riley finished for him. She was still laughing. "Scott thought he was protecting me. Besides I got him back." Riley walked past Scott and put his arm around Amanda. "Do tell." "I wouldn't mind hearing this myself," Hanson said, grinning. "Traitor." "Let's just say he left me in the dust. When I finally caught up to him, I took Sugar and left him with Lavender." "Will you marry me?" Riley said. "Why don't you let Amanda finish the story," Hanson said. "Sure, sorry. Go on." "So when he finally caught up, he was upset." Riley laughed. "What's the matter, Harris? Seabiscuit too slow for ya?" They all laughed except him. "Boy, you really showed him." "I did. Didn't I, Scott?" "She rides like a lunatic. Weaving around trees. She even did a few jumps." "Jumps?" Hanson said. "Just small ones. Nothing major," she said, quickly dismissing it. He made a face, which told her he wasn't too happy to hear that. "So I guess you won't be giving Lavender out for anymore rides. Huh, Pierce?" "Bite me." "So hostile." "I'm going to take the horses inside and give them rubdowns." "Need help with old Seabiscuit?" "Why don't you quit while your ahead?" "I would, but you give me so much material to work with." "Why don't you take the horses inside? I'll be there in minute." "Guess the funs over. Always a pleasure, Amanda." He kissed her hand. "That's enough, Casanova. Or I'll call Sam myself," Hanson said. "Sorry, didn't realize she was spoken for." He walked into the barn, leaving Hanson and Amanda staring at each other. "Amanda, I'm sorry about earlier. Riley's right, I was being an ass." "Apology accepted. I hope to see you again, Scott." "Okay. Bye." He went into the barn and Hanson looked at her. "What?" she asked. "I do believe he's softening." "I think so too." "Man, I wish I could have been there to see the look on his face after you left him with Lavender." "It was pretty funny." "I'm glad it went okay. I was nervous because he seemed like he didn't want to do it." "You're right about that. He told me he didn't want to." "No sugarcoating there." "It's fine. It's not like I don't deserve the anger." "He looked at her, and she felt her pulse quicken. "Well, I guess I should be going." "I'll walk you." "Oh that's not necessary. My car's right over there. What could happen?" "Riley could show up again." "I've known some flirts in my day, but he takes the cake." She chuckled. "He seems quite taken with you. Though I can't say I blame him." She looked at him. "That sounds like *another* compliment." "It does. Doesn't it? Guess that makes us two for two." She smiled. "I guess so. Maybe we're on a roll." He looked at her. "Maybe we are."

Ross and Sabrina walked into the station and were practically jumped by Linda. "Well, took you long enough. What, were you grinding the beans yourself?" "No, Juan Valdez was. He says to stop being a pain in my ass." Linda took the drink from him and walked away. "You're welcome," he said to her backside. She ignored him. "I get no respect around here." "If it makes you feel better, I respect you." "What? No. I don't want you to respect me. I want you to—" "Ross!" "What? I'm just saying." "Saying what, Sheriff?" Andy was there now. "That I . . . never mind. Where are you coming in from?" "Mrs. Haugtry's." "Don't tell me. Sammy?" "Believe it or not, no. She needed the panel on her storm door changed." "So this is what we're reduced to? Changing storm doors?" "Well, it's not like there was anything else going on. Besides, I'd feel bad saying no. Not like her husband's around to do it anymore." "Yeah, I know." "I'm gonna go finish that filing I've been workin' on." "Bye, Andy." "See you around, Sabrina." "Ross, I'm gonna get going. I want to get to Landy's before they close." "I wish you didn't have to go." He kissed her. "Me too, but duty calls." He watched her leave. Linda came up behind him. "If you don't put a ring on that girls' finger . . ." "Ree-lax, Linda, that's my plan." "Good. Just make sure it doesn't take twenty years this time." He looked at her and laughed.

Emily was busy typing at her computer. She had yet another paper due. At this rate, she would be totally fried by the time the semester ended. The phone rang, and since she was busy, she let the machine pick up. "Em, it's me. If you're there, pick up. If you're not there, you can't pick up." She smiled. "Hi, Scott." "Hey, there's my girl. What were you doing?" "Working on another paper." "Sounds like fun." "Oh it is. Anyway, what's up?" "Well, you wanted to know how things went with my mother." She paused. "Scott, you just called her—" "My mother? Yeah, I know. I did earlier too. Riley was flirting." "Again?"

"He can't help himself, I think it's genetic. Anyway, I asked him to stop flirting with my *mother*." "Wow." "Yeah, that was basically everyone's reaction." "Who else was there?" "Just Dad." "How were they?" "They seemed okay. Though I left them alone to rub Sugar down after the run Amanda gave her." "Wait, your mother rode Sugar?" "Yeah, I'll get to that in a minute. They both seem to be hiding something." "Like what?" "I don't know, but I'm going to find out." "Wait, I want to hear about her riding Sugar." "Oh right. Well, I was being a dick. She told me she hadn't ridden in a few years, so I gave her Lavender." "You didn't?" "I did." "What happened?" "Lavender was moving slower than usual, and I couldn't stand it so I rode ahead." "How far ahead?" "To the lake." "Scott!" "I know, I know. Like I said I was being a dick." "When she finally caught up to me, she was pissed. She knew I gave her Lavender on purpose. The next thing I knew, she's riding away on Sugar." "What did you do?" "I went after her. After, we had a good laugh about it and rode back together." "Who did you ride back?" "Lavender." She laughed. "I like her. Sounds like she doesn't take crap." "Yeah, tell me about it." "So will you see her again?" "Probably. Not for a while, though, since I'll be busy with school." Anyway, enough about that. I miss you." "I miss you too." "Brad hasn't been sniffing around you, has he?" "No." "Good." "How's Sam doing?" "Would you believe she and Riley have been burning up the phone lines?" "Really?" "Yeah, she calls him during her free period, and he calls her at night." He whistled. "How the mighty have fallen." "I think it's sweet." "I guess it is. Anyway, to change the subject, I'll be driving back to Morrisville tomorrow with Dad." "I thought you weren't leaving till Sunday?" "That was the original plan, but I figured it couldn't hurt to get back a day earlier and get some things done." "Guess so. Well, I'd better get back to my paper." "Okay. Em?" "Hmmmm?" "I love you." "I love you too, Scott."

Sam was talking to herself while she typed. "Stupid Mr. Excitement. He wouldn't know excitement if it came up and bit him in the ass. 'Just a little project to keep your minds sharp,' he said. Yeah, I've got something that'll keep your mind sharp, idiot." Just then, there was a knock at her door. "Who the?" She got up and looked through the peephole. She couldn't believe it. *Riley?* She opened the door and was greeted by a sexy grin. “Hey.” “Hey, yourself. What are you doing here?” “I was bored, so I decided to take a drive.” “It’s like three hours?” “All right, so I was *really* bored.” “Well, come in. I was just in the middle of a tirade on one of my professors.” “Oh which one?” “Calculus.” “Mr. Excitement?” “Right.” “Can I get you anything? A drink?” “Sure, you got any soda?” “Coke, ginger ale.” “Coke, please.” “Comin’ up.” “Sorry to interrupt your work.” “Are you kidding? I needed a break badly. I was moving on to four-letter words.” “Why’s that bad?” “I was going to put them in the report.” He laughed. “Yeah, I could see that being a problem.” She handed him his drink. “So miss me?” “I think we established that during our multiple phone calls.” “True but that was with words. I’m looking for something of a more physical nature,” he said with a sexy seductive grin. “Oh, what did you have in mind?” He pulled her down onto his lap. “I like your style.” “Right back at you.” They kissed with a heat that could melt ice. Soon both her top and bra were off, then his shirt. “How you feelin’, handsome?” she asked as she opened his fly. “Pretty stiff.” She smiled. “I can see that. How about I help you relax?” “I’d be grateful.” “How grateful?” “I could show you *after*.” She smiled and reached into his jeans, seeking him out. When she found him, she pulled him out and looked at him. “You gonna take a picture?” “No, smart-ass it’s just . . . never mind.” “What?” “It’s nicer looking than some others I’ve seen.” He chuckled. “Did you just compliment my penis?” She laughed. “I did. Believe me, you wouldn’t believe what’s out there. Some are downright scary.” He laughed loudly. “I’ll take your word for it.” “Now where were we?” “You were complimenting my penis.” “No, before that.” “Oh. I believe you were about to give me a happy ending.” She smiled. “That’s right. I was.”

Sabrina had mostly everything she needed and was headed to the check-out counter at Landy’s. She knew all the cashiers by name. “Hey, Agnes. How’s things?” “Oh fine, Sabrina. The usual, you know.” “Hmmm, I do.” She was placing her items on the belt. “You’re here kind of late, aren’t you? Usually you come earlier?” “Yeah, today sort of got away from me. I had a few stops to make. I bumped into Susan at the post office.” “Oh right, I heard she was back. Nice girl. Always liked her.” “Me too.” “I wonder if she and Ross will get back together? I never did understand why they broke up. They made such a nice couple. Didn't they?" Sabrina paused. "Ah, sure. Guess it just didn't work out." "Guess not." Agnes finished bagging the groceries. "Nice seeing you, Sabrina." "You too, Agnes. See you next time."

Sam and Riley were entangled in each other on the sofa. "Anyone ever tell you that you've got gifted hands?" "You're no slouch in that department either." "I aim to please." "And please you do." He kissed her. "I really missed you, Sam. So much that it's kind of scary." She laughed. "Is this your idea of post-coital conversation?" It was his turn to laugh. "Don't take it the wrong way. I meant it as a compliment." You know the way I was with women." "Yeah." "I never felt nervous with anyone before. I'd just be with them. With you I feel all sorts of things." "Like fear?" she joked. "I know it sounds bad, but hear me out. Being with you makes me feel good because for the first time I'm interested in *your* wants and needs. I've never cared about that before." "I know what you mean, Riley, because I feel the same way." "That's real good to hear."

Sabrina was unloading the groceries when Pete and Dave came out to help her. "Here let me get those, Ms. T." "Thanks, Pete." "I've got these," Dave said, holding up six bags. Pete was only holding three. "Show off." "Pete, you can take one of mine," Sabrina said as she held up five bags. "Well, that's just embarrassing." "You can eat some spinach and carry more next time," Dave teased. "Up yours." "Now is that any way to talk in front of a lady?" "Play nice, you two." "Sorry, Ms. T." They brought the packages into the kitchen. "Thanks, guys." "No problem. Glad we could help, Ms. T," Dave said. "Hey, can you believe that Riley's visiting Sam again?" She was surprised. "So soon?" "It's just not right. He was my idol," Dave said. She tried hard not to laugh. "He's definitely smitten." "He's not just smitten, Ms. T. He's *goooone.* As in 'cuckoo cuckoo for cocoa puffs' gone." This time she could not stop herself from laughing. "It was a good run," Dave said. "That it was," Pete replied. She looked at them and shook her head.

Chapter Sixteen

Scott couldn't wait to get back to Morrisville. Not because he loved school but because the sooner he went back, the sooner he'd graduate. His father had let him sleep late today. "Thanks for letting me sleep in, Dad." "Well, I figured it being your last day and all, what the hell." "I'm making French toast. So go wash up, and by the time you are done, it will be ready." "'Kay." He took a quick shower and went back into the kitchen. "So what did you and Amanda talk about?" Hanson flipped over the French toast. "Nothing much." "*Riight.*" "What?" "Just that I get the feeling you two are hiding something." He flipped the French toast. "Paranoid much?" "I don't think so. I think something happened the day you two talked." "Like what?" "Dunno exactly but I'm working on it." "Well, let me know when you crack the case, Sherlock." He grinned. "Believe me, you'll be the first to know." "Well, breakfast is ready, so put away your magnifying glass and cap for now."

Riley woke up in Sam's tiny bed, alone. And he didn't like it. *Now I know how it feels.* He looked over and saw a note;

Mornin' Handsome,

I had an early class that I couldn't miss. After class, you'll find me in the library. I have a paper to finish. There's yogurt in the fridge, help yourself. You could also hit the cafeteria for something heartier.

Hotly yours,
Sam

He smiled at the way she had signed it. He began thinking all kinds of naughty things. *Later,* he said to himself. He sat up, rubbed his eyes, and glanced at the clock. It was almost nine. He had slept late. Most likely because they had spent most of the night talking and cuddling. Which is something else he *never* did. He got to shower. While lathering up, he imagined Sam all soapy and wet along with him. When he was done, he toweled off and got dressed. He opened the fridge but couldn't bring himself to eat a yogurt. Instead, he decided to hit the cafeteria for some real food. He got the breakfast special of two eggs, home fries, bacon, toast, and coffee. He sat down and started eating. *Not bad for cafeteria food,* he thought to himself. After he finished, he bumped into Brad on his way out. Literally. "Whoops, sorry I didn't . . ." Brad trailed off when he realized who it was. "What are you doing here?" Brad asked. "And a pleasant good morning to you too." "Sorry, not the way I meant it." "That's okay. I drove up last night to see Sam. She had an early class, and I'm meeting her at the library." "Right." They both were quiet. "Riley, about what happened between Scott and me." "Yeah?" "I told him I was wrong." "That was big of you." "Not one of my finer moments. Believe me, I don't hit on other guys' girls." "Could've fooled me." "Anyway, I'm glad things worked out. Em is crazy about him." "I believe the feeling is mutual." "Yes, well, he made his feelings known to me and everyone within earshot. Right after he punched me." Riley grinned. "So I heard. Looks like your chin's healing nicely." "I'll live." "Anyway, I gotta go see my girl." "Sure, tell her I said hi." "Sure." *Not.* "Oh and thank her for the other night." "The other night?" "Yeah, she told me to not do anything stupid. Which, of course, for us guys is like daring us to do something stupid. Anyway, after making a complete ass of myself with Em, I went to see Sam and she and I talked." "Did you?" He was feeling something. What the hell was it? "She gave me some solid advice." "What was that?" "Stop being an idiot." He grinned. "Sounds like my girl." Brad looked at him. "Pierce was right. You have got it bad." "Gotta run. Later." He stood outside, trying to talk to himself. "My girl? Where the hell did that come from?" Some of the students passing by were staring at him. "What? Haven't you ever seen a guy talk to himself before?" He started walking and then realized he had no clue where the damn library was. So he asked a student. She gave him directions and her phone number. She was cute, and in the old days, he would have definitely tapped that. As she walked away, she gestured *call me* with her hand. He looked down at her number and crumpled it up and tossed it in a nearby trash bucket.

After he ate, Scott went into the barn to feed Sugar, and Sabrina came in. "Hi, Scott." "Hi." "So today's the day, huh?" "Yeah. Don't remind me." She smiled. "Oh come on, it's only three months till graduation. It will go like that." She snapped her fingers. "I hope so." "Riley back yet?" "Nope, not yet. He's probably . . ." He stopped short of what he had been going to say. "He's probably what?" "You know." "No, I don't know," she teased. "Come on, Sabrina." "Scott, if you're doing it, then you should be able to say it." He laughed. "Fine. They're probably doing the horizontal mambo." She laughed. "Probably. Anyway, to change the subject, have you spoken with Emily?" "Yeah, last night. I gave her an update on what's going on with Mom." She looked at him. "And yes, I realize I called her 'Mom.' It's not the first time." "It isn't? That's progress." "I guess." "She must have been thrilled." "I think she was more shocked than anything else. She also told me that you guys talked the day she came to see Dad. "Yes, we did." "That was nice of you. I mean you don't even know her. Did she say anything about her and Dad?" "Just that he was upset." "Yeah, join the club." "Look, Scott, far be it for me to tell you how to feel or what to do, but I really think Amanda's trying." He said nothing, just listened. "How did your ride go yesterday?" "Bad at first. I was a complete A-hole. I put her on Lavender." "You didn't?" "I did. I apologized . . . eventually. After, she borrowed Sugar and made me eat her dust." She laughed. "Good for her. Serves you right for giving her Lavender in the first place." "Anyway, I apologized and we actually laughed about it." She noticed his face was softer now when he spoke about her. "I'm glad. It will take time for the scars to heal." "Yeah, tell me about it. I just hope it's worth it in the end."

Sam was typing away on her laptop. She had done the necessary research and was putting it all down on paper for Mr. Excitement. Which was also putting her to sleep because again this was calculus, and it was incredibly boring. Plus she hadn't gotten that much sleep between Riley's being there and having to get up early for class. *Riley.* She smiled at the thought of him. The night of the party he looked good *with* his clothes on, but after seeing him naked, he looked even better *without* clothes. And boy was he gifted. The things he could do with those lips of his, hands, not to mention his tongue. Her body quivered at the thought of it. This is one guy she would never tire of. *Hold up . . . did I just think that?* Speak of the devil, she looked up, and he was walking toward her. He had a great walk. Not quite a strut or swagger, more a combination of the two. "Hi." "Hi, yourself." "You left." "I had class. I left a note." "I know. I didn't like it." "What, the note?" "No, waking up alone." "Oh." "Just cosmic karma, I guess." "Huh?" "All those times I left before the girl I was with woke up." "I'm guessing you didn't leave a note." "You guessed right. Anyway, how's the paper going?" "It's going. And so is my energy level. I'm fading." "Need me to get you something? Coffee, PowerBar, Red Bull?" She laughed. "Maybe a latte?" "You got it. I'll be back." He leaned down and kissed her. "That should hold you till I come back."

Ross wasn't exactly sure what he was going to say to Susan when he saw her again, but he knew he needed to talk to her. He decided to head over early; that way, it wouldn't be as crazy as it could sometimes get there in the afternoon. He told Linda he was going out and would be back shortly. It was a quick walk to the post office, and he was standing on the front steps second-guessing himself when fate interceded. "Hello, Ross." He turned around, and there she was looking as pretty as ever. "Hi, Susan." "What are you doing here?" "I'm ah . . . here to talk to you." "Oh, I guess Sabrina told you I was back?" "She did." "Well, I was just on my way to Perk for my morning caffeine fix.

Care to join me?" "Sure." They started walking. "So when did you get back?" "About a month ago. I was in the Canandaigua branch and put in for a transfer maybe six months ago. It finally came through last month." "It's been a long time, Susan." She stopped walking to look at him. "It has, hasn't it? You look good, Ross." He stood across from her now. "And you look just as pretty as when we met." "Thank you." They both stood standing quietly for a moment. "Susan . . .before you say anything, there's something I need to say first." "Okay." "I want you to know that I never used you. I was with you because I enjoyed being with you. End of story." She smiled. "I never thought that, Ross. Just like I hope you know that the reason why I stopped seeing you wasn't because I stopped caring but because I had started caring too much." "Look, Susan, you don't have anything to feel bad about. I was the one who was hung up on someone else." They arrived at Perk. "That's just it, Ross. I did feel bad. I couldn't understand why you weren't feeling more. Then I started to put it together. I realized you had feelings for someone else, but I didn't think it was Sabrina. Then little by little I began noticing how you were around her." "Susan—" "No, it's okay. When I realized that it was Sabrina, I just couldn't believe it. The truth is that by the time we broke up, I was a little bit in love with you, that's why I left. If I saw you every day, I'd have never have gotten over you." "God, Susan, I'm sorry." "Please don't be, I didn't tell you to make you feel bad. Just to clear the air. I'm okay with it, with all of it. Besides, if it hadn't happened, I would never had met Rob." "Is that the guy you're serious about?" "Yes, he's wonderful." He smiled. "That's great. I'm very happy for you, Susan." "I'm happy for me too. But there's something else I need to say to you." "Oh?" "I want to thank you." "Thank me? For what?" "For being who you were. Who you are." "I'm sorry, I'm not exactly following you on this." "What I mean is, when we were together, you always treated me with respect, even though you had feelings for Sabrina. Some guys would have just used me for what they could get." "You sound like you're going to nominate me for Man of the Year or something." She laughed. "No, nothing like that. I just wanted you to know that you're a special man, Ross. I knew it then, and I know it now. I'm happy for you, Ross. I know how crazy you are about her. I hope it works out the way you want it to." "Thanks,

Susan. Rob is lucky to have you too." She leaned over and stretched a bit to kiss his cheek. "Well, I guess I should head back." "What about your caffeine fix?" "My break's over." "Let me run in and get you something. What do you want?" "Mocha Sensation." He laughed. "What's so funny?" "That's Linda's drink." "Well, it's really good. Ever try it?" "No, I like my coffee without fancy names attached to it." She laughed. "Start walking back and I'll catch up." She was almost back at the post office when he caught up. "Sorry, line was so damn long." He handed her the hot cup. She inhaled the steam and took a sip. "Hmmm." "Glad you are enjoying it." "It's great. Thanks." "Sure. Well, I'll let you get back inside and keep the mail flowing." "I'm glad we talked." "Me too." This time, he leaned over and kissed her on the cheek. "Rob's a real lucky guy." She smiled. "Thanks, Ross. Sabrina's a lucky woman too." "Take care of yourself, Susan." "You too." She went inside, and he walked back to the station.

Sam was trying to focus, but it was just so damn boring. She needed that coffee. "Hey, Sam." "Hey, Em. You're here awfully early, aren't you?" "No, it's almost eleven." "What? Oh crap. I thought it was like nine." "Yeah, two hours ago. How long have you been working?" "Right after Mr. Excitement's class." "That long? Are you crazy?" "No, just desperate to finish this shit. I'm losing it." "All right, deep breath. Breathe in, then out. In through your nose and out through your mouth." Sam did as she was told but felt no better. "It's not working." "Give it a minute." "What I need is for Riley to bring me my latte." "Riley? He's here?" "In the flesh," he said from behind. "Hey, Em." "Riley." He handed Sam her drink. "What took you so long? I'm dyin' here." "You're welcome," he said, slightly annoyed. "Sorry, just stressed to the max right now." "I can see that. You said you wanted a latte, and the machine in the cafeteria wasn't working, so I had to go out to that local coffee place." "You mean the Grind?" Em asked. "Yeah. I asked around and they told me to go there." "That's a bit of a walk," Sam said. "Which is why it took me a while." She looked at him. "You went through all that for a latte?" "No. I went through all that for *you*." "Aw, that's so sweet," Emily said. Sam was practically inhaling her latte. "Ah, this is better than sex." He looked at her. "I take offense at that." "Sorry, let me rephrase. This is better than sex with *other* guys." "Now that's better." She giggled. "So, Riley, when did you get here?" Emily asked. "Late last night. Kind of a spur-of-the-moment thing." "I think it's really nice that you surprised Sam." "It was. Wasn't it? Romantic even. I get extra points for that, right?" Sam shook her head. "What is this, Scrabble?" Emily laughed. "Hey, not every guy would go in search of a coffee bar to get your drink." "That's true." Sam let out a relaxing breath. "I feel better already. I can feel my brain defogging." "Are you almost done with this stupid paper?" he asked. "Almost. Good thing, 'cause it's due today." "Sam, what did I tell you about leaving stuff for the last minute?" Emily said. "I know, but I just couldn't motivate myself. Every time I tried, I'd feel my eyes closing." "I believe that's called sleeping," he teased. "A few more equations, and I'm done." "Well, I'll let you finish and be alone with Riley." "Hey, Em, you don't have to go." "I've got to get back anyway." "No, it's okay. I want to take a walk before my next class. Get some sunshine." Riley spotted Brad talking to someone by one of the bookcases. "Great. What is it with this guy? He's like everywhere," he said. "What, you saw him already?" "Yeah, in the cafeteria. I bumped into him, literally." "How cozy," Sam teased. "Not funny." Brad spotted them. "I think he's coming over," Sam said. "What are you worried about? You two are pretty tight from what I hear," he said, sounding slightly annoyed. "Huh?" "Your little chat after he put the moves on Em." "Brad talked to you after that? You didn't tell me, Sam?" *Great.* "That's 'cause there was nothing to tell. He was upset, needed a shoulder to cry on. That sort of thing." "Yeah, that's the sort of thing I don't like." "Ree-lax, okay?" "Hey, Sam, Riley, Em." "Brad," Emily said. "Hey, Brad," Sam said. "Are you following me?" Riley asked, annoyed. "No, just happens to be a coincidence." *Coincidence my ass.* "Right," he said, sounding pissy. "It is a library, and I am a student, so it makes sense that I'd come here to . . . oh, I don't know . . . get a book or two." "He has a point, Riley," Sam said. He gave her a look and she shut up. "So, Em, how's it going?" Brad asked. "Busy. You?" "Same. How are things with Scott?" "They're really good. Thanks for asking." "Sure. I don't know if he told you, but I gave him my sister's number." "Well, that was generous considering he decked you," Sam teased. Brad laughed and Riley grew warmer. *Christ, I'm jealous.* "I'm sure Scott appreciated it, Brad,"

Emily said. "He seemed to. He said I wasn't a complete asshole after all." The girls laughed. "Sam, I'm heading out now," Emily said. "Okay, Em." "Bye, Em." "Bye, Brad." "Well, I guess that's my cue to leave." "'Bout time," Riley mumbled. "By the way, Sam, I just wanted you to know how much I appreciated your support the other night. Not to mention the much-needed beer. "Beer? You had beer with him?" Riley asked. "*He* had *a* beer. I had nothing." "Anyway, I appreciate the assist. If ever there's anything I can do for you, just ask." Riley rolled his eyes. "Thanks, Brad. I might just take you up on that." She said it in an almost flirtatious tone. *What the fuck*? He was getting more steamed by the minute. "I hope you do. Anyway, see you in class." He left and Riley stared at her. She was trying to type but felt his eyes burning a hole in her forehead. "What?" she asked, annoyed. "You have to ask?" "Actually, I do. 'Cause I don't know what bug has suddenly crawled up your ass." "First of all, there is no bug up my ass. Second, you don't know? Pleeze. I might just take you up on that one day, Brad," he said, using a higher-pitched voice and batting his eyelashes. "I was not doing that eye thing. Besides, he was just being polite." "Bull, he was flirting with you. And you flirted right back." "I did not." "Don't try to play a player, Sam." "Fine, so I was flirting. I'm sure you flirt too." "Maybe I do but not in *front* of you." "Why are you getting so bent out of shape about this? Are you jealous?" "Don't be ridiculous. It's just he gets on my last nerve. I'm still pissed at him for what he tried with Em." "As far as I'm concerned, he's made up for that. He hasn't tried anything else, and he gave Scott his sister's number." "Well, let's nominate him for sainthood." "What is with you? You're being a total jerk right now. And I have to finish this." She got up, closed her laptop, and grabbed her backpack. She poked her finger into his chest, hard. "So when you're through being a jerk, give me a call. If I'm not home, then maybe it's 'cause I'm out with Brad." She huffed and walked out, leaving him standing there.

Chapter Seventeen

Scott packed up a few things he wanted to take back with him and was ready to go. He double-checked his wallet for Brad's sister's phone number since he intended to call her. He finished loading the truck and went back inside. He wanted to call Amanda before they left since he knew he'd be busy the first few weeks. He dialed her number. After several rings, her machine picked up. "Hi, you've reached Amanda *and Sam*. We're not home right now. So leave a message, and we'll get back to you." The machine beeped. "Amanda, it's Scott. Listen, I'm driving back to Morrisville this afternoon. Just wanted you to know. I'll try calling another time. Take care. Bye." He hung up and scratched his head. "*Who's Sam*?"

Scott used the bathroom and went outside. He looked for Riley, but there was no sign of him. He had hoped he'd be back before he left. Which was really weird. "You ready?" Hanson said. "Yeah. I guess." "What's the matter?" "I just tried calling Amanda." "And?" "I got her machine." "Why did that upset you?" "It didn't upset me, just got my wondering." "This is like pulling teeth here. About what? Just say it." "Fine. The message says you've reached Amanda *and Sam*." Hanson felt himself tense. "Who's Sam?" "How the hell should I know? Most likely her boyfriend or could even be her husband." "You think she's married?" "You say that like it couldn't happen." "No, it's just it threw me for a loop." *Me too*. Hanson thought to himself. "Oh good, Riley's back. I wanted to talk to him before we left." Hanson looked at him. "Did you just say you were glad to see Riley?" "Yeah. Weird, right?" "I'll say." "He can be a pain in the ass, but he's helped me a lot lately. First with Amanda, then with Em." "Which you still haven't told me about." "We patched things up. That's all you need to know." Riley got out, slammed the car door, and kicked his tires. "Oh boy, someone doesn't look happy," Hanson said. They walked over to him. "Hey, glad you made it back before I had to leave." "Yeah, sure. Whatever. Have a nice trip back." He walked into the barn. Scott and Hanson looked at each other and followed him. He was filling up buckets with fresh feed. "I did that already," Scott said. "Then I'll do it again," he said with an attitude. "Who pissed in your cornflakes?" Scott asked. "None of your fuckin' business." "Sounds like somebody has a bug up his ass," Hanson said. "Why does everyone keep saying that?" "Probably 'cause it's true." "Fuck you, Pierce." "Sorry, you're not my type." Riley moved past him, carrying two buckets. "I told you, I did that already." "And I told you I'm going to do it again. You got a problem with that?" "No, but you seem to. Wanna talk about it?" "No, I don't wanna talk about it." Scott looked at Hanson. "Dad, could you?" "Sure." He walked out. "Okay, what happened? Pete said you went to see Sam." "I did." "Come on, Riley. Do I have to pull it out of you?" "Fine! You wanna know what happened. I fucked up. That's what happened." "Well, I know that. I want to know *how* you fucked up?" "You have such faith in me." He laughed. "I have none 'cause you're a guy and guys screw up. As Sam would say, spill." "You aren't going to let this go. Are you?" "Nope." "Well, once again your buddy Brad is involved." "Brad? How?" "He came to talk to Sam that night after he hit on Em. They talked, she comforted him, she even gave him a beer." "Shocking," Scott teased. "Anyway, I felt pissy about it but didn't understand why at first." "That's 'cause you're *sloooow*." Riley sneered and continued. "Then in the library after I had walked half a damn mile to get her a stupid latte, he shows up." "What is with that guy?" "I don't friggin' know, but it irks the shit out of me. I even asked if he was following me." Scott looked at him. "Paranoid much?" "Yeah, I know. Sounds a bit nutty." "A bit?" "You wanna hear the rest or not?" "Sure." "Em was there." So they were talking, Brad is thanking Sam for being there, blah, blah. Then he says if you need anything just ask. And she says, 'Oh I might just do that.' She was being all flirty and fluttery." "Fluttery?" "You know, the thing they do with their eyes." "Oh, right. Then?" "Then I really screwed myself. I acted like a dick to Brad, she got mad, then I got madder. Then she got really mad. Poked me in my chest, saying that when I was through being a jerk, give her a call." Scott looked at him. "Go ahead. I know you are *dying* to say it." "I told you so." "You suck." "That may very well be. But I'm also right." "Crap, I know it. So now what?" "Well, the tides have changed. Not so long ago, you were helping me with Em, and now I'm helping you with Sam. How the mighty have fallen." He rolled his eyes. "Don't give me that crap. Just tell me what I have to do." "Well, off the top of my head, I'd say stop being a jerk." "Right."

Sam was good and pissed, and it was all Riley's fault. "Not jealous my ass." "All right, class, settle down." "I am *sooo* not in the mood," she mumbled. "I assume everyone has their papers?" Some students mumbled. "What's that? I can't hear you?" "Yes, Mr. Benson." "That's better. All right, please place your papers on the left side of the desk." One by one, everyone brought up their papers. When it was Sam's turn, she wasn't paying attention. "Ms. Stewart, I said *the left side of the desk*." "Sorry, Mr. Benson. I wasn't thinking." "That's obvious." *So's that really big zit you're trying to hide*, she mumbled to herself.

Hanson and Scott decided to take Riley with them on the drive back to Morrisville. It would give him time to cool off and, more importantly, stop him from refeeding the already-full animals. Sabrina came out with a bag. "Scott, I packed a few things, so you wouldn't have to worry about dinner your first week back. It's a casserole. Just nuke and eat. Then there's grilled chicken, veggies, and sauce for pasta." "Thanks, Sabrina. You're the best." She smiled at him. "There's also pie and cookies." "I hate to leave." She laughed. "See you at graduation before you know it." "Okay." He hugged her and got into the truck. "All set?" Hanson asked. "Anybody need anything before we go?" "Yeah, a DeLorean," Riley said sarcastically. "I could lend you the movie," Scott joked. "Bite me." Hanson rolled his eyes. "Don't make me regret this, you two." "It's him, Dad. He's all moody now that Sam is mad at him." "Hey, you were just as bitchy when Em was pissed at you." "You two cut it out. Got it?" Hanson said, frustrated. Sabrina leaned into the car window. "Drive safe. And try not to kill them." "I'll try." She laughed as they drove away.

They had been on the road about an hour, and Riley wasn't talking. He just kept thinking about Sam. "Let me guess, you're beating yourself up for the hundredth time?" "Fuck off." "You two keep this up, and I'll leave you *both* on the side of the road." "So you gonna tell me what happened between you and Sam?" Hanson asked. "Scott can fill you in." "Basically, he was an idiot," Scott said. "Hey, wasn't so long ago *you* were the idiot. And if I remember correctly, you were crying in the barn." Hanson slowed up. "What??" "I wasn't crying, I had something in my eye." "Yeah, they're called tears. Don't let him bullshit you, Hanson." "Hey, I was fucked up, all right. The shit with Amanda and then Em." Hanson grew annoyed. "You know I'm getting real tired of asking this. What did you do?" "I—" "He banged her up against her door." "You're upset so I am going to let that one slide, Riley. But if you ever talk about her like that again, I will knock your block off. Got it?" "Yeah, I got it. Sorry." "So what in God's name made you treat her that way?" Hanson asked. "I wasn't thinking straight." "Which is why I told him *not* to go see her. But he didn't listen." "No, I didn't. Believe me I felt like shit afterwards. Anyway, what about Sam?" He told them what had happen. "Sam's right, you were being a jerk," Scott said. "Takes one to know one." Hanson grinned. "So you were a jealous ass? Must have felt weird since you were always the 'love 'em and leave 'em' type." "You have no idea how weird. At first I didn't even know what it was that I was feeling. I've never been jealous before. There was never any reason for it." "Different girls, no attachments, no need. Right?" Hanson said. "Exactly, but with Sam it's different." "We've all been there, Riley," Hanson explained. "Even me." "So what do I do now?" "Start by apologizing. Then you gotta romance her." "Not this again." "He's right, Riley. Women love it." "Were you that way with Amanda?" "You bet your ass I was." "Flowers, and not ones you pick from the garden," Scott said. "Real ones from the florist." "Right. Anything else?" "Yeah, explain things to her the way you did to us, and she'll understand," Hanson said. "Great, why didn't I write it all down?" They laughed.

Amanda tried calling Hanson, but he didn't pick up. So she tried Sabrina next, who picked up after a few rings. "Hi, Sabrina, it's Amanda." "Amanda, hi. How's it going?" "Okay, I guess. I was out doing errands, and Scott called. I tried reaching them, but no one picked up. Did they already leave?" "Yes." "I figured that. Oh well. I guess I'll talk to him when he has time." "I'm sure he'll give you again soon." "You're probably right." "So I heard about your Annie Oakley impression." "Annie Oakley?" Amanda caught on and laughed. "He told you?" "Yes. I can't believe he put you on Lavender!" "I know. A lovely animal but way past its prime. At least if you're interested in moving forwards." Sabrina laughed. "Yes, we rarely ride her anymore. We just walk her around to keep her in shape." "What did Scott say exactly?" "That he was eating your trail dust." "Well, after I ate his, it was no more than he deserved." "I couldn't agree more." "When he finally caught up to me, he was upset. He sort of said he was worried about me." "Sort of?" "Well, he didn't come out and say it, but I could read between the lines." "That's great." "I think so." "I think little by little he's warming up to you." "Well, that's something I guess." "Sabrina, you've been so supportive. I don't know how to thank you." "I know a way." "Oh?" "How about coming for lunch. We can get to know each other better. If you're interested?" "Sure." "Why don't you come by Sunday?" "What time?" "Say noonish?" "That's perfect. See you then."

The guys arrived at Morrisville and parked in the lot. Scott grabbed his stuff, and Riley grabbed the food. "Why don't you guys come up and hang for a bit? We can nuke Sabrina's casserole." "Sounds good to me. I'm starved," Riley said. "I wouldn't say no to Sabrina's casserole before driving back," Hanson said. "I got the trip back, Hanson." "Thanks, Riley. That would be much appreciated." "No problem. It's the least I can do. After the way I acted." "What about me? What do I get for my heartburn?" Scott asked. "A nice big roll of Tums." "You're an ass." "That I am." They were outside Scott's room when they bumped into his friend John. "Hey, man, I was just coming to see if you were back yet." "Just got back now. How's things, John?" "Same ole, same ole." He looked at Hanson and Riley. "Oh, John, this is my father." "Nice to meet you, Mr. Pierce." Hanson laughed. "Mr. Pierce was my father, call me Hanson." "All right, Hanson." "And this pain in the ass here is Riley." They shook hands. "So tell me, does Pierce bust your balls as much as he does mine?" Riley asked. "You bet he does. Sometimes I just want to wear earplugs." Riley laughed. "Now that's a good idea. I might have to try that." "You two done?" "Nah, we're good for another hour at least," John joked. "I like your friend, Scott," Riley said, smiling. "Yeah, he's a regular riot." "So, Scott, what's up with that Emily babe?" "You met Em?" Riley asked. "Yeah, when I drove this one here back home so he could be there for her birthday." "That was real nice of you." Riley said. "Yeah well I'm a real nice guy." "Sure you are, when you aren't being an ass. Which is almost all the time." "You see the abuse I take, Riley?" "I do, and I take plenty myself, believe me." "If you two are done, there's a casserole I'd like to be eating. John, you interested?" "Did you make it?" "No." "Then I'm interested."

Ross walked down the hall to check on Andy's progress with the filing. The closer he got to the file room, the louder Andy's singing got. "I'm on the edge of *gloooory* and I'm hangin' on a moment of truth, out on the edge of *glooooory*." Ross stood there, shaking his head. He walked up behind him and tapped his shoulder. Andy jumped. "Damn it! Do you always have to do that?" "No, I just like to. I was just checking on how the filing was going." "Real good." "That's great, Andy. Good job." "Thanks, boss." "It's getting late. Why don't you take off?" "You sure?" "I'm sure." "Thanks, see you. Mañana." Ross grabbed his jacket and closed his office door. He flipped off the lights and locked the front door.

The guys devoured Sabrina's casserole. Scott was staring at the empty casserole dish. "Man, this was supposed to be dinner for the week." They eyed the empty dish. "You aren't gonna cry again, are you?" Riley joked. "Cry?" John asked. "Never mind, Riley's just being a dick because he's in the doghouse with Sam." John leaned back in the chair. "What'd you do?" "Let's just say pea green is not my best color. I acted like jerk because I was jealous." John laughed. "Haven't we all at one point or another. I mean, the things we go through for women. They have no idea." "You got that right, pal," Riley said. "Things were so much easier when my motto was love 'em and leave 'em." John looked at him. "Wait, are you saying what I think you're saying?" "Riley's a reformed womanizer," Hanson said. "The term is player, Dad." "Oh excuse me. *Player.*" "So let me get this straight. You had what every guys dreams about. A different girl whenever you wanted, no commitments, no worries, and you gave it all up? For some girl?" Riley didn't like hearing Sam referred to as *some girl.* "No. I gave it up for *the girl.*" Hanson's, Scott's, and John's mouths all dropped. "Are you serious?" John asked. "Yeah, I am." "Riley, I know you like Sam a lot—" "I'm nuts about her." "Okay, fine. So you're nuts about her but that doesn't mean—" "So what? You're saying you don't feel the exact same way about Em?" "Em?" John said. "Your *pal,* Em? You and her are together? When the fuck did this happen?" Scott looked at him. "On break." "Must have been *some break,*" John said. "Tell me about it. He falls for Em, I fall for Sam, and Ross and Sabrina end up together." "Who the hell are they?" "Em's Aunt and the local sheriff. He's been in love with her since they were kids." "Sounds like they're putting something in the water up there. I'd better stay away." They all looked at him and laughed.

Emily hadn't seen Sam since she bumped into her at the library. She tried calling but just got the machine. So she went to see her. When Sam opened the door, she could tell something was up. "Where've you been?" "Here." "Okay, why didn't you answer when I called?" "I didn't feel like it." "Why? Did something happen?" "Yeah." "What?" "Riley's a jerk, that's what happened." "What did he do?" Sam told her. "And then I picked up my shit and left his ass there." She smiled. "So I have to ask. Was there any reason for his being upset?" "What? No." She didn't sound too convincing. "Sam?" "Well, maybe I was being a little flirty. Sometimes I just can't help myself. I like the attention." "Who doesn't? But, Sam, to flirt with Brad in front of Riley—" "I know. It wasn't cool. I don't know why I did it." "I do." "Okay, so enlighten me." "You wanted to see if he'd get jealous." Sam remained quiet. "Well, are you going to say something?" "No." "Why?" "Because you're right." Sam sat on the sofa. "Why did you want to make him jealous?" "'I don't know." "Don't laugh. It's not funny. I mean, I've never been the type to care if a guy got jealous or not. In my defense, though, he was acting pissy before that." Emily shook her head. "What? "You can't possibly be that dumb." "Lately, my IQ seems to be dropping." "You're crazy about him." "I am not. I like him *a lot,* and the sex is off the charts." "It's not just sex and you know it." She took a deep breath. "You know I hate it when you're right." "I know."

John and Scott walked Hanson and Riley to the truck. "So you and Emily, huh?" John was still trying to get used to it. "Yeah." "I should have never said she was hot. It made you notice." He laughed. "So, John, how do you stay friends with him?" Riley asked, grinning. "He pays well." Riley laughed. They were at the truck and Hanson unlocked the doors. "Well, I guess this is it till graduation." "Yeah," Scott said. "Study hard, stay safe. I love you, son." "I love you too, Dad." They hugged. "Someone pass me a Kleenex," John joked. "I *really* like you, man," Riley said. "Next time Scott comes around, come with him. We can all go drinking at Jake's." "Sounds like a plan." Hanson shook John's hand. "Nice meeting you, John. Take care." "Great meeting you. Safe drive back. Thanks." He got in on the passenger side, since Riley was driving back. He and Scott were standing next to each other. "Well, it's been real, Pierce." Scott laughed. "It definitely has. Thanks for everything, Riley. I mean that." "Sure, I'm glad things are better." "Yeah, me too. I hope you're able to smooth things over with Sam." "Yeah, me too." They shook hands, and Riley got behind the wheel and closed the door. "Dad, call me when you get back." "Will do." Scott and John watched as they drove away. "Your dad is cool." "Yeah, he is." "Riley's a real smart-ass. I like him," John said. "That doesn't surprise me since it seems like you two were separate at birth." This made John laugh. "So anything else happen on break that I should know about?" Scott paused. "Well, my mother showed up." "I had to ask."

Sam was feeling better after her talk with Em. "So you know what you have to do. Right, Sam?" "Yeah, yeah. I need to come clean with him." "Right. The sooner the better." "Do you think he's miserable too?" "Yes, Sam. I'm sure he is." "Good, that makes me feel better." They laughed. "Well, if the crisis is over, I'm going to head back." "Sure. Thanks, Em." "Please you don't have to thank me, Sam. I love you." "I know. I love you too." Em left, and Sam decided to watch a movie before bed. She opted to watch *How to Lose a Guy in Ten Days.*

Somehow it seemed fitting since the romantic leads were both relationship challenged.

Riley once again broke the sound barrier, much to Hanson's dismay. "Do you always drive like this or is it just because I'm in the car?" "I tend to drive a little fast." "A little? I think we lost all four hubcaps back there." "Very funny. I'm only doing eighty. I wanted to make up some time and get us home sooner." "How about doing seventy and getting us home in one piece?" "You got it." They drove for a while after that in comfortable silence. Which, eventually, Riley broke. "So how are things with you and Amanda?" "Why the heck does everyone keep asking me that?" "Dunno, maybe 'cause they can see you still have the hots for her." "You think so?" "No, I know so. It's as plain as the nose on her gorgeous face." "Are you done?" Hanson asked. "Nope, just getting warmed up. We talked about Sam so now it's your turn." "There's nothing to talk about." He looked at him. "There isn't. I mean, of course I still find her attractive." "Dude, she's hot." He ignored him. "The bottom line is she came back for Scott." "You sure that's the only thing she came back for?" "It doesn't matter since she's got another guy." "How the hell do you know that?" "Scott called her and got her machine. The message says you've reached Amanda *and Sam*." "So you think he's her boyfriend?" "Could be or maybe her husband." "That would suck balls if it were true." Hanson agreed but said nothing. "So I guess this means neither one of us has a shot, huh?" Hanson let out the biggest belly laugh. "Riley, you're fuckin' hilarious." "Who said I was joking?" They looked at each other and laughed again.

Sunday morning arrived, and Sabrina was busy getting ready for Amanda's visit. She was preparing the fresh fish she bought. She'd grill it when she arrived. She was also baking pear tarts. Hanson stood by the door; she saw him and motioned him inside. "Morning, Sabrina." "Morning. I see you made it back all right." "No thanks to Riley. That boy drives like a lunatic." He sniffed the air. "Is that pear I smell?" Yes, I'm making your favorite tarts." "And you weren't going to tell me?" he teased. "I was going to put some on the side for you." "Please do. So what's the occasion?" "Oh I invited Amanda over for lunch." "Really? Seems you two are getting kind of chummy." "Well, seems like she needs a friend." "So what time is she coming?" "Noon. Will you be around?" she asked him. "I might be heading into town for some things. If I'm around, I'll stop by and say hi." "Okay." He walked out. She shook her head and smiled. She'd bet money on the fact that he would be.

Amanda was both happy and excited while driving to Sabrina's. She had been taken aback by the invitation at first. After all, they hardly knew one another. Although she had liked Sabrina from the start. Not very many people would have opened their door to a total stranger. Then her mind wandered to the kiss she and Hanson had shared. She touched her lips in remembrance. When she arrived, she was hoping to see Hanson but didn't see him. She walked toward the barn. She went inside and saw Lavender on her left and Sugar in the stall on her right. "Hello, ladies. Miss me?" She walked over to each of them and petted them. Lavender nuzzled her and Sugar butted her shoulder. "We sure showed him. Didn't we girls?" She smiled at the memory and realized it was her first with her son since she had left. "Bonding with your girlfriends?" She turned to see Hanson standing in the doorway, hands in his pockets. He motioned toward the horses. She smiled. "Believe me, we did plenty of bonding the other day." He smiled. "I believe it. Sabrina told me you were coming for lunch." "Yes." "You're in for a real treat. Don't tell her I told you, but she made her pear tarts. They are just pure heaven." "Hmmm. Sounds good. So how did it go with Scott?" "Oh fine unless you count Riley almost doing us both in with my truck." "Why was he with you?" "Long story but the short of it is he screwed things up with Sam." "His girlfriend, right?" "Right. And well, he came back from seeing her in a piss-poor mood. Anyway, Scott and I figured it would be better to take him along." "What happened?" "He was an ass." "Doesn't sound that bad." "A *jealous ass.*" She laughed. "Sam didn't appreciate his attitude, so she told him off and left him standing in the library." "Poor Riley." "I tend to agree. The guy was a complete mess. And the kicker is that he was a former womanizer." "I believe the term you should be using is player." He smiled. "Right. Anyway, he was real upset. At one point, we were in Scott's dorm eating. It was me, Scott, Riley, and John, Scott's friend. John couldn't figure out why Riley would be so quick to give up every guy's dream. Different women, no attachments, sex up the yin yang. So John says,

'Man, you gave that up for some girl?' And that's when he shocked the shit out of all of us. He says, 'No, I gave it up for *the girl*.'" Her eyes grew wide. "Are you serious?" "Dead serious." "Wow." "Wow is right." "So what will he do?" "A whole lot of begging if he's smart." She laughed loudly. "I can remember you begging on more than one occasion." "Yeah, so can I." She laughed again. "There's isn't a man alive who hasn't begged or crawled over broken glass one time or another." "Well, I hope things work out between then." "Me too. Anyway, Scott's back at school and classes start Monday." "I know. He left me a message." "He told me." "I was so sorry I missed his call. I was out doing errands." *With Sam? Hanson thought to himself.* "Errands, right. Well, I'm sure he'll call when things calm down." "I actually think he will. We had a few laughs that day. Which felt good." "I know." "I told him about the slap, Hanson." "Why?" He asked me what happened that day between us." "He's been asking me too. You didn't tell him about—" "The kiss? No, I didn't. I just said we were both angry, did a lot of yelling and I slapped you. I told him it wasn't one of my finer moments." "Yeah, not one of mine either." They looked at each other. "Anyway, Sabrina will be wondering where I am." As she was walking out, he grabbed hold of her hand. "Who's Sam, Amanda?" His question hit her like a ton of bricks. "Scott said when he called your machine said Amanda *and Sam*." All of a sudden the barn walls were closing in on her. Everything seemed to be getting darker. He looked at her with concern in his eyes. "Manda, you're white as sheet. You okay?" *I'm going to pass out* was her last thought before everything went dark.

As she came to, she heard voices. "She's coming 'round. Manda, can you hear me? Come on, honey, let me see those pretty brown eyes of yours." She heard him and focused on his voice. Slowly her eyes opened. "That's it, attagirl." Her eyelids fluttered a few times before staying open. "You gave us quite a scare." She was lying on the sofa with Sabrina standing over her. Hanson was sitting beside her, holding a damp cloth to her forehead. She reached for the cool cloth. "Leave it on a while." She nodded. "What happened?" "You fainted." "I never faint." "Well, then say hello to never," he said sarcastically. "Hanson," Sabrina chided him. "Sorry, it's just you went white as a sheet, and next thing I knew, you were dropping like a stone." "Let me get her some water." Amanda tried to get up and grew dizzy. "Whoa, easy. Take it slow." Sabrina came back with water. "Here, drink it slowly." She sat up a bit, and he braced her back while she drank. "I'm sorry to be so much trouble." "Nonsense," she said. "You just gave us a scare. When Hanson carried you in here, I didn't know what to think." "Neither did I." "Why did you faint?" he asked. "I don't know. That's never happened before." "You got that way after I asked about Sam." She closed her eyes, for she remembered all too well. "Hanson, can I speak to you a minute?" Sabrina said. "Sure. Be right back, Manda." She pulled him into the dining room. "I get the feeling that Sam is the reason she fainted. Why don't you leave us alone for a while? Maybe she'll talk about it with me. I have a feeling she might not open up if you're around." "I guess you're right. I've got to get some things at the Feed N Seed, anyway." They walked back into the living room. She was sitting up now, damp cloth removed from her forehead, and color returning to her face. "'I've got some errands to run, but I'll be back soon. Don't leave till I get back." She nodded. He cupped her chin in his hand. "You scared the crap out of me. Don't ever do that again." "I'll try not to." She smiled. Sabrina watched them together. "Amanda, I'll be right back." "Okay." She walked Hanson outside. "What I have to do won't take long." "No worries. We'll have a nice leisurely lunch. I'll take good care of her." "I know you will." He started down the steps. "Hanson?" "Yeah?" "I saw your face when you brought her in. You still love her, don't you?" "God help me, but I think I do."

Chapter Eighteen

Hanson drove into town, replaying what had happened over and over again. All he could think about was Amanda dropping like a stone. In those moments, as he held her limp body and raced toward the house, he had never been so scared in his life. He drove over to the Feed N Seed and parked. He went inside and asked for Tom, the owner. He was told he could find him around back. He saw Tom talking to Charlie Ross. Who happened to be Ross's biggest fan or so he'd heard from Sabrina. "Hanson." "Tom, how's business?" "Can't complain. It's been good as of late." Hanson looked at Charlie. "How 'bout you Charlie?" "Five by five." Hanson smirked. "Charlie, I told you—" "I know, I know. Speak English." "Right. So what can I do for you?" "I need a few things." "All right, Charlie can help you with whatever it is you need." "Thanks, Tom." He started walking away and turned back around. "Remember, Charlie—" I *knooow*, speak English," he said, annoyed. Hanson chuckled. "So what do you need?" "About two-dozen bags of fertilizer and a dozen bags of chicken feed." "Anything else?" "Yeah, toss in six bags of miracle grow for good measure." "You got it. Give me twenty then meet me out back." "Okay."

Back at the house, Amanda felt steady enough to sit at the kitchen table while Sabrina grilled the fish. "Sabrina, I'm so sorry." "Would you please stop apologizing? You fainted, you didn't steal the family silver."

She smiled. “I know it’s just—” “Just nothing. Forget it.” “Okay.” “So why don’t you tell me about Ross?” “What do you want to know?” “Everything?” She laughed. “That might take a while.” “I’ve got time.” “All right. Well, for starters we all grew up together, me, Ross, my brother, James, and his wife, Rebecca.” “Scott and I talked briefly about the crash.” “Yes, it was a horrible blow to us all. Ross and James were very close. Like brothers.” “How sad.” “Even sadder was my niece becoming an orphan overnight.” “Scott talked about her too. He seems very taken with her.” “The feeling is mutual, I’m sure. Anyway, we all grew up together and were best friends.” “So once you guys hit the teen years, things changed?” “Not right away.” “See, Becca had slowly been developing a thing for James, but he was too dumb to notice. Not that I should be casting any stones since I was just as clueless when it came to Ross.” “So how did she get James to notice her?” “There was this school dance, the kind you got dressed up for. Becca wanted to wear a dress that would stop traffic and get James’s attention. She hit this vintage clothing shop and found this great cocktail dress.” “Oh I love anything vintage. So much style and class.” “The dress was a real showstopper. Off the shoulder, fitted bodice, and flared out.” “What color was it?” “Lavender.” “When we got to her house, she came out. I swear I heard my brother’s heart stop beating.” “How romantic.” “It was. All I can say is after that, he always noticed her.” “What about you and Ross?” “Ross and I are a very different story. He was crazy about me, but I never knew.” “Sometimes it’s hard to see something from the inside. It’s easier to notice from the outside looking in.” “I guess so. Years went by, we dated and were in relationships, but his never lasted very long.” “Because he was in love with you.” “Yes. He told me that he would try and get over me by seeing other women, but none could compare to me.” “Wow.” “Yeah, I know.” “So how did you finally find out?” “It was the morning after Emily’s twenty-first birthday party. Ross had slept in the guest room. I went to wake him and found him wearing only boxers. “Hubba hubba!” She laughed. “He has great abs. I mean definition up the wazoo.” “I’m gonna need more ice water,” Amanda joked. “Coming up.” She got out the pitcher from the fridge and poured. “So he was in his boxers, looking all hot and—” “And well, I couldn’t help looking.” “He caught you?” Sabrina laughed. “Oh yeah, and he loved every minute of it. He went on and on about how studly he was. So then I said he'd be a good catch one day, make some girl very happy." "Then?" "Then he grabbed me said he didn't want *some girl*, he wanted *me*. Then he kissed me. And not just any kiss, this was a 'knock your socks off, ruin you for any other man' kiss." "Wow." "Wow about sums it up. Things got hot and heavy fast. Before either of us knew it, my top was on the floor, and he was playing with my breasts and . . ." She looked at Amanda. "Don't stop on my account," she said, smiling. "I couldn't breathe, let alone think." "Thinking's overrated." "You sound like him." "Then what happened?" "Then Emily called us down for breakfast." "Damn." "It was after that that he told me he loved me." "What did you say?" "That I love him, just not the same way." "What about now?" "I'd say I'm definitely in the falling stages." "That's the best time. Not being able to keep your hands off each another, all the great sex." "I assume you're remembering a similar time with a certain foreman of mine?" "You assume correctly." "So I have to ask because I've always thought Hanson to be someone who'd be quite capable in the bedroom." "Sabrina!" "What? I mean he's in good shape, has strong hands." Amanda shook her head, smiling. "Oh come on, I just told you about Ross fondling my breasts." She laughed. "All right, yes, he knows how to use his hands. And he's a great kisser." "I knew it." She looked at the fish she was grilling. "Well, looks like the fish is done." She plated it with couscous and zucchini. "Wow, this looks wonderful. You really didn't have to go to all this trouble." "Nonsense. It's been ages since I've had a friend over." "It's been a long time since I've been called that." "What? Friend?" "Yes." "I hope I'm not overstepping here, but it seems like you could really use one." "I really can." "Well then, friend, let's eat."

Hanson sat on the hood of his truck, waiting for Charlie. It was going on twenty minutes, and he wasn't out yet. He heard rattling and saw him racing a flatbed toward him. "Sorry, man, Tom pulled me to help Mrs. Daughtry do something." "What? Search for Sammy?" "No, but that dog of hers couldn't get any dumber." Hanson grinned. "I know it irks Ross to no end." At the mention of his idol, his face brightened. "You know he broke up a fight here a couple of weeks ago, right?" "I heard something about it." "It was awesome. These two guys were going at it because one of them had tried to pick up the other's girlfriend." "Idiot," Hanson said. "I know, right? I mean, lame doesn't begin to cover it. Anyway, neither one would listen, so he tossed one of them into that barrel. It was so cool." "I'm sure it was a sight to see." "Definitely was." Charlie started loading up the truck. "Let me give you a hand." "Thanks, appreciate it." "Not a problem." When they finished, he tipped him. "Thanks, Hanson." "You're welcome." "See you next time."

Sabrina and Amanda were enjoying their fish. "So do you want to talk about what happened earlier?" "It's a long story." "We've got all afternoon." "Okay. After I left, I ended up in New York. I figured I had a good chance there. I arrived with little money and big dreams. I got a job waitressing to pay the bills. The pay wasn't great, but it was enough to get me a furnished room not far from Times Square." "That makes sense since all the theaters are nearby." "Exactly. I hustled and got some callbacks for Off-Broadway. One day, I was on my way to another callback, and while crossing the street, I realized that I was in the direct path of an oncoming taxi. I remember closing my eyes and thinking that I was about to die." "What happened?" "I was pushed out of the way and landed on the ground, hitting my head in the process. When I awoke I was in emergency with a mild concussion. The nurse told me that a Good Samaritan had saved me. Our story was the talk of the ER. He had also been injured but would be okay. I told the nurse I wanted to thank him. She said she'd arrange it. Sometime later, a good-looking guy peeked from behind my curtain." "Let me guess, Sam." "Yes. We got to talking and hit it off right away." "The next day he showed up when I was being released and took me home. After that, we became good friends. Thinking back, I don't know where I would be today if he hadn't helped me." "Did he know about Hanson and Scott?" "Yes, I told him. He never judged me about it. Though he did think I should have contacted them." "How long were you friends?" "A couple of years. After a while, we moved in together." "Oh?" "Rents being what they were, it just made sense, so I moved into his place. We respected each other's privacy, and it worked out well." "Did you ever think that he wanted more?" "He went on dates, so I didn't really give a second thought." "Maybe he was trying to get over a certain someone."

"An astute observation." "Yeah, too bad I wasn't as astute when it came to Ross." "I found out how Sam felt when it was too late." "What do you mean too late?" "He told me before—" "Before what?" She got up and went to the window. Sabrina heard her take a deep breath. "Before he died." She stood, speechless. "He had been feeling tired a lot, exhausted even. When he finally went to his doctor, they told him he had cancer." "I don't know what to say." "Neither did I when he told me." How long?" "Not long enough." "Before he died he told me he loved me. That he had fallen in love with me that day in the hospital." "Oh how sad." "He was the best friend I've ever had." She wiped away her tears with the back of her hand. "You said Sam saved you. You weren't just talking about that taxi. Were you?" "No. Sam was the one who finally got my depression diagnosed. He had a friend who was a physiatrist. He couldn't believe that I had been dealing with depression, waitressing and performing. He prescribed some meds, and I began to feel better almost immediately. It's funny, but I never realized just how bad I felt until I began feeling better." "Well, I think depression grows steadily worse the longer it's left untreated." "Yes, that's what he told me. I'd wake up every day drained and my entire body aching. I felt like an old woman. It was horrible." "I'm glad he finally convinced you to see someone." "So am I." "I think after that we need some dessert. Pear tarts okay?" "Pear tarts sound great. Sabrina?" "Yes?" Thanks for not judging me." "Why would I do that? We've all made mistakes." "I'm so glad we met." "Me too."

Hanson got out of his truck and yelled into the barn for the guys. Max, Pete, Dave, and Riley came out. "You guys want to help me unload?" "Sure." "Get started, I'll be right back." He walked to the house and knocked. "Come in." He found them sitting at the kitchen counter, eating pear tarts and sipping tea. "Well, you look a whole lot better." "Thanks, I feel better." "Glad to hear it. Sabrina, I have the guys unloading the stuff I got from Tom." "Great, thanks. Could I interest you in a tart?" "I thought you'd never ask." She smiled. "Can I get it to go? I need to help the guys." "Sure, I'll wrap it for you." She got up and went into the cabinet. He looked at Amanda intently. So intently she felt herself blush. "You know, you took ten years off my life earlier." "I'm sorry. I'm fine now." "Glad as I am to hear it. We still need to finish that conversation." "I'll come see you before I leave." "I'll be waiting." "Here you go, enjoy." "Thanks." Amanda watched him walk out. His backside did make a nice exit. She looked at Sabrina who had obviously caught her staring. "I've always thought he had a nice butt myself." They both laughed.

A while later, Sabrina was walking Amanda out. "This was a lot of fun. We must do it again. But next time, I'll take you out for lunch, since I don't want you cooking every time I visit." "Oh I don't mind. I like to cook." "Sam liked to cook too. God, I miss him so much sometime." "I'm sorry, Amanda." "He died over a year ago, and I still haven't changed the message on the machine. It still says Amanda *and Sam.*" "That's why you fainted. Hanson wanted to know who Sam was." "Yes. Scott left a message and he heard it. He must have told him." "So Hanson thinks you're *with* Sam." "Most likely." "So was it Sam's death that finally made you contact Hanson?" "You're good you know that." "It's a gift." She smiled. "Sam was after me to contact him for years, but I refused. Once I got my depression under control, I began seriously considering it. Then Sam got sick and—" "And that was that." "Until he died. That's when I realized that life is too short and that I had to at least try." "I'm glad you did." "So am I." Sabrina hugged her and heard the phone ringing. "I've got to get that. Could be Nico." "Go, we'll talk soon."

Sabrina grabbed the phone. "Hello?" she said, a bit out of breath. "Oh am I interrupting a clandestine moment with your sheriff?" "No, I was just running for the phone." "What a pity. Anyway, I'm calling because Pony Express just delivered your sketches." She ignored his sarcasm. "And?" "*And* they're fantabulous." "You weren't put off by the sashes?" "At first, but then they began to grow on me. Sashes are different. They aren't belts and not exactly scarves." "That was my thinking too." So I'm going to show these to a few clients who are coming in this week. I think they might be interested in wearing them to the Guggenheim Fundraiser this summer." "Wow, I didn't think you'd be showing them this fast." "Why not? They're fresh, new, and scream 'wear me.' Anyway, I need to run. I have a meeting." "Thanks, Nico." "Honey, you do not have to thank me. Ta-ta." "Ta-ta, Nico."

Amanda walked into the barn to find Hanson and the guys arranging the bags of feed. "Careful, Dave, you might break a nail." "Screw you, Pete." Hanson was grinning, when he turned around and saw Amanda. "Gentlemen, we have a lady present, so watch the language." Riley caught sight of her and let go of a bag of fertilizer, which almost landed on Steve's foot. "What the fuck, man?" Hanson looked at him. "Sooorry." "It's okay. I curse when I'm pissed too." Riley stood next to her now. "And what a sight that must be, all fire and smoke coming from those eyes." Hanson had to agree. He'd seen Amanda mad, and she was definitely fire and smoke. "Hey, Finn, flirt on your own time," Pete said. "I'm taking my union ten." "We aren't union," Max said. "I believe she's here to speak to *me*," Hanson said. Riley looked from Hanson to Amanda and back to Hanson. "Can't blame a guy for trying." "I can't but Sam sure could. And aren't you in hot enough water as it is?" Hanson said trying not to grin. "That's a low blow." Riley said. "Looks like my break is over." She laughed. "Boys, I'll be at my place if anyone needs me for anything," Hanson said.

After they left, the guys started talking. "So could you be any more desperate hitting on her?" "I wasn't hitting on her. I was just being friendly." "Yes, *very* friendly," Pete said sarcastically. "Besides, I don't go after women who are already taken," Riley said. "Taken? By who?" Dave asked. "Can you be that clueless?" Pete said. "Huh?" "Anyone with eyes can see the boss is still crazy about her." Dave looked at him, then the others. They all nodded. "The air crackles anytime they're around each other," Riley said. "You think they'll end up together again?" Steve asked. "Not sure. There's a lot of water under that bridge," Max said. "Maybe too much," Riley said.

Chapter Nineteen

Amanda and Hanson sat at the kitchen table. "Can I get you something to drink?" "Normally I'd say no, but I could use some wine." "You still a fan of reds?" "Yes." "How's a nice Pinot Noir sound?" "Perfect." He got out a bottle, uncorked it, and poured it into two wine glasses. "Manda, if you don't want to tell me about Sam, you don't have to." She nodded and he took sip of wine. "Listen, I'm sorry if I was pushing earlier. I didn't mean to. It's just when Scott told me about the message I got—" "Jealous? Is that what you want to hear?" "Yes. No. I don't know." She sipped her wine now. "Are you sure you're ready to hear this?" "As ready as I'll ever be." "I met Sam in New York when he saved my life." "What?" "I wasn't paying attention while crossing the street, and the next thing I know, I was being shoved out of the way of a speeding taxi. When I woke up I was in emergency." "You're damn lucky to be alive." "Don't I know it. That's when the nurse told me that someone had pushed me out of the way and had sustained some minor injuries in the process. I asked to meet him, so I could thank him." "Let me guess, Sam?" "Yes, over time we became friends." "Friends?" "Yes, *friends*. Nothing ever happened between us. Even though we did end up living together for a time." He felt jealous of a man he'd never even met. "That must have been cozy." She frowned. "It wasn't like that, Hanson. He dated women." "What about you? Did you date men?" "No, I never met anyone who could compare to . . ." She let her words drop off. "So obviously you still live with him." She could feel herself choking up. "No," she said in a lower voice. "Then why is he still in your message? Why didn't you change it?" "Because Sam died from cancer. I haven't been able to change the message. He stood in shock. "'Manda—" "I need some air." She stood on the porch, staring at the setting sun. "Manda, I—" "When Sam died, I lost my best friend. Not a day goes by that I don't miss him." "I know what that's like. I still miss James." "I'm sorry he died so young." "Me too." They stood there quiet for a few minutes. "I'm sorry Manda. I didn't mean to be a jerk, it's just—" "You thought we were together." "Yeah." "Well, we weren't." "Excuse me, but I'm finding it real hard to believe that a man could live with a woman and not have feelings for her." "You always did have good instincts. Sam did have feelings for me. I, on the other hand, never did." "That must have been hard on him?" "I never knew just how hard until he got sick. There was never any reason for me to think anything. He never said anything." "He wouldn't have. He was probably afraid he'd lose you if he did." "How did you find out?" "He told me, when he got sick." She was crying now. He turned her so she faced him. He used his fingers to wipe away her tears. "I'm sorry you lost him. Sounds like he was a good guy." "He was. He was always after me to contact you. Before he died, he really pushed for it. He'd get mad when I didn't. Said I was as stubborn as a mule." "I'd have to agree." "I wanted to come back. I did. You don't know how many times I picked up the phone to call but then . . ." "Then?" "Then, I'd get cold feet. I figured you'd just hang up." "I probably would have." "You'd have had every right to if you did." "You hurt me, Manda. Real deep." She closed her eyes. "I know. I'm not going to say I'm sorry anymore because it just seems so inadequate a word." "So how did you end up in New York?" "After I left, I sang at various places and saved as much money as I could. When I finally had enough saved, I decided New York was the place to go." "Makes sense since Broadway is there." "Yes, but I never made it. I only worked Off-Broadway." "I'm sorry." "Why are you sorry?" "Because I hoped that you hadn't left in vain. That at least something good would have come out of all of it." "You mean after what I did, you still wanted me to make it?" "As crazy as it sounds, yes. I loved you." She felt herself coming undone. "Oh, Hanson." She started crying and the tears just kept coming. It seemed the floodgates had opened, and she was crying eleven years' worth of tears. Seeing her this way nearly broke his heart. All he could do was take her into his arms and hold her while she cried.

It seemed like she had been crying forever. He sat holding her while she wept. "Manda, honey, I'm going to pick you up and carry you inside. Okay?" She merely nodded. He pulled her to him and lifted her up with ease. He brought her into Scott's room and laid her on the bed. Her sobs seemed to be easing. "Be right back." He went to the kitchen, refilled her wine glass, and brought it to her. "Here drink this." She sat up and sipped. He sat on the edge of the bed, looking at her. Most women looked like hell after crying, but not her. Without saying a word, she handed the empty glass back to him. "I don't think you should drive back in the shape you're in." "I'll be fine. Just need to pull myself together. I'm sorry I came apart like that." "No need to apologize. Rest for a bit. You can drive back later." She did feel drained all of a sudden. "All right, I'm too tired to argue." "That'd be a first," he said, trying to coax a smile from her. The corners of her mouth turned up slightly. "Rest. I'll be back in a bit." She lay down, promising herself that she would only rest for half an hour, but the minute her head hit the pillow, she was out. He stood watching her sleep, and for the first time was jealous of a pillow.

Hanson went to go talk to Sabrina, who was in her office. "Having fun?" he asked. "Oh yeah, a ball." He smiled. "Amanda told me about Sam." "Good, I'm glad. Since it seemed to be weighing heavily on her." "She started crying and didn't stop until she ran out of tears." "Poor thing. Sounds like it's been a long time coming." "I know the feeling," he said. "Are *you* okay?" "Sure. Why?" "You just listened to your ex-wife talk about her life after she left you. Couldn't have been easy hearing it." "It wasn't, but once she started crying, I just—" "Melted?" "In a way, yeah." "Did she leave?" "No, I didn't think she should drive like that. So she's resting in Scott's room." "I think that's a good idea. So now that you know, does it change anything for you?" "You mean how I feel?" "Yes." "No." "I see. Hanson—" "Look, Sabrina, about what I said earlier." "You mean when you said you still loved her?" "Yeah."

"What about it?" "I don't want her to know." "Why not? Maybe if you worked through the issues, you could try again." "I doubt it." She came very close to telling him the reason Amanda left. *No, it's not my secret to tell.* "Hanson, you know I love you, right?" He felt himself blush slightly at her sentiment. "Sure." "So please hear me out, since I have your best interests at heart." "All right." "I think what Amanda told you about Sam is only part of the story. I think there's *more*." He looked at her. "You mean you *know* there's more." "Fine, I know there's more. When the time is right, she'll tell you the rest. Trust me when I say she's had a rough time." "She's not the only one."

Riley sat by the phone. He knew he had to call Sam and beg like a dog for a bone, but he did have his pride after all. *Screw pride.* He picked up and dialed her number. After five rings, the machine picked up. *Crap, she's screening.* "Sam, it's Riley." Nothing. "Sam, pick up." Still nothing. "Fine, I'm calling to apologize. I've never felt jealous before, and that's the God's honest truth. It threw me. I'm sorry for being a jerk. I hope you'll want to call me back because I miss you." After he hung up the phone, he sat there looking at it. This would be something else he'd never done before. *Wait.*

Hanson checked on Amanda who was out like a light. He looked down at her and watched the peaceful rise and fall of her chest. *Why did you have to leave? I loved you, so much. It hurt like a bitch. Still does.* She stirred, and he knelt down next to her and lightly touched her cheek with his fingers. *So soft. Like silk.* He got up, closed the door, and went into the kitchen. He'd just let her sleep. She could go back in the morning.

Later, after he had showered, he turned to see her standing in his doorway. "Hey, Sleeping Beauty." "Hi. How long was I out?" "Couple of hours." "I thought you were going to wake me?" "Seemed like a better idea to let you sleep." She tried not to focus on the fact that he was only wearing a towel. "What time is it?" "Near ten." "I need to get going." "You can't mean to say you're going to drive home now?" "Sure. Why not?" "How about because just a few hours ago you were an emotional wreck?" "Key words in that sentence, *a few hours ago*." She stressed the last part. "Doesn't matter. No way are you driving home tonight. I won't let you." "Excuse me? You won't *let* me? I don't recall asking your permission. I come and go as I please." "That's pretty damn obvious." "You know I'm getting pretty damn tired of you always throwing that up in my face every time you get pissed." "So don't get me pissed." She shook her head. "Were you born this big a pain in the ass?" "Most likely." He grinned. "Seriously, please don't drive tonight. Stay in Scott's room. Go back in the morning when you're fresh." She was having a hard time focusing on anything but his chest, which was covered in tiny water droplets that glistened in the soft light coming from the lamp. *God, he looks good enough to eat.* "Manda? Did you hear what I said." "Yeah, sorry. All right, I'll stay. "Good, you'll need something to sleep in. I'm sure one of Scott's jerseys will do the trick." He searched through several drawers. "I swear, I don't know how that boy finds anything." "I'm sure he has his own system." He looked at her. "Yeah, then just toss it in the drawer system." She laughed. He finally found one. "This okay?" "Yes, thanks." As he handed it to her, their fingers brushed and sparks flew. "I'd better go wash up," she said, wanting to get out of there before she made a fool of herself. "Sure. 'Night, Amanda." "'Night, Hanson."

He lay in bed unable to sleep because he couldn't stop seeing her in that jersey. *Should have let her sleep in her own clothes.* He glanced at the clock and got up. Maybe some warm milk would help. Who was he kidding? That wouldn't help. He walked quietly into the kitchen and got out a small pot to heat the milk in. As he did, the door to Scott's room opened and Amanda came out. "Did I wake you?" She shook her head. "No, I couldn't sleep. Probably because I slept too long before. *Or because I kept imagining licking those water droplets off your chest.* "You can't sleep either?" "No." "Why?" *Because I kept imagining you in that goddamn jersey and nothing else."* "Probably just wired from all the excitement today. I'm heating up some milk. Want some?" "Sure, why not." She sat while he heated up the milk. He was staring at her legs, which he imagined wrapped around him. He handed her the milk and sat down. "Something's missing," she said. He knew just what she meant. He got up and took something out of the cabinet and placed it in front of her. "Oreos! My favorite." "I know." "I thought you didn't like them?" "I don't, they're Scott's." "He has good taste in cookies." She took a cookie, pulled it apart, began licking its creamy center. He couldn't help looking at her tongue and imagining it licking other things. "You still eat them that way, I see." "There's only one way to eat an Oreo and *this is it*." He laughed. "What? Why are you laughing?" "Because Scott eats them the same way and says the same thing." "Really? Must be genetic." "Must be." She finished the cookie and pulled out another. He wasn't sure how much more he could take. "Well, I'm feeling tired, I think I'll turn in." "Okay, I'm still not tired, so I'll just savor some more cookies." *I'd like to savor you.* 'Night." "'Night." He went into his room, shut the door, and let out a long, hard breath. *When did eating Oreos become so erotic?* He lay down and tried to sleep, and sometime later she knocked and came in. She stood in the doorway then began walking toward the bed. She didn't speak, but her eyes told him all he needed to know. "Manda." She got on top of him. "I've been thinking about this ever since you kissed me that day." "Me too." "I wanted to jump you, earlier," she said, making him laugh. "Why the heck didn't you?" "I didn't think you wanted me." He took her hand and placed it on his manhood. "*That* is how much I want you." "Hanson?" "Yeah?" "Can you please just be kissing me now?" He took her mouth, and she tasted like cookies and cream. "You taste like dessert." "Then eat me." He flipped her on her back, and they both reached for the jersey at the same time, pulling it off. He looked at her now-exposed breasts and touched them gently. "God, they're even more amazing than I remember." He savored each nipple with his tongue. "So long. It's been so long and it feels soo good," she said. "It's going to feel even better real soon." He worked his way down and started eating her just as she had eaten that Oreo. "You still know how to use your tongue." "Just like riding a bicycle." She laughed. "I've missed you." "Me too." He continued until she screamed his name in ecstasy. Then he positioned himself on top and reached into the nightstand for a condom. "What the f*uck*?" "What?" "You aren't going to believe this." "No condom?" "No condom." "Please tell me you're on the pill?" "No." "Damn it!" "Sorry, I haven't been with anyone, so there's been no need." "It's okay, I may have an idea." He got up and went into Scott's room." She followed him in. "What are you doing?" "Looking for condoms. He's a twenty-something-year-old guy. He's got to have them somewhere." She laughed. "Aha! Found 'em." "Thank goodness." "I can't believe I had to raid my son's nightstand for rubbers." She laughed. "Neither can I." He looked at her. "It's been a while, since I needed them." "I understand." He got back into bed with her. "God, you are so beautiful." "You always could make me believe that." "Because it's true. Come here, beautiful." She went to him and they melted into each other's arms.

Sam was still in bed when she heard knocking at her door. She looked through the peephole and saw Riley standing there with flowers. She opened the door. "Sam." "Riley. What are you doing here?" "I was in the neighborhood and wanted to bring you these." "They're nice." *Nice?* "They're from the florist." "Okay, so they're *really* nice," she said sarcastically. "I called you last night." "I know." "I left a message." "I know." "A really nice message." I listened to it." *This is going well. Not.* "What did you think?" "Of what?" "Of what I said." "It was okay." "It would have been better if I had gotten you instead of the damn machine." "I doubt that." *Ooookay.* "Look, I'm trying here." "I know." "Could you please stop saying that." She almost smiled. "You gonna put those in water or throw them out?" "I'll give them a drink. After all, they're innocent," she said, walking away. "Unlike me. Right?" "Look, Riley, I don't want to fight." "Good that makes two of us." She filled a vase with water. "You acted like a real jerk the other day." "I know, and I admitted that in my message." She put the flowers in the vase. "Look, I acted like a jealous jerk, and I'm sorry. That's all I can say. The rest is up to you." He started walking out. "Wait." He turned back around. "I'm afraid," she said, before she could stop herself. "Me too but maybe we'd both be less afraid together." He looked at her, she at him, and then they rushed into each other's arms. "This is crazy, Sam. I haven't been able to sleep since our fight," he said, while smothering her with kisses. "Me either." "I promise I'll work on the whole jealous thing." "I don't mind you getting jealous. I just mind you being an ass." He smiled. "I promise to work on my ass." She laughed. "I'm sorry too. The way I acted with Brad was wrong." "So we good?" She smiled. "We're good." "What time is class?" "A little over an hour." "Hmmm, doesn't give us a whole lot of time." "I'm up for the challenge if you are." He looked down at his jeans. "Oh I'm up for it." They laughed.

Chapter Twenty

Sam and Riley maximized their time by taking a shower together. The water wasn't the only thing heating things up. As they stood there, he turned her around so that her soapy backside faced him. He spread her arms on the shower wall and entered her from behind. She thought she'd die from the sheer pleasure it gave her. "I don't think I'll be able to last long. You've got me way too turned on." "It's okay, I feel like I'm nearing the finish line myself." He kissed her neck as he pumped into her. She turned around, and he kissed her breasts and played with her nipples. She wrapped one leg around him, and the angle had his strokes hitting her G-spot. It was unlike anything she'd ever felt. The pressure continued to build until she felt an explosion of ecstasy. She nearly collapsed, but he held her up while he himself came tumbling down after her. When they were toweling off, he looked at her. "What?" "That wasn't your run-of-the mill orgasm." "Nope. Congratulations, handsome, you found the fabled G-spot." "G-spot? I thought that was a myth?" She laughed. "Nope, it exists." "Well, I'll be damned." She got dressed and was getting her books together. He had put his jeans back on but not his shirt. "Hmmm, I do love the way you look in jeans." "I thought you liked me in nothing?" "Oh I do. A girl can like more than one look on her man." "Your man?" "Just an expression. Forget I said it." She was trying to run out the door. "Sam, wait." "I have to go. I'm already late." "Hold up a sec. Is that how you feel?" She hesitated. "'Cause if you do, it's okay because I consider you *my* girl." She couldn't help but smile. "You do realize how ironic this whole thing is?" He grinned. "Believe me, I do." "So okay then. You're my man." "And you're my woman." They both smiled. "I've gotta go," she said. "I can't stay, gorgeous, I've got things to do." "It's okay. Call me later?" "Try and stop me." He grabbed her and planted the hottest, most mind-searing kiss on her lips. "That ought to hold you till I get back here again." "And if not, there's always phone sex." "Oh I looove the way you think." "I know. Later, handsome." Just like that, she was gone. He stood thinking about that phone call and grinned widely.

Hanson and Amanda lay tangled in the sheets. "That was . . ." she said. "It sure was," he said. "I feel so relaxed," she said. "Me too," he said. "In fact, I haven't been this relaxed in years," she joked, making him laugh. "I guess we're relaxed enough to sleep now." "Definitely." He held her, and they fell asleep that way. When she woke up, she was alone but feeling great. They had made love twice more, and each time was better than the last. She got up and looked at herself in the mirror. She looked like a well-satisfied woman. Her lips slightly swollen, hair messy, and her face flushed with color. She put the jersey back on and walked into the kitchen. That's when she saw the note on the table.

'Manda,

Had some chores to take care of. Be back soon.

Hanson

She was in such a good mood she decided to make breakfast. She opened the fridge and noted that there wasn't a whole lot in it. She did manage to find a couple of eggs, some cheese, and bread for toast. "It's not fancy but it'll do." She beat the eggs and added milk to make them creamier. After searching his cabinets for plates and silverware, she set the table. She didn't want to cook the eggs until he got back so she decided to shower. While she was rinsing herself off, she thought about their night together. She could almost feel his lips on her body, and she shuddered. Then she heard the door open, and he peeked from behind the curtain. "Mornin'." He was grinning from ear to ear. "Morning." "Sorry I had to leave, but there were some things that needed to be done that couldn't wait." "I noticed you set the table." "Yes, I thought I'd make us breakfast before I leave." "You're going to cook?" She rolled her eyes. "Don't sound so surprised. I do cook you know." "Sure, whenever you are being forced at gunpoint." She laughed. "Oh stop, I cooked when we were together." "Manda, Eggos don't count." She laughed. "Sure they do. Besides, I'm in such a good mood, I don't care." He shrugged. "I won't complain since I'm usually the one to do the cooking around here." "Really? Because your fridge was pretty empty." "Always is after hurricane Scott blows through. That boy eats me out of house and home." "How do cheese omelets sound?" He grabbed her face and gave it a lip-smacking kiss. "Sounds delicious." She dried herself off, put the jersey on, and walked into the kitchen. He stared at her. "What?" "Ah, if you want to actually eat, you'd better put something else on." She looked down at herself. "Why?" "If you have to ask, then I guess I didn't do a good enough job last night." "Believe me, I have no complaints about last night," she said, smiling. "Good, but you still need to change." She went into Scott's room, put her clothes on, and came back out. "Better?" "Much."

They sat at the table and enjoyed their omelets. "Best omelet I've had in a long time." "I'm glad you enjoyed it." She stood up and started to clear the table. He touched her hand. "I'll clean up." They stood that way, still feeling the electricity between them even after spending most of the night making love. "I'd better get going. "All right." So I ah . . . I guess I'll . . ." "It's okay, Hanson. You don't have to say anything. Just kiss me good-bye." They kissed until they were both forced to come up for air. "I've . . . got . . . to . . . go." "I know. I just can't get enough of those lips." "Me either." They kissed again. This time he pulled away. "Okay, okay. You need to leave. *Now.* Otherwise I won't be responsible for what I do next." She licked her lips." "Please *don't* do that," he said, sounding almost as if he was in pain. She smiled. "Sorry. I'm going." She grabbed her purse, jacket, and ran out the door. He stood in the doorway and watched her walk to her car. She looked back and waved before getting inside. He watched as the trail of dust grew faint.

Riley pulled in as Amanda left. "So how did things go with Sam?" "We're good." "I'm glad." Riley was grinning at him. "What the hell are you grinning at?" "I think you know." "Why don't you enlighten me?" "Well, let's see. It's noon, and Amanda was leaving, so either she got here real early or she stayed overnight. Plus you have that 'I just got laid' look." "*Careful, Riley.*" "Hey, I mean no disrespect to you or Amanda. I'm just stating facts. So you two back together?" "No just seeing where things go." "Hmm." "Hmm, what?" "Just that you sound like Sam and me when we first hooked up. We were all just take it as it comes, it's no big deal. The truth was we were both full of shit." "So you're saying Amanda and I are full of shit?" "Yep." Hanson laughed in spite of himself. "*Plus* you have a history together *and* a son. Speaking of Scott. What are you going to tell him?" "I don't see why we have to tell him anything. We're both adults. Neither one of us has to clear who we sleep with." "I didn't say you did. It's just he's not an idiot. He's going to figure it out eventually." "Yeah, but by then whatever this thing is will have run its course." "Run its course? You wish. Listen, you're calling her by a nickname, which I assume is from when you were together before. Believe me this thing is *not* going away." Hanson rolled his eyes. Even though deep down he knew Riley was right.

Scott sat in class doodling what his center would look like. He wanted something he and Emily could be proud of. Wow, had he just envisioned a future with Em in it? *Riley's right. I'm as gone as he is.* He mumbled to himself. "Mr. Pierce, would you care to enlighten us." "I'm sorry, Mr. Brady. What?" "Would you care to enlighten myself and your classmates as to what it is that has your attention so focused." "Nothing, just doodling." The class laughed. "I see. Well, don't let us stop your artistic moment." "Thanks, I won't." He joked. Mr. Brady's face soured. He walked back toward him and grabbed the drawing from him. "What is this?" "An equestrian center. Well, at least it will be one day. I plan on opening one." "I had no idea you were so ambitious since you hardly ever show any ambition in here. While your goal is admirable, Mr. Pierce, could you perhaps focus your attention on the here and now." "Yes." "Good. I will hold on to this until class is over. You may reclaim it then." Scott frowned at him behind his back. "Man, you're lucky he didn't write you up," John said. "Nah, he's all bark, no bite." "Think so?" John said. "Mr. Ryder, is there something you'd like to share with the class?" "No." "Good, then let's get on with today's lesson."

After class, Scott walked up to Mr. Brady's desk. "Ah, Mr. Pierce. I assume you'd like your drawing back?" "Yes." He handed it to him. "You know, I must say it looks to be very impressive if you succeed in doing it. I enjoy horses myself." "You do?" Scott asked, sounding surprised. "Don't sound so surprised, I do have a life outside this academia." *Could have fooled me.* "Believe it or not, I hope you do succeed, Mr. Pierce." "Thanks, Mr. Brady. You're okay in my book." Brady looked at him and blinked. "Well, I'm glad you think so, Mr. Pierce. I'll sleep better knowing that fact. Good day." Scott walked out and bumped into John. "What the—" "Just making sure you didn't get your balls handed to you by Mr. Happy." He smirked. "Mr. Happy? I like that." "Thanks. I just came up with it. "So what happened?" "Nothing. He was just busting balls. He actually said he likes horses." "Well, color me shocked. I didn't think he liked anything," John joked. "I know. I'm hungry. Let's go get some lunch." Sometime later, they sat in the cafeteria, eating burgers. "So you never did tell me what went down with your mom." "That's right I didn't." "Sarcastic much?" "Sorry, it's just a touchy subject." "I'm sure it is. When you're ready, I'm here." "Thanks." They ate in silence for a bit. "So you and Emily?" "Haven't we already had this conversation?" "No, we had a half-assed conversation where your friend told me you were with her." "He's not my friend. He's just . . . hell, I don't know what he is." "Sure, whatever you say. So what gives?" "With?" "Emily." He said nothing. "Come on, Scott. Throw me a bone." "Why should I?" "Because I haven't gotten any." "And whose fault is that? If your relationships went beyond a month you, might just get some." "Stop acting like a dick and tell me." "Fine, if it will shut you up." John made the motion of zipping his lips. Scott told him the whole story. The dinner, the dress, the kiss, everything. He sat there, mouth gaping. "You gonna say anything anytime soon?" "Yeah, how did you get someone that hot?" Scott gave him a shove. "I'm kidding. I know how you got her. I opened up my big fat mouth. That's how." "Yeah, thanks for helping me see the light, man." "Yeah, sure, that's what friends are for. And if you start singing that song, I swear I will smack you." He grinned. "You know me so well, John." "I do. So just how crazy about her are you?" "She's all that, a bag of chips, *plus* dip." John laughed hard. "So it's safe to say you are completely gone over her." "*Completely*. I've never felt this way about anyone." "I believe you. What's it like?" "Amazing and scary at the same time." "Sounds intense." "It is but so worth it." "Yeah. See, I can never get past the fear." "You know what, John? One day you'll meet someone who'll make you want to stop running." "Maybe." "So you getting psyched about graduation?" He smiled. "Are you kidding? I can't wait." "I know, me too. Three months can't go fast enough."

Chapter Twenty-One

Two weeks to graduation

Scott finished packing and looked around the room. You would never know two guys had lived here for four years. All that remained were his six boxes. His roommate, Ted, the one who liked classical music, was already gone. They had exchanged numbers and promised to stay in touch. Scott grew to like him very much. It was because of him that Scott had a new appreciation for classical music, well, at least for some of it. He had done well in all his courses and was even getting an achievement award. He knew it would make his dad proud. His thoughts shifted to his mother. Should he invite her to graduation? On one hand he felt she didn't deserve to be there, while on the other, she had been trying really hard to make things up to him as best she could. He'd have to give it some more thought. One thing he was sure of was that there was something going on between his parents. Whenever he brought one up to the other, they got weird. Most likely because they were sleeping together. He wasn't sure how he felt about that either. "One thing at a time." "See what happens when I'm not around? You start talking to yourself." He turned around to see Riley grinning. "Hey, you're late." "Yeah, sorry. Four-car accident on I-81." "Yeah, I figured. Anyway, I'm all packed and ready to go." Riley looked at the boxes. “You sure got a lot of shit for a guy.” “And for a guy, you sure talk a lot of shit.” He grinned. “Man, I hate to admit this, but I missed busting your balls.” “Well, call me crazy, but I think I missed you busting ‘em.” “Um, are we having a moment?” Riley asked. “Yeah, and it’s totally freaking me out.” He laughed.

They were on their way back, and as usual, Riley was driving above the speed limit. “You better slow down. Unless you want to get a ticket.” “You sound like your dad. That night we dropped you off he was all, ‘Slow down or you’re going to get us killed.’” “How fast were you going?” “Near a hundred but I told him eighty.” He grinned. “We talked about your mom.” “Oh?” “Yeah, he’s got it bad for her. You know that, right?” “Yeah, I’ve been thinking that. I mean, whenever I bring her up, he gets weird. So does she.” He looked at him. “Don’t expect me to confirm anything.” “I wasn’t asking you to.” “Speaking of your mom, are you going to invite her to cap-and-gown day?” “I’m thinking about it.” “Yeah? Well, think faster. It’s two weeks away. Mind if I put in my two cents?” “I won’t bother saying no ’cause you’ll just say it anyway.” “So true. I think you should invite her. She missed a lot when you were growing up.” “And whose fault is that?” “Hers.” “I hear a *but* coming.” “*But* I don’t think this should be added to the list.” “I hate to admit it, but you’re probably right.” “’Course I’m right. I’m always right.” Scott just rolled his eyes.

When they got back, Ross was getting out of his squad car. “Hey, Scott, back already?” “He’s *baaaaaack*.” Scott looked at Riley. “You’re an idiot.” “Takes one to know one.” Ross looked at them. “Nice to see nothing’s changed. So, Scott, soon you’ll be donning your cap and gown.” “That’s right, and getting my award.” “Award?” “Yeah, some achievement thing.” “Well, now that’s something to be proud of.” Does your dad know?” “No, I want him to be surprised.” “I’ll keep it to myself.” “Thanks, Ross.” “Now if you’ll excuse me, I’m gonna go see my lady.” They watched as he practically skipped to the house. “Maybe your friend John’s right. Maybe there is something in the water here.”

Sabrina was in her office with the door partially closed. He peeked in and saw that she was on the phone, looking annoyed. “Yes, I understand, Mr. Peters. No, that’s not the way we do business. I’m sorry you feel that way. If you change your mind, please call. Good day.” She hung up and wanted to throw something. "Looks like I picked the right time for a visit." She looked up and tried her best to smile. "Oh boy, it's worse than I thought. What did Peters do this time?" "He complained that the milk he received was not fresh." "That's bullshit." "I know. I was this close to telling him that." "Why didn't you? We don't need his shitty attitude or his business." "We?" "That's right. We. Let me call that asswipe back and tell him a thing or two." She looked at him. "What?" "I love it when you get all tough. It's very sexy." He put his arms around her. "Really? Well, allow me to continue being sexy." "Please do." He kissed her and the air sizzled. "Ross." "Yeah?" "I have to finish this." "Sometimes you are such a joy kill." "I'm sorry. How about if I said I'll make it up to you?" "Well, that would depend on the how." "Well, I don't want to spoil it, but let's just say it involves the phone and some naughty talk." "Honey, you'll have me at hello." She laughed.

Scott and Riley were just about finished putting everything in its place. Hanson walked in and stared. "What the hell is *that*?" He was pointing to an oddly shaped chair. "A chair." "Chair? Looks like a damn lima bean." Riley's mouth twitched. "That's why they call it a beanbag chair, Dad." "Stupidest thing I've ever seen." "Maybe, but it's comfortable as hell," Riley said while sitting in it." "Scott, I'm gonna get going. I told Max I'd help him when I got back." "Sure. Thanks for the ride and help unpacking." "Not a problem. Later."

After he left, Hanson decided this was a good time to talk to him about inviting Amanda. "Scott, I want to talk to you about something." "Okay." "It's about graduation." "What about it?" "I wanted to know if you're going to invite your mother." "I haven't decided yet." "Okay, well, it's in two weeks." "I know, Dad." "Look, I'm as confused about all this as you are." "Could have fooled me." "What's that supposed to mean?" "Do I have to spell it out?" "I think you should." "Fine. There's something going on between the two of you. Isn't there?" "Yes." "I knew it. Why didn't you tell me?" "Because, first of all, we're both adults. And second, it's really nobody's business." "How long?" "Since you went back to school." "Wow, you didn't waste any time." "Scott—" "No, I mean I had a feeling that you were back together but—" "Technically, we aren't." "What?" "Back together." "Oh so you're just fucking?" Hanson's face grew angry. "You're upset, which is the only reason why I'm not knocking you on your ass right now. I'm going to ask you to calm the hell down and watch your mouth." "Why should I? Once again you kept something from me. First the letter—" "I explained that." "Yeah, you wanted to protect me." "That's right I did." "Okay, so what's the excuse this time? Too busy getting your rocks off to fill me in?" "*Scott,*" he said, teeth clenched. "That's your mother you're talking about." "Oh please, she's another one. All this time, and she said nothing." "I asked her not to." He looked at him. "Look, your mother and I we have a history, which complicates thing." Scott put his jacket back on. "Where are you going? We're not done." "Out for a ride."

Scott rode Sugar hard and ironically ended up at the very same spot that he and Amanda did. He remembered how afraid he'd been that she'd hurt herself. He cared. He never stopped caring. What would he do about it? In the past few months, she had shown just how serious she was about making amends. She would call and speak to him each week and even visit him at school. He remembered one such visit not that long ago.

Amanda stood at the door, holding two bags of groceries. She hoped that Scott wouldn't be too upset with the surprise visit. She knocked and he opened the door, surprise clearly on his face. "Amanda, what are you doing here?" "I know this is a total surprise, and if I've overstepped please tell me. I had this crazy idea about cooking you dinner." "Who is it, man?" She heard the baritone voice coming from inside. "It's my mom." "No shit. Really?" He got off the couch and came to the door. This tall, very good looking blond guy was standing before her, smiling. "Hi, I'm John." "Amanda. I'd shake your hand, but as you can see, they're full." He slapped Scott's arm. "What's the matter with you? Here, let us get those." "Thanks." "Sure, come on in." Scott was giving him the eye, but John wasn't paying him any mind. "I apologize for just showing up. I didn't realize you'd have company. I'm just going to go." "No way. We have no special plans. Ain't that right, Scott?" Scott hesitated but then answered, "No, no plans at all. Though from what I remember, you said you don't like cooking." "True, I did say that. But I'm willing to do it for you. There's more than enough. You'll stay, won't you, John?" "You bet I will." "Great. So point me to the kitchen, and I'll get started." "It's right there." She eyed the small kitchenette area. "Oh I see." "Dorms, no one really cooks," John said. "Apparently not. Well, I'll just make the best of it." "We'll help," John said. "We will?" Scott asked. "Sure." "Okay, if you don't mind. You can slice and dice the tomatoes, peppers, and onions." "You got it." John passed Scott a knife. "What the hell are you doing?" he asked, whispering while Amanda was cleaning the chicken. "Chopping." "You know what I mean?" "Look, the woman came all this way to do something nice for you." "I know but—" "But nothing." He took a minute before speaking again. "You're right." "'Course I'm right."

They sat down to eat. "This looks great," John said. "It really does. Thank you." "You're welcome." They started eating, and she was encouraged by their satisfied sounds. "This is delish." "It's really good. What is it?" Scott asked. "Drunken chicken." John laughed. "So what the bird has a hangover or something?" She laughed. "In a way. See you cook the chicken in beer." "Which is how it got its name." "Right." They ate and talked about many different things. "So Scott told me that you used to be a singer." "He did?" She looked at him, surprised that he even talked about her at all. He shrugged. "We were just talking one day." "Well, I was a singer. Mostly I sang in bars and cabarets." "Sounds cool." "It was." "Do you still sing now?" "Oh I haven't sang in a very long time." "Well, how about belting out a tune for us." "John, there's no music," Scott said. "So? A good singer doesn't need music. Isn't that right, Amanda?" "That's true but it's been years and I'm—" "Afraid?" he challenged, her knowing she wouldn't back down. "Certainly not." "So then, what should I sing?" "Whatever you want." "Any requests?" "Something old," John said. "All right. *Stars shining bright above you, night breezes seem to whisper I love you. Birds singin' in the sycamore tree, dream a little, dream of me.*" They listened to every word. Her voice smooth like velvet. When she finished, she giggled. "Definitely out of practice." "If that's out of practice, I'd hate to hear how you sound *in practice*." "What song was that?" Scott asked. "It's an old World War II song, 'Dream a Little Dream.'" "Why didn't you ever go pro?" "I tried but it's very difficult. I did sing in some Off-Broadway shows." "Really?" Scott asked, curiously. "Yes. That was after working my way up from off Off-Broadway." They laughed. "You gotta sing another one," John said. "I'm flattered but one song is enough for today. Besides, I have to clean up." "The only thing you're going to do is put your pretty little self on that sofa. Scott and I will handle cleanup." "John's right. It's the least we can do." "All right, if you insist." She sat on the sofa and smiled to herself.

After all the cleanup was done, John decided to give them some time alone. "Listen, this has been great, but I'm going to head out now." "Really, John? Do you have to go?" "Yeah, I've got some things to take care of." "Like what?" Scott asked suspiciously. "Like shaving my legs." Amanda laughed. "You know, you are starting to sound more and more like Riley." "Good, I like him." "I know. There's no accounting for taste." "Amanda, thank you for everything. I enjoyed your wine-o chicken." "You're very welcome. I'm glad you enjoyed it." "Scott, I'll see you tomorrow." "Later, man." He left. "What a nice guy." "That's 'cause you don't know him." She smiled. "You seem to be winning everyone over. First Riley and now John." "Oh please," she said. "Seriously, if Riley had been here to hear you sing, I'm pretty sure he'd have left Sam for you." She laughed. "You're being silly." He smiled genuinely. "I guess the drunken chicken was a bad influence." They laughed together, which was nice. "Thanks for making dinner, Amanda." "You're very welcome. It was my pleasure." Scott's thoughts came back to the present, and he knew just what he would do.

Chapter Twenty-Two

When Scott got back, he went into the house to talk to his dad. Since he wasn't there, he decided to call Amanda. After several rings, the machine picked up. He noticed that her message no longer said Amanda *and Sam.* Just as he was getting ready to leave a message, she picked up. "Hello? Hello?" "Amanda, it's Scott." "Scott, hi. Sorry I was doing something and couldn't get to the phone right away. What's up?" "Well, I'm calling to invite you to my graduation." She was speechless. "Amanda, are you there?" "Yes, just near speechless." "I guess you weren't expecting me to invite you?" She felt tears forming. "Are you kidding? Just try and stop me." He smiled. "Good, it's two weeks from today. The ceremony starts at nine. I have to be there by eight." "Okay. I can't tell you how much this means to me." "I never thought you'd ask." "To be honest, I almost didn't." "What made you change your mind?" "I realized that I didn't want you to miss any more important moments than you already have. The tears fell and she sniffled. "Are you crying?" "Yes." He wasn't sure how to handle this. "Amanda, please don't cry." "I'm sorry, I can't help it. I just never thought you'd ask me." "I'm glad I did." She smiled. "Me too." "See you in two weeks." "See you then."

Hanson had walked into the tail end of Scott's conversation with Amanda. "I see you're back." "Yeah." "Good ride?" "Yeah, cleared my head." "Good." He started walking away. "Dad?" "Yeah?" "I'm sorry about before. I was out of line." "You were *very* out of line. If you had been any other guy, I would have knocked your block off for talking that way about her." He looked at him. "You really do love her. Don't you?" "Yeah, I really do." "And you think this time is gonna be different?" "I don't know. I just feel we lost eleven years, and that's enough." "I hope it works out." "So do I." "So I just invited her to Graduation." Hanson breathed a sigh of relief. "Well, that's a relief. When I came in and heard you ask if she was crying, I feared the worst." "I guess the way I acted earlier made you think that?" He nodded. "What made you change your mind?" "It kind of goes back to what you said. She missed eleven years of important events. Did I really want her to miss another?" "Well, I'm glad you calmed down and thought things through." "Yeah, me too. I'm going to go call Em now."

Emily was studying like crazy. She had several finals coming up and was super stressed. The phone rang, and she was thankful for the break. "Hello?" "Hey, beautiful. Miss me?" "Actually, I'm in the middle of studying, so I haven't had time to miss anyone." "Ouch. You really know how to hurt a guy." "Would it help if I promised to kiss it and make it better?" "It might." They laughed. "So what are you studying for?" "Economics." "Ah, Mr. Excitement." "The very one. I don't think I'm going to do that well. It's just hard to stay focused on something so boring." "You'll do fine. Just do your best." "Thanks, I feel better already." "Anytime. So how's Sam?" "She saves everything for the last minute, so she's super stressed." "Why does she do that?" "I don't know. How's Riley?" "Still being a pain in the ass, he's fine." She laughed. "It was nice of him to help you bring your stuff back." "Yeah, he even helped me unpack." "Really?" "Yeah." "So to change the subject, I invited Amanda to graduation." "Good, I'm glad. She deserves to share in the day's happiness." "I think so too. I found out that Dad and her are . . . well, they're . . ." "Sleeping together?" "Yeah." "You don't have a problem with that, do you?" "At first. I mean, I just I don't want him to get hurt again." "Scott, he's a grown man. It's his decision." "I know." So is she coming?" "She is." "Good, I'm glad." She said. "Yeah, it was the right thing to do. Anyway, I'd better let you get back to studying." "Okay." "Good luck on your exams." "Thanks. Can't wait to see you at graduation." "Me too. Riley is going to pick you girls up that day." "Okay, I'm sure Sam will get the details from him as we get closer." She said.

Graduation Day

Scott stood, looking at himself in the mirror. He was having difficulty with his tie. "Here, let me do it." "I got it, Dad." "No, you don't. That knot looks like a pretzel twist." His mouth curled up. "Fine, you do it then." Hanson untied the knot and redid it. "There now, that's more like it. What do you think?" "I think it's just a smaller pretzel." They looked at each other and laughed. "Smart-ass." "Till the day I die." "Yeah, yeah. So your mother's meeting us there." "You spoke to her?" "Last night." "Dad?" "Hmm?" "How are things going between you?" "Very well." "You seem happy." "I am happy." "Riley's taking care of getting Sam and Emily, right?" "Yeah, he already left." He looked down at his watch. "With the way he drives, he's probably already there." Scott laughed. "Wouldn't surprise me if he was. Ross is bringing Sabrina, right?" "Yeah. We're all set." He looked at him. "Ready, Graduate?" "*So* ready." "Then let's hit the road."

Riley pulled at the collar of his shirt. He hated dressing up. He was nearly to the girls' school when he saw a rest stop and pulled off the main highway. He wanted to get Sam something. He went inside and thanked his lucky stars when he found a tiny flower stand. He grabbed an assorted bouquet, paid, and was walking back out when he spotted a candy counter. He grabbed a Snickers bar, her favorite, and was on his way once again.

When he arrived on the campus, he grabbed the flowers and went into their building. He knocked, and Sam was the one to greet him. The way she looked took his breath away. She wore a jade-green scooped-neck dress that fell a few inches above her knee, showing off her great legs. She had matching jewelry that caught the light and sparkled. On her eyes, green shadow. She looked amazing. "You look gorgeous." "This old thing? Why, I only wear this when I don't care how I look." He smiled. "I'll bet." "You're looking all GQ yourself in that suit of yours." "Don't remind me, uncomfortable as shit." He pulled at his tie. "What's behind your back?" "Nothin'.'" "Right, so show me your hands then." "Make me." "Okay, I will." She grabbed his tie and pulled him in for a hot, steamy kiss. When she pulled away, he could barely remember his name. "You win." He handed her the flowers and Snickers. "Flowers *and* chocolate? What's the occasion?" "*You.*" "Isn't that sweet," Emily said from the doorway of her room. "Sweet *and* sexy. A dangerous combination." She pulled him in for another kiss. "Keep this up, and Em will have to wait in the car fifteen minutes." She looked at him." "Just fifteen?" "Well, we are in a hurry with Dimples graduating and all." She laughed. "True. Though, I could do quite a lot to you in fifteen minutes." "Oh no doubt." He bit her bottom lip. Emily got between them. "Okay, break it up, you two." He looked at her. "Spoilsport." "Sorry but we have a graduation to get to." Riley looked at Sam. "She does have a point, gorgeous." "Those fifteen minutes will have to wait til later." They laughed.

Sabrina was ready to go. Ross called to say he had to make an unplanned stop at the station to help Andy handle something. He sounded very annoyed. He'd be a few minutes late. Which wasn't a problem since they had given themselves plenty of time. Sabrina checked herself in the mirror. She had fixed her hair differently today by sweeping it up into a twist. Her dress was purple with a sweetheart neckline, accented with a Y-necklace of amethyst crystal. She ran the necklace through her fingers, wondering if Ross would recognize it. She checked her purse, grabbed her cardigan, and went outside to wait for him. That's the way he found her, sitting on the porch swing, rocking back and forth. For a moment, he was reminded of another time when she sat waiting for him in the same porch swing. *It was Sabrina's sixteenth birthday, and she was all dressed up for her party. "Hey, Brina." "Hi, Ross." She got up and gave him a hug. "Happy Birthday, Sweet Sixteen." "Thanks. How do you like my dress?" He looked at the cobalt dress she wore. "Is it new?" "Better, I made it." "Really?" "Yep. Mama had a box of old dress patterns, so she helped me make it." "It's really nice, Brina." "It is, isn't it? I feel good about it because it's something I made." "You always were good at sewing." "I think this is just the beginning for me, Ross." "What do you mean?" "This is what I want to do." "What, like a designer?" "Yes. Oh I know I won't be famous like all those big-name designers but I don't need to be." "If anyone can do it, you can." "Thanks, Ross." "So where's James?" "Right here." They shook hands. "Hey man, ready for the wild party?" "How bad could it be?" Ross asked. "I don't know, but if they ask us to play pin the tail on the donkey, we're leaving." "Stop it, you two. I'm sixteen, not six." "Whatever you say, sis." James looked at her. "Don't go getting a big head or anything, but you look pretty." She smiled. "Thanks, big brother." "Well, Dad needed me to help him with something, so I'll see you inside, Ross." Ross took her hands. "I want to give you your gift." "Okay." He took out a small package wrapped in tissue paper. "I hope you like it." Inside a velvet pouch, was a lovely Y-necklace with amethyst crystals. "Oh, Ross. It's beautiful. But it's too expensive." "Nah, try it on." He said. "Can you help me?" "Sure." She lifted up her hair, so he could fasten it. In doing so, he grazed her skin. "There. Turn around." "It looks . . . beautiful on you." "I love it, Ross." "And I love you, Brina." The words were out before he could stop them. "I love you too, Ross." She hugged him. If only she loved him the way he did her. He closed his eyes and dreamed of the day when maybe she would.*

Sabrina was knocking on his window. "You okay? I was knocking forever. You were a thousand miles away just now. Where were you?" "Your sixteenth birthday." "Whatever made you think of that?" "The way you were sitting on that porch swing, it reminded me of how you looked that day." "You remember that?" "I remember *everything*." "Then you must remember this." She held up the necklace. "You still have it?" "I was going through my drawers and found it. "I thought you lost it." "No, never. I told you I'd treasure it always. I had put it in my drawer for safekeeping." "It still looks beautiful on you." "Thanks. You said you loved me that day. Do you remember, Ross?" "Yeah, I do." "You didn't mean it the way I thought you did. Did you?" "No." "I also remember saying that I loved you." "You did. You don't know how badly I wanted you to mean it the way I did." "I was a sixteen-year-old girl who didn't fully understand or appreciate what it meant to have someone like you love them." He looked at her. "Ross, tell me you love me." "You know I do." "Say it, please." "I love you, Brina." She cupped his face in her hands. “And I love you, Ross.” He stood speechless. “I’m sorry you had to wait so long to hear it.” “Say it again.” “*I love you.*” He kissed her and scooped her up into his arms. “What are you doing?” “What do you think I’m doing?” “Ross, we can’t. What about Scott’s graduation?” “We’ll arrive fashionably late.”

Chapter Twenty-Three

Amanda arrived on campus very early but she didn't care. She'd rather be early than late. She got out of her car and followed the signs to Morris Gardens, which was where the ceremony would be held. The stage was set up, and hundreds of chairs were arranged on the lawn. She imagined Scott looking handsome in his cap and gown, receiving his degree. She wanted a bird's-eye view, so she walked all the way down to the first row behind where the graduates would be sitting. She sat there thinking about things past and present. It had been a long hard road but here she was. At her son's graduation. She thought of Sam and felt herself tear up. "I wish you were here, Sam. I'm happy but I'm scared too. I don't want to disappoint him. I've done enough of that for one lifetime." Her phone vibrated. "Hello?" "Manda, where are you?" "I'm in Morris Gardens. I got us seats right up front." "Okay, be there in a minute." She stood up so he would see her. There were a lot more people sitting down now than when she had arrived. She spotted Hanson and waved to him. "You weren't kidding about being up front," he teased. "I didn't want to miss anything." He looked at her. "I understand." "You look handsome in that suit." "Thanks, but I feel a bit ridiculous. I miss my worn-in cotton shirts and jeans. Besides, I'm not the only one who looks good. You look great." "Oh stop. I'm a mess. I changed like ten times, and I'm still not happy with what I'm wearing." "You look beautiful, relax." "I'm trying." He started massaging her shoulders. "Boy, are you tense." "Why so nervous?" "You're joking, right?" "It's all going to be fine, "Manda." "You didn't make him invite me. Did you, Hanson?" "No, Manda I didn't." She looked at him. "I swear. Now try to relax." He kissed her. "I'll try." "Try harder." He kissed her again, this time for longer. "Better?" "Yes." "Good." "So where's Scott?" "He's in the great hall. They wanted all the graduates to meet up there." "What about everyone else?" "If you mean the gang, they'll be here soon." "Good. I still can't believe it. Our boy is graduating." "He's not a boy, Manda." "I know, but I still can see him trying to make mud pies in the microwave." He smiled. "I know what you mean."

Scott had his gown on but the cap was giving him trouble. "How the hell does this thing stay on?" "Got me," John said, shrugging. "Some help you are." "Hey, cut me a break the last time I had to wear one of these was back in high school." Scott laughed. Eventually, one of the girls took pity on them and gave them some bobbiey pins." "How do I look?" Scott asked. "Smart, which is a big improvement over how you usually look." John said trying not to grin. "Smartass." Scott said also trying not to grin. "Takes one to know one." John said smiling. "So is your Mom coming?" "Yeah, she is." Good, I think you did the right thing by inviting her." "Yeah, I think so too." Scott said.

It was nearly time for the ceremony to begin. Riley, Sam, and Emily sat next to Hanson and Amanda. Ross and Sabrina were further back because they arrived later. Suddenly, "Pomp and Circumstance" began to play, and everyone rose to get a better view of the graduates. They saw Scott and were able to wave to him. Emily blew him a kiss, and he pretended to catch it and place it over his heart. Sometime after the opening remarks, the awards were given out. Scott received his Academic Achievement Award, much to the surprise of his father and mother. "Did you know about this?" she asked. "No, he didn't tell me." After that, it was time to begin reading the names of the graduates. Since Scott's last name started with a P, everyone knew it would take a while. Finally, the moment they had all been waiting for came. "*Scott Pierce*." Everyone jumped up and cheered. Riley and Sam whistled while Amanda cried tears of joy.

When the ceremony ended, it took a little while for everyone to wade through the crowds and find their friends and loved ones. Scott eventually hooked up with everyone and received his fair share of hugs, kisses, and handshakes. "Scott, you didn't mention you'd be getting an award," Hanson said. "I wanted it to be a surprise." Sam and Riley came up behind him. "Shocked the shit out of me," Riley joked and Sam slapped his arm. "Okay look, all kidding aside, you did good. Real good. Congratulations." "Thanks, man." Hanson took him aside for a minute. "I wanted you to know that I couldn't be any prouder than I am at this moment." "Thanks, Dad." "I think your mother is hanging back because she thinks you didn't really want her here." "What?" "I'm just telling you what she told me." "I'll take care of it." He walked over to her. She was talking to Emily. "I'm just so happy I could be here." Amanda was telling Emily. "I'm glad Scott decided to invite you." "Well, I think his father might have had a hand in it." "No, he really didn't." Scott said from behind making them both turn around. "I invited you because I wanted to, Amanda. Okay?" She smiled. "Okay." "Sorry I wasn't able to introduce you two." "Your dad took care of that." You've found yourself a lovely girl, Scott." "Don't I know it." He said smiling at Em. "Hey Em, could you come here a minute?," Sam asked. Sure, Sam. Excuse me, Amanda." Em gave him a kiss before walking away. "She's a special girl, Scott." "She definitely is." He said watching her laugh with Sam. "Then again, you're a special man." "Ah well, I mean, thanks." "If you're smart, you won't let her get away." "Don't worry, I don't plan on it." "Good, you're already smarter than I was." He looked at her, and for the first time, felt sympathy for all she had lost. "Hey, we're all heading to Sabrina's to celebrate. Did you want to come?" "I'd love to." "Good, see you there."

Scott and John were talking. "Listen John, I'm not one of those idiots who says they'll keep in touch and then doesn't." John looked at him. "You're not? Damn, here I thought I was free and clear." "You're a jerk." "True, but I'm *your* jerk." "Anyway, we have some celebrating to do." John said. "Yeah, we do. You could make that visit we talked about. Hit Jake's." "Sounds good but . . ." "But what?" "You gotta get that shit with the water straightened out. I don't need to start drawing hearts with initials." Scott looked at him. "That was only one time."

"That I saw." "So drink bottled water." "Right. So when should I come out?" "The sooner the better." Riley walked over. "Sooner the better what?" "He's making me promise to visit." John said. "God, I hate it when he gets attached." Riley said grinning. "You two belong together," Scott said looking at them. "I was just saying to Scott that the only way I'm coming to visit is if the water thing gets fixed." Riley laughed. "You still think there's something to that?" John looked at all the paired off couples around them. "Ah yeah, I do."

A few hours later, everyone was back at Sabrina's. Since she had prepped everything the day before, all that needed to be done was pop everything in the oven. Pot roast, roasted potatoes, and green beans almondine were all on the menu. "Sabrina, everything smells great," Amanda said. "Thanks. Since we'll be eating soon, have the guys set the table." "Hey, Hot Stuff!" Sam yelled. "*Yeah*." All the guys replied and she laughed. "Sorry. *My* Hot Stuff." Riley grinned widely. "Yeah, gorgeous?" "We need you guys to set the table. Dinner's almost ready." "No problem." They set the table, and in no time at all, everyone was seated and enjoying Sabrina's meal. "Brina, I have always loved your roast." "Who are you kidding? You've always loved *everything*," Hanson joked. "That is true." He leaned over and kissed her. Riley and Scott made gagging noises and got slaps from both Emily and Sam. "So, Scott, how does it feel to be a college graduate?" Ross asked. "Good. I can't wait to get started." "Started? On what?" Hanson asked. "You know, the horse center I told you about." "Yeah, but that is going to take money. A lot of it. So how will you swing that part of it?" "By taking out a loan." "A loan, huh? You have no credit, no bank is going to approve it." "They will if I have a co-signer." "That'd be me, I take it." "Yeah." "We'll talk about it another time." "So you won't co-sign?" "No, that's not what I'm saying. It's just you aren't talking about opening up a lemonade stand." "I know, Dad. I'm not planning on doing this tomorrow. First, I plan on working a ranch. Get a little more experience." "Plus, Brad gave Scott his sister's number. She owns a ranch down in Kentucky," Emily said. "Who the heck is Brad?" Hanson asked. "This guy at Em's school. He has the hots for her," Riley said. "Scott decked him." "No way!" Ross said. "Way. Knocked him on his ass, man," Riley said, grinning like a proud papa. "Ah, guys, getting off topic here," Amanda said. Hanson picked their conversation up right where they left off. "So you're going to ask Brad's sister for a job?" "The thought did cross my mind." Amanda had been listening patiently, waiting for the right time to enter the conversation. "Scott, when the time comes, I'd like to invest in your center. I'd be more than happy to help out any way I can." They looked at her. "'Manda, you don't have to do that," Hanson said. "I know I don't have to. I want to." She paused to look down the table at the faces staring back at her. "It's no secret to anyone here that I was hardly mother of the year. Leaving was the biggest mistake of my life. I know that nothing can ever really make up for all the hurt and pain I've caused, but I am trying. I want to invest because I believe in his idea and in him." Up until now Scott hadn't spoken because he wasn't sure he'd be able to. He never expected her to make such a gesture. Let alone say all those things. She believed in him. "I don't know what to say." "You don't have to say anything. Just consider it. If and when the time comes, just ask. Okay?" "Okay. Thanks." "Well, I think we've had enough serious conversation for today," Sabrina said. "I agree, this is a celebration." Ross stood up, glass in hand. "I'd like to propose a toast." Everyone stood. "Scott, we are all very proud of you. May all your dreams come true. To Scott." "To Scott!" everyone said, as they clinked their glasses together.

A while later, Amanda looked at her watch. "I should get going." "Why don't you stay over?" "Tempting, but I have an early meeting tomorrow." "You know, you still haven't told me what it is you do." Scott joined them. "What are we talking about?" "I was just saying how your mother never told us what she does." "Well, it's no secret." "Then you won't mind sharing it with us," Hanson teased. "Course not. I'm an agent." "Real estate?" "No, talent." "Isn't that kinda hard?" Hanson asked. "I mean, I know how badly you wanted to make it." "In the beginning, but then after a while, I felt good about it. I figured if I could help other people achieve their dreams . . ." "You'd be giving them the help you never got," Scott said, feeling a bit sorry for her. "In a way, yes." "How did you become an agent?" "Sam. He knew people." "Course he did," Hanson said, sounding more than a little jealous and feeling guilty since he was jealous of a dead man. "I worked alongside a really great agent, Estelle. She taught me all the tricks of trade, and when she retired, she gave me all her clients." "Is that the same Sam who was on your machine?" Scott asked. Her face grew sad. "Yes." Scott could tell that this was a sensitive subject, so he didn't push it. "I'll walk you out," Hanson said. "Can I get a minute with Amanda?" "Sure, I'll be by the car." "Do you mind if we walk a little?" Scott asked. "Not at all." "What did you want to talk to me about?" "What you said in there." "Oh?" "I . . . those things you said. Did you mean them?" "I did." "I wanted to make sure." "I understand." "Not sure you do. See, all those years you were gone there were times I wanted—no, needed—someone to believe in me." "Your father didn't?" "He did but I needed—" "Your mother." "Yeah." She felt her eyes growing misty. "I—" "I know I was an ass to you at first." "You? Never." He laughed. "Anyway, I'm glad I gave you a chance." "So am I, Scott. So am I." "Thanks for believing in me." He kissed her cheek. A few tears ran down her face. "I hope those are the happy tears?" "They are." "Good." Scott walked her back to his dad. He had seen what transpired between them, and it almost brought a tear to his eye. They walked over to her car. "Drive, safe." "I will. Thanks, Scott. You've made my day, year, and decade." He laughed. "I'm glad. We'll talk soon." "We sure will." She so wanted to hug and kiss him good-bye, but she decided not to push her luck. "So the ice has definitely melted between you." "Yes, thank God." "I'm glad things are progressing." "So am I. Believe me. I was worried." "To be honest, so was I." "Soon he'll be hugging and kissing you every time." "I can't wait for that day to come." "And I can't wait to have you in bed again." She felt herself flush slightly. "You're insatiable." "Don't pretend you don't love it," he said, smiling sexily. "No, I won't because I do." She pulled him in for a long hot kiss. "That was one hell of a kiss." "I'm glad you approve." "Definitely, do. So much, I want to carry you back inside and ravage you." "I wish I could but—" "I know, I know. Early meeting. Joy kill." She laughed. "I promise to make it up to you." "I'm going to hold you to that," he said, grabbing her butt and squeezing it gently. "I'm sure you will."

Two weeks later, the day of Nico's visit arrived. While putting the sheets on the bed, Sabrina thought of a time when she had only been working for Nico about six months. *"No, James, I can't come this weekend. I know it's July 4. Yes, I know we always do the picnic and fireworks.*

No, I don't think my job is more important than family." Nico came in. "James, please, this is a really big deal. I can't just leave Nico stranded. No, I'm not the only designer here but . . ." Nico could see she was getting upset. "James, I can't be there and that's that. He hung up on me." "Well, you did have a bit of a 'tude." She looked at him. "Oh so now you're going to start?" "I never start, merely finish." She felt the sides of her mouth curl up. "My brother is upset because—" "Because you can't make some Mayberry Independence Day Extravaganza." "It's something we've done together since we were kids." "Oh how touching." "Well, let him be upset," she said, annoyed. "He'll calm down." "You think so?" "I do. Listen, if it's really that big a deal, I can get Edgar." "Edgar?" she asked, sounding unnerved. "What, you disapprove?" "Well, no I mean he's talented but—" "But?" "But he's got no people skills." "True. Still—" "Look, I committed to working with you this weekend, and that is what I'm going to do. James will get over it." He looked at her and smiled. "Good, now go have fun in Mayberry." She looked at him, confused. "Huh?" "There is no client coming this weekend. I made it up." "You made it up?" "I needed to see how serious you were about all this. I can't have someone who won't fully commit." "Another test?" "Yes, a necessary one." "My brother is pissed at me because of your stupid test." "Oh don't worry about him. I'll have him eating out of the palm of my hand in no time." He asked for the number and put the call on speaker. "James, this is Nico, Sabrina's handsome and available boss." She almost choked. "I'm calling to clear the air." James said nothing. "Your little Mayberry thing is still on." "I don't understand." "No, so I'll explain. Your sister just passed another one of my tests that I like to give from time to time." "Tests?" "Yes, see, in our line of work one must not only be creative but dedicated as well. I needed to see if your sister was ready for the level of commitment this job requires. I'm happy to say that she is. You're very fortunate to have someone like her to call family." "I know. I'm sorry I got so upset, sis. It's just I wanted to see you. I miss you." Sabrina felt her eyes tear up. "Oh, if only my brother were so open." She looked at him. "Nico, you don't have a brother." "I was speaking hypothetically of course. Anyway, no worries, Jimmy, she'll be there." "Jimmy?" she said knowing damn well James hated being called that. "What, you don't mind my calling you Jimmy, do you?" "Nope, not at all." She rolled her eyes since no one had gotten away with calling her brother that since eighth grade. The phone rang and brought her thoughts back to the present. "Hello?" "Tis I." "Where are you?" "I'm on some backwoods dusty road." "That's Apple Road. Just take that all the way down till you can't go anymore, then hang a right." "Would that be Pear Street?" he said sarcastically. "No, and watch the sarcasm." "Oh fine. I'll be there in two shakes of a lamb's tail, cowbell, or whatever it is you have there." She couldn't help laughing as she hung up. She went downstairs, and Emily was in the kitchen pouring herself a drink. School had ended for her a week ago. She had been dividing her time between training and being with Scott. Riley and Sam had been spending a lot of time together as well. "Hey, Em. Good ride?" "Yeah, we went up to the lake. So where's Nico? I thought he'd be here already." "He should be here soon. He was on Apple Road when he called." "You must be excited since it's been so long since you've seen him." "You know much of the wake and funeral are a blur, but I think I remember him. Was he the one wearing a veil?" Sabrina laughed. "Yes, he was channeling Marlene Dietrich. One of his favorite actresses." "Who?" "Don't let him hear you ask that." "Okay, I won't." "Anyone here? I made it to Mayberry." "He's here." "I'll be right out. I want to wash up a little. Get some of this trail dust off me." "Okay." Sabrina walked out to see a shiny red BMW being unloaded by a portly, slightly balding man. "Nico!" He turned and smiled broadly. "I made it! Though it was one wild ride. You could have warned me about Apple Road." "I figured a city boy like you could handle a simple country road." "That was no road, it was barely a trail." "Stop exaggerating." "I never exaggerate, only embellish." "Sure, Nico." "I'll need help with my bags." She looked at the growing pile of luggage. "Haven't you ever heard of packing light?" "*This* is nothing. I left loads back home. Who knows what to pack for rustic living?" "This is hardly rustic, Nico." "Honey, for me this is about as rustic as it gets." "Let me go get the guys to help with your bags." "Make sure they're careful, those are Louis Vuitton." She rolled her eyes at him and Emily came out. "Hello, Nico," she said, smiling. "Goodness is this Emily?" "Yes." "My dear, you're all grown up." "Well, I think the last time I saw you I was ten, and you were wearing a veil." "I was channeling Marlene Dietrich." "Well, you nailed it." He looked at her. "You know Marlene?" "Of course, she was amazing." "You know, it's so refreshing that someone your age knows and appreciates the greats." "How could anyone not? *Blue Angel, Shanghai Express, Morocco*." "I love that one!" "The scene where she's dressed in men's clothes and kisses another woman. So provocative for that time." Sabrina cleared her throat. "Don't mind me, I'll just go inside and eat the scones I made." "Someone sounds jealous. Excuse me for having a moment with your lovely niece. Come here and give daddy some sugar." She smiled and hugged him. "I'm so glad you're here." "Me too. "Let me get the guys to haul in your trusso." "Don't get smart." She walked away smiling and came back with the guys. "Nico, this is Dave, Pete, and Riley. Guys, this is Nico." "My, my, they do grow them handsome out here, don't they? No wonder you never came back." She shook her head. "I haven't had this much eye candy since I went to Cher's farewell concert." "You got to see it? Man, I couldn't get tickets," Riley said. Nico's gaze was transfixed. "You like Cher?" Riley looked at him. "Who doesn't?" "So true, but I supposed there are those with no appreciation for her talent and flare. What's your favorite song?" He thought for a minute. "Hard to say. 'Turn Back Time' or 'I've Found Someone,' most likely." "Will you marry me?" Sabrina tried not to laugh. She looked at Riley and wasn't sure whether he wanted to laugh or run. "Sorry, Nico, but Riley doesn't play for your team. He has a girlfriend, Em's friend, Sam." "Drat, once again trumped by a pair of ovaries." "Guys, if you could please take Nico's bags up to the guest room." They looked at the rather large pile of bags. "Are those all yours?" Dave asked. "Yes. I don't believe in traveling light." The sides of Dave's mouth curled up. "That much is obvious." "No one likes a smart-ass, Dave." "I do," Riley said grinning. "You would," Pete said. "Boys, those are Louis Vuitton, so please be ginger with them." "Louis who?" Riley asked. Nico looked at him. "How could someone so handsome be so clueless?" "Just a wild guess but probably 'cause I'm not gay." "Touché," Nico said, laughing. "We'll be in the kitchen if you need anything." "Careful, Pete, you don't want to give yourself a hernia." "Shut up, Dave." As they walked back into the house, Sabrina pulled Emily aside. "How did you know that stuff about Dietrich?" "I Googled her." She laughed. "Smart." The guys were hauling in Nico's bags and cursing. "What the hell is in here?" Pete asked. "Mine feels like a boulder." "You two want to cut it out," Riley mumbled. "Mine aren't exactly light either." Emily and Sabrina couldn't help but giggle. These guys carried sacks of feed and moved around hay bales for a living. The girls went into the kitchen and found Nico on his cell. "No, I don't want Kristie to handle that. She's awful with florals. Have Cecily work on it. Right. I'll check in again later. Tootles." He hung up. "I swear, there's no rest for the fashion weary." "What's going on?" Sabrina asked. "What's going on is that Kristie was about to make a big mistake on the new line." "Kristie? I thought you said she was good?" "She is very talented but little common sense." "Well, sounds like you got things sorted out." "Yes, Cecily has a real eye for knowing just how big to make the flowers without it looking like my grandmother's old sofa." "So can we please have scones now?" Emily asked. "Let them eat scones!" he proclaimed. "Sorry, always wanted to say that." "You know, it's a wonder you didn't go into theater with all your theatrics," Sabrina teased. "Keep this up and I'll have the guys put my bags *back* in the car." "Pleeze, idle threats don't become you. Besides, I know you're just dying to hear about the guys." "Well, that's true. All right, I'll stay, but only if I get to hear all the *really* juicy stuff." "By juicy you mean—" "Sex, darling. What else?" "Well, seeing how I sleep with neither Riley or Scott, that might prove difficult." He snorted out a laugh. "Oh how I've so missed you."

Scott was on the phone with John. "So are you coming?" "What's the matter, miss me?" "Yeah, my heart aches." "Smart-ass." "Til the day I die." "Yeah, well keep it up and you'll be dyin' a whole lot sooner." Scott laughed. "So come. Nico's here." "Who's Nico?" "Sabrina's old boss. I hear he's a trip." "You haven't met him yet?" "No. Em and I had gone out for a ride, and when we came back, he wasn't here yet." "So I should come for Nico?" "Not unless you want to switch teams?" "He's gay?" "As the Village People." "I got no problem with that. Anyway, I can be there tomorrow around four." "We'll all hit Jake's. It'll be fun." "Sounds good. See you then."

Scott walked up toward the house and went inside. "Anybody home?" he said jokingly. "In the kitchen." As he walked in, he saw Emily, Sabrina, and Nico sitting at the table, having tea and scones." "Well, looks like I made it just in time. Hope you saved some for me." "You can have some of mine, carbs go straight to my thighs." Scott laughed.

"You must be Nico." "I see my reputation precedes me." "Definitely, I've heard a lot about you." Nico's face lit up. "Have you? Only good things I hope." "Sure." "Well, my dear Emily, you've certainly lassoed a good one." She smiled. "I sure have." She and Scott smiled at one another. "Ah, young love. How I miss those days." "You aren't that old, Nico," Emily said. "Bless you and you're right. I'm still in my prime. After all, they do say life begins at forty." "Then your life must have started years ago," Sabrina teased. "You know, I don't remember you being this bitchy." Scott and Emily laughed. "So, Scott, tell me more about this horse center of yours." "Well, horses have always been a passion of mine, so I'd like to incorporate that into a place that has it all. Breeding, lessons, training, etc." "Sounds like hard work." "It will be a lot of work, but some of the best things have to be worked for." "So true. I like you, Scott. You seem to have a good head on those broad shoulders of yours." "Thanks, Nico." They sat, ate scones, and listened to some of Nico's stories "That was the last time I used spandex in my designs." They all laughed. "So, Scott, how serious are you about our lovely Emily?" Emily blushed. "Nico!" Sabrina said. "What? I can't ask? She and I have bonded over Marlene. That's for life. So how 'bout it, Scott?" "I'm in love with her." "Oh darling, anyone with eyes could see that. What I want to know is it kismet?" "It sure feels that way," he said, smiling affectionately at her. "Oh wonderful. I can't wait to attend the wedding. I'll have to wear a white veil this time." Sabrina rolled her eyes. "Nico, they've only be dating a few months." "I know, I know, and I'm not rushing things. It will happen when the time is right. For now, just enjoy one another." Riley, Pete, and Dave finally finished bringing all his bags upstairs. "All done," Riley said, wiping his brow. "Did I make you work up a sweat, handsome?" He grinned. "What?" Nico asked. "Sam calls me that." "Well, what can I say? I call 'em as I see 'em and evidently so does Sam." "He calls her gorgeous," Em said. "Does he? I'm so jealous since I hoped you'd call me that." Everyone got really quiet. Then Nico started laughing. "You should have seen all your faces. Priceless." He kept on laughing and they joined him.

When John arrived the next afternoon, it was later than he had said. Scott was waiting for him outside. "Traffic?" "Yeah. So where's you know who?" John asked. "Nico?" "Yeah. He's not going to hit on me, is he?" "Only if you know who Louis Vuitton is." John looked at him. "Louis who?" "You're safe." "Come on, let's go get you settled." "Sounds good. I can't wait to have a nice cold beer." Meanwhile, Nico was also getting ready. When the guys had asked him to join them, he was tickled pink. He showered, lotioned, and spritzed himself with cologne. When he was finished, he looked in the mirror. "I look fine if I do say so myself. Too bad they're all straight. Oh well." He shrugged and walked out the door. The guys were waiting for him by the barn. *God, look at all these delectable men. And I can't have a single one of them.* " "Nico, this is John. John, Nico." "Pleasure." "Oh no the pleasure's mine," he said, smiling at John. "I can't wait to meet the rest of your friends, Scott. So far they have the makings of the next Abercrombie and Fitch ad." Riley pulled him aside. "Ah you sure about this?" "What?" "Bringing Nico. I mean he's gay." "I didn't think you had a problem with that." "I don't. It's just he seems more like the martini-and-jazz type while Jake's is more a—" "Beer-and-peanuts type of place?" "Exactly." "Don't worry. It'll be fine." They drove to Jake's and when they arrived Nico stood outside staring. "My. Rugged, isn't it?" "Told you," Riley said under his breath. "You know, it's not polite to mumble, handsome." "Sorry, it's just I told Scott this wasn't your kind of place." "Oh and what exactly is *my* kind of place?" "You know those fancy places where you come out hungry." Nico smiled. "Look at you, two days and you already know me. Damn you for preferring ovaries to testicles." Riley laughed. "Now let's go in and have some fun." He shot ahead of them, sashaying his hips as he walked. "That man is a trip," Riley said. "He sure is." They walked inside and saw him already cozying up to Jake while he made him a martini. Jake said something and Nico laughed. "Looks like Jake's got the situation well in hand," Hanson said. "Hey, Jake." "Boys, Nico here is quite the character." "Don't we know it," Riley said, grinning. "Oh stop, little old me? I'm just your average Joe." Jake grinned. "I've only just met you, but I can see there's nothing *average* about you, Nico," Jake said back. "Oh my you do go on, Capt'n Butler." "Is he flirting with Jake?" Scott asked. "Looks that way," Riley said, grinning. "Jake can hold his own," Hanson said. Jake was smiling. "I love that movie." Nico looked as if he was about to wet himself with delight, while the guys just stood with their mouths open.

Jake looked at them. "What? It's a friggin' classic." "It certainly is. What's your favorite scene?" "When Rhett has had enough of Scarlett's pining for that pansy-assed . . ." He paused and looked at him. "No offense." "None taken. Ashley was a pansy. A big one. Go on." Jake could not help laughing. "When he had enough of her pining for Ashley, and then he carried her up those stairs to show her who rocked her best." Nico sighed. "That scene caused quite the controversy back then." "So what's your favorite scene, Nico?" Jake asked. "Ah, well I have several but I'll narrow it down." "Okay, shoot." "It's the scene where she's in the garden, trying to eat a rancid radish. Then vows to never go hungry again. It's woman power personified." "I like the scene where Rhett dumps her after he's had enough of her shit," John said. Scott looked at him. "No wonder you're single." John gave him a quick shove. "So enjoying your visit, Nico?" Jake asked. "Yes, I've met so many fine men, unfortunately they're all straight." Jake laughed. "Yeah, I could see that being a problem for you." "Oh it's just horrible. Here I thought I could maybe meet someone have roll in the hay and all I get are men who wear flannel." "Why is that bad?" Scott asked. "Because my young horse whisperer gay men wouldn't be caught dead in flannel." "Why not?" Asked John. "Because all that plaid is just a nightmare." At that moment, Ross walked in. "Well, look who the cat dragged in. How's it hangin' Harris?" "Slightly to the left. You?" Jake grinned. "To the right." "Gracious, stop teasing me pleeze. My heart can't take it." Nico joked while sipping his martini. "So another cat in a tree?" "Cat my ass. I was actually doing something important." "Oh yeah what finding Sammy again? Jake joked. "Who's Sammy? Some runaway?" Nico asked. "No, a big dumb dog who belongs to an even dumber woman." Jake answered. "She's a nice lady who lost her husband recently." "The poor dear." "That poor dear allows her dog to get loose every other week, and then Ross is the one who has to find him," Jake said. "And instead of saying no, he comes to the rescue again and again." "Well, I'm sure it's because he feels bad for her," Nico said. "Thank you. See, he gets it." Nico had tears in his eyes. "You okay, Nico?" "I'm fine. It's just so sweet that you care about her. Look at me tearing up, like Tammy Faye Baker. This is terrible." "Why?" Hanson asked. "Because my mascara isn't waterproof." "He's wearing mascara?"

John said. "Shut up, John." Jake handed Nico napkins. "Here you go, buddy." "Thank you, Jake. I'm all right now. Sometimes I'm just overcome with emotion." "It's fine, Nico. No worries," Jake said. "You are just the sweetest man, Jake." "That's not what the ladies say," Ross joked. "Up yours, Harris." "Gentlemen, please. No fighting on my account. Jake, can I get another martini? Extra olives this time?" "Comin' right up." "You're the best." A while later, after his third martini, Nico was definitely buzzed. "So I have something I want to ask all of you." "Okay, what is it?" Ross asked. "Well, would someone explain to me what's so great about vaginas?" Most of the guys spit out their beer. "What? What did I say?" Riley patted him on the back. "Nothing, don't mind them. You're in luck because I happen to be an expert on the subject." "I had a feeling you would be, handsome," Nico said. "Let's get you another martini, and I'll tell you all about it." Sometime later, Scott and John were nursing another beer. "I can't believe he asked that," John said. Scott was laughing. "I know." They couldn't help overhearing the end of the conversation. "And that, my friend, is why I'll go for women every time." Nico sat staring at him. "My, I had no idea that was even possible." "Believe me, it is." "Well, if you'll excuse me, I need to tinkle." "What the hell did you tell him?" John asked. "We just chitchatted about the G-spot." "G-spot?" "That's a myth," John said. "Sorry to bust your bubble, my friend, but it's not. I found it." "What? Who?" Ross asked nervously. "Breathe, Ross," Jake said. "No way. I've been searching for years and have never found any woman's G-spot. It doesn't exist." Riley grinned. "Maybe 'cause you didn't know where to look," Riley countered, sounding cocky as hell. "What's going on?" Jake asked. "Riley's saying he's found the fabled G-spot." Jake blew out an exaggerated breath. "Bullshit! No one can find that damn thing." "Yeah? Well, I'm telling you that I not only found it, but I rocked it." "Prove it." He pulled out his phone and hit a key. "Hey, gorgeous, it's me." "Hey, I thought you were out with the guys?" "I am." "Okay, so what's up?" "Well, first I'm going to put you on speaker so they can all hear you. Okay?" "Sure." "Right, so you're now on speaker. Anyway, they don't believe that I found your G-spot." "Oh really?" "Yes, they think I'm just blowing smoke up their asses." She laughed a deep-throated laugh, and he felt himself harden. "God,

I love your laugh. It's so damn sexy." Scott rolled his eyes. "Focus, Riley." "Right, sorry." "Hey, Sam." "Hey, Dimples." John looked at Riley. "Dimples?" "Tell you later." "So, Sam, is it true?" "Damn straight it is." Riley's grin grew wider. "Thanks, gorgeous." "Sure thing, handsome, we'll talk later?" "Count on it." He hung up. "Satisfied?" "My, my, it seems Sam is the one who's satisfied," Nico said, trying to contain his chuckling. "She is but then again so am I." "Rub it in, why don't you," Jake said. "I think I just did." Hanson stood up. "Well, if Riley's done tooting his own horn, I'd like to get going. Sunrise comes early." "Well, this has been so much fun. Jake, I can't thank you enough for hosting a pleasurable evening." "Glad you enjoyed, Nico. Hope the rest of your visit is as much fun." "Oh I'm sure it will be with handsome men such as yourself to entertain me. By the way, just out of curiosity, who is your Scarlett?" "There is no Scarlett." "I find that hard to believe." He eyed Jake's expression carefully. "Wait, there was someone. Wasn't there?" "Yeah, there was." Nico looked at him. "Oh my, you aren't over her?" "Nico," Ross said. "No, it's okay. I do still have feelings for Scarlett . . . er . . . Angela." "So why don't you play out your favorite movie scene with your lady love." "*Niiico*," Ross said again. "What? You want him to waste years the way you did with Sabrina?" "Low blow, Nico," Jake said. "No, he's right. I should have told Brina a long time ago. I let fear of rejection rule me. That was my mistake. Those are years I can never get back. If you still have feelings for her, do something about it." "Our illustrious lawman is right," Nico said. "Maybe it'll work out, maybe it won't, but only one way to find out," Ross said. "I can't." "Can't or won't?" Nico asked. At that moment, Ross noticed a magazine sticking out from behind the counter. A magazine that oddly looked a lot like *Cosmo*. "What's that? "What?" "That magazine." "It's nothing. Just something they sent me in the mail." Ross leaned over and grabbed it. "Hey, give it back." Ross looked at it and shook his head. He held it up and showed the guys. "*Cosmo*? Maybe there's hope for me yet," Nico teased. "It's not what it looks like." "Really? 'Cause it looks like *Cosmo*." Ross said. "Maybe he plays on my team after all," Nico said to Ross. Jake rolled his eyes. "Would you all just shut the fuck up so I can explain?" "Touchy too," Ross said, grinning. Jake gave him a look that could freeze ice. "Fuck you." "Does

Cosmo approve of that language?" "Up yours, Harris." "Either start explaining, or Nico's going to start picking out curtains," Riley joked. "I'm not a curtains kind of guy. I prefer drapes and valances," Nico joked back. Jake was growing more frustrated. "*This is a woman's magazine.*" "I think we've established that," Scott said, grinning. "The reason I got it is because of *this* article." He tossed the magazine on the bar and pointed to it. "One Hundred Ways To Give Your Man Pleasure Through *Fellatio*. Just imagine. That's one hundred days of different blow jobs," Jake said. They all stood quiet until finally Riley spoke. "Jake, I think I'd like to borrow that when you done." They all laughed.

Chapter Twenty-Four

The next day, Nico and Sabrina were sitting on the porch while Nico nursed a wicked hangover. "I'm telling you, Sabrina, I haven't had that much fun in years." She smiled at him. "I can see that. I haven't seen you this hungover in years." "Oh it was all Jake's fault. He makes the best martinis. Tell me, how ever did you manage such a long, dry spell with all these good-looking available men around?" "Because I run a farm and—"Oh stop, you're giving me a headache." "You already had one." "Well, you're making it worse." While Sabrina and Nico sat outside, Emily was in Sabrina's office, wishing she'd never suggested she'd spend the summer training. Since it meant having to deal with idiots like Mr. Peters. "Yes, Mr. Peters, I understand what you are saying. No, Taylor Farms is not in the habit of delivering subpar product. My aunt is in a meeting and won't be available until tomorrow. No, of course not, Mr. Peters. I assure you if there is anything to this we will . . . What? No, I wasn't implying you were being dishonest. I . . ." She rolled her eyes. "Since you're so dissatisfied with how I'm handling the situation . . ." She paused to take a deep breath. "Fine, I'll have her call you." She hung up and dropped her head on the desk. "Me and my big mouth." She walked outside to her aunt and Nico. "Hey, sweetie, what's wrong?" Nico asked. "Asshole Peters, that's what's wrong." "Who's that?" he asked. "A very difficult customer."

"Oh I've got a few of those myself." "So still want to take over?" "Yes, I'm not going to let a jerk like him stop me." "Bravo! Marlene would be proud." "Thanks." "So, Nico, you've asked us both about our men. Now it's your turn," Em said. "Moi?" "Yes, and don't play dumb, it doesn't become you," Sabrina said. "I never play anything, least of all dumb. I'm not seeing anyone right now." "Why not?" "I'm just growing tired of the whole dating scene." Sabrina eyed him. "You never got over him, did you?" "Who?" "You know who. Do you want me to say his name?" "No." Emily looked at him. "Who's she talking about?" "Someone from long ago." "Someone he was in love with." He let out a long, drawn-out breath. "His name was Francois. We met during Fashion Week in Paris." "How romantic," Emily said. "It was the best two weeks of my life." "So what happened?" "Life." "I'm not sure I understand," Emily said. "Let's just say, we both had different visions of what the future held." "I'm sorry." "Aren't you sweet. It was a long time ago." "Do you ever think of him?" Emily asked. "From time to time. It's for the best." "Then why do you sound so sad?" Emily asked. He shook his head. "Do I? I'll be all right." "I'm sorry I asked." "No, it's fine. As a matter of fact, I'm going to take a walk. Be back in a bit." "Sure." After he had gone, Emily sat down next to her aunt. "I don't think he's over him, Aunt Sabrina." "No, I never thought so either." "It's so sad." "It is, but sometimes love isn't enough."

Riley was mucking out one of the stalls in the barn when Nico came in. "Hey, you okay?" "Peachy." "You look blue to me." "And blue is so not my color." The sides of Riley's mouth curled up. "What's eating you?" "Love. What else?" "I'm starting to feel like everyone's cupid around here." "Why is that?" "Well, Scott fucked up with Em a while back and needed me to help bail his ass out." "He's lucky to have a friend like you." Riley grinned. "Did I say something funny?" "No. Well, yeah. See, Dimples and me had a rocky start." "Dimples? Oh, you mean Scott. Adorable nickname, by the way." "Well, you can thank Sam for that one. Anyway, we mostly got on each other's nerves in the beginning." "Really? I couldn't tell." "We're a lot better now. Believe me." "Oh I do." "Then there was Hanson and his troubles with Amanda." "The ex-wife who's not so ex, right?" "Someone's been busy catching up on the gossip around here." "Honey, knowing is half the battle." "Right you are. Then there was Ross with Sabrina." "Oh please, don't get me started on that one." "I hear you. Now you." "No need to add me to your list of the lovelorn. I'm fine." "You don't seem fine." "I was just remembering someone, that's all." "I take it you loved this someone." "I was young and naïve." "Relationships aren't easy. I can only imagine how being gay complicates things even more." "You are very wise for someone so straight." He grinned. "Thanks, but I think Scott, Sam, and Em would disagree." "Why is that?" "Mostly 'cause I've been an ass with Sam recently myself." "You? No?" "Yes, and I am lucky she forgave my stupid ass." "Now you have me intrigued. Do tell." He preceded to tell him about the time he got jealous of Brad and acted like an complete ass. "And that's the story, Lorrie." "Well, I could see why you were jealous since this Brad sounds like a tall drink of water in the desert." Riley looked at him. "Remember, I am gay." They both laughed. "Sam forgave me, and we've been tight ever since." "So you love her?" "Love isn't a strong enough word for how I feel about her." "My, my, this sounds serious." "It is, but let's get back to your younger, more naïve days." "I met Francois in Paris during Fashion Week." "Wait, they have a week about fashion?" Nico tsked. "We really must broaden your horizons." He grinned. "Go on." "Fashion Week in Paris is simply fabulous. Talented people come from all over to see new collections from the latest up-and-coming designers. I met Francois at the Armani show." "Hey, I know him." "There may be hope for you yet. Anyway, it was love at first sight. At least for me. We started talking about silk dupioni, and before either of us knew, it was dawn." "Wow." "Wow is exactly how I felt." "So what happened?" "We began a passionate affair, which I won't go into further details with you." "Thanks for that." "Of course when the show ended, I had to go back to New York." "And I'm guessing Francois stayed in Paris." "Right you are. I'm impressed." "Hey, I'm not just another pretty face," Riley said, smiling. Nico laughed. "Evidently not. And so, my dalliance with Francois came to an end." "Didn't you guys ever hear of long distance?" "Oh we tried that. He came to New York and I went to Paris but . . ." "But?" "As you said, relationships are difficult, and gay ones are even more difficult." "What went down?" "I am very open about being gay. I am proud of it and see no reason to hide it." "Let me guess, he didn't feel the same way?" "Sadly, no. He wasn't closeted, but he wasn't going out of his way telling people we were together. I couldn't understand why. I thought he was ashamed of us, of me. So we ended things." "Ever see him again?" "A couple of times at various shows. I usually left before we had a chance to talk. "Why?" "I don't know." "I think you do." "Seeing him, it's difficult." "Yeah, because you still have feelings for him." "I do." "So practice what you preach and do something about it." "Touché, my handsome young friend." "Anyway, I have to get back to work." "Of course, I apologize for taking up so much of your time." "Hey, no apology necessary. That's what friends are for." "Oh I love that song!" Nico said, beaming. "Me too." Nico looked at him raising his eyebrow in surprise. "Ah, that stays between us right?" "I'll take it to the grave." "Good to know." "Anyway, I'll let you get back to work. Ta-ta." Riley watched him sashay towards the house and laughed.

Emily was back at her Aunt's desk, running payroll. This was easy compared to her earlier call with Asshole Peters. Scott came in. "Hey, you almost done?" "Ten minutes." "I'll wait." "So still think you don't need any training?" She gave him a look. "What? Hey, you said it." "I did and you were right." "Can you repeat that since it's not something us guys hear often." "You were right. There's a lot more to this than I thought." "You've got time. You aren't graduating till next summer." "I know it's just . . . I want Aunt Sabrina doing what she loves already." "I know, but despite what you think she is." "I know but she loves designing more." "That's true, but I'm willing to bet that if the chips were down, she'd pick this again." "You think so?" "Yeah, I do. She grew up here, it's in her blood. Just like it's in yours." "You're right, but I still want her to have her dream." He leaned in and kissed her. "She will." She smiled at him. "I love you." "And I love you." "What's say we knock off for the day and get some dinner." "Sounds good."

Nico was feeling better after his talk with Riley. So much so that he decided to take a drive into town. "Nico, are you sure you don't want me to come with you?" "Darling, I navigate the wild streets of Manhattan every day." "Yes, I know but—" "I'll be fine." He didn't tell her about his plan to see Ross. "Take your phone and if you need anything—" "Yes, yes I'll call. Gracious, I'm gay not stupid." She laughed. Her concern seemed warranted when he got into town and somehow got turned around even though their streets were the size of an aisle at the supermarket. "This is ridiculous!" He parked, got out, and began walking. On his way, he passed a woman on the street. "You look lost." "Bless you for caring. I'm trying to find the local lawman. I seemed to have gotten turned around." "No, you're going the right way. It's just another two blocks." "Thank heavens. I've been searching forever." "Not a problem. In fact, I work at the station. I just stopped off to get my caffeine fix for the day." "What luck! I'm Nico." He put out his hand. She shook it. "I'm Linda. So what business do you have with Sheriff Harris?" "Oh no, it's nothing like that. I'm a longtime friend of Sabrina's and I'm visiting this week." "How nice." "Oh it has been." "Tell me all about it," she said. "Surely, but first do you mind if I have a sip of that drink?" "Sure." He took a sip, then another. "What is this? Crack?" "Nope, but it sure comes close." "What is it?" "It's a Mocha Sensation." "It certainly is. I must get one. Which way to paradise, darling?" She chuckled. "Follow me." Linda and Nico came into the station, chuckling. "I'm never going to forgive you, Linda, for making me eat half of that double chocolate muffin. Carbs go straight to my thighs." "Your thighs are fine." "You really think so? I mean, I am rather portly." "I like portly men. My husband, Ed is portly. I like him that way. There's just more to love." He chuckled. "I never thought about it that way." Ross had been listening to their conversation, trying not to laugh. "Hey, Nico, what brings you here?" "Well, I was just taking in the sights, and wanted to come by and see where the action happens." Linda nearly snorted. "Action? The most action we have is when Andy imitates Lady Gaga." He laughed. "She needs help with her fashion sense, but her songs are catchy. I love 'Alejandro.'" "And Andy would love you for saying that," Linda said. "So I see that Linda has corrupted you," he said, looking at the drink in his hand. "Thankfully so. Without my daily Starbucks fix, I've been starting to twitch. Thanks to this lovely assistant of yours . . ." Ross snorted rather loudly. "What? Did I say something funny?" "He doesn't think I'm lovely." "Nonsense, you're a gem." "That's 'cause you don't work with her," Ross mumbled. "Anyway, she had me taste this tempting libation and I was hooked." "I can see that. Why don't you come back into my office." "Surely, but don't I get a tour?" "There's not much to see." "Let me be the judge." "Okay, follow me." Ross gave him what he liked to call the five-cent tour. Andy was in the file room singing and dancing along to what was probably another Lady Gaga song. "That's Andy." "I assumed that since he's singing a Lady Gaga song." Ross grinned. "Does he do this often?" "Too often. My office is down the hall. Go on inside, be there in a minute." "Fine." Nico went in and looked around the small but tidy room. He liked a man who kept his working space neat. While looking around, he noticed several pictures of Sabrina, Emily, Hanson, Scott, and Jake. One in particular caught his attention. It was Sabrina, James, and Ross when they were teenagers. "When was this photo taken?" "Oh way back in the day. I think I was fifteen and Brina was thirteen or something like that." "You all look so happy." "We were. Sometimes I look at that picture and wish I had known then what I know now." "If you did, what could you have done differently?" "I wouldn't have let James fly. I would have taken his keys." "It was tragic. So young, so full of life." "I know. I still miss him." "I'm sure you do." He looked at the picture again. "You loved her then, didn't you?" "That obvious, huh?" "Yes, to anyone with eyes." Ross laughed. "And here I thought I had done such a good job hiding it. But everyone knew, James, Hanson, Jake, even the women I tried dating." Nico laughed. It's funny they all knew but not Brina. She was clueless." "She's a brilliant designer, but sometimes she's a little slow." Ross grinned. "Speaking of Sabrina, I think it's time for us to have a chat." "Sure, what's on your mind?" "Me, nothing. I know you have things on yours." "So what, you're psychic now?" "No, just perceptive." "What do you want to know?" "How you *really* feel about her working for me again." "Well, I—" "Please be honest." "Before I say anything, I just want you to know that I like you *a lot*." "I know. I'm very fond of you too." "I love Brina and I couldn't be prouder of her." "Nor I." "I know it's just—" "Just?" "Working from here will only get her so far. In the end, she'll need to work alongside you in New York." Nico looked at him. "I'm right, aren't' I?" "You are." "I knew it." "Take it easy. Remember, this is all hypothetically speaking." "No, it's not. 'Cause you and I both know it's going to happen. Her time is coming. She's earned it." "I couldn't agree more. You love her very much, don't you?" "I'd die for her." Nico felt himself tearing up. "Yes, I believe you would. That's why I know when the time comes I can trust you to do the right thing." "You mean walk away?" "Heavens, no. You belong together." "Sorry, you've lost me." "Oh heavens, did you think that's what my visit today was all about? Wanting you to step aside when the time came?" "Yeah." "I'm sorry if that's the impression I gave. I know you would never hold her back." "No, I wouldn't. I want her to succeed." "As do I. Though I want to assure you that I will not push her into doing anything she doesn't want to do. I want her designing *and* married to you." Ross looked at him. "You do plan on marrying her, don't you?" "Geez, you sound like Linda." "Well, good, because she's right." "Calm down, Nico, of course I plan on marrying her." "Well, that's a relief. So what are you waiting for?" "Hell, I'd marry her tomorrow if I could." "They why don't you?" "It's too soon for that kind of talk, Nico." "My dear Sheriff, haven't you waited long enough?" "I have but she hasn't. Hell, she only just told me she loved me a few weeks ago. She's not ready. It would only scare her away." "How do you know unless you ask?" "Because I know *her*." "Nonsense." "No, it's true. She hesitated when I asked her to go on a date." "Maybe she needed a leg wax?" Ross looked at him. "What? It would deter me. Hair is *sooo* unattractive." The corners of Ross's mouth were curling up. "Believe me, she's crazy about you." "You really think so?" "I know so. The way she talks about you, she lights up whenever you enter a room." "She does?" "Oh stop. Now you're just fishing." He smiled. "Anyway, I should get back. Sabrina probably thinks I'm lost in an apple orchard somewhere." He laughed. "Why would she think that?" "Never mind. Plus I know your time is valuable." Linda came in. "Sheriff, we got a problem." "If it's animal related, I'm not interested." "Nope, this one's strictly human." "Then I'm interested." Nico couldn't help smiling. "So what's the problem?" "The Woolsey boys are back at it again." "Damn it. What's it gonna take with those two?" Linda shrugged. Ross turned back to Nico. "Sorry, Nico." "No worries, we had our talk, and I think we're both on the same page." "Yeah we are and thanks." "For?" "For being a good friend to her and to me." He was obviously touched because he hugged Ross. "Oh, Sheriff, you are one in a million. If she doesn't marry you. I will." He laughed. Nico turned to face Linda. "Darling, I'm in town till Saturday. Are you interested in another coffee date?" "You bet I am. Come by any time." "Is tomorrow too soon?" "Honey, you had me at coffee." He laughed.

Scott sat staring at the phone. He knew he had waited too long to call Vanessa. By now she wouldn't remember who he was. That's if Brad had actually told her about him. With what had gone down between them, he doubted it. Still, he picked up the phone and dialed her number anyway. It rang several times, and then the machine picked up. *You have reached Carlton Ranch. Please leave a detailed message, and we will return your call promptly. Beep.* "Uh hi, this is Scott Pierce. Brad suggested I give you a call. I also attended Morrisville. Please call me at (607)557-0587. I look forward to hearing from you." Riley came in and saw him on the phone. "Who was that?" "I was leaving a message for Vanessa, Brad's sister." "You mean she wasn't waiting by the phone since spring for your call? Shame on her." "Can the sarcasm, Riley. I'm not in the mood." The phone rang and Scott reached for it eagerly. "Hello?" "Scott, this is Vanessa Carlton." "Oh hi, thanks for calling back so quickly." "Sure. So Brad mentioned you'd be giving me a call." "Yeah, sorry, I meant to do it a whole lot sooner." "That's okay, things happen. So you attended Morrisville?" "Yeah, I just graduated in June." "Congratulations." "Thanks. When did you graduate?" "Let's just say a ways back." He laughed. "I can take a hint." "Good, we'll get along fine," she said, laughing. While talking, Riley motioned to him that he'd come back later. "So Brad told me that you have a nice ranch down in the Bluegrass State." "It's smaller than some of the ranches here, but I'm proud to call it mine." "Sounds great. I can't wait to have my own one day." "Brad mentioned that too. He also mentioned that you gave him a nasty right hook." Scott grew nervous. "Oh well . . . er . . . he . . . I . . ." She started to laugh. "Relax, I'm not going to exact vengeance on behalf of my brother." "You're not?" "No, he told me he that he hit on your girlfriend. So the way I see it, he deserved to get clocked." "Er, I don't know what to say." "Then don't say anything. Let me do the talking." "Okay." "How would you like to take a trip down here?" "Are you serious?" "Yes, I could show you around." "Wow, that would be great." "So how about Saturday?" "This Saturday?" She laughed again. "Unless you'd prefer one next month." He knew she was teasing him.

"Just tell me where and I'll be there." "Great. Text me your info, and I'll pick you up at the airfield. I'm looking forward to meeting you, Scott." "Likewise. By the way, I have a friend who just so happens to be visiting. Would it be okay if I brought him?" "I don't see why not." "Great! See you, Saturday." "See you then." Scott hung up and practically ran into Riley on his way. "Whoa where's the fire?" "Sorry, I'm going to Vanessa's ranch on Saturday! I'm soo excited!" "I couldn't tell," he teased. "I gotta go tell Dad, Mom, Em, and—" "Maybe you want to send out an announcement?" "Will you ever stop busting my balls?" "The day I stop busting them is the day I stop caring. Think of it as my own personal hallmark card." Scott rolled his eyes. "I think I'd rather get the card." Riley laughed. "So you're heading down Saturday?" "Yep, and I'm taking John with me." "Sounds like a plan. So looks like Brad came through after all, huh?" "Yeah," Scott said begrudgingly. "You still don't like him. Do you? "Nope." "Me either." They laughed. Scott told everyone about his trip. His father and his mother, she had screamed so loud he thought they had heard her all the way in Seneca. He saved telling Emily for last. "Oh, Scott, I'm soo excited for you!" She hugged and kissed him. "I know. Me too! I can't wait to get down there." He paused. "Of course, I'll miss you." "I'll miss you too, but you'll be back before you know it. Oh, you're going to miss Sam." "She's coming?" "Yep, she's arriving Saturday afternoon." "Anyway, I'd better go tell John that he's making a trip to the Bluegrass State." "Hey, wouldn't it be nice if he met someone down there?" "God, you are such a hopeless romantic." "Hey, it could happen." "We're talking about John. The guy who breaks out in hives at the mention of love." "You and I both know why that is. He was obviously hurt badly by someone he gave his heart to." "Again, I repeat. Hopeless romantic." "What you don't agree with my theory?" "Oh no, I definitely do. He was hurt bad once upon a time." "He's never told you anything?" "Never, and I doubt he will." "Well, I hope one day he meets someone who makes him as happy as I am with you." He smiled and kissed her. "I hate to break it to you, Em, but John has a better chance of getting struck by lightning." She laughed.

Scott found John up near the milking center. "Hey, what's up?" "I just got invited down to Louisville to see a ranch." The guys whistled.

"You must be in seventh heaven," Pete said. "I am." "Wait, is this that guy's sister?" John asked. "Yeah." "So Brad came through after all." "Yeah, he did." "So when you heading' down, Scott?" Max asked. He looked at John. "*We* are heading down on Saturday." John looked at him. "We?" "Yeah, I told her you were visiting, and she said I could bring you." "And were you ever going to ask me?" "I'm asking now." "You're so controlling." Scott laughed. "So what's the deal?" John asked. "We're going to fly into Bowman Airfield, and she'll pick us up there. You down?" "Sure, why not? I've got nothing better to do," he said, sounding sarcastic. "Cheer up, John. Maybe you'll meet someone." He paused and then said, grinning, "Yeah, a horse." They all laughed.

Chapter Twenty-Five

Scott and John arrived at Bowman Airfield. Bowman was about five miles from downtown Louisville. Carlton Ranch was about fifteen miles from there. "Man, talk about a small airport," John said. "It is, but it's a hell of a lot easier than flying into Blue Grass Airport in Lexington and then driving nearly seventy-five miles here." "Definitely easier." "So what does Vanessa look like?" "I don't know." "What do you mean you don't know?" "I was so excited about everything, I forgot to ask." "That's just great. We're in a strange place, and we haven't a clue what the person picking us up looks like. For all we know, she could be toothless and have warts." Scott looked at him. "You really need to stop reading those *Lord of the Rings* books. Not everyone looks like Gollum." At that moment, John's eyes happened to look toward the entrance, and a tall, slender woman began walking toward them. As she walked, the sun hit her brown hair, showing off its fiery highlights. It was pulled back and up into a high ponytail. She wore cat-eye sunglasses. John secretly hoped that this was Vanessa. "Scott?" "Vanessa?" She nodded and took off the glasses. "Sorry I'm late." "No worries. We haven't been waiting long." John stared. *Hazel.* Her eyes were hazel. She looked at him. "So I take it this is your friend." He still said nothing. "Does he speak?" "Usually." He gave him a kick. "Er, sorry." She smiled and put her hand out. "I'm Vanessa." "John, nice to meet you." He shook her hand, but continued to hold it. Normally she'd have pulled it away herself, but for some reason she liked how it felt. They stood like that until Scott decided to break it up. "You two going to let go of each other's hands anytime soon?" he joked. They both awkwardly released the other's hand. "So are you ready for a tour?" "You bet." She smiled. "I'm parked out front." She walked ahead of them. As they walked, Scott murmured to him. "You're right, very unattractive." "*Shuuut* up." The drive through downtown Louisville was enjoyable. The bluegrass blew in the summer breeze and looked like ocean waves flowing over the fields. They passed several ranches, which must have cost the owners a small fortune to operate. "This is amazing," Scott said. "It is beautiful. We call this Ranch Row." "What do you think of the views, John?" she asked. "They're great." The truth was he wasn't looking at the famed bluegrass views, only at her. "When do we get there?" "It's just a few miles more." "So, Scott, why don't you tell me what got you started on this path." "Well long story short, my girlfriend's father gave me his horse. And that was all it took." "I know what you mean. It was the same for me." Vanessa's eyes locked onto John's in the rearview mirror. "I'm sorry, John, we're being rude by talking about something you have no interest in." "I'm interested." *Boy am I interested.* "I know more than you think since this is all he talks about." She laughed. "Sort of like being brainwashed." He laughed. "Yeah, I guess so." *God, she has a great smile.* "Well, I hope you two won't be disappointed when you see my ranch. It's a lot smaller than these." "Vanessa, there's no way I could ever be disappointed," Scott said. "Me either," John said looking at her in the mirror. Scott grinned as he looked out the window. It appeared that his friend John had been hit by the lightning after all. During their tour, Scott had been full of questions, which Vanessa gladly answered. John didn't mind so much, since he enjoyed listening to her talk. Her voice was equal parts sexy and sultry, with a hint of Southern that only came out once in a while. It was the kind of voice that could tie a man in knots if he let it. And right now he felt like a pretzel. "Why don't we go back to the house and get something cool to drink?" "Sounds good." "Why don't you two head up and I'll catch up with you in a bit? I want to take a walk around the place." "Okay. See you later." The truth was he needed some time away from her. He had to get a hold of himself. Vanessa and Scott sat in her office. "So what do you think of my ranch?" "Are you kidding? I love it!" "Well, I'm glad to hear that because I want you to come work for me." "Work for you? Here?" "Unless you want to work down the road at the Parson place." "What? No of course not. I just . . . wow . . . I wasn't expecting this." "Well, I recognize potential when I see it, and I'm not one to waste time." "Yeah, I can see that." "The position I have in mind is junior foreman." He said nothing, just listened. "You'd be working alongside Ray, our head foreman. Ray's a great guy, really knows his stuff. He used to work in rodeos and was trainer to a few Triple Crown contenders. You'll learn a lot from him." The man sounded like a god to Scott. "I can't wait to meet him." "So when can you start?" "Is immediately too soon?" She laughed.

John ended up in the equestrian center. There were several people in the midst of getting lessons, but one stood out. A teen with long strawberry-blond waves cascading down her back. She wore a riding outfit complete with crop. Although she was young, he could easily see that in just a few years, she'd be real heartbreaker. "Hey, how goes it?" he said to her. "Okay so far. Are you here for lessons?" "No, I'm here visiting with a friend. He's talking to the owner." "Oh you mean Vanessa." "Yeah. I'm John." He extended his hand. "Eve." "Nice to meet you, Eve." "So what's your friend talking to Vanessa about?" "Horses, what else? Probably gonna marry one someday." She laughed. "That bad?" "You have no idea. I went to Morrisville with the guy. Sometimes he would neigh in his sleep." She laughed again. "I like you, John." "Thanks." "Eve!" John saw an instructor calling her over. "Well, I'd better let you go." "Will you be here tomorrow?" "Well, we're leaving, but I could probably stop by." "Cool." He watched her trot over to the waiting instructor. When he got back to the house, he knocked on Vanessa's office door and went in. "You two still at it?" "Sorry, we could talk about this all day." "No kidding." "So where've you been?" Scott asked. "The equestrian area. I made a friend." "A horse?" Scott joked. "No, that would be *your* idea of making a friend." Vanessa laughed as Scott gave him the finger. "Teenager, long strawberry blonde hair. "That's Eve. She's one of our more serious students. She's been in shows and won a few trophys." "That's impressive." John said. "How old is this girl?" Scott asked. "She started later than most of our other students, but she more than makes up for it in talent and enthusiasm. I believe she's turning fifteen soon. Actually, Eve has always had a crush on my brother." "Brad?" Scott said. "Brad, the guy who hit on Em?" He looked over at her, wondering if he shouldn't have mentioned it. "Don't worry, I know what my brother did." "She's got a crush on him?" Scott asked incredulously. She gave him a look and then he backpedaled. "Not that there's anything wrong with that. He's a good-looking guy." John looked at him. "You should sit down before you hurt yourself." Which made Vanessa laugh. "You two can relax. I know my brother isn't your favorite person." "Nope, he broke the bro code," John said. She looked at him. "The bro code?" "Top three rules of the bro code are you don't date someone your friend dated. You don't sleep with anyone your friend slept with, and lastly, you don't hit on another guy's girl." "Guys follow this code?" "Sure. Unless they're a complete asshole." John realized he had just called her brother an asshole, and he winced, thinking she was about to plow into him. "I couldn't agree more." He couldn't believe his ears. "I told my brother he was a jerk for doing that." Most women would have made excuses or defended their brother, but not her. Where had she been his whole life? "I'm sure she'll meet some guy her own age and forget all about your brother," John said. "I'm not so sure. She's been crazy about him since she was five." "That long?" Scott asked. "I thought she would have outgrown it by now, but she still insists that one day they'll end up together." "Poor kid. She's about to find out the hard way that life doesn't always hand you what you want," John said. "How's your brother been handling it?" "Brad's idea of handling it is by *not* handling it." "For once, I'm on Brad's side. It's awkward," Scott said. "I get that, but one day he'll have no choice. Anyway, it's getting late. Let's have some dinner. You guys are leaving tomorrow, so you'll want to pack and get to bed early." The next day they sat on the porch, sipping iced tea, admiring the beauty of Carlton. "This place is amazing," Scott said. "It's pretty cool." "And I'll be working here. Imagine junior foreman." "I don't have to, since you've been doing enough imagining for both of us." He smiled. "Yeah, I have." John looked down at his watch. "I'll be back." "Going to see your girlfriend?" "Jealous?" "Of a fifteen-year-old?" "Oh that's right, you're only interested in horses." "Ha-ha." "Come on, I'll introduce you." When Scott and John found Eve, she was adjusting her jodhpurs. "Hey, John." "Hey, Eve. How's it goin'?" "Good. I nailed all my jumps yesterday." "That's great, Eve." She eyed Scott. "Who's the guy with the dimples?" "This is the friend I was telling you about." "Oh the one who'll marry a horse someday." Scott punched his arm. "Pay no attention to this idiot. I'm Scott." "Eve." "Yeah, I know. Beautiful horse." "She is gorgeous. Wish she was mine but she's not. She's Vanessa's. Her name's Ginger." Scott put out his hand to her, and she licked it. Then she nudged him with her head. "She likes you." "All horses like him. He's like a distant relative," John joked. "Up yours, John." "Is that anyway to talk in front of an impressionable young lady?" That made Eve laugh. "Impressionable? Me? You guys are a trip." "So, Eve, Vanessa mentioned that you have the hots for Brad." Scott frowned at him. "What? I'm just asking." "I'm going to marry him someday." "Does Brad know that?" John asked, smiling. "Brad's in denial but he'll come around." "Anyway, we should get going to the airport." "Will you be coming back?" "Scott's going to start working here next month, and I'm sure I'll be visiting him." "And Vanessa," Scott mumbled under his breath. "What?" John said. "Nothing. You'll definitely see us around." "Cool. Well, have a safe trip back." "Thanks, Eve." John and Scott walked back up toward the house. "Nice girl," Scott said. "Yeah, and she's going to be a real looker very soon." Scott looked at him. "Yeah, you're right. She is. I wonder if Brad knows what he's in for?" "Probably not since he's in denial." They laughed. Vanessa was waiting outside to say bye. "Well, I hope you enjoyed your visit." "Are you kidding? I'll be talking about it for days." John looked at him. "Who are you kidding? You'll be talking about it till you're back again." Then he mimicked a gun and shooting himself in the head. Vanessa laughed. "So I'll fill Ray in." "Great, can't wait to meet him." Scott grabbed Vanessa and hugged her. John stood there, feeling more than a little envious. "You know, I deserve one of those just for listening about ponies for the past two days." "Yes, you do." She smiled and hugged him. John had never known a hug could feel so good. As they pulled part, she moved left to kiss him on the cheek, but he also moved the same way and their lips met. It was only for a moment but the air crackled around them. They stood staring at one another, not speaking. "Er, John, we should get going. Don't want to miss our flight." "Yeah. Take care, Vanessa." "You too, John." Scott pulled him into the waiting taxi, and just like that they were on their way. She stood and touched her lips the whole time she watched the taxi drive up the path. Later, when they were seated on the plane, Scott looked at him. "So what that was all about?" "I haven't a clue." Scott looked at him. "Dude, the air sizzled when you two kissed. I mean, it was crazy." "I know." "You look a little freaked out." "That's 'cause I am freaked out. See, I told you this would happen. I visited you in Cupidsville, and now I'm acting like the rest of you." "You seem upset." "That's 'cause I am!" "Who screwed you over, John?" "Leave it alone, Scott." "I won't. For four years, I watched you date countless women only to have you ditch them the minute things got remotely involved." "I'm not into relationships, lots of guys aren't." "Yeah, but I think someone hurt you, right?" "You don't know what you're talking about." "Then tell me." "Look Scott, I know you're trying to help, but you can't." "So you're just going to run from Vanessa?" "No, because there's nothing to run from. I just met her for Pete's sake." "That's bull, and you know it. I saw your face in that airport." "Leave it alone, Scott." "Whatever, but this thing isn't going away. I'm going to be working there and you'll be visiting." "I'll cross that bridge when I get to it." "Knowing you, you'll burn that bridge so you won't have to deal with crossing it." "I'm putting my headphones on now." "Fine." They sat in silence the rest of the flight.

Nico's bags were packed and loaded in his car. "I can't believe how fast the week went," Sabrina said. "Time just flies whenever people are with me." "Yes, though not fast enough." "Even though you've been bitchy, I'm still going to miss you." "Special sheets, freshly baked scones, special dinners. You're right. I've been such a bitch." He laughed. "Oh I do love you," he said, smiling. "I love you too. Looks like some other people want to say bye too." He saw Riley and Hanson walking toward them. "Nico, safe trip back. It's been a real pleasure getting to know you," Hanson said, shaking his hand. "I feel the same way. I've enjoyed my visit immensely. Especially our time at Jake's. Speaking of which, keep hitting that G-spot, Riley." "I intend to," he said, grinning. "Do

I even want to know?" Sabrina asked. "Of course, just ask your sheriff. He'll tell you all about it." Riley was trying very hard not to laugh. "Well, I guess I should make my exit." "Wait!" Emily was walking briskly toward them. "Sorry, got stuck on another happy phone call with asshole Peters." "Oh, honey, tell him to stick it where the sun doesn't shine." "I'm very tempted, believe me." "I've enjoyed spending time with you, Nico." "As have I, my dear. You are just lovely, and if Scott doesn't put a ring on that finger, I'll come down here and personally knock some sense into him." "Thanks, I'll miss you." "I'll miss you too. Call me anytime to discuss anything. Mostly I'm interested in the juicy stuff." She smiled. "I will." He got into his car. "Alas, parting is such sweet sorrow." They stood waving as he drove away. "Did he just quote Shakespeare?" Riley asked. "He sure did," Hanson said, smiling and waving. "That man is a trip," Riley said, laughing. "He sure is," Sabrina said, smiling.

A few weeks later, Emily was heading back for what would be her last year at SUNY. She had spent a good portion of the summer training. "You ready to go, Em?" Scott asked from her doorway. "Just about." He stood staring at her. "Why are you looking at me like that?" "Because you're beautiful and I love you." She walked over to him and kissed him. "Keep that up and we won't make it to the car." She looked at the clock. "We've got time." "Even if we didn't, I'd make time." He picked her up and carried her to the bed. "Are you trying to seduce me, Mr. Pierce?" "No, I'm *definitely* seducing you, Ms. Taylor." She laughed as he laid her down on her bed. With each kiss, he removed a piece of clothing until she was naked beneath him. "You are just sooo beautiful. How'd I get this lucky?" "The same way I did. Scott?" "Yeah?" "I wish it could always be this way." "It will, Em. That I promise you." They made tender love, and when it was time to leave, they came out. Riley was waiting by the car. "What the hell are you doing?" "Riding shotgun." "Again? Why can't you make your own trip?" "'Cause annoying you is a lot more fun." "You're a dick." "But you love me anyway." He smiled. "I feel lots of things towards you, Riley, but love isn't one of them." "Everyone gathered by the car. "I'll miss you," Sabrina said. "I'll miss you too. I'll be back on break before you know it." She hugged her as did Hanson. He pointed at Scott. "If this one gives you any trouble, just call me and I'll take care of it." Scott looked at him. "Whose side are you on, Dad?" "Hers." She laughed and got into the car. Riley opened the back door. "Where do you think you're going?" Hanson asked. "He's going to see Sam." "Again?" "That's exactly what I said." "I think you just enjoy busting Scott's balls." He laughed. "Well, that's an added bonus." "Just try not to kill each other." "No worries, we've moved past that stage." "Oh good, that's a relief," Hanson said, grinning.

Six months later

Scott sat atop Sugar, anxiously awaiting the arrival of an Arabian that was being delivered. After many years, Ray was finally able to convince Vanessa to try their hand at thoroughbred racing. Ray had worked in the industry for a time, so he knew the ins and outs. A truck appeared way down the road, and Scott took off to tell Vanessa and Ray that it was coming. "I hope we're doing the right thing, Ray." "Ain't like you to get cold feet, Nessa." "I know, but this is a big gamble with a high price tag if it doesn't work out." "It'll work. Besides, if it doesn't, he'll make a fine addition to the local petting zoo." She laughed. "Ray, you're terrible." He grinned. "I know." They saw Scott approaching, riding like Paul Revere himself. "The Arabian's here!" "I could've sworn you were about to tell us the British were coming with the way you were riding," Ray joked. "I'm excited." "We couldn't tell," Vanessa teased. After several minutes, the truck pulled in and two men got out. "Delivery for Ms. Carlton." "That'd be me. You can put him in the paddock for now." "Sure thing." After they left, Vanessa, Scott, and Ray stood, staring at their magnificent Arabian. "So how does it feel to be the proud owner of an Arabian, Nessa?" "Pretty damn good, Ray." "I think he's the most beautiful horse I've ever seen," Scott said. "Hey, you think one day we'll be standing in the Winner's Circle at the Derby?" Scott asked. "That's the plan, son," Ray said, sounding hopeful. He looked over at Vanessa and nodded at her. "So, Scott, there's something I wanted to talk to you about." "Sure." "Well, you've been doing a great job here." "Thanks." "You've not only proved you're hardworking but that you're eager to learn too." "The boy's a sponge." "You make learning easy, Ray." "Still, Ray and I have talked it over, and we'd like you to be assistant trainer." He stood in stunned silence. "I don't know what to say." "Say yes, thunderhead." He smiled. "Of course it's yes." "There's one more thing." "Okay." "Ray would like you to assist him with training our newest addition." His eyes grew even larger. "Are you serious?" "Yes, it was Ray's idea." "Scott, you've got something real special when it comes to horses, and I think it would be beneficial for all if you helped train him." "I won't let either of you down." "We know you won't, Scott." "So before we go any further, we need to come up with a name for this beauty." "I got it," Ray said, smiling. "Since he's got all our dreams riding on him, how about Dreaming?" "I like it," Vanessa said. "I do too." "All right, Dreaming it is. And may he one day, bring us all the way to the Derby."

Epilogue

Five years later

Scott, Vanessa, and Ray stood taking in the beauty of Churchill Downs. "I can't believe we're here," Vanessa said. "Neither can I. I feel about as nervous as a cat in a room full of rockin' chairs," Ray said. "I second that," she said. "Would you two relax? We got this. Dreaming can't lose." "You sound awfully sure of yourself, Scott." "You bet your ass I'm sure. Er, sorry, Vanessa." She laughed. "No apology necessary. I'm glad you're so confident. It helps make up for the fact that Ray and I are so nervous." "Listen, we worked too hard, for too long, not to win. Dreaming won't let us down. He wants this as much as we do. Trust me," Scott said. "From your lips to God's ears, son," Ray said, smiling. "The race will be starting soon, we should get to our box," Vanessa said.

Sabrina stood in her office, staring at the dress Sam was modeling. Something wasn't quite right with it. "Do you want me to twirl some more?" She smiled. "All the twirling in the world won't help. I'm sorry, Sam, I don't know what's bothering me about it." She looked down at herself. "Looks good to me, but then again, I'm just the model." "Sam, you're never just the model, you are the showcase." Sam laughed. "You sound just like Nico." She laughed. "I meant to." "Do you ever think about how it all started for you, Sam?" "How could I not? It was so comical." "You and Em were supposed to meet me for lunch." "But Em got stuck working, so it was just the two of us." "Nico's model Simone got sick last minute, and he couldn't find anyone to replace her." "I walked in and the next thing I knew I'm being stripped and dressed like a Barbie doll. I told him he was crazy. I had no experience how could I model." "You were a natural and everyone fell in love with you." "I still can't believe the name he and Riley came up with." Sabrina smiled. "Mocha Muse." "Speaking of Riley. How is he?" "He's good. He's going to come to Paris for the show." "That'll be romantic." "If we can get away from everyone." "I'm sure Riley will have a plan." "I still can't believe we're married." She laughed. "I'm still getting used to it. Though I definitely love being married. And that's something I never thought I'd hear myself say." "Anyway, enough about me. What about you? What about Ross? Any chance you'll get back together?" "I doubt it. Ever since we broke up, we're like two strangers." "I'm sorry, Sabrina." "So am I, but life doesn't always give you a happy ending." Sabrina sat down at her desk. "Why don't you go change? We'll get Nico's opinion when he comes back from his meeting. "Sure." Sam walked out and Sabrina's phone rang. "Sabrina Taylor." "Hi, Aunt Sabrina, bad time?" "No, actually you're stopping me from taking a pair of scissors to a dress Sam's modeling." "I hope you wait 'til she's out of it?" She laughed. "No worries, your BFF is safe. So what's new?" "The bank finally approved the loan." "That's wonderful, Em! How did you get them to do that?" "The only way I could get them to approve it was by lowering the amount." "By how much?" "Half." "Half? That's not enough, is it?" "No, but Vanessa found me a private backer who'll lend me the rest." "How did she find out?" "Hanson and Amanda were visiting Scott and he told them about it." "So Scott knows?" "Yes." "Who's the backer?" "I don't know." "What do you mean you don't know?" "The only condition was he had to remain anonymous." "I'm not sure I like that." "I didn't either until Vanessa assured me this person was completely trustworthy." "So she knows him then?" "Yes." "That's great, Em!" "I know, which is why I called you. I wanted you to be the first to know." "Your father would be so proud." "You think so? Didn't he always want to keep things the way they were?" "Yes, but in order to keep the farm competitive, it needs to keep up with the other dairies, which in all honesty we both know it hasn't." "To change the subject, Uncle Ross came by earlier this week." She paused. "How's he doing?" "Okay, I guess. I'm sure he misses you." "How can you be so sure?" "He's loved you since you were kids that kind of love doesn't die." "Things change, Em." "Not this. I see it in his eyes when he asks about you." She remained quiet. "Aunt Sabrina, why don't you call him?" "You know why." "The only thing I know is that two people who clearly still care about each other are apart." "We're apart because Ross got tired of sharing me with my career." "For which he was very wrong. Just like Scott was wrong with the way he handled things with us. As far as I'm concerned, we're better off without them." "Who are you trying to convince, Em, me or you?" She said nothing. "The truth is, I still miss Ross." "Sometimes I ask myself if losing him was worth it?" "Of course, it was. Designing has always been your dream. You so deserve this." "Thanks, honey, but what good are dreams if you have no one to share them with." "They both remained quiet." "Well, I should get back to work." Em said. "Me too, I need to figure out what's bugging me about this dress." "Congrats again on the loan. Keep me posted." "I will. Aunt Sabrina?" "Yes, honey?" "Why is it still hard sometimes?" "Because you still love him honey, and sometimes love hurts." "It's been a long time, I thought it would be better by now." "If it's one thing i've learned is that as much as time can heal, it can also hurt too." Sabrina said thinking about Ross. "Yeah, well at least the dairy keeps me busy. "Em said. "How about I take some time off soon and we drown our sorrows in a few pints of Cherry Garcia and Cookie Dough?" "That sounds great. Love you, Aunt Sabrina." "Love you too. Bye."

Scott, Vanessa, and Ray stood in the Winner's Circle. Dreaming had done it. He'd won the Kentucky Derby. "I still can't believe it!" Scott said excitedly. "Neither can I!" Vanessa said. "This wouldn't have happened if you hadn't worked on me, Ray." "Ah you would have done it eventually, Nessa. You just needed a push." She laughed. "More like a hard shove." It was his turn to laugh. Brad was working his way through the crowd. "Nessa!" "Brad! You made it!" "Yeah, sorry I missed it but my flight was delayed." "No worries, you're here now." "So how does it feel, sis?" "Amazing. Thanks for being here, Brad." "Like I'd be anywhere else," he said, grinning. He looked over at Scott and Ray. "Hey, Ray, Scott. Nice to see you again." They shook hands. "Nessa!" Brad turned around to see the most gorgeous young woman in a striking hat walking toward them. "Who's that?" he asked curiously. "Eve, silly." "That's Eve?" "Yes, Brad." He couldn't believe his eyes. *Why, only yesterday she was well a teenager, and now today she was a woman.* "I didn't recognize her without her jodhpurs." Vanessa laughed. "She does look very different. Very grown up." "*Very.*" "Nessa!" You won the friggin' Derby!" "Well, Dreaming won. We all just went along for the ride." Brad couldn't stop himself from staring. "Scott! Are you as happy as I am?" "More." She laughed as he pulled her in for a hug. "Hey, Ray." "Eve, you look great." "You do," Vanessa chimed in. "I love the dress and the hat is just gorgeous." The lavender dress brought out her hazel eyes, peaches-and-cream complexion, and strawberry-blond hair. The hat was a deeper shade of lavender with a single fuchsia orchid on it. In a word, she was stunning. "Thanks, Sabrina did an amazing job." "Sabrina made them for you?" Vanessa asked. "Yes, well, I had asked Scott to see if she'd have time to make me something." What she was leaving out was that she had gone to Scott and asked him for help. She was tired of Brad seeing her as a child. She wanted him notice her, and she figured the Derby was the place to do it. "Well, you look amazing." "Thanks, Nessa." "Hello, Eve." "Hi, Brad." He reached for her hands and held them out. "Look at you. You look beautiful, Eve." "Thanks, Brad." He was staring at her. "Something wrong?" "No, it's just . . ." "Just?" "I'm not used to seeing you look so . . ." "So?" "So grown-up." "Oh." "She felt her heart swell. "Thanks, Brad." "You're welcome." Later that evening, everyone was back at Carlton to celebrate Dreaming's win. Vanessa and Ray were trying to get Scott to call Emily. "Just call her, Scott," Vanessa said. "Things are awkward now." "And whose fault is that?" Ray asked. "Mine." "Damn right. I still can't believe you gave her that old 'come or else' speech." "I didn't say it like that, Ray." "No, but in the end that's what you basically meant." "She still doesn't know that the money is coming from you, does she?" Vanessa asked. "No and she's not going to." "Why the hell not?" Ray asked. "If she knew, she wouldn't take it." "I'm not so sure about that, Scott," Vanessa said.

"Look, I know you two mean well, but what Em and I had is over." "Son, pride has left many a man lonely." "I'm with Ray. *Call her.*" "I'll think about it." Later that evening, he excused himself from the party and got up the nerve to call her. "Emily Taylor." He froze for a second. "Hello?" "Hi, Em." It was her turn to freeze. "Scott?" She couldn't believe her ears. "Why are you calling?" "Can't I just call to see how you're doing?" "Sure, except you haven't done that in years." "I'm sorry." "I'm busy so what's up?" "We won, Em." "Oh my God!" For that one moment, they forgot all the hurt and pain of the past. "Scott, you won the Kentucky Derby!" "Well, Dreaming did have a little something to do with it." She laughed. "Nice that you give him some credit." He laughed. "You were the first person I thought of after the race. I wanted to hold you. But you weren't there." "Whose fault is that?" "Mine." She paused. "Well, since we're sharing news, I have some of my own." "I got the loan." "That's great, Em. How did you do it? I thought the bank was set against it?" "They were, but I convinced them to lend me half." "Where will the other half come from?" "An anonymous backer." He could hear Vanessa in his head. *Tell her.* "I'm not sure I like that." "That's exactly what I thought, but Vanessa vouched for them." "Whoever this guy is, I'd like his number." "What makes you think it's a guy?" *Shit.* "I don't know, just the first thing that popped into my head. If Vanessa said he's solid he is. Not that you need my approval." "You're right, I don't." "Look, Em, I didn't call to fight." "Then why did you call?" "To give you the best news of my life." "It's been three years, Scott." "And in those three years not a day has gone by that I haven't thought of you. I tried to forget you, but I couldn't. I miss you, Em." She hesitated. "What do you want me to say? "Say you still care. Say you miss me too." "I'm very happy for you, Scott." "That's not all and you know it." "I have to go, Scott." "Em, let me come visit. We can talk." "Why? Nothing's changed. You're still down there and I'm still up here. Unless you plan on coming back?" He paused. "You know I can't. We just won the Derby. There will be all sorts of things to handle." "Right. So once again, Scott Pierce's life trumps everything else." "Come on Em, I—" "Please tell Vanessa I'll be in touch to set up the wire transfer." "Em, please." "Take care of yourself, Scott." She hung up before he could say anything else. "That was smooth." He turned around to see Vanessa standing in the doorway. "How long have you been standing there?" "Long enough. "Yeah, well what's done is done." "That's bullshit! That girl was the love of your life, and as far as I can tell she still is." "It's not that simple, Vanessa." "Yes, it is. You love her, you get her back." "It won't work, not this time. So forget it." "God, why are you being so stubborn?" She was in his face now, making gestures with her hands. "You aren't gonna hit me, are you?" The sides of her mouth curled slightly. "I would if I thought it would knock some sense into you." "Em said she'll call you to set up the details for the wire transfer." "Fine." "Vanessa, I need you to promise that you won't tell her about the money." "Scott . . ." "Promise me." "All right, fine. I promise. But *you* should tell her. Now if you'll excuse me, I have a party to get back to." Back at the party, Brad had been watching Eve all night. *She's twenty, get a grip*. Eve stood chatting with a bunch of trainers. One of them, Seth, was being a little too friendly and Brad didn't like it. "Hey, little brother, what's eating you?" "Nothing. Why?" "Well, you're shooting daggers with your eyes at poor Seth." "There's nothing poor about him. Seth's got a rep." "Eve's just enjoying the attention. She's too smart to fall for his crap." "She's naïve." Vanessa laughed. "Eve is a great many things, but naïve is not one of them." He looked over and saw Seth's hand slinking lower on her backside. She was laughing at whatever he was saying. "Brad, she can handle herself." He stood up and started walking in their direction, and Vanessa grabbed his arm. "What are you doing?" "Stopping her from making a mistake." "Aren't you overreacting?" "No, Seth's a jerk." "I'm telling you, Eve can handle herself." They looked over at them, and Seth's hand was now resting on her ass. "Looks like Seth is the one doing the handling." "Brad, don't start something you might not be able to finish." "Stay out of this one, sis." He walked over to them. "Excuse me, I wonder if I could borrow Eve." "Sure, but don't borrow her for too long." Brad wanted to wipe that grin off his face. Without thinking, he removed Seth's arm from Eve's backside and led her outside. "Brad, what the hell are you doing?" "I could ask you the same thing." She pulled her arm free. "What?" "Why are you letting that jerk feel you up." "He's not a jerk." "*Riiight*. So is he your man now?" "What? *Nooooo*, of course not." "You might want to tell him that. Since he seems to think he owns you. Or at least your ass." "He just got a little carried away. I was going to tell him to stop but you showed up and pulled a caveman act." His temper was slowly rising. "Well, I'm glad to hear that otherwise if he kept moving south he'd have ended up touching your—" "How dare you?" "I dare because I'm your friend. I care about you." "Care. That's all you ever do, Brad. Care about me as a friend." "Well, you are my friend." "Well, aren't I lucky to have a *friend* like you." "That's right you are. And when I see some jerk taking advantage I'm going to say something." "Well, you did, so we can go back inside now." "You need to stay away from him, Eve. Guys like Seth are only after one thing." "At least he treats me like a woman, not a kid." "Do you hear yourself? This isn't some game, Eve. Not all guys respect no when they hear it." "What makes you think I'll say no? Maybe I want him too." "You can't possible want a jerk like that." "You haven't a clue as to what I want, Brad. I can take care of myself. This conversation is over." She turned around and started walking towards the door when he grabbed her and pulled her into him. "What the hell are you doing?" "Ever since the Derby, I haven't been able to get this one thought out of my head." "Oh and what would that be?" "This." She managed to take another breath before his lips came crashing down on hers. Their lips created a blazing heat together. He tore his mouth from hers to catch his breath. "Damn it, Eve. This can't happen." "But it is, go with it." She pulled him in for another smoldering kiss. He knew he shouldn't be kissing her, but he couldn't help himself. She tasted like heaven. He finally tore his mouth from hers. "Eve, listen to me. I know you've always had a crush on me but—" "It's more than that. I'm in love with you, Brad." He stood speechless. "You don't mean that." "I do!" "Look, kid—" "Don't do that. Don't try and push me away. You felt something just now. I know you did." "Maybe, but that doesn't make it right." "What's wrong with it?" "I'm too old for you, Eve." "That's bullshit. Twelve years is no big." She pressed her curves into him. "Eve, don't." "Why, because you know you won't be able to resist? Well, good. I've waited my whole life for you Brad. I'm tired of waiting." "Eve, you don't know what you're saying." "Yes, I do." She wrapped his wavy hair around her fingers. "Kiss me, Brad. Kiss me like there won't be a tomorrow, only today." He made a noise that sounded like a growl. "*Eve . . .*" "Would you rather I go back inside to Seth?" He answered her not with words but with a kiss so deep and full of passion that her legs nearly gave out. "God help me, I want you Eve." "Then take me, Brad. I've always been yours."

A week had passed and Scott was growing more depressed by the day. He'd been doing a lot of thinking since talking to Emily. He had to admit that something was missing. Not something, *someone.* He knew damn well who that someone was. He had let his pride rule him and been a fool in the process. *Now what?* Judging by their conversation, she was still angry with him. Not that he blamed her. It would take a hell of a lot to win her back. If that was even possible. No, he'd find a way to win her back. Even if he had to crawl across broken glass to do it. His cell rang. It was Ross. Seeing his name gave him an idea. He'd help himself and Ross at the same time. "Hey, talk about perfect timing." "Oh?" "Yeah, you're the first person I'm telling this too. I'm going to get Em back." "Well it's about damn time. What brought this on?" "Vanessa gave me a swift kick in the ass." "That'll do it." "What about you, Ross?" "What about me?" "You still think you're doing fine without Sabrina?" "She's the stubborn one, not me." "Sure she is." "Look I didn't call to talk about Brina." "No, I'm sure you didn't, but here's what I'm going to. I'm going to spare you any more time being miserable." "I'm not miserable." "Really? When was the last time you went on a date?" "Ah . . ." "And when was the last time you went to Jake's?" "A month ago." "Yeah, you're happy as a clam. My point is, you have done jack shit since you lost her." "I'm hanging up, Scott." "What's the matter, truth hurt?" "I'm fine." "Yeah, well, so am I. But you know what? I'm tired of being *fine.* I want to be more than just fine. I know you've been telling yourself you're okay without her because that's exactly what I've been doing, but we both know we're full of shit." "Scott, I appreciate what you're trying to do but—" "Do you still love her?" "I—" "It's a simple question, Ross." He let out a long breath. "Yeah, I do." "Then it's time to man up." "Scott, things with Brina . . . they can't work. There's no room for me in her life." "*That* is exactly the type of bullshit thinking that got you into this mess in the first place." "It's too late, Scott." "It's only too late if you let it be too late. You love her, fight for her. Like I plan on doing with Em." "So what's it gonna be, Ross?

There was a long, silent pause before he finally answered. “I think it’s time we got our girls back.”

Second Thoughts

A Buttermilk Falls Story

Deborah Flace-Chin

Chapter one

Vanessa sat cross-legged on the sofa with Scott and Ross. Scott had convinced Ross to come down to Kentucky, so they could come up with a plan to get Em and Sabrina back. "So that's our plan. What do you think, Vanessa?" She looked at them for a minute. "I think…it's a bold move. Though it may take a while to convince them to take you back." "Yeah, we know." "So when are you guys going to put this plan into action?" "First I need to get someone to fill in for me at the station." Ross said. "Will that be a problem?" "It shouldn't be. I hardly ever take time off and I've got a slew of days accumulated. Plus, the Police Chief in Seneca owes me a favor." Ray came in. "Who's this?" He said pointing to Ross. "Ray, this is Ross." They shook hands. "So you're the *other* idiot." "That's me, Mr. Idiot." Ray smiled. "The guys were just sharing their plan with me, Ray." "Well, it took you long enough to make one." "We're slow." Scott joked. "No kidding. So what's the plan?" "Ross is going to New York and I'm going back home." "For how long?" "As long as it takes." Scott said. Ray looked over at Ross. "What he just said." "Well, sounds like you two got your work cut out for you." "They do but I really think they've got a good chance at getting them back." Vanessa said. ""Ross where will you end up staying?" She asked. "I haven't thought that far ahead. I know I can't afford a hotel for more than a few nights." "Too bad you don't have anyone you could stay with." "Yeah, I know." Scott thought a minute. "God, we are so stupid." "No arguments here." Ray said grinning. "Funny, Ray." "Who said I was kidding." "Cute. Ross, you can stay with Nico." "Hey that's a great idea. Do you think he'd be okay with it?" "Only one way to find out."

Nico was eyeing a cocktail dress, made by Sabrina, modeled by Sam. "I adore it. Don't you fair Sam?" "It's really cute." His phone rang. "Stamas Designs, Nico speaking." "Nico, it's Ross." "Dear Sheriff, it's been far too long." "Yeah, sorry about that, it's just talking to you reminds me of…" "Say no more, I completely understand. So to what do I owe this pleasure?" "Well, I'd thought you'd like to know that I'm through being miserable and have a plan to get Brina back." Ross had to hold the phone away from his ear because Nico was screaming so loud. "Oh this is wonderful! If you were here, I'd kiss you!" "Well, it's funny you mention that because that's why I'm calling." "Oh?" "I'm going to be staying for as long as it takes to get her back and…" Nico dropped the phone. "Sorry, I was just taken aback by your bold announcement." "Yeah, that makes two of us." "When will you be here?" "As soon as I can arrange someone to take my place." "That soon?" "Yeah, enough time's been wasted. Don't you think?" "Heaven's yes." "Anyway, I was wondering if I could stay with you?" "With moi?" "I know it's a lot to ask but..." "Nonsense, mi casa, es su casa." "Thanks Nico, I was hoping you'd say that." "Of course, you can stay as long as you like." "It might be end up being a few weeks?" "Still fine. I simply adore you Sheriff, you must know that?" "I'm starting to and thanks again, Nico. It means a lot to have your support." "It's something you will never be without, dear Sheriff. Now I'd love to talk more about it but I'm in the middle of a design session with Sam. Call me when you're leaving so I know when to expect you." "Will do. Oh and Nico." "Yes?" "Don't mention any of this to Brina. I don't want her to know." "Never you fear these luscious well moisturized lips are zipped." Ross tried not to laugh. "Thanks, speak to you soon." "Ta Ta, Sheriff." "Ta Ta, Nico."

After the session with Nico ended, Sam went into the ladies room to change. When she was nearly done dressing, her cell rang and she saw that it was Riley. "Hey handsome." "Hi, gorgeous. What are you up to?" "Just finished a design session with Nico. I'm getting dressed."

"I wish I was there to help t you stayed *undressed*." "You have a one track mind, Mr. Finn." "Yeah, and don't pretend you aren't on that track with me, Mrs. Finn." She laughed. "Fine, I won't. "So what are you up to?" "Nothin' much." She heard lots of horn honking. "Where are you? It's awfully loud. "Outside." "I know that. *Where* outside?" "Look out the window." She did and saw him standing by a street light. "You're here!" "Yep, come down and give Daddy some sugar." "I'll be right down." When she got to the lobby he was already there waiting for her. "Hey, hotstuff. Miss me?" She threw herself at him and smothered him with kisses. "I guess that's a yes." "You know I did. I can't believe you're here." "Neither can I especially since I just went out to get milk." She laughed. "That's a long way to go for milk since you work at a dairy." "You're telling me." "You're so silly, come upstairs." "Yeah, sure." On the ride up he held out his hand and in it was a Snickers bar, her favorite. "How do you always know when I need one?" "That's easy, because you always need one." They walked into the office and Nico was standing by the water cooler. "Hey Nico." "Well, if it isn't the handsome, Mr. Finn. You know no one brings a smile to my face the way you do." "Ah I bet you say that to all the boys." "I do no such thing. So sweet of you to surprise Sam." "How do you know it's a surprise?" "Because our Chocolate Muse tells me everything and she didn't mention that you were coming." He looked at her. "*Everything*?" Riley said sounding nervous. "Oh come now Riley, there's no need to be embarrassed. After all, you're the man who found her g-spot. In the straight man's world you deserve an award." "Yeah, I guess I do." "Let's go into my office. There's something I want to tell you both." "Sure." They went in and sat on his cognac colored leather sofa. "So it seems that both our fearless lawman, and illustrious horse whisperer will be making a play to get their lady loves back." "Really? Both of them?" "Indeed." "Scott's an asshole. He hasn't called me in weeks." "Bitter much." Sam said looking at him. "Could it be that you're missing him?" Nico asked. "Me? Miss that jerk? No way, I just miss busting his balls." Nico looked at him dubiously. "The gentleman doth protest too much, me thinks." "Speak English, I hate that Shakespeare crap." Nico looked at him with surprise. "Just because I'm on a farm, doesn't mean I'm not edumacated." Nico laughed. "I do love your sense of humor,

Riley." "Thanks, I try." "Hopefully, they'll be back together before you know it." "I don't think so, Nico." "Riley?" "Sam, you gonna sit there and tell me that you think Em is going to take his sorry ass back? After what he pulled? Ross might have a chance but not Scott." "You know I'm very curious as to why you think Ross has a chance but not Scott." Nico said. "Ross lost Sabrina because he was afraid of losing her to this new life of hers. Whereas, Scott lost Em because his new life took over. Any way you slice it, it's fucked up." "Well, I had no idea you could be so philosophical." "It's a side I don't show often." Nico grinned. "As much as I hate to admit it, I think handsome here is right. Em was devastated and she's still really pissed at him." "Yes, I fear that they will both have their work cut out for them. However, I'm a firm believer that love conquers all." "Then you should be back with that guy you met in Paris." Riley said. "What guy?" I didn't know you met someone?" Sam asked. "It was many years ago. I don't like to talk about it. Now back to the subject at hand, we really need an event, one that will bring everyone together." How 'bout a séance?" "Less sarcasm, more realism, please." Nico said sounding annoyed. "What we really need is a wedding. Nothing rekindles the flames of an old love like a wedding." "That may be true, Nico but no one is getting married anytime soon." "Well, I'd gladly volunteer but who would I marry?" He looked at Riley. "Don't look at me."

About the Author

This is Deborah's first published work. She resides in Glen Cove with her husband, Mark. Deborah currently works as a conference center coordinator at a law firm in New York. In her free time, she enjoys reading, watching classic movies, and spending time with family and friends.